The Wanderers on Earth

Book II of the *Mission from Venus Trilogy*

The Wanderers on Earth

Book II of the *Mission from Venus Trilogy*

Susan Plunket

COSMIC EGG
BOOKS

Winchester, UK
Washington, USA

JOHN HUNT PUBLISHING

First published by Cosmic Egg Books, 2020
Cosmic Egg Books is an imprint of John Hunt Publishing Ltd., 3 East St., Alresford,
Hampshire SO24 9EE, UK
office@jhpbooks.net
www.johnhuntpublishing.com
www.cosmicegg-books.com

For distributor details and how to order please visit the 'Ordering' section on our website.

Text copyright: Susan Plunket 2019

ISBN: 978 1 78904 532 1
978 1 78904 533 8 (ebook)
Library of Congress Control Number: 00000000

A CIP catalogue record for this book is available from the British Library.

Design: Stuart Davies

UK: Printed and bound by CPI Group (UK) Ltd, Croydon, CR0 4YY
US: Printed and bound by Thomson-Shore, 7300 West Joy Road, Dexter, MI 48130

We operate a distinctive and ethical publishing philosophy in
all areas of our business, from our global network of authors to
production and worldwide distribution.

Contents

Also in this series

Mission from Venus : Book I
The dark side has infiltrated many governments and much of the world of finance. The mission from Venus threatens their planned takeover of Earth. Failing a takeover, the dark lords will cause the planet's destruction through nuclear war to prevent Earth from ascending to the fourth dimension on the path of light. The volunteer wanderers are all that stand in the way.

Published : October 25 2019

Paperback: 978-1-78904-170-5
Ebook: 978-1-78904-171-2

Chapter 1

Rose

The psychiatric inpatient unit was sterile and cold, a gray world. Rose closed her eyes to shut it out, and tried to imagine the smell of salt air mixed with the fragrance of a seaside rosebush, lavish with wild pink roses. When that didn't work, she tried to feel the sea itself rushing up to greet her toes. But she couldn't hold onto the sensation. Her mouth was dry, and she felt drugged and quivery, a stranger to herself. After twenty-four hours shivering in a hospital gown, they had finally returned her clothes. Resting behind her eyelids, she again tried to piece together how she'd got here. Two policemen had taken her from Washington Square Park. They said she'd been dancing in the fountain and hallucinating. Had she? She did remember sitting on the edge of the fountain, under the embracing curve of the night sky, looking up at the stars, because it was unusual to be able to see stars in the sky over New York City, but they had been visible that night. Gazing up at them had reminded her of something. Then it had come to her, almost casually, not just the crumbs of a memory but a whole long-ago conversation, where she was walking with a man and asking him if the stars seen from Earth would look the same as they did from Venus. As she spoke to him, she turned to meet his violet eyes, the same violet as her own.

"Venus," she said out loud. "Did I once live on Venus, forty million kilometers from Earth? Was I actually walking with a man on Venus? A man with violet eyes? And asking him about the stars?"

Where had this memory, if it was a memory, come from? Had it always been there, lodged in a hidden fold of her deep mind? After having lived all of her nearly twenty-one years with the feeling that there was something important she had to remember, something more than important, something crucial to her existence, the revelation that she might have had a previous life on Venus arrived like a cup of life-saving water after a journey across a desert. Certainly, this would have been cause enough for dancing in a fountain.

The restless cough of her roommate drew her mind back to the present. She pulled her sweater tighter around her heart and turned her mind back to the night the police had picked her up. Yes, before they arrived, she had been sitting under the stars, on the edge of the fountain, breathing the moist air as it poured over the ledge to mingle with the leftover scent of the day's tourists, and she'd been reliving a conversation from another world. Trying to digest the memory of that strange conversation, she'd closed her eyes and let her mind hang, suspended between Earth and Venus. When she'd opened them, it was as if another memory had come to life. The man with violet eyes was standing in the fountain in front of her. He offered his hand. She took it. They walked deeper into the fountain, and stood, the arks of water falling on them, like a baptism or a marriage blessing. But when she had tried to explain this to the police, they said there was no man, that she'd imagined him. Figuring she was psychotic, they hauled her out of the fountain and took her to the Bellevue emergency room.

Unpleasant as the hospital was, at least the experience at the fountain, which landed her here, had provided her with two more pieces of her own puzzle. She'd once lived on Venus and she definitely had a twin flame whose violet eyes were very like her own. If the man she'd once spoken to on Venus wasn't really there, as the police claimed, then he must have been a thought form created to look like him. And someone had sent it, either one of her spirit guides to help her figure out her true identity and purpose for being on Earth or an enemy of the light, one of the dark lords who wished to harm her by making her appear crazy. Either way, even being with a thought form of him convinced her that she had a twin flame and stirred in her a passionate desire to reunite with him. If he was on Earth, she'd find him. Until now, he'd only appeared in dreams, or in the overlapping edges between waking and dreaming, leaving her always longing for him.

"You have a visitor," the nurse said, interrupting Rose's reverie. She leapt up when she saw her father, and threw her arms around him. Hunter's presence restored her to herself. Relief washed over Hunter as well. He knew she had always been a fanciful child, making drawings of an imaginary violet planet, and telling him of invisible friends and light beings who visited her in her dreams, but no one had ever labeled her psychotic before or put her in a mental hospital. And, he'd observed that in recent weeks, on the cusp of turning twenty-one, Rose had spoken less of dreams about dark lords and light beings or the planet with the pink-gold sky. And the Amazon deliveries of books on twin flames, spirit guides, and Earth's ascension into the fourth dimension had almost stopped. Hunter hoped she'd finally outgrown these interests, which had long concerned him. When she was ten, right after Jacqueline ran off with his best friend, Hunter had taken her to see a child psychiatrist, who'd said that Rose's fantasies were an attempt to escape from the pain caused by her narcissistic mother abandoning her. Hunter had wanted to believe him.

"I'm sorry I didn't get here sooner, darling. The hospital only reached me in London yesterday afternoon."

"Dad, it's OK. I'm fine. This was a mistake. Can we go home now?"

"The doctor said you can leave, since you agreed to a voluntary admission."

"I did?"

"Apparently you were co-operative, and even charming on admission, regaling the young resident in the emergency room with all kinds of stories about higher dimensions."

Without knowing it, Rose stopped breathing for a moment. She knew it worried her father when she talked about other dimensions or exhibited strange abilities. She'd been trying for years to filter herself, ever since the incident at The Neue Galerie, when she was a child.

The Neue had been having an exhibit of Art Deco Clocks. Hunter collected Art Deco pieces, and he'd taken Rose along with him to see the clocks. She'd been about ten at the time. While they strolled around, Rose noticed that Hunter kept returning to look again and again at one clock in particular. Rose walked right up to it, and, before Hunter could stop her, put both hands on it. Just by touching it, she'd known all about the person for whom the clock had been made, how he had died, and that he had been Hunter's great-great uncle. She was relaying this to Hunter when the museum guard walked up. When he heard what ten-year-old Rose was saying he was stunned, and handed Hunter a sheet with information about the clock. Rose had told Hunter everything that was on the sheet, and more. Shaken by the incident, that's when he'd taken her to that psychiatrist, who told him that Rose had an ability called psychometry, which meant that she could discover facts about a person by touching an object which they'd owned or used. Rose knew she could do this, but she thought everyone could.

"The doctor is signing the paperwork now, so we should be able to leave soon," Hunter said.

Rose sneezed. "I'll be happy to get out of this freezing air conditioning." When she was a child she'd told Hunter that air conditioners gave off a bad energy. He'd asked her how she knew that, and she'd told him she could see it.

"Stop being ridiculous," Jacqueline had snapped at Rose, for what turned out to be one of the last times. A week later Rose came home from school with her babysitter and found the note from her mother on the table in the foyer, informing them that she had left. Rose was in fourth grade at the time. That night the housekeeper told Hunter that she'd seen Jacqueline get into a car with her luggage, a car driven by his best friend. All Hunter said was, "So he's gone too."

The minute they were out in the street, all the light which had been locked out by the hospital walls, burst on them, bouncing off Rose's blonde hair and painting her skin a rosy pink. Hunter marveled at her resilience, and once again relief washed over him. If he ever lost her, it would be the end of him. He hailed a taxi. Rose hopped in, and Hunter slid in beside her and gave the handsome young Greek driver their address.

"I have to get ready and go over to the UN. Orientation for my internship is this afternoon. And they're having a Bar-B-Que for all the interns."

"Darling, are you up to that?"

"Of course. I'm looking forward to it. Interns are coming from forty different countries to work together on global warming." Without knowing why, she was especially excited that there would be an intern from Jerusalem, a place she had often asked Hunter to take her. They'd traveled to many countries together, but somehow never to Israel. Hunter had been surprised when Rose chose the internship at the United Nations, as she'd spent most of her previous semester at The New School, writing a paper about the five permanent members of the United Nations Security Council, railing against them. Her thesis had been that as the biggest arms dealers in the world, the five permanent members: China, Russia, The United States, The United Kingdom and France, were all misusing their power for profit, and were responsible for the deaths of millions of people around the world. She particularly hated that the Saudis were bombing Yemen killing innocent civilians, many of them children, with arms sold to them by The United States.

"Their greed is really ignorance," Rose had told him. "They don't understand that what they do to others, they also do to themselves." When she said this, Hunter thought for the millionth time, *she has a heart as big as the sky*.

Unfortunately, there was one entity who wanted that big heart stopped. Darpith had been observing Rose since her birth, ever watchful for an opportunity to slip through the quarantine around Earth, and manipulate some weaker being into causing Rose's death. Since he had determined early on that Rose could not be turned to the dark side, he had decided to eliminate her. But it had been challenging, since the light Rose radiated drew people to her, and made them care for her, all except her mother, Jacqueline. Darpith had used Jacqueline several times to injure Rose. Playing on Jacqueline's vanity, he had fed her thoughts which provoked jealousy of her daughter, and caused her to neglect and endanger Rose. He'd nearly succeeded in breaking Rose's neck in Washington Square Park when she was twelve months old. Jacqueline had set her on top of the ladder to the slide. Instead of facing Rose so she could go down the slide, Jacqueline carelessly faced her backwards on top of the ladder. One forward lean, and Rose would be on her face on the cement below her, with a broken neck. Relishing this thought, Darpith distracted Jacqueline, filling her mind with thoughts of her power and beauty, and of how Hunter didn't appreciate her, and only loved Rose, and how she should punish him for that. Unconscious of her actions, or where her thoughts were coming from, Jacqueline plopped Rose high up on the ladder and stepped away to look in her bag for her compact and lipstick. Seeing her mother walk away, Rose had reached out for her and started to tumble forward but another mother saw Rose, and caught her just in time. Rose's cry brought Jacqueline to her senses and she dropped her bag and hastily took Rose from the woman's arms. The woman didn't reproach her, but said only, "What beautiful violet eyes your daughter has." Darpith cursed them all.

After Jacqueline was gone from Rose's life, Darpith and his

minions searched for other ways to kill Rose. It got more difficult once Rose was old enough to pray and meditate, because when called, the Chohans of the Light were free to intervene. Darpith's latest attempt had succeeded in landing Rose in a psychiatric hospital, where his plan was to have her die of an accidental overdose. If only she hadn't uttered that prayer for help, Darpith thought, Portia and Saint Germain, Chohans of the Violet Ray of Transmutation, wouldn't have been allowed to intervene. But Rose, who lay on a table in the emergency room, had prayed for help, and they'd come in answer to her call. Resplendent in long, flowing, violet robes, shimmering with light, they were invisible to everyone except Darpith. And although Darpith was invisible to everyone else they could see him in the corner of the room, controlling the resident's mind, directing him to give Rose a lethal overdose. To stop Darpith, Portia and Saint Germain directed the Violet Ray of Transmutation into Rose's eyes and out into the eyes of the resident. Rose held the resident's eyes with her own, arresting him with their beauty. As soon as the Violet Ray struck the resident's retina and moved deeper to penetrate his pineal gland, Darpith lost control of him and he dropped the syringe containing the overdose. It shattered on the floor. In a rage, Darpith fled the emergency room, more determined than ever to destroy Rose. His only consolation was that he had managed to get her into the emergency room by using that thought form of her twin flame. Maybe he could fool her again? He reminded himself that the battle for Earth would be won by sowing dissension, feeding greed and turning the weakest-minded to the dark side. Those who could not be ensnared onto the path of service to self would be slaughtered. First, he would eliminate the wanderers, like Rose, to prevent them from spreading their message of unity. Once they were gone it would be easier to sow dissention. Next, he would bring all the positively oriented humans, those who understood that all are one, over to the dark side. Failing that, he would kill them.

Once that was accomplished, it would be child's play to lure the weaker minded humans onto the dark path, and set them against one another using that orange puppet he'd set up in the White House with the help of the Russians. He would enslave them all using their own egos. The lure of money, power, drugs and sex, would take care of the rest. Then all beings on Earth would bow to his will.

Though he believed his plan was well thought out, Darpith had failed to realize that there might be other dark lords on Orion with their eyes on Earth, others, every bit as ruthless as himself, who would take great pleasure in enslaving him, as well as all of Earth. Veldemiron, for one, was watching Darpith, biding his time and making his own plans to enslave the humans.

Chapter 2

Ephraim

Ephraim had chosen to complete his military service in the Israeli army before applying to college. As a pacifist, he'd been given a desk job. He detested war and killing, and could not find it in himself to hate or distrust the Palestinians or the Iranians. In fact, he cared about their welfare as much as his own. His real interests were writing and music. Relieved now to be finished with his military service, he was hungry for a bigger life. Since boyhood he'd been writing songs and science fiction stories about far off planets, time travel, and beings with magical powers. Many of his songs and stories were about light beings from Arcturus, the Pleiades, and the Violet Planet, who visited Earth to bring messages to the humans. But his favorite of everything he'd written was a story about an Israeli boy from Jerusalem, and an American girl from New York, meeting, and discovering that they weren't actually human but extraterrestrials who had come to help save Earth from the dark lords. He worked on this story off and on for years, never quite able to let it go. It was the writing sample he'd submitted with his application to NYU. Soon he'd be on his way there to study writing and music. For as long as he could remember, he'd felt something pulling him, tugging on his heart, drawing him toward New York City. At last he would see this place of his longings.

Ephraim's parents, Daniel and Rachael, were less enthusiastic about his choice to study in New York. They wanted him closer to home, partly because not only did he have episodes where he blacked out, but he was accident prone as well. At least that's how they saw it, especially after he'd nearly drowned at age eleven, in a boating accident, the summer they vacationed on Corfu. The three of them were out on the sea, in an Aegean blue sailboat with brass fittings and stylish rigging. Ephraim was standing in the bow, enjoying the feeling of the boat running before the wind like a dancer. Daniel was at the tiller. Rachael closed her eyes and leaned back, thinking what a joy it was, for once, to feel a harmony among the three of them as they relished the experience of the boat, the wind and the water.

But suddenly the wind changed. Daniel lost control of the tiller. Rachael's eyes jerked open, as the mainsail swung around knocking Ephraim overboard. She screamed when she saw him go over the bow and disappear. He knew how to swim so there shouldn't have been a problem, but he got what felt like a cramp in his leg. It was so painful, he wasn't even able to tread water. Not realizing this at first, Daniel just threw him a rope. The pain in Ephraim's leg intensified and he began sinking. As he lost consciousness under water, Ephraim slipped the bounds of his rational mind and was transported to another world where he saw things he would never again forget. An array of beings of all kinds, some tri-pedal, others quadrupedal, many with sensors and tentacles, blue skinned and green skinned beings, many twelve or fourteen feet tall, strolling beside beings four feet high who walked on three legs. All of them were moving under a pink–gold sky toward an archway into a huge temple. Ephraim's eyes fixed on one bipedal pair with violet eyes like his own. He watched them walk along, holding hands, communicating telepathically. He understood their silent exchanges, as they telegraphed their thoughts back and forth about a mission to Earth, to awaken the humans to knowledge of their divinity and save them from the dark lords. The man called her *Soonam*. The name pierced Ephraim's heart. He wanted to get closer and hear more. But he was distracted by something happening in the archway into the temple. A being with long white hair, wearing a purple robe and a pendant of a star tetrahedron, was gesturing to him. Yes, he was sure he was being summoned. He wanted to ask the being what he was witnessing, but he was unable to speak. It was then he heard the message from the white-haired being. *It is not time for you to die. You are a wanderer on a mission to Earth. Go back.*

The next thing he knew, someone was grabbing him, pulling him from his reverie, hauling him up out of the water, and pushing him onto a hard surface. He felt a powerful pressure on his chest and back, then water rose up inside him and gushed out of his mouth. Where was he? Where was the violet-eyed couple he'd been listening to? Where was the white-haired man in purple robes? What mission to Earth were the violet-eyed couple talking about? What was a wanderer? Ephraim was dazed and longed to return to the scene by the temple to hear more. But it was gone. He held onto one word, *Soonam,* and that night and for many nights after, he fell asleep with this name on his lips, trying to compose a song around it.

Seeing Daniel jump in to save Ephraim, two Greek fishermen had come to their aid and brought the unruly mainsail under control. As they worked to bring the frisky sailboat to heel, the Greeks kept up an easy banter, talking themselves through the task. Rachael admired their steady ingenuity. She liked Greek men, imagining something of the ancient gods in them. Despite working hard, Greek men seemed to have plenty of time for dreaming, loafing, smoking and playing jokes on one another. Life was gentle on sundrenched Corfu, and everyone, young and old, took time to taste the sweetness. If you asked a Corfu native, "How far to the village?" the reply was invariably, "Two cigarettes." Rachael smiled to herself at the thought of using pleasure to measure distance. This whole near drowning event seemed too violent for Corfu. Something felt off about what had happened. That evening, sitting on the terrace, surrounded by the richness of their seventeenth century Venetian style hotel, sipping Retsina, a plate of figs, bread and olives before her, Rachael wished she could erase the feeling that it hadn't been just an accident. It reminded her of too many other weird incidents surrounding Ephraim, and that scared her.

Was it only a coincidence that just before they'd gone sailing, she'd been reading the part in *The Tempest* about the shipwreck? The concierge at the hotel had loaned it to her, explaining that Corfu was the island which Shakespeare had in mind when he wrote it. Of course, it was a coincidence and not a premonition, she told herself. It's magical thinking to say it was a warning, let alone a premonition. She picked up a fig, and was biting into it, when Daniel walked up and tossed an opened pack of Greek cigarettes on the table. She looked up at him in surprise. He hadn't smoked in over eleven years.

Later, as they were getting ready for bed, Rachael put her hair brush down and said, "Another eventful family vacation."

Her attempt to minimize what had happened that day fell flat. Daniel would not be jollied.

"I've gotten used to living in a house on fire, with Ephraim," he told her. "But what hurts is that I can never get close to him. It's as though he's always half in another world."

"He's only eleven, be patient. He's going to do great things," Rachael said, less certain than she sounded.

"But he's strange in ways that I don't understand. He nearly drowned, and he wasn't even scared. Does he think he has nine lives?"

Whenever they were vacationing with Ephraim, Rachael noticed that time seemed to stretch out and slow down. She suspected that Ephraim was manipulating it, but dismissed the idea as ridiculous. At first it had been accidental. If he was enjoying something, he'd unconsciously slow time down to make the pleasure last. And if he was uncomfortable in a situation, he'd speed time up. He assumed everyone did it. As he grew out of childhood, he found he could not only slow down and speed up time, but he could stop it and rewind it as well. He experimented and noticed that time existed in one space, one dimension, and he wondered if he could manipulate it across dimensions. Ephraim attuned himself to each place he visited with his parents and stretched time, or shortened it, as it suited him. On vacations, it often felt to his mother as if he was on a mission to discover something, or find someone. It had been like that when they visited both London and Tokyo. He walked in the streets as if he was expecting to see an old friend come around the next corner. There were secrets in his heart, as yet not unlocked. Rachael understood this, but it made Daniel impatient with his son.

The year they went on vacation to Mumbai, Ephraim had insisted they take the ferry to Elephanta Island to explore the caves and see the six-meter high statue of Shiva. When Daniel asked him why he wanted to go there, in particular, he had no answer other than, "I feel drawn to the place." Daniel preferred more specificity, and had trouble sympathizing with his son, who so often seemed to have one foot in an invisible world. And it was on Elephanta Island, while walking back to the ferry, surrounded by pesky monkeys, that Ephraim had his first blackout. He'd been fifteen at the time when he suddenly lost his eyesight. First, he found himself in total darkness, then he lost consciousness completely. People swarmed around, offering advice and help to carry him to the ferry. Ephraim regained consciousness, and his eyesight, on the boat ride back to Mumbai. But Rachael noted a far-away look in his eyes, that never left him.

Ephraim had been observing the monkeys, and attempting to manipulate time in order to discover where he'd seen them before, for he knew he had, and he suspected it was in the place with the pink-gold sky he so often dreamed about. What he didn't remember was that he'd seen the monkeys while he was a creature of the Fifth Dimension, on Venus, while viewing the hologram of Bereh's parents the day they all learned where they'd be incarnating. On Elephanta Island he wasn't able to complete the time manipulation, and he blacked out. When he came too, he realized his manipulation failed because the memory must have involved another dimension, and it was most likely impossible to manipulate time across different dimensions. He was overjoyed at this. It was another proof that he had once existed in a different dimension, and that he was in fact a wanderer as he'd been told in the vision he'd had when he nearly drowned off the coast of Corfu, four years earlier. Furthermore, because he'd remembered the monkeys, he now knew that memories from other dimensions were somewhat accessible. He also suspected that what he'd seen during the near drowning was also a memory.

As Ephraim regained consciousness after the blackout on Elephanta Island, Daniel looked at his smiling son, and shook his head. Later when they were alone, he said to Rachael. "Did you see the look on Ephraim's face when he regained consciousness? There was not even an instant of bewilderment or concern for what had happened."

"I guess we could be glad for that," Rachael answered, attempting to close down any further line of inquiry, as had become her habit. She did this to protect Ephraim, to make him seem more normal than he was. Intuitively she understood that he shouldn't be too different, shouldn't stand out too much, that it could be dangerous.

After the incident on Elephanta Island, Ephraim felt closer to knowing his true identity as a wanderer than he ever had. Unfortunately, his blackout had not gone unobserved by the dark side. Darpith had instructed his minions to monitor all the wanderers on Earth. One of them saw Ephraim lose consciousness, but hadn't acted quickly enough to take control of his mind or finish him off. In future, he would be ready, and could perhaps even cause Ephraim to blackout so he could slip in and gain control of him while he was unconscious.

Because of his strange dreams, Ephraim was somewhat aware of the dark side and suspected he was under attack. Many nights he dreamed of visiting temples where light beings warned him to be on guard, especially if he blacked out again. They also showed him ways to protect himself. Sometimes in his dreams he saw the girl with the violet eyes, who was also being shown how to protect herself. One morning he awoke with the words *Master El Morya* on his lips. The name sounded so familiar. He had been dreaming of a white temple high in the Himalayas where he was among friends, listening to El Morya who stood in the middle of a huge temple in his long blue robes, wearing a gold turban with an agate on it, right over his third eye. His bronze skin, close clipped beard and piercing blue eyes were all familiar to Ephraim. Sure that this wasn't a dream but that he had actually been there, he jumped out of bed and googled Master El Morya to discover that he was an ascended master, Chohan of the Blue Flame of the Will of God. Ephraim read on and learned that El Morya had lived many lifetimes on Earth, one of them as Melchior, one of the three wise men at the birth of Jesus, another as King Arthur, another as Abraham, the first Hebrew patriarch in 2100 B.C. Somewhere he'd heard all this before. He even felt he'd met El Morya in a different life. Ephraim's nightly adventures in his dreams were becoming more real than his waking life. More and more he felt that they weren't just dreams.

Since his blackout on Elephanta Island at age fifteen, the frequency of his dreams about visits to temples, where he met with masters of light, had been more and more frequent, and he began asking himself why he had come to Earth. His memories and dreams of light beings and superpowers, his ability to control time, and even his childhood so called "accidents" must all be a part of the reason for his incarnation on Earth. But what was it? He was also sure he wasn't alone on this mission. He felt certain that others had come from another dimension with him, and one in particular, who was very dear to him. His dreams of the violet-eyed girl had made that clear. And then there was the feeling that someone wanted to prevent him from discovering that purpose, even if they had to end his life to do it. For a long time, he'd sensed that clues to his destiny lay in New York City. Now, about to turn twenty-one, he would finally get there. With great joy and anticipation, he lifted his duffle bag and guitar out of the trunk of his parent's blue Volvo, hugged them goodbye and walked into the airport.

Chapter 3

Natasha

"I don't like it one bit, Masha. Work as a model? I forbid it." Igor slammed his palm down on the breakfast table, jiggling the tea cups on their saucers.

"But Natasha sees it as an opportunity to travel, and to live and work in New York for a time, while she's still young, before she settles down."

"Her place is here in Moscow with us. Just the thought of her going is ruining my breakfast."

Masha doubted that as she watched Igor sprinkle powdered sugar on his blintz and take a bite.

"What? She's just going to up and leave university, when she's only half finished, because she's won some contest. Nonsense. And twenty is too young to go abroad alone."

"And you're too old fashioned, my darling," Masha told him between sips of fragrant tea. "Young people don't do everything in a straight line nowadays. One can take a leave for a year and return to finish college later."

"Alexei and Clara did everything in a straight line. Why does Natasha have to always give us headaches?"

Igor wasn't wrong. From birth, there had been something different about Natasha. Even playing hide and seek with her brother and sister, and sometimes on family outings, she'd frighten them all by suddenly disappearing. It felt as if she'd vanished into thin air. Then just as suddenly, she'd reappear, wearing an innocent look. She, in fact, had had no control over it as a child. The mere suggestion to hide during a game of hide and seek caused her to disappear. When she vanished, she found herself under a pink-gold sky, with different parents, who were made of light, and lived in a big stone mansion. They always told her the same thing, that she could not stay just then, as she had a job to do on Earth. They would send her back, but they seemed sad to do it. And she was sad to leave them.

Igor didn't want to look too deeply into Natasha's invisibility, lest it lead to even more unanswerable questions, so he decided her disappearances were out of her control, and started ignoring them. He wanted Natasha to be normal. And if he had to overlook a few oddities, so be it. But she wasn't normal, and the whole family knew it, which was the real reason he didn't want her far away in New York, modeling, and maybe taking drugs that would affect her in who knew what way. The memory of the time she'd nearly died, as a five-year old, from ingesting something in her school lunch, was still too real. None of the other students had even gotten sick from eating the same food. Natasha told them that it was the dark lord who had tried to poison her.

"Stop making up stories," Igor had snapped at her. "There's no such thing as a dark lord. Your head is always full of crazy ideas. You're getting too old for that now that you go to school."

But Natasha had insisted that the dark lord would have killed her if the pink man and lady hadn't come when she called them to help her. "They filled me with light to save me. And the dark lord fled because he was afraid of their power."

"Enough nonsense," Igor had bellowed.

And the poisoning had not been the only frightening incident during Natasha's childhood. There was the time she fell through the ice while skating at a friend's pond outside Moscow. The temperature was minus twenty-three degrees Celsius, and the pond had been frozen solid for weeks. It was impossible that the ice could have cracked. But it had. One minute Natasha had been skating along, the next, she was under the freezing water and her friend was screaming. Somehow Natasha was out of the water and lying on the ice next to the hole before any of the adults arrived. If Natasha had called the pink man and pink lady for help, and they had somehow rescued her, she didn't mention it to Igor. But that night, while putting an extra quilt over her, Masha asked Natasha if the pink man and lady had come to save her, and if, now that she was a little older, they had told her their names. Ten-year-old Natasha answered her mother that they were called Paul the Venetian and Lady Ruth, and that they wore long, rose-colored robes with aquamarines all along the bottom. And their eyes were aquamarine colored too.

"And did they help you when you fell through the ice today?" Masha asked her daughter again.

"Yes. I knew they were coming because I smelled roses. They levitated me out of the hole in the ice, and chased the dark lord away. You see, he melted the ice with his will but I didn't notice it in time."

Masha kissed her daughter on the top of the head and said into her hair, "Thank heaven for the pink man and the pink lady, my love."

Because he was aggravated, Igor swallowed the last bite of his blintz with less concentration on it than usual. How could so many freak things happen to one girl? No, it wouldn't do. New York was a bad idea. He was certain. Thankfully, Masha understood his fear. And over the years she had come to accept that Natasha was different from Alexei and Clara. Truth be told, she'd suspected it even before Natasha was born. Her dreams during pregnancy had been of an ethereal world with a pink sky. She had seen her future daughter walking there, looking much as she looked now on Earth, except there, she was made mostly of light, and she was much taller, maybe twelve feet tall, and her features were even more delicate than her human face, which was lovely enough. So, it hadn't surprised her that when Natasha began to talk, around age two, that she told them of other worlds which she visited in her dreams, and of the people she met there. She spoke often of magical beings wielding rays of light of different colors. Her favorite was the pink ray where the pink man and lady lived, as she had called them as a child. Once, when she'd been about ten or eleven, Natasha drew a picture of a temple made of pink light floating over what looked to Masha like the photographs she had seen of the Statue of Liberty in New York Harbor. Natasha named her drawing *The Temple of the Sun.*

"Could she have seen a photo of the Statue of Liberty?" Masha had asked Igor. Or, she thought to herself, had Natasha traveled there in her dreams? Was this the home of the pink beings, Paul the Venetian and Lady Ruth?

"This new devil," Igor said in loud voice, "modeling in New York. Why did this American company have to come to Moscow?"

"We can't control the world, Igor."

Representatives from a fashion house in New York, called Ralph Lauren, had arranged with Moscow University to offer all the students, both men and women, an opportunity to compete for a year-long job working in New York as designers or models. They would choose five men and five women in each category. Natasha had entered for design, but they had chosen her to be a model. Her height, five eleven, her long neck, her oval face and gray-gold eyes, made her a perfect fit for their brand. Though disappointed about not being chosen for design, she had long wanted to visit New York. If modeling was the path, so be it. The only thing that could have stopped her would have been a chance to go to Mumbai. For years she had been having a recurring dream of a young Indian man in Mumbai, standing on a cliff, gazing down at the shimmering Arabian Sea below him. The dreams had started one winter night after she'd been skating with friends in Gorky Park. An Indian boy, skating near her, had suddenly turned into pure light then become flesh and blood again. None of the other skaters had seemed to notice, as they'd been distracted by a woman screaming. Most people would not have believed their eyes had they seen it happen but Natasha did believe it, and furthermore, the boy was strangely familiar to her, in a wonder-filled way. She suspected that he was the same Indian man standing on the cliff above the Arabian Sea in her recurrent dream. She'd had the dream for the first time the very night that she saw the boy turn into light. This experience was one of the many things about her life that she could not yet explain to herself. But she knew deep down that there was an explanation for everything. If she couldn't go to Mumbai to search for him, at least she would go to New York. Perhaps the path to Mumbai was through New York.

While Natasha was busy convincing her father to let her take this opportunity, Darpith and his minions were also busy. They were making plans to prevent her from ever arriving in New York. They knew that Arjuna, the man in Natasha's dreams, was living in Mumbai but would soon be moving to New York to study astrophysics. The two light beings could not be allowed to meet. *Perhaps a plane crash,* Darpith thought.

Chapter 4

Arjuna

Aastha wanted Arjuna to enter government work after he completed his studies. "So you'll have a safe profession." She placed a plate of warm nan on the wooden table next to his dinner. They were eating in the garden under the flowering lime tree. Arjuna didn't answer his mother immediately, but breathed in the sweet scent of the lime flowers. He never openly disagreed with her, or lost his temper, or even raised his voice, but instead, gracefully contrived to bend the arc of the conversation to his wishes.

"Yes, government work is secure," he agreed, "and good, if it suits the person." He broke off a piece of warm bread and dipped it in the fragrant sauce. "Sublime," he said, smiling at his mother and closing down the discussion of government work.

If she noticed the way Arjuna managed to turn the conversation around, Aastha didn't remark on it, but went on cutting up a juicy mango. She had a quiet heart. However, she did fret over him since in the almost twenty-one years of his life, she'd nearly lost him several times. The first time, he'd been a small boy of three, playing in their garden, when he was bitten by a poisonous snake. Only the fact that Aastha's sister was visiting had saved Arjuna. After changing careers several times, her sister had gone to medical school, and that had been the perfect fit for her. The day of the snake bite she quickly made several incisions near the bite wound, and she and Aastha sucked out the poison before taking him to the hospital. Arjuna later told them that the snake was friendly at first, coming closer and closer, but then suddenly it had struck, sinking its fangs into his leg. Aastha was shaken. In all the time that she'd lived there, and tended her walled garden, she'd never seen a single snake, let alone a clever one, pretending to be friendly so it could come close enough to strike a toddler.

A few years after the snake bite, Arjuna was hit by a car while he and some friends were playing ball in the street. Though there were many witnesses, none could agree on the make or even the color of the car, let alone the description of the driver. Some were convinced it was a woman, others equally sure it had been a man driving. One person even said there had been no driver at all, that the car had moved on its own. It was as if a veil of confusion had been dropped over the witnesses. The only thing they all agreed upon was that the car had come out of nowhere, and it had struck Arjuna in a deliberate and vicious attempt to hurt him. No one was ever apprehended. After the accident, Arjuna lay in the hospital in a coma for several weeks, hovering between life and death. Darpith watched with satisfaction from a corner of the hospital room, waiting for an opportunity to finish the job. Perhaps some weak-minded doctor or nurse would be susceptible to mind control, and could be induced to smother Arjuna if only the mother would clear out. But Aastha stayed. She sat at Arjuna's bedside and prayed for help. After one long, hot day, she fell asleep in her chair, still holding Arjuna's hand, and she dreamed of a beautiful, young, light being with green eyes the color of emeralds. He wore a green cape over a shirt woven of many colors of light, and stood over Arjuna, wielding a light ray the same emerald green as his eyes. He spoke to her in a soft voice as he directed the light emanating from his palms to mend all the broken bones in Arjuna's body.

"My name is Hilarion," he told her, "I have come because you called out in your prayers and asked for healing for Arjuna."

In her dream, Aastha could see the bones knitting back together as the emerald light entered them. After he mended the bones, Hilarion channeled the emerald light into the center of Arjuna's brain, into an area, which her sister later told her, was his pineal gland. As he did this, she saw two intersecting pyramids which surrounded Arjuna's body, one facing up and one down, begin to spin in counter rotating fields.

From his corner, Darpith watched in a rage, despising Hilarion but afraid of him. Hilarion was aware of Darpith, and what he was trying to do, but wished him no ill, understanding that Darpith served the Creator in his own way — on the negative path. That would change, Hilarion knew, when Darpith evolved to reach the sixth dimension. For after the sixth dimension there is no way forward, except on the positive path of service to others. Unable to bear Hilarion's light, and full of hate, Darpith fled back to Orion.

Aastha awoke to see Arjuna opening his eyes and starting to speak to her.

"I dreamed of Master Hilarion. How wonderful it was to see him again," Arjuna told her.

Aastha's eyes filled with tears which rolled freely down her cheeks.

"Yes, Arjuna, I, too, saw him, in my dream, but who is he?"

"He is a master of the Green Ray of Healing, but that's all I remember. I must have known him in a past life, as I've never seen him in this life," Arjuna said.

After that, for the rest of her life, whenever Aastha performed puja, she included Master Hilarion in her prayers.

Arjuna seemed different to Aastha after the accident and the encounter with Master Hilarion. Though still a boy of only twelve he was somehow more serious and adult, as if he was half in another world. But if possible, he was even more loving. Aastha wondered how Arjuna could have known a light being in a past life. As a Hindu, she believed in past lives but what kind of life allowed one to meet beings made of light, who had magic healing powers? She asked herself why Arjuna was so different from other children. "Maybe it's because he's had to grow up too quickly without a father," she told her sister. But she didn't believe that herself. Despite all her prayers that Arjuna have a normal life, she knew there were things about him that weren't normal. And she knew that her dream of Hilarion was no ordinary dream. If only Siddharth had lived to help her raise their son, he would have been able to explain these mysteries to her. Like the time, when he was only six years old, that Arjuna had doubled all the plants and trees in her garden. Knowing his mother's love for her growing things, Arjuna surprised her for her birthday by duplicating every one of her plants and trees so she had twice as many. This had frightened more than surprised her. How had he done this? When she asked him, he told her he had no idea how. He had just wished very hard for it. She assured him that she was grateful his gift but gently reminded him that his wishes were powerful, and he needed to be careful what he wished for, especially around other people. Now she could smile about it, because he exercised self-discipline and discretion when using his ability to duplicate, but back then, before the coma, she had been frightened for him. What if the wrong people learned of his talents, because duplication, was not the only one.

She had also seen him change things, and even himself, from one form to another. In his early teens, when she'd questioned him about this ability, he told her that he'd been shown in a dream that he could transform things. It scared her to hear this, so she asked him nothing more about it until their trip to Moscow when he was fifteen. It was their first ever vacation together, and they'd saved up for it for several years. Arjuna had begged to visit Moscow. He said he wanted, especially, to go ice skating. Aastha knew he had been collecting photos of families in Moscow, ice skating, for many years. He told her he felt as if he'd been there, and seen families skating in Gorky Park in person, maybe in a past life. Aastha understood that this was important to Arjuna, and so they went.

They flew from Mumbai to Moscow. Aastha watched as Arjuna took ice skating lessons in Gorky Park. He was awkward at first, but after a few lessons he caught the knack of it. Near the end of their week, they stayed later at the skating rink one day, and at dusk saw colored lights come on under the ice. Arjuna's soul delighted in the beauty of the colored lights as they fell on a girl skating toward him, and for a moment he transformed and was no longer a teenage Indian boy, but a light being soaring to a height of twelve feet. Aastha screamed when she saw it happen, and all eyes turned to her. It was not by design, but, none the less, her scream prevented anyone else from noticing Arjuna's transformation. Almost anyone else, that is. The teenage girl who had been skating toward him looked at him just at that moment. A flash of recognition passed through her as the air around the boy glowed a soft pink and he turned into light. The next moment, the light being was just a boy again.

Arjuna and Aastha returned to Mumbai and spoke no more of Moscow or ice skating. He knew he had frightened his mother. But on his own, he went over what had happened in Gorky Park. He'd been watching a girl skating toward him. For a moment, her gray-gold eyes had fixed on him, just as the lights of many colors coming from under the ice lit up her face. She was achingly familiar to him. He looked at her, bathed in light, and felt himself lose his flesh, and become pure light as his soul rushed out to greet her. He did not understand that he had appeared to her in his fifth dimensional light body. The joy of the feeling obliterated everything. After that, he longed to make that feeling his permanent state, and to find that girl.

After Moscow, Arjuna focused his high school studies on physics and metaphysics. As he searched for answers to understand how he had transformed into light, he could feel ideas living at the edges of his mind, ideas he couldn't approach directly but which sometimes approached him. Then he would take hold of them and write them in his journal before they slipped away again. He thought there might be a clue to what had happened to him in one esoteric alchemical treatise he read which explained that the merkaba surrounding humans in the third dimension has counter rotating fields spinning at nine tenth the speed of light, but in higher dimensions the merkaba spins at the speed of light itself. Had seeing the Russian girl caused his merkaba to momentarily achieve the speed of light? It was one theory he entertained. He felt sure the concept of Unity, of accepting all beings as one, was also connected to it in some way. His dreams provided more clues, especially the ones about reincarnation and light beings gathering in temples in the sky over Crete and Egypt, above the Himalayas, on the planet Venus, and even in the rings of Saturn. He wrote them all down sitting in their garden by the lime tree, under the stars.

A few years after their trip to Moscow, Arjuna was accepted at the Indian Institute of Technology in Mumbai, where he chose to study astrophysics.

"What is astrophysics?" Aastha asked her son.

"It's the science that studies how stars, planets, and even galaxies and nebulae are born, and how they live and die. It uses the laws of physics and chemistry to understand the lives of these great beings."

Aastha nodded, remembering how when he had first learned to talk Arjuna had told her, "People are made of stars."

When he wasn't studying, Arjuna relaxed at the gaming center near school. His favorite virtual reality game was *Fifth Dimension*. It was a game about light beings with different super powers, coming together from all over the galaxy to help humans awaken to their true identity as Divine beings. Arjuna especially loved missions where he joined forces with other light beings around the globe. Together they rescued humans from the clutches of the dark lords. But he was finding it more and more difficult to pull away from the game, often playing all night, growing more and more involved in the battle against the dark side.

He let himself give in to his obsession with *Fifth Dimension*, rationalizing that soon he'd be leaving Mumbai, and the gaming centers in New York might not have *Fifth Dimension*. He'd applied to be an exchange student, to spend his junior year of college at Columbia University in New York City, taking courses in their astrophysics program. His department chair had just informed him that he'd been accepted. Even though it was his second choice, he was over the moon. His first choice had been to study at Moscow University. But he reminded himself, that the most direct path isn't always a straight line. He had not bought into the illusions of linearity, or permanence or congruence either. Maybe the way to find that grey-eyed golden-haired Russian girl was through New York.

From Orion, Darpith observed the pattern of movement of these four incarnated light beings, Rose, Ephraim, Natasha and Arjuna. He knew that all four would soon be in New York City unless he stopped them. If they found one another and reunited, it would increase their power, and awaken their memories of their true identities as Fifth Dimensional beings who had come to Earth on a mission. He could not let that happen. He would set more of his slaves on the task of preventing any reunions.

Chapter 5

Horus

When Adjo completed his work on the extension of the Suez Canal he was offered a job in Iran, redesigning Tehran's underground transportation system. Amisi didn't want to leave Cairo and move to a country where women were even more repressed than they were in Cairo. In Tehran women weren't even allowed to attend public sports events. Soccer matches, or, as Horus called them, football matches, were important to her because Horus loved the game. At age ten he lived for it, and Amisi adored watching her son play. His strength never seemed to wane, despite often running six or seven miles up and down the field in the course of a single game. And when he performed a header, he leapt so high into the air it looked as if he was unbound from Earth and about to take flight.

"He can play football in Tehran," Adjo told her, "the Iranians are also obsessed with game."

"But I won't be allowed to go to his matches."

"You can dress like a man and go. That's what women do there. You might enjoy it," Adjo teased, smiling at the thought of Amisi dressed like a man.

"And my flower shop?" Amisi put her hands on her hips and tilted her head playfully.

"I promise you, you will not have a life without flowers."

So they'd moved, and had lived in Tehran for ten eventful years, when at twenty, Horus had been chosen for Iran's national soccer team. Now, about to turn twenty-one, he would play for Iran in his first World Cup.

As it turned out, Amisi had fallen in love with the Persians and their culture, and had made many friends, both through Adjo's work and her own. One of the many Persian stories she

29

loved was about an ancient battle, when the Persian army won a victory by wearing so much gold armor that the sun reflecting off it blinded their enemy. And she shared the Persian love of roses and rose oil. Instead of opening a flower shop in Tehran, Amisi planted roses in the extensive walled gardens behind their home. She sold the many varieties of roses which she cultivated to flower shops all over Tehran. Growing in her garden there were not only white, yellow, peach, orange, pink, fusia and deep red roses, but also roses with many different subtle and intoxicating fragrances. Each week, while her roses were in bloom, Amisi held a tea in her garden, and hosted all the flower shop owners. Wearing her lucky dress, which had a full skirt and a pattern of pink roses, she stood behind a long table covered with a white cloth on which she placed her samovar surrounded by delicate tea glasses, plates of thin cookies made with lemon and rose water, and a bowl of tiny sugar cubes with small silver tongs. She loved that Persians sweetened their tea by placing a little cube of sugar behind their front teeth and sipping the tea through it.

Within a few years, roses came to rival even blue lotuses in Amisi's affections. When she mentioned to Adjo that ounce for ounce, rose oil was more valuable than gold, he encouraged her to learn the process of producing it. She and her best friend, Mahin, spent months researching how to make rose oil before embarking on the new venture. Mahin also shared Amisi's interest in soccer. Horus had grown up playing soccer with Mahin's son, Ali, who was as passionate about the game as he was. Ali loved playing so much that when he broke his toe during a match he bought larger soccer shoes to accommodate the splint, and played despite the break.

But life hadn't been all roses and football. Horus had had several serious injuries, both on and off the soccer field. Each time he was laid up with an injury he'd turn his attention to his other interest, the piano. Like his father, Horus favored Schubert above other composers, and during the course of his many injuries learned to play all twenty of Schubert's piano sonatas.

As serious as Horus's football injuries were, something even worse had happened. When Horus was fourteen, he was abducted on his way home from school. After dropping Ali off at his house, Horus was walking toward home when two men came out of the hedges, took hold of him, and pushed him into the back seat of a car. The gardener across the street chanced to look up from his trimming to wipe his brow, and saw the two men push Horus into the waiting car and drive off. The gardener recognized Horus as he regularly helped Amisi with her roses. Something was wrong with what he had witnessed, and he strained to see the license plate number as the car pulled away. He scribbled it down with his bit of pencil, in between items on his list of gardening supplies, and ran to Amisi. Amisi immediately rang Adjo, who notified the police. Road blocks were set up, but the car had already slipped through. After a harrowing three days for his parents, Horus reappeared on their doorstep, confused, and unable to tell them what had happened, his mind a fog.

Unbeknown to them, Darpith's slaves had planted the idea in a couple of thugs that they could get a huge ransom for Horus. Once the thugs had Horus, Darpith's minions took complete control of their minds and instructed them to brainwash Horus, alter his values and turn him to a life of greed and crime. For three days they held him in a house only two miles from where he lived. They tried, and failed, to seduce him into joining them in their life of crime. First they tried drugging him with opiates, hoping to get him addicted, but the drugs didn't have the desired effect. He never asked for more, or even seemed to enjoy them. Similarly, the promise of power and riches failed to entice him. Finally, they brought in three young prostitutes who attempted to seduce him, but to no effect. His heart and mind were incorruptible. Horus's love for soccer, and his dreams of a girl made of light, had shown him what real love was. Neither the thugs, nor Darpith's slaves understood love for anything other than themselves, so they couldn't fathom why Horus cared for none of what they offered him. Furious at this, Darpith's minions pushed the thugs aside and wiped Horus's mind of the previous three days, then decided to go even further, and instructed the thugs to kill him. But something went wrong, Darpith's slaves momentarily lost mind control of the thugs who got into an argument and started beating one another up. Horus watched. He might have just stood there, paralyzed by his own confusion, but something welled up from the recesses of his mind, and told him that he must ask for help in order to receive it. Immediately after his prayer calling for help, he heard a voice, a pure tone riding on a wave of blue light, which organized itself into a pair of beings made of light. Wearing a long robe the color of lapis lazuli and a gold turban with a large agate set in it over his third eye, one of the beings bowed to Horus. His bronze skin, piercing blue eyes and close clipped beard were all familiar to Horus, but from where? Beside him stood a goddess with a flame of light coming out of her third eye and dancing in front of her forehead. She held a sword in her right hand and touched the top of his head with it opening his mind. Horus knew instantly that the pair were Amerissis and El Morya. He bowed to them in recognition.

"Escape while they are distracted," Amerissis told him.

"It is not the will of the Divine that you die now. You have a mission to fulfill on Earth, and you must survive to accomplish it," El Morya added. "Run. Now."

Horus did not want to leave them. He felt such joy in their presence. But they urged him on and he tore himself away, and ran like he had wings under his feet. Feeling a force guiding and protecting him, he didn't stop running until he arrived at his own door. All he remembered of the three days was being with El Morya and Amerissis. How could they be so familiar and so dear to him when he didn't even know where he had seen them before. But their message that he had a mission to accomplish on Earth, was information that didn't entirely surprise him. He had long suspected that he had a special purpose.

Darpith tortured his slaves for losing control of the minds of the thugs and allowing the young light being to escape. For several days he feasted on their pain, before turning his attention to a new plan to corrupt Horus. Crippling him so he could no longer play soccer should create enough bitterness to lure him to the dark side.

At first, Amisi and Adjo didn't connect the kidnapping with the other strange incidents in Horus's life. But once things settled down again, they admitted to one another that this was yet one more thing that they didn't understand about their son. Where had he been, and why didn't he have any memory of those three days. Thankfully, the years following this incident were less harrowing. Now, as he was about to turn twenty-one, Horus was on the brink of international fame as a soccer player. Secretly, Amisi feared this. Since the summers of his childhood, which they spent on the Caspian Sea, she had known that Horus's speed, strength, agility and endurance were beyond human.

Every summer they rented a summer home on the Caspian Sea. Mornings, while Adjo worked for a few hours, and the beach was still empty, Amisi accompanied Horus along the flower lined path from the house to the sea. One morning, a few months after Horus's abduction, Amisi was lounging on her striped canvas chaise watching Horus swim, when she saw him leap straight up out of the sea, forty feet into the sky, flip his body over and dive back down into the water below him. Frightened, she rose and walked to the water's edge. Horus emerged from the water exhilarated to face his mother. She wanted to warn him not to let anyone know he could do such things, but the words stuck in her throat. They exchanged a long look, and understood between them that this should be kept private knowledge within their family. That he could leap to such heights with ease delighted Horus. It reminded him of something he couldn't quite piece together but which involved leaping from water and diving to delight someone, perhaps the emerald-eyed girl he so often dreamed of. When they got back to their summer house for lunch, Horus made a quick note in the book of clues which he'd started keeping after his abduction when he learned that he'd come to Earth on a mission. Each entry in the book was a piece of the puzzle, which he hoped would help him recover his lost memory and illuminate his mission. Often the clues came during physical activity, and sometimes in dreams. What mystified him most was the feeling that he was only half of himself, that part of him was missing. The only time the feeling went away was when he dreamed of the tall girl with ebony skin and emerald eyes. Then he felt whole. In his most recent dream of her she'd been walking toward him, and he'd been so overjoyed to see her that he'd leapt forty feet into a pink sky, and perfectly executed three flips before landing face to face with her smile. He wrapped up the feeling from the dream and carried it next to his heart for days, trying not to let it wear off.

Horus was especially excited that the World Cup was being held in England because he'd been having a recurrent dream for the last several years of a park in London, where he saw a little dark-haired girl feeding swans. He didn't recognize the child, but he knew he'd seen the park and the swans somewhere before. It bothered him not to know where. He'd never been to London in this life. Amisi told him that recurrent dreams were especially important, and that she believed we could dream of our past lives. The night before he left with his team for London, he again dreamed of the little girl. This time she turned and looked directly at him, as if she knew he was watching her. Her emerald eyes were the exact same green as his own, but more than that, they were eyes he knew well. He startled and awoke with his heart pounding.

Only once before had he had such an intense experience of recognition. It was about a year after his abduction and discovery that he was on Earth for a mission. He was traveling with his parents to Tokyo, where his father was doing a consulting job. While Adjo was in meetings, Amisi asked Horus to accompany her to a large park with salt water ponds. She wanted to study the placement of flowers in the Japanese gardens in the park, and especially to see the irises which were world famous. Horus, then about fifteen, had the job of photographing the gardens for her. He was walking along with her snapping photos on his phone of whichever flowers she pointed out, when they came to a bridge over one of the saltwater ponds. The bridge led to a tea house in the middle of the pond. Without knowing why, he walked ahead of Amisi, crossed the bridge and entered the tea house. His eyes immediately went to a Japanese mother and daughter, sitting across from one another, having tea and cake. The girl, who looked his age, felt him staring at her, and smiled, flashing her orange-gold eyes at him. They reminded him of an orange diamond he had once admired in Tehran. Amisi followed Horus into the tea house and suggested they sit down. She could feel the air vibrating around Horus. The girl's mother also seemed to sense the connection between Yosiko and Horus. Amisi ordered tea. Horus could not stop himself from staring at the girl, who was, at her mother's direction, now trying to keep her eyes lowered, but was barely able. They were seated about twenty feet from Horus and Amisi, well inside the limits of each of their energy fields which extended out from the two wanderers to a distance of fifty-five feet. Both Horus and Yosiko felt one another's energy and recognized something familiar and comforting. The hostess was at the girl's table conversing with her mother, who she seemed to know. Perhaps she was a frequent customer. The mother and daughter rose to leave, and passed right next to Amisi and Horus's table. Without thinking, Horus reached out and grasped the girl's hand, sending a noticeable shock wave through both of them. Amisi apologized in the few words of Japanese she knew, and Horus dropped the girl's hand. Yosiko's mother bowed slightly, giving Amisi a look which conveyed that she was not a stranger to unexpected events surrounding her daughter. After the mother and daughter left the tea house, Amisi questioned Horus about his reaction to the girl.

"What made you touch her? Did you think you knew her?"

"I don't know. I was drawn to her, not romantically, but in some other way. I felt a force pulling me into the tea house even before I saw her. Did you see her eyes, so unusual for a human, like orange diamonds? I think I grabbed her hand so she would look at me, and I could see her eyes up close. I've seen those eyes somewhere before."

As he lay in bed that night at their hotel, Horus sifted through his feelings about the girl. The feeling was nothing like the love and passion he felt for the emerald-eyed girl he saw in his dreams. What he mainly felt for this girl, with the orange diamond eyes, was a deep familiarity, friendship and a shared purpose. But how could it be? Was she part of the mission, too, and if she was, did she know it yet? He had heard her mother called her Yosiko. He determined to return to the tea house and leave a note for her, telling her of his feeling that they might be comrades on a mission, and giving his address in Tehran. He would ask someone at the concierge desk to translate it into Japanese. Hopefully Yosiko would receive the note the next time she was at the tea house.

Amisi, too, had thoughts that night of the girl with the orange diamond eyes. She lay awake for hours. Maybe this girl had superpowers, too, and maybe they knew each other in some different dimension. The girl's mother certainly wasn't shocked at the exchange between her daughter and Horus. Maybe she had experienced strange things over the course of her daughter's life just as Amisi had with Horus. Thankfully, so far, Horus had managed over the years to use his physical abilities in believable ways, so as not to draw too much attention. With this comforting thought, she finally fell asleep.

Over the next six years, Amisi prayed that this pattern would hold, and that no attention would come to Horus beyond that which any national footballer received. But as the time came closer for the World Cup games, where Horus would be on the world stage, visible to all, friend and foe alike, Amisi's fear began to grow.

From Orion, Darpith observed Horus's increasing fame with both distain and anticipation. He had tried repeatedly to permanently maim Horus, hoping to create bitterness in him so he could more easily be turned to the dark side. So far, he'd failed, and had had to content himself with corrupting weaker minded humans, and torturing his slaves. But the World Cup was a new opportunity to crush Horus's dreams by permanently crippling him and ruining his career. Darpith relished the thought of the pain that would inflict, and the bitterness he hoped would ensue, hopefully enough bitterness to open Horus's mind to the dark path. Still, he knew that there are those who are destroyed by misfortune and those who are not. He hoped Horus was one of the former.

Chapter 6

Mary

Mary had been a determined, headstrong child. At first Charlotte assumed Mary had inherited those traits from Robert's mother, Maggie, but by the time Mary was in lower school, Charlotte had revised her thinking about the origin of her daughter's character. In her second year of school, the headmistress requested that both Charlotte and Robert come in for a meeting.

"Several of the girls have reported that Mary has an identical twin, and that they take turns coming to school," the headmistress informed them.

Robert laughed at the idea. "I assure you we have only one daughter."

"But Mary seems to have no memory of some of the lessons," the headmistress said, "and many of the children have reported seeing two of Mary."

"Young children sometimes imagine things. And yes, concentration can be a problem for Mary," Charlotte said, hoping to explain away any strangeness about her daughter.

"We'll have a talk with her about paying attention in class," Robert said.

That night Robert gave Mary a stern talking to about paying attention in class, and added, with a meaningful look, "and no funny business."

The headmistress sensed that Lord and Lady Merton were trying to hide something, but she let it go for the moment. Maybe the other girls had just imagined seeing two of Mary, but then, so many of them had told the same story.

The truth was that when Mary wanted to escape from school, she doubled herself, and left her double in the classroom while she slipped outside to a nearby park. The problem was that some of the girls had seen her in class and leaving the building at the same time. The first time she doubled herself, at age six, it had been accidental. Bored in class, she imagined herself escaping and sitting outside in a tree, and it had happened. She'd found herself up in a tree, and no one seemed to notice that she'd been absent. She climbed down from the tree and peeked in the classroom window, and saw herself sitting at her desk. After that she'd doubled herself intentionally.

Her parents had acted more baffled with the headmistress than they actually were. Could Mary possibly be able to double herself? Charlotte wondered. Wasn't that just a made-up power that superheroes had? Even by age six, they knew Mary wasn't an ordinary child.

Charlotte worried what Mary might do next. She said so many strange things about planets they'd never heard of. At first they dismissed this as a child's fantasies. But as she grew older, her beliefs about the way life should work increasingly diverged from the British mainstream, and particularly, from the views of her paternal grandmother, Maggie. Maggie's feet were solidly rooted in a world ruled by the British aristocracy. Mary valued her grandmother for her strength and outspokenness, but she had no use for any kind of class system. The idea of elites, and non-elites revolted her. This resulted in many family discussions, since her father was a member of the House of Lords, and the causes which Mary supported usually involved championing the less fortunate. Despite often being at loggerheads with her father and grandmother, Mary loved them both deeply. It was her grandmother who had brought her the large quartz crystal from her trip to Brazil, when Mary was five. She placed it on her bedroom window sill and watched the way it separated the light rays into the colors of the rainbow when the sun shone through it. At certain times of year, in the late afternoon, the crystal filled her walls with many rainbows of colored light. The colored light rays helped her imagine other worlds, where light beings lived.

She made up stories about beings living on different rays of light, and wrote them down and put them in her secret box. She especially loved the blue ray beings, and many of her stories were about a man wearing a turban and a long blue robe who used blue light to do magic things. At first, Charlotte and Robert had encouraged Mary's writing and enjoyed her fantastical stories of beings who lived on light instead of food, and who could heal themselves with their intention, and travel about the Universe by adjusting their vibration. But by her teen years, when the fantasies hadn't given way to more adult writing, their concern grew. Sensing their concern, she stopped sharing her work with them.

Mary's other grandmother, Georgina, was Charlotte's mother, and a Jungian analyst. Mary was most comfortable when she was with Georgina who was the one member of the family who still encouraged her to write down her fantasies, and never seemed troubled by anything she said about other dimensions, light beings, or dark lords. Mary told Georgina things she would never have shared with Maggie. Her two grandmothers were night and day. Despite this, a kind of detente existed between them. Georgina liked Maggie, even appreciated her as a kind of relic of a bygone era. And Maggie secretly admired what she considered Georgina's bohemian life style, except when it influenced Mary. What would have been a clash of titans, in two less admirable women, was a mostly peaceful competition for their granddaughter.

Around the time Mary was applying for college, Maggie came for lunch one Saturday, and asked if Mary would be joining them.

When Robert told her that Mary was out with Georgina, Maggie gave a little pony-like snort. "Out saving the downtrodden?"

"Don't be spikey, Mother."

"Well, what is Mary going to do with her life? I don't like that woman's influence on her."

"By 'that woman', I assume you mean my mother," Charlotte said, walking into the drawing room.

Maggie didn't even blush, but inquired, "Has Mary decided where she wants to study?"

"She's been accepted at The University of Saint Andrews. It was her first choice," Charlotte told her mother-in-law.

"But, why would she go there? No one in our family has gone there," Maggie said.

"She wants to pursue Middle Eastern studies, and they have a strong program," Robert answered.

"I thought she'd outgrown her obsession with Cairo and the Middle East after your vacation there last year."

"Hardly, she just learned not to discuss it with you," Charlotte said, not without a touch of pleasure.

Mary had gone off to Saint Andrews, and apart from a couple of health scares: one serious accident on the soccer field, and an inexplicable fever which was initially unresponsive to treatment, her time there looked uneventful from the outside. In fact, it had been far from uneventful. Darpith had waged war on her. Only her long relationship with Amerissis and Master El Morya, Chohans of the Blue Ray, had prevented her death. Each time Darpith had penetrated the quarantine around Earth, and poisoned, infected, or physically injured Mary, she had called on El Morya and Amerissis, and their legion of blue flame angels. Once summoned, they were free to help and arrived instantly, their blue sapphire and diamond encrusted robes around their shoulders. Darpith was no match for them. As masters of the Blue Ray, they wielded the power to align Mary with the will of the Divine. Although they were free to help if summoned, they could not tell her her true identity. She would have to awaken to that knowledge herself. Darpith clung to the hope that one time, she would forget to call them, and he would pounce and kill her. For although she knew enough to ask for help, she as yet had no idea that her true home was in the fifth dimension, and that she herself was every bit Darpith's equal.

Now, about to turn twenty-one, and having graduated from Saint Andrews, Mary was back in London looking for a job and a flat, and anticipating her independence, but not so much independence that she hadn't asked her father to use his connections to get her tickets to the World Cup, which the United Kingdom was hosting for the first time in decades. She loved football, or as the Americans called it, soccer, and had played it all through secondary school and college. Tall, strong and fast, she was an excellent player. She also liked the game because it stirred up feelings of someone, someone just out of memory's reach, who she felt was calling to her from far off, almost from another world, a world somehow connected to the pyramids. Although this didn't make sense to her, she accepted it.

It had been because of this tugging on her heart that she'd asked to visit Cairo and see the pyramids. So, when she was seventeen, they'd taken a family vacation to Egypt. While packing for that trip, Mary had imagined meeting a young man there, who would be standing before the pyramids, waiting for her. But when at last she stood before them herself, in the sweltering heat, the air rippled and what she saw was a little boy in khaki shorts and a white shirt, holding the hand of an elegant woman wearing a gossamer dress with a pattern of blue lotuses on it. It felt to Mary as if she was seeing ghosts. Where had she seen this exact pair before? The air rippled again and they were gone.

The image stayed with her all day. That night, she asked for the gift of a dream to help her understand what she'd experienced. Georgina had taught her to do that, explaining that Jung believed that the dream was a small hidden door into the soul.

"The unconscious sees beyond this dimension," Georgina had told Mary, "it knows far more than the conscious mind. You must ask for the gift of a dream when you want information from the unconscious. When you ask your unconscious for help, and give it your attention, it becomes your ally."

Mary had often followed Georgina's advice and enlisted her dreams to help guide her. Her unconscious did not disappoint her. That very night it rewarded her with the gift of a haunting dream. She awoke in the dark with a start, the dream images still before her eyes.

Two serene, elegant beings, who looked like they were partly made of light, strolled together under a pink-gold sky. They were maybe twelve or fourteen feet tall. Their black skin shimmered in the soft evening light. On top of their long slender necks, emerald-green eyes shone out of their light-filled oval faces. The man paused and withdrew something from the pocket of his elegant floor length robe to show the woman. Balanced on his palm, it looked like a bubble, until it expanded into a life size scene. It was the very scene Mary had viewed standing before the pyramid that morning. The dream woman turned her emerald eyes, which were the exact same shade of green as Mary's own, toward Mary, and sent her a telepathic message. "You are me in another dimension. Wake up to your true identity, reunite with our twin flame, and accomplish the mission for which you incarnated in the third dimension. Use your intuition." As she said this, she cast her eyes lovingly toward the man standing beside her under the pink-gold sky.

Mary sat up in bed and hugged herself to make sure she was made of flesh and blood. For a moment, she wasn't sure of her name or which woman she was, the one in her dream or the one sitting in the bed, or both. If the tall woman walking with the man under the pink sky was her, was it her before she'd incarnated or some future version of her? Was the man in the dream her twin flame? Had he been sharing a scene which he himself had witnessed, and then preserved in the bubble so he might show it to her. Was it so that she would remember that scene later when she was Mary? Could the man in her dream be the little boy in the scene in front of the pyramid? If so, was he alive on Earth now too? He must be, if she was to reunite with him. Was that why she'd been drawn to Cairo, because she had once known that he was there? She got up, opened her journal and sketched everything she could remember from her dream vision, as Georgina had taught her to do. The dream made sense of the feeling she'd had all her life that half of her was missing. She drew the couple again and again until dawn broke in the sky, and she heard the call to morning prayers ring out across Cairo. As she stared at her drawings of the man, she knew without a doubt that he was the other half of her, and she must find him. He'd been at the pyramids when he was a child, but he could have been visiting from someplace else, as she was. And by now he could be living anywhere. At least part of her purpose was clear. She would search for this man and try to learn why they had come to Earth. How she would find him she didn't yet know. But she would follow her intuition as Georgina had instructed.

It was her intuition that led her to ask her father for tickets to the World Cup. So when they were having cocktails before dinner, and Robert set his martini on the table, reached into the inside breast pocket of his dinner jacket, and handed her two tickets to the Iran-Ireland game the next day, her heart jumped and banged against her ribs in excitement. Georgina, who was dining with them, was the only one who noticed Mary's outsized reaction as she pulled the tickets from their envelope and saw the word, *Iran*.

"Darling," Georgina asked, "are you particularly following Iran's progress in the games?"

"Not really, but there is a player who interests me, an Egyptian, born in Cairo, raised in Tehran, who is on the Iranian team. He plays with such agility, strength and speed that I love watching him."

Georgina smiled at her granddaughter, but said nothing. Although Robert had gotten her two tickets, Mary had a feeling she should go alone to the game the next day. Unless maybe

Georgina could be persuaded. Something was coming near and Mary knew it. She would not sleep that night.

Chapter 7

Ewen

Aidan's column had become more and more political over the twenty-year period since Ewen's birth. During those years, *The Irish Times* sent him abroad to live and work on three different occasions. Once to Istanbul, where they lived for two years, when Ewen was ten, then to Karachi for three years when he was fifteen, and finally to Mumbai, when Ewen was eighteen. In each city, Caitlin made a comfortable home, and taught Ewen to appreciate the marvels of different cultures.

Wherever they lived, Ewen's favorite activity remained the same, making and remaking objects, changing their shape from one thing to another, reshaping a clay dog into a dolphin, a person into a tree. Observing his son's activity, Aidan joked to Caitlin, "Ewen will either be a sculptor or a shape shifter when he grows up."

Caitlin stopped peeling potatoes and looked up long enough to give him her, "don't go there" face.

Once, as a toddler, while he was playing at her feet, Ewen casually told his mother that he knew there was an easier way to change the shape of things.

"Really?" was all she said, but she felt like someone had walked over her grave.

Though he didn't know how he did it, Ewen had accidentally changed some things, even living things, from one form to another when he was a child. The first time it happened, he and Caitlin had been walking along the beach beside the Irish Sea, looking out over the water, when a blue backed bass leapt up out of the water, and changed into a collared dove. Then it flew over to them and circled their heads before soaring skyward. Caitlin asked five-year old Ewen if he had made that happen.

"I thought the fish wanted to experience the sky, and that's why it leapt up. I imagined it turning into a dove, to make its wish come."

Caitlin felt both awe and fear ripple across her scalp, and right down to the ends of her long, curly brown hair. She had to think about what to say to Ewen, and caught herself just in time, before her anxiety burst out and frightened him.

Ewen felt for all creatures, and wanted them to be happy. Once he was old enough to understand that meat came from animals, he refused to eat it, telling his parents that raising cattle for meat was destroying the rain forest and making it harder for Earth to breathe. So they all stopped eating meat. At first Aidan had missed his Irish stew, but Caitlin got creative in her cooking, studying the cuisine of whichever country they were living in, and all three of them happily survived as vegetarians. While living in Mumbai, Caitlin surprised herself by publishing a vegetarian cookbook, Aidan's politics deepened, moving further to the left, and Ewen continued to develop as a sculptor. Now, at nearly twenty-one, he had been studying for the past two years at the L.S. Raheja School of Art in Mumbai. And in a few weeks he would be leaving to attend the Royal College of Art in London.

It made Caitlin uneasy that Ewen was going so far away. She and Aidan still had another year in Mumbai. She wasn't a mother who smothered her child, but Ewen had given them some frights over the years. Since his early teens he'd been into gaming, sometimes obsessed with it. One evening Ewen went off to a gaming center, and when after nine hours, he still wasn't home, Aidan had gone looking for him, and found him in a frightening state, unresponsive to his own name, red-eyed and lost in a virtual reality game called *Orion*. Not only did Ewen not respond to his own name, he didn't seem to be able to hear anything at all, except the instructions coming from the game. He had lost his identity, and the game was controlling him. Aidan tore the head phones and goggles off Ewen and forcibly removed him from his chair, at which point Ewen collapsed. Aidan carried him to a cab. He remained unconscious for the next twenty-four hours, though the doctor couldn't find anything wrong with him, beside the fact that his vitals were low and his skin was a greyish color. "Keep him quiet and let him rest," was the best the doctor could do.

Caitlin, terrified for Ewen, sat by his bed, holding his hand, praying, calling out to whatever higher power she could think of to save her son. It felt like whatever had a hold of him was pure evil. Ewen no longer even looked like himself. As she prayed, begged really, for a miracle, someone answered her. She clearly heard a gentle male voice say to her: "Place both hands on him, and repeat, *you are the resurrection and the life.*"

Then a female voice spoke urging her to use the mantra she had been given. "Do it now. Speak the words you are the *resurrection and the life* and keep repeating it. We have come in answer to your prayer to help Ewen, but it will be better if you participate."

Caitlin did as she was instructed, and a gold light began to surround Ewen. Seeing the light, she let out an involuntary scream, which brought Aidan running. Together they watched as Ewen's body became transparent and absorbed the golden light through a central tube running the length of his body from about six inches above his head to six inches below his feet. As he absorbed the golden light a sphere that looked to Caitlin like DaVinci's drawing of the Vitruvian man formed around Ewen and filled with golden light coming from both the top and bottom of the tube. The gold was especially bright in the area of Ewen's heart. The gray color left his skin. They could see the gold light moving into his head, into the center of his brain. When the gold light entered his pineal gland, Ewen regained a kind of consciousness, but did not open his eyes and seemed to be focused on an internal world. Unaware of his parents, he spoke instead to beings who were invisible to Caitlin and Aiden, calling the invisible beings Lord Sananda and Lady Nada. With his eyes closed he saw them clearly standing beside him, Sananda's dark skin shimmering next to the milky white of Nada's arms emerging from her gold and purple robe. Her long, dark-red hair hung to her waist and was held in place by a slender circlet of gold. Sananda's shoulder length brown hair was unbound. From his palms poured out a golden light, like an eternal fountain. Ewen thanked them for resurrecting him and told them of his joy at seeing them again. Sananda raised his hand over Ewen in blessing. Breathing softly, Ewen slipped into a peaceful sleep.

Darpith watched and listened to all this from a corner of Ewen's bedroom. He'd almost had this young light being completely in his power, until the mother had called out, asking for help, and Lord Sananda and Lady Nada had answered. Darpith knew he was no match for Sananda and Nada, and he feared the gold Resurrection Flame. He didn't understand its workings. In fact, Darpith knew nothing of love for others or of self-sacrifice or resurrection. All his many lives, he had been devoted only to self-love. He cursed them all and withdrew, for the time being.

While Ewen slept, Aidan researched the names Lord Sananda and Lady Nada, and discovered that according to esoteric lore they were ascended masters and Chohans of the Resurrection Flame. When he told Caitlin she said only, "How does our son know two ascended masters?"

"So, you believe in ascended masters now?" Aidan said, smiling at her.

Caitlin nodded, "And in miracles too."

Several hours later, when Ewen awoke, he told his parents that the strange thing was that *Orion* wasn't one of his usual games. Someone he'd never seen before had challenged him to play, and he'd felt compelled, which wasn't like him. At first it had been exciting, but very quickly it was as if the game had taken over his will, enslaving him. He'd tried to stop playing, but grew too weak to break free. He'd fought the feeling at first, but then he'd passed into a state beyond caring. Aidan forbid him to ever play *Orion* again, no matter how compelled he felt. Caitlin wanted to ban all gaming, but Ewen charmed her out of that position. Aidan agreed with his son that the danger was connected to the game *Orion*.

It was at this same gaming place, near Raheja, that Ewen met Arjuna, not long before both of them were to leave Mumbai, Arjuna, to take up his studies in astrophysics at Columbia University, in New York City, and Ewen, to study sculpture at the Royal College of Art, in London.

Ewen paused before the entrance to the gaming center. He hadn't been playing much since the incident, but that evening he decided to check out the latest virtual reality and multisensory feedback effects that had been added to his favorite game, *Fifth Dimension*. As he was about to put on his headgear and goggles, he noticed the guy next to him, who was already deep into *Fifth Dimension*. There was something familiar about him. Ewen sat down and logged in. He glanced over at his neighbor's screen and saw that he had also reached level five, which meant they could play together. Once you reached level five in the game you were an acknowledged light being on a mission from Venus, and you could work with others to fight the dark lords using your superpowers. Ewen requested permission to link in to his neighboring gamer's group of light fighters. Permission was granted. The gamer looked sideways for a moment to see who had joined. Ewen smiled, and Arjuna returned it. Then they both became absorbed in a battle with a particularly devious dark lord for the soul of a young Japanese girl, Yosiko, who did not yet know she was a light being. The rules forbid them to tell her her true identity, but they could offer aid since she had requested it, and they could give her clues. Ewen stared at Yosiko and felt something new stir in him, a feeling of protectiveness toward her he'd never felt before for anyone. Suddenly he wanted desperately to save her. He charged the dark lord. Arjuna took advantage of the moment to duplicate Yosiko a hundred times, hoping to confuse the dark lord as to which was the real Yosiko. Sensing that Ewen was somehow connected to Yosiko, Arjuna was certain that Ewen would know which Yosiko was the real one, even if he created a thousand of her. Currents of white light emanating from Arjuna's fingers forced the dark lord back, while Ewen created a wall of violet light and shapeshifted all hundred Yosikos into different species to further confuse the dark lord, so they could escape with the real Yosiko into the fifth dimensional positive zone. As he did this, Ewen turned the real Yosiko into a kitten and tucked the tiny creature inside his jacket, and flew her to the healing temple. Once there, Ewen turned the kitten back into Yosiko. She looked at him with such love in her eyes that Ewen never wanted to be parted from her again. But she needed healing. Her head was on fire from resisting the dark lord's attempt to control her mind and enslave her. In the temple she could receive light from the green ray beings. Ewen didn't want to leave, but Arjuna reminded him it was a game they were playing, and Yosiko was only a character. It didn't feel like that to Ewen, but reluctantly, he returned with Arjuna to the action of the game to answer another call for help. This time the call came from a being called Natasha. She was on an airplane bound for New York, and it was about to crash. After this rescue attempt it would be Arjuna who had to be reminded that Natasha was only a character in the game.

They played for several more hours before Ewen asked Arjuna if he'd like to go eat something. Arjuna agreed without hesitating. He felt drawn to this fellow gamer in a way he'd not felt with any other human before. Neither of them consciously knew that they had been friends in the fifth dimension, on Venus, where they were known as Toomeh and Bereh, but both felt an uncanny connection. They left the gaming center together and walked toward a nearby restaurant frequented by students. Arjuna spoke first.

"It's exciting to be in a virtual world where so many more things are possible." Arjuna paused before adding, "And so hauntingly familiar."

These last words caught Ewen's attention.

"What seems so 'hauntingly familiar' to you about *Fifth Dimension*?"

"The abilities to use light for protection, to mutate, regenerate, and duplicate, to become invisible at will, to have incredible speed, agility and strength, to be in a battle with the dark side. I sometimes feel that all these powers would be possible for us, if we knew how to access them. But more even than the powers, it's the idea behind the game, that there are those who would turn Earth to the dark side, and must be stopped by light beings who have incarnated as humans but don't know that they're light beings. When I play the game, and engage in the battle against the dark lords, it feels more real than my ordinary life."

What was it about Arjuna, Ewen wondered, that was so familiar. But the waitress came with warm nan and sag paneer, and they tucked into it.

"Do you play other games besides *Fifth Dimension*?" Arjuna asked.

"Not usually. Something feels familiar and true about *Fifth Dimension*. I keep going back to it, like I'm looking for a hidden message in the game."

"I know what you mean." Arjuna nodded.

They finished dinner, and kept talking, not wanting to part, and finally agreed to meet at the gaming center the next day. Then Arjuna remembered it was his birthday, and a family celebration had been planned.

"Tomorrow is my twenty-first birthday too," Ewen said.

That they shared a birthday somehow didn't surprise either

of them, but both would think about it later as somehow a key to his own mysteries. They exchanged cell numbers and parted, agreeing to meet soon at the gaming center before they left Mumbai in a few weeks. Both of them dreamed that night of traveling to a temple in the Grand Teton Mountains in Wyoming, and being addressed by Lord Lanto and his twin flame Shoshimi who taught them how to wield the yellow Flame of Illumination. Lanto and Shoshimi reminded them they were light beings, incarnate as human, and that they must remember this when they awoke in the morning back in their human bodies. Shoshimi also told them that various aids were in place to stimulate their memories, including virtual reality games.

Chapter 8

Yosiko

Yosiko was Umeko and Kosuke's only child. The three of them lived a gentle and ordered life in their large, comfortable apartment in Tokyo. When Yosiko was still small, Umeko began teaching her the art of flower arrangement, including how to choose the correct vase for each season, and where it should be placed in a room for that time of year. Yosiko had also been instructed in the art of the tea ceremony, and on how to select the appropriate cup for each person. Proper pattern, color and sleeve length of a kimono based on the person's age and sex had also been part of her education. Even her dolls had kimonos with the long sleeves suitable for maidens. Kosuke, too, participated in Yosiko's education by teaching her painting and calligraphy, and sharing with her his passion for Chijimi linen. She often traveled with him to inspect rare pieces.

Despite the care, and attention to detail which characterized her upbringing, Yosiko's life had not been without repeated trauma. There was the time when she was seven that she accompanied her father all the way to Chijimi snow country. After his business was concluded, Yosiko had asked to go skiing, and Kosuke had obliged her even though it was already late afternoon. The concierge where they were staying arranged everything, and within an hour they were riding up the mountain behind their guest house in a gondola. The late afternoon sun glistened on the snow-covered slopes below them. The skiers traversing the mountain looked like small moving dolls from the gondola. Their guide was explaining something to them, when suddenly the gondola jerked to a stop. First it began to swing wildly, then to slide backwards down the mountain, toward another gondola waiting at the base. The gondola picked up speed as it roared down the mountain, dumping Yosiko onto the floor. Kosuke threw his body down on the floor covering her to brace for the crash. Their guide wanted them to jump out, but it was still a fifty foot drop into the snow below from a fast-moving vehicle. They could see sparks flying from the cables above their heads and both men knew a fire could break out any moment. They could even be electrocuted when the crash came. But Kosuke said it was too dangerous for Yosiko to jump. The guide nodded. Kosuke tightened his arms around Yosiko's little body and reassured her. All three of them were knocked unconscious when they crashed and the gondola burst into flames.

Rescuers pulled them out and carried them to the inn, where Kioko, a young woman doctor, who was also staying there, examined them and treated them for shock, ordering that they be kept warm and hydrated, and explaining that they would require rest for their concussions. In the next few days Kioko's care and gentle manner made a deep impression on Yosiko, so much so that on the train ride back to Tokyo, she told her father that she wanted to be a doctor, like Kioko, when she grew up. She also told him that Kioko had had help from the same violet light man who had helped save Hoshi's paw. "I recognized his violet eyes and robes and his reddish hair and mustache," she told her father.

"And how did the violet man help Kioko?" Kosuke asked his little daughter.

"He put his violet flame in her hands so when she worked on our pyramids it would help them spin again."

"What pyramids?"

"The three pyramids surrounding our bodies. Two of the three need to spin. After the accident ours weren't spinning correctly, but the violet light fixed them."

"What did she say to the violet man."

"She bowed to him and called him Saint Germain, and thanked him for coming when she called him. I was happy to see him again too."

Though surprised that Yosiko knew the violet man, as she called him, Kosuke only bowed his head slightly toward her in acknowledgement of what she had said, and asked no further questions about him or the pyramids. He was, in fact, less mystified at this than one might have expected.

Darpith's minions had failed to make good on the opportunity with the gondola to kill Yosiko. He was enraged when he received the report of their failure, and subjected them to a hideous form of mental torture, feasting on the picnic of their pain. But even that was not enough to slake his rage that the young doctor had summoned Saint Germain. Of all the Chohans of the Seven Rays he feared Saint Germain and the Violet Ray of Transmutation the most. Now he would have to wait until his minions could again slip through the quarantine around Earth in order to make another attempt to wipe out this little light being.

Yosiko and Kosuke returned to Tokyo with no further incident, and although Yosiko's appreciation of Chijimi linen continued to grow over the years, she declined to take over her father's business. Her heart was set on being a doctor and on working with Saint Germain and the violet ray. The way the human body could heal a broken bone, or a deep cut, or fight viruses and bacteria made her feel a tremendous respect for it. Meeting Kioko and seeing Saint Germain again had strengthened her resolve, but even before that, Yosiko had been enthralled with living bodies of all kinds. She loved how starfish, which she called "sea stars," could regenerate injured limbs, and how they housed most of their vital organs in their arms, rather than in their central body. And there had also been that time with her kitten, Hoshi, when Saint Germain, Lady Nada and Lord Sananda had regenerated his little paw. Even though her parents tried to tell her afterwards that the vet had sewn it back on, she remembered the streams of violet and golden light she'd seen entering Hoshi's tiny body. In her dreams she saw beings regenerate their limbs after losing them in battles where they wielded light. She filled her sketch books with images from these dreams. The idea of regeneration became an obsession for her. By age thirteen Yosiko was staying after school every day to work in the biology lab. She felt there must be a way to empower humans to regenerate missing limbs as well. If only they could learn to use light like Saint Germain and Lord Sananda and Lady Nada.

When she began majoring in biology at the Tokyo University of Science, Yosiko saw it as the first step toward fulfilling her plan to be a doctor. Umeko and Kosuke were delighted for her. But when she was accepted at King's College in London for medical school, they were far from happy. How could their love protect her across such a distance? It had been clear to them from early in her life that she was somehow different from most people, and also, that their love was among her most powerful protections. Even from the time of her pregnancy, Umeko had suspected that Yosiko was not completely a human baby but connected to some other realm. They learned the truth of this suspicion when Yosiko was five. She had been asking for a kitten, and for her fifth birthday they got her one, a lovely little fellow with green eyes and a white star on the gray fur of his tiny chest, right over his heart. She named him Hoshi, which means star. Hoshi followed Yosiko everywhere, ate from her hand and curled his tiny body up on her pillow to sleep at night. When she returned from school each day he was at the front door to greet her. One afternoon when Hoshi was about six months old, Yosiko came home, and Hoshi wasn't at the door to meet her. Something was wrong. She, Umeko, and their cook searched the house. There was no sign of him. Yosiko wondered if he could have slipped out when cook went into the garden to gather herbs. Cook had been instructed never to leave the door ajar, but maybe this once she had forgotten. Yosiko burst through the back door and ran into the garden, followed by the cook and Umeko. They heard Hoshi crying and found him under a peony bush, his paw caught in a rat trap. The cook freed him, but his front paw was almost completely severed and he was losing a lot of blood. She wrapped him in her apron and bound his paw with a clean dish towel. The vet couldn't save his little paw and amputated it. That night as Hoshi lay beside her head, Yosiko promised him a new paw. She set her heart and mind on it, praying as hard as she could, calling out to the universe for help. She fell asleep and dreamed of three light beings. Two were moving within golden light, a man and a woman, wielding a golden flame. The third light being wielded a violet flame, directing it to Yoshi's arm where the paw had been severed. She saw the light entering Hoshi through a central tube running the length of his small body. The light was resurrecting his paw. The violet and gold light filled both Hoshi's upward facing pyramid and the downward facing pyramid which intersected it to form a star tetrahedron. Yosiko stared at the spinning tetrahedrons around Hoshi, and they felt oddly familiar to her. When she awoke, Yosiko tore off the bandage and saw Yoshi's perfect little paw restored. Scooping him up and kissing him, she ran into her parents' room to show them. She told them that she had prayed very hard, and her love had called the light people who made Hoshi's paw grow back. When the cook arrived that day she was given a two-week vacation before she could see Hoshi, and was later told that the vet had sewn the paw back on. After this, Umeko and Kosuke were on high alert for what else their daughter might pray for. They cautioned her about wishing too hard for anything, especially in front of other people. But she was five, and her stories could still be passed off as fantasy, at least for a little while longer. When she reached the age of reason, they would have a serious talk with her.

Yosiko understood her parents concern for her, and did her

best over the years to be discrete with her talk of light beings and regeneration. She knew her parents feared that if her ability was discovered powerful people would try to use her to their advantage. They didn't suspect, however, that there were dark lords in higher dimensions set on turning Yosiko to the dark path, and failing that, would take her life. Yosiko, however, by the time she was a teenager, had her suspicions. Her dreams had warned her. Only the previous night she had been out talking with another student at a party, a cute guy, almost too cute to be real, who was really into her. Yosiko could feel herself becoming enthralled. He offered her a pill, telling her it would make her feel great. She hesitated.

"Don't you trust me?" he pressed.

"It's not that."

"Then take it," he said, leaning into her.

Yosiko felt herself weakening. She liked him and she didn't want to seem a prude. But why was it so important to him that she take this pill? She turned away for an instant to collect herself and in that moment, he dropped the pill into her drink. When she turned back he'd changed his tune and said, "Never mind the pill, finish your drink then let's get out of here." He chatted to her while she sipped her drink, then, pretending to be playful, he grabbed her and pulled her to the exit. Once outside he pushed her into a waiting vehicle and the driver sped off. Yosiko felt something taking over her mind. She fought against it, but it was a powerful dark presence. The car pulled into an empty lot near a warehouse. As the guy dragged her out of the car she suddenly saw a hundred of herself. Was her mind playing tricks? But her captor seemed to see them, too, and in his confusion accidentally let go of her just as a wall of violet light surrounded her. She struggled to hold onto her mind as all one hundred duplicates of her turned into different animals. She looked at her body and saw that she had become a tiny kitten and was being lifted by gentle masculine hands and placed inside his jacket next to his heart. The next moment they were in the air, flying. When they landed, he lifted her from inside his jacket and looked into her eyes, which were the same orange-gold as his own. He changed her from a kitten back into a girl, and laid her down in a temple of healing. When she awoke the next morning, she was in her own bed. What stayed with her the most from the experience was looking into those eyes, the same orange-gold color as her own, and the feeling of never wanting to be parted from them.

Darpith angrily dropped his disguise as the handsome young Japanese man who had crashed the college party and drugged Yosiko. He resumed his reptilian form and raged against his bad luck. Furious at the young light beings for rescuing Yosiko, Darpith returned to Orion and tortured a few dozen of his slaves.

Yosiko was to leave for London in a week, and much as she had been looking forward to this now her mind was full of the man who had rescued her, and his orange-gold eyes, so like her own. She knew he had parted from her at the healing temple only reluctantly. She had felt it. It was like nothing she had ever experienced before. There had been that time in the tea house when a boy had grabbed her hand sending an electric charge through her, but that had been more the feeling of an old friend than of a lover. When she received his note the next time she went to the tea house, she had wanted to answer it but her mother had taken it and burned it.

The night before her departure for London, while her human body slept, Yosiko's guides took her to the Temple of the Blue Ray, high in the Himalayas. There, along with many others in their light bodies, she was shown how to align her will with the will of the Divine in her. Some of those present for the training were strangely familiar, but her heart leapt when she saw the orange-gold-eyed man who had rescued her. They communicated telepathically to make a plan. But the next morning, back in her human body, she struggled to remember what it was. All she could recall was a feeling of tremendous joy, and one word, which she struggled to hold onto, *Toomeh*. But what did it mean? What language was it? She resolved to try harder to remember what happened at these temple visits, for this had not been the first. The beautiful feeling from her night journey stayed with her all day, and it was with a happy heart that she packed for London. Hoshi was now fifteen, relatively old for a cat, and more beloved than ever. It tore her heart to say good-bye to him. She wept into his soft gray fur, kissed his white star, and promised him that she would see him again.

Chapter 9

Movie Night

Rose made several good friends among the interns at the UN. Her closest friend was Lia, a girl from Jerusalem. The two of them started a weekly movie night for their intern group. Tonight, it was Rose's turn to have everyone over and they were planning to watch *Mississippi Burning*. Lia asked if she could bring a friend who had just arrived from Jerusalem to study creative writing at NYU. Everyone agreed.

Her father was in London on a business trip so Rose had their West Village brownstone to herself. She bustled around washing apples and grapes, setting out chips and salsa and rearranging the chairs and sofas in the living room to face the large screen she'd set up. The doorbell rang as she was about to pour the popcorn into the warm oil. Dashing to the entrance she paused a second to smooth her wild, curly, blonde hair in the foyer mirror before swinging the door open.

"Lia! Come in," Rose said, before she saw the man standing beside Lia.

"Rose, this is my friend Ephraim from Jerusalem," Lia said, turning toward the handsome violet-eyed man.

But neither Rose nor Ephraim heard her. Time stopped as their violet eyes met. The world moved away and only they were left standing face to face, unable to move or speak. Echoes of another world began beating inside each of them like a second heart. When he telegraphed to her "I know you," Rose felt herself breaking apart into tiny stars.

"You are my light house, the one I have been walking over the Earth seeking. I have slowed time down in every city I visited all my life to search for you, without knowing it was you I was searching for."

Rose stared at him, her eyes polished by tears. Another being, inside her, seemed to be using mental telepathy to answer him. "I have seen you standing at the edge of my dreams. Are you real this time?"

Ephraim heard her thought with his heart and his body nearly burst into flames. "I am real flesh and blood standing before you in the doorway."

Lia didn't know what was going on, other than that the two of them were staring at one another, dumbstruck.

"I smell something burning," she said.

Rose dragged her eyes from Ephraim's face to try and focus on what Lia was saying, but it was like returning from another universe. After a delay, the words registered in her brain.

"Oh, it's the oil for the popcorn," she said. The whole house could have burned down before Rose moved had not Lia grabbed her arm and dragged her toward the kitchen.

"Don't touch the pan," Ephraim shouted from behind them, the protectiveness he felt for Rose already sounding in his voice, "just turn off the burner." He spoke calmly but inside he was dying of tenderness for her.

The rest of their group arrived to find the front door wide open and followed the sound of voices into the kitchen, where the three of them stood by the stove, Rose glowing as if her skin was shedding light, Ephraim gazing at her, bells sounding in his body, and Lia wearing a bemused expression. Even someone with the most lumbering imagination could not have missed the connection between Rose and Ephraim. Assessing the situation, Lia took charge. "I think we should start again with a new pan for the popcorn."

"Yes," was all Rose could manage. She pointed up to the hanging rack of pots and pans and Ephraim reached up for one. Everything that had once been familiar to Rose was now altered. The kitchen was still her kitchen, but it felt different and it looked different. Lia poured the oil into the new pan and when it started to smoke she added the popcorn. Someone offered to shake the pot once they heard the corn begin to pop. Rose stood staring at Ephraim, afraid he might disappear if she took her eyes off him. Somehow a large bowl appeared and someone dumped the warm popcorn into it. Someone else found the salt while Lia got the movie rolling. It all happened in a daze for Ephraim and Rose. When they sat down to watch the movie, Ephraim took the seat next to Rose on the sofa, but neither of them saw anything on the screen. They sat side by side communicating telepathically about their lives on Earth so far. When he shared his near drowning off the coast of Corfu and the vision he had of the two violet-eyed beings walking under the pink-gold sky toward a temple, she stopped him, and telepathically sent him a detailed description of the temple. But it was when he telegraphed the name *Soonam*, the name he'd heard while he was drowning, that her soul flowed out of her eyes into his. With irresistible tenderness, he put one finger on her cheek to wipe away her tears.

"These are not tears," she telegraphed to him, "this is the whole universe and a thousand lifetimes."

He took her hand. As their fingers intertwined they knew themselves to be a single being, a single grain of sand, twin flames. Though they had both had inklings throughout their lives that they were not of this time, and both of them had suspected that they had come to Earth on a mission, they didn't yet remember what that mission was. But they knew that their meeting was a big step toward figuring it out.

Still absorbed by the intensity of the movie, everyone but Ephraim left soon after it ended. Rose turned to him still holding the word *Soonam* in her heart. Why was it so comforting and familiar? Ephraim read her thoughts. "Shall I call you by this name?"

"Yes. Call me by my name."

He said out loud, "Soonam." At the sound of her true name,

spoken by him, her mind burst its third dimensional limitations burning away every confusion about this lifetime. She searched in the ashes until she found his name, *Attivio*. The word rose up out of her throat like a phoenix. When he heard her speak his name, he stepped forward and embraced it like a new self.

Soonam took his hand and led him upstairs to her bed.

"We have much to figure out, but not this night," he said as he lifted her in his arms and laid her on the bed. "Your hair, it's like wheat and starlight," he whispered into the shell of her ear. Lying beside her, he ran his hands over her body tracing her soft curves through her cotton dress. When she moaned at his touch he unbuttoned the bodice of her dress and slipped it over her head. For a moment, he rested his head on the pillow of her breast, covered only by a thin lace bra. As she moved his head aside and sat up to unhook her bra, his lips brushed her nipple and another moan escaped her lips. He pulled off his shirt and jeans, pressed her back on the bed, pulled off her underwear, and gazed at her naked body, at once familiar and strange. It was made of flesh and light, and not of light alone. Her eyes beckoned him and he lay upon her, the sweetest weight she'd ever known. Welcoming him inside her, she opened to him, body and soul, until he reached the sweetness of her being and knew her to be himself. After a separation of twenty-one Earth years they were again one being. Their sexual union opened the memory of their identity as citizens of the Violet Planet. Touching Attivio heightened Soonam's power of psychometry. She saw them training on Venus for this mission to Earth. She saw their first meeting on the Violet Planet and images of their friends throughout this galaxy and in distant galaxies. By morning, nothing of their past lay hidden, extinguished or forgotten. They now knew themselves to be wanderers to Earth who had come on a mission. They knew also that they were not the only ones, but had come with a group and they felt an urgency to find the others. As to their fifth dimensional powers, they'd have to see what they could recover and what would work in the third dimension now that they knew they were from another time and place. Neither of them brought up the dark side, but that topic could not wait much longer. They could sense the dark lord's anger at their reunion and knew he meant to destroy them.

Chapter 10

More than a Game

Natasha was trying to fall asleep when the turbulence began. First in Russian and then in English, the pilot's voice came over the loud speaker informing them that they had encountered some unexpected turbulence and instructing them to fasten their seatbelts. The flight had taken off from Moscow, headed for New York's JFK, less than hour before, in clear skies. Ten minutes after his first announcement the pilot told them that the turbulence had passed and they were free to move about the cabin. Feeling too excited to sleep, Natasha scrolled through the selection of available movies and chose an old classic, *Dirty Dancing*.

Darpith summoned the minions who had caused the turbulence and threatened them. "I told you to wait until the plane was over the North Atlantic Ocean, so it would go down in the water and all evidence would be lost. Get it right this time or you'll suffer the consequences."

While Darpith was threatening his slaves, Arjuna and Ewen were in Mumbai, at the gaming center, playing *Fifth Dimension*. They had just delivered the Japanese girl to the healing temple and were headed back to answer another distress call. This time it came from a young Russian girl in an airplane flying over the North Atlantic Ocean on its way to JFK International Airport in New York City.

During the final song of *Dirty Dancing*, the captain came over the loud speaker again and instructed all the passengers and flight attendants to fasten their seatbelts because of new turbulence.

Natasha glanced at the girl in the seat next to her and saw beads of sweat on her forehead. When cups, glasses, books and computers started bouncing, falling off tray tables and hitting the floor of the aircraft, Natasha herself started to sweat. She whispered a prayer calling for help from her old standbys, the pink man and lady, now known to her as Paul the Venetian and Lady Ruth. The prayer came easily to her lips and calmed her. Natasha in turn, tried to reassure the girl beside her.

Paul the Venetian and Lady Ruth heard Natasha's call and knew at once that Darpith was behind the turbulence and what his aim was. As the Chohans in charge of *Fifth Dimension* that day, they informed the players, Arjuna and Ewen, that the trouble was once again the work of Darpith and his minions from Orion.

"We're on it," Arjuna responded.

Lady Ruth reminded Paul the Venetian that neither Arjuna nor Ewen yet knew the extent of their superpowers. They still believed they were just playing a game and that Darpith was but a game adversary.

"That's why we're using the game," Paul the Venetian told Lady Ruth. "When they're playing *Fifth Dimension*, they accept their powers as a natural part of the game."

In fact, all the Chohans of all the light rays responsible for planet Earth had together created *Fifth Dimension* for this purpose, hoping that playing it would awaken the wanderers and they would remember their mission and their true home in the fifth dimension.

Conditions inside the aircraft were becoming worse, the plane was violently bouncing up and down now, and one side had partly caved inward like a bent tin can. The pilot tried to reassure them, but passengers and crew alike were terrified. Natasha continued to call for help from the light beings. Ewen and Arjuna could simultaneously see conditions both inside and outside the plane on their screens, and when Arjuna spotted Natasha he instantly recognized her as the girl he'd seen ice skating in Gorky Park six years before. This recognition shook him and he froze, causing Ewen to ask, "Are you alright?"

"I know the girl on the plane calling for help."

Paul the Venetian and Lady Ruth heard this and immediately appeared on the screen of *Fifth Dimension* to address Arjuna directly.

"You are correct. You do know her and you and Ewen must work with us to save this plane from Darpith and his minions. Don't allow yourself to be swept away with feelings. Think rationally about what powers you can employ through *Fifth Dimension* to save the passengers and crew.

"*Fifth Dimension* isn't just a game?" Arjuna asked.

"Again, you are correct. It is a game and it is more than a game. Play it like a game for now, but play to save lives."

Arjuna and Ewen had often sensed that *Fifth Dimension* was more than a game and that the beings who led the game were actually real beings in some other dimension. There was something so familiar about them. And it was strange, too, that they both had dreams of meeting these beings in ethereal temples, suspended above the Earth.

As Arjuna and Ewen viewed the damage to the plane, a new character appeared on the screen requesting permission to join the game. She identified herself as Ederah of Venus. Ewen did not want any interference and suspected this was a trick by Darpith to infiltrate their plans, but when Arjuna saw that she looked remarkably like the Russian girl he'd seen skating in Gorky Park he insisted that she be allowed to play. Rather than delay, Ewen agreed. When he actually looked at Ederah of Venus a flash of recognition passed through him as well, and he, too, smiled at her in welcome.

Back inside the plane it appeared to her fellow passengers as if Natasha had passed out. In fact, aroused by her desire to save her fellow passengers, she had unknowingly shifted into her true state as the higher dimensional being, Ederah. Seeing Ederah awaken and split off from Natasha, Lady Ruth had guided her into the game to work with Arjuna and Ewen.

The three of them were observing the wind currents around the plane in order to make a plan, when they spotted four of Darpith's minions creating the turbulence. Ederah instantly made herself, Arjuna and Ewen invisible. Both Arjuna and Ewen realized at once that this must be one of her superpowers. Though they were now invisible to anyone else they could see one another.

"Good move," Arjuna told her.

Her answering smile pierced his heart. They saw that the turbulence encircled the plane and moved with it like an aura. The three of them stayed just outside of the aura to confer. Ewen said he could change the plane into a large bird shape which could dive out of the turbulence. Arjuna, angry at the threat to the Russian girl's life, wanted to capture the minions, but Ewen pointed out that their first priority was to save the plane.

"We need something to distract them," Ederah said, "long enough for Ewen to change the plane into a bird shape and slip out of the turbulence."

"Ederah, can you make the plane invisible?"

"No, it's shaking and moving too much."

"What about the sun? Can you make it invisible so the sky will be black, even for a few seconds? Arjuna asked her. "They may lose their ability to keep control of the plane if they can't see it."

"I can do it for a few seconds, long enough for them to be startled and for Ewen to take control of it and shape shift it into a bird," Ederah answered.

"Good. Once it's a bird shape, Ewen can enter the bird's head/cockpit to protect the pilots from any attempt on their lives. Ederah, will you help me protect the bird/plane on the outside from any further attempts by Darpith to crash it?"

Ederah nodded. Arjuna was so emboldened by her presence,

that he felt capable of anything. She was, for him, like a fresh sword in battle. The fact that she looked so like the Russian girl confused him. There was no time to think about that now, but later he would ask himself if the Russian girl was somehow playing the game with them as the character Ederah of Venus.

"Ready, Ederah?" Ewen asked.

She nodded and suddenly the sky went from sunny and bright to a complete blackout, frightening Darpith's minions and breaking their concentration on the plane. Ewen connected his energy to the plane at the moment of blackout and acted swiftly to change it into a bird, then he entered its head/cockpit. Ewen remained invisible to the pilots. When the sky lightened again a few seconds later the minions had lost sight of the bird/plane. Instantly they began to fear Darpith's retribution. With the plane nowhere in sight, they had only their fear to bite on.

Arjuna and Ederah flew beside the large bird shielding it with light protection all the way to Kennedy International Airport. Although the sky was empty and clear, the nearness of Arjuna, flying beside her, gave Ederah the feeling of being surrounded by doves. And Arjuna, who kept turning to stare at her luminescent radiance was so disassembled that he nearly broke apart into light beams.

Before the plane came onto the air controller's radar Ewen changed it back into a plane shape. Once it had landed safely, Arjuna and Ewen took off their gaming gear and stared at one another. They both looked around for Ederah, but there was no one at the gaming center resembling her.

"That was too real," Ewen said.

Arjuna nodded. "I have to know if a plane from Moscow, which went through such extreme turbulence that it was dented, just landed at Kennedy airport," he said.

"How much more than just a game is *Fifth Dimension*?" Ewen said aloud.

"I wonder," Arjuna said, "and why does Ederah of Venus

look so much like the Russian girl who was on the plane. I once saw her ice skating in Gorky Park when we were teenagers."

"You've been to Gorky Park? You didn't tell me that."

"There are lots of things I haven't told you yet." Arjuna laughed.

"Ditto."

The question of Ederah of Venus, Arjuna tried to stuff into a deep corner of his heart. At least Natasha, he knew, was real, he'd seen her in Russia. Both men sat for a moment in their gaming chairs, Arjuna focusing on Natasha, and Ewen remembering the Japanese girl who they'd rescued on the previous mission. For a moment, he saw again her eyes, soft and lustrous, and felt himself melt.

They'd been playing *Fifth Dimension* so long that their human legs were stiff when they finally stood up. Ewen stretched his back. "Let's have a last bite together," he said, "I leave for London in a few days."

Arjuna nodded. In two days, he himself would leave Mumbai for New York City.

As Ewen and Arjuna sat down to their dinner in Mumbai, Natasha picked up her luggage in New York, and went through customs where she was met by a young woman from Ralph Lauren who accompanied her to the apartment the company was providing. She was still half out of it, trying to understand what had happened to her on the flight, and why she felt so in love with the Indian man she had often dreamed about over the years, and had again dreamed of on the flight. In her dream, she'd been working with him and his friend to keep a plane from crashing. And, she'd learned his name. Arjuna.

Chapter 11

The World Cup

Amisi and Adjo checked into their London hotel the day before Horus's first World Cup game. The room was done in shades of pale green and ivory and overlooked Hyde Park. Amisi opened the French doors onto the balcony and walked out to be greeted by a sea of green treetops. She spread her arms wide to embrace them. Adjo was already unpacking and hanging up his trousers. Walking back into the room Amisi suggested they have a cocktail on the terrace before going down to dinner. The gin arrived in two tall glasses, with tonic on the side in real glass bottles which made a satisfying sound when Adjo opened them and poured the tonic over the gin. Fresh lime completed the drink and they toasted to Horus's success in the game the next day. Adjo's phone rang and he set his glass down on the terrace table between their chairs. It was Horus. He'd already been in England with the Iranian team for a week.

"How was your trip?" Horus asked.

"Smooth, and there was no trouble with immigration from the minute we said we were visiting because our son was playing in the World Cup," Adjo said. "How are you feeling about tomorrow's game?"

"Excited, confident, and a little nervous," Horus answered. What he didn't tell his father was that he had been having dreams that he would be under attack in the game from some outside force, and that someone in the stands would try to intervene to save him from serious harm. Amisi took the phone to wish her son good luck.

The same day that Horus's parents arrived in London from Tehran, another person who would become important in Horus's life arrived from Mumbai. Ewen had come to study at The Royal College of Art. When he checked into his dorm room, his roommate, Tom, who was also originally from Dublin, told him he had two tickets for the Iran-Ireland game the next day and invited him to go. A chill went up Ewen's spine as he accepted the invitation. He made a note of it, but hadn't a clue what the chill was trying to tell him. But he'd long ago learned to listen to signals like this from his body.

While not having chills up her spine, Mary felt as if her stomach was full of butterflies from the moment she awoke. Leaning her head back under the shower she rinsed the soap out of her long black hair and planned her outfit for the day. She wanted to dress in green, red and white, the colors of the Iranian flag. She was glad that she had decided to ask her grandmother, Georgina, to accompany her to the game. Georgina was calm, intuitive and accepting of even the strangest happenings, and Mary didn't want to be alone when whatever was going to happen that day, happened. She knew something was coming close and that it had to do with the young Egyptian player on the Iranian team. Her stomach was still fluttering after her shower, so she had only a cup of tea before leaving to meet Georgina at the tube station for the ride to the stadium.

"Good morning, darling," Georgina said as Mary kissed her on both cheeks. Georgina noted Mary's white blouse, green skirt and red sweater, smiled and said nothing.

Ewen and Tom ate breakfast together in the dorm's cafeteria. Buttered toast with jam, soft boiled eggs, bacon, and tea with milk, were a wonderful treat for Ewen after his Mumbai breakfasts of plain roti. Tom wore a T-shirt with three big stripes of orange, green and white, meant to evoke the Irish flag. Ewen wore what he always wore, blue jeans and a black T-shirt. Wolfing the last of his toast, Tom urged Ewen to finish up. Ewen smiled at Tom's excitement and downed his tea. Practically at a trot, they headed off to the tube station, with Tom telling Ewen about Ireland's star player, Tylor, and explaining that no one was anywhere near as fast or agile, except maybe the Egyptian guy, Horus, on the Iranian team. Ewen perked up his ears at the mention of the Egyptian player. For a moment, he saw the pyramids and a small boy standing before them holding the hand of a lovely woman in a large sun hat, wearing a sheer summer dress with a pattern of blue lotuses on it. He shook his head and wondered how that had popped up. His life had been so full of strange occurrences that he'd learned to take them in stride and wait for their meaning to become clear.

Amisi and Adjo rose early and breakfasted on their balcony. Adjo hired a car to take them out to the arena. Traffic was heavy and the players were already on the field awaiting the playing of the national anthems when Amisi and Adjo slipped into their seats. Amisi searched the lineup for Horus and easily spotted him as the tallest player on the team. She whispered a prayer for his safety, success and anonymity. Iran won the coin toss and chose to attack the goal at the opposite end of the field from where, not only Adjo and Amisi, but also Mary and Georgina, and Ewen and Tom were seated. Ireland kicked off, but Iran immediately gained possession of the ball and drove it down the field toward Ireland's goal. As Iran's striker, Horus was out front controlling the ball until his teammates could join the attack. Mary stopped breathing without realizing it. Georgina touched her hand and she exhaled. Sitting a few rows behind Mary, Ewen's eyes were also glued to Horus. There was something so familiar about him that Ewen wondered if he'd met him before. But he didn't think he would have forgotten such a figure, so tall, strong and agile, and one who seemed to glow with an inner light. Mary was on the edge of her seat as she watched Tylor harry Horus and steal the ball. She didn't like Tylor and sensed something dark around him. Ewen had a similar feeling toward Tylor, who seemed to be enveloped in a dark shadow.

What both Mary and Ewen were picking up about Tylor was a result of several weeks' work by Darpith who had effectively taken over Tylor's mind to stoke up his aggression and greed for fame and money. Darpith so relentlessly fed Tylor the thought that he could only win the game by crippling Horus, that it became a belief for him. To permanently cripple Horus, Darpith had instructed Tylor to put a metal plate with a retractable blunt tipped blade in it in the toe of his shoe. Even as the game was in progress, Darpith was controlling Tylor's mind, promising him glory when Horus was maimed.

During the whole first half of the game, play was intense and neither team scored. Tylor continued to harry Horus, and fouled twice trying to injure him. Next time he had to succeed. All through the halftime break Darpith continued to fill Tylor's mind with visions of riches from advertising campaigns and world fame. The coach glanced at Tylor in the locker room and thought he looked distracted. He approached Tylor to have a word, but Tylor stood up and headed for the bathroom.

When the teams took the field after half time, both Mary and Ewen again locked eyes on Horus. Sitting beside her, Georgina observed Mary closely. Never one to dilute her feelings, Mary was almost shimmering with a complexity of emotions Georgina could not quite name. It was Iran's turn to kick off for the second half and the Iranians maintained possession, driving the ball toward the goal with expert passing. Amisi was relieved that so far Horus, though he had played well, hadn't appeared to have any skills beyond what a human had. There had been no extraordinarily high leaps, unusual headers, or displays of superhuman speed. She hoped this would continue. Ewen chewed his bottom lip as he watched Horus handle the ball, trying to understand why he seemed so familiar, like a brother or best friend, and physically familiar, too, in the powerful, graceful way he moved. Both Mary and Ewen leaned forward in their seats as Horus closed in on the goal. Both saw him shift his gaze from the goalie to Tylor who was coming up fast on his left side.

When the accident happened, Mary jumped out of her seat and Amisi let out a scream. Horus went down hard from a kick to his shin. Tylor was about to fall on Horus when Ewen, without thinking, shapeshifted Tylor, momentarily, into a lifelike blowup doll of himself, making him light enough to be blown a few inches to the left of Horus's body before he fell, thus preventing him from landing on top of Horus's already damaged leg and crushing the already splintered bones. It happened so fast no one noticed Ewen's intervention. No one, except Mary, who saw Ewen's energy as it moved right over her head toward Horus and Tylor. She turned in the stands in search of the source and saw Ewen a dozen rows behind her. A shock of recognition went through her. But desperate to see what was happening to Horus, she turned her attention back to the field where he lay unconscious. The referee held up a red card indicating a serious foul by Tylor. A stretcher was brought out onto the field and Horus was lifted onto it and carried off. Amisi and Adjo made their way to the locker room, explaining that they were Horus's parents.

When she saw Mary go completely white watching Horus carried off the field, Georgina stood and took her arm to guide her out of the stadium.

"I need to know where they are taking him," Mary said.

"Yes, we'll find out," Georgina said.

She walked Mary around to the players' exit where they saw the ambulance driver waiting. Georgina asked him which hospital he would take the injured player to. The driver looked at Mary leaning on Georgina, her face completely drained of color and her body shaking, and decided they must be family.

"Kings," he said.

"Thank you," Georgina answered before turning to Mary and telling her that this was not the time for whatever was going to happen between her and the injured player. Mary nodded. She would go to King's Hospital later.

Ewen left Tom in the stands and made his way around to the back of the stadium to find the ambulance. He encountered Mary and Georgina just as they were leaving. When his eyes met Mary's, he felt again the same electric current run through him as he had earlier when she looked up at him in the stands. Mary too felt the jolt.

"I know you," Ewen said. As he spoke, a vision of two tall beings with ebony skin and emerald eyes flashed before his eyes.

"Yes," Mary answered, as she too saw his vision, and realized she was one of the tall beings. Was this man before her the other one? No. That didn't feel right. Could the injured player be the other one? Click. Yes. So, she had known Horus before in some other life where they were very tall and dark skinned with emerald eyes.

"Do you know where they're taking him?" Ewen asked.

"Is he a friend of yours?" Mary replied.

"It's hard to explain," Ewen began.

"Try," Mary said.

"The moment I saw him on the field today, he was familiar to me," Ewen said.

"You sent energy to the field right after the accident," Mary said. "What were you doing?"

"I didn't want Tylor to fall on Horus's leg and crush it further."

"And?" Mary pressed, "I saw your energy. I know you did something."

"I shapeshifted Tylor into a blowup replica of himself and the air moved him enough so he didn't land on Horus. It happened without me consciously willing it." Ewen was surprised that he'd spilled this out. But he trusted this girl who'd been able to see his energy.

"You're able to shapeshift," Mary said, more as a statement of fact than a question.

"Yes, ever since childhood."

Mary smiled hearing this, introduced herself and gave him her cell number. If Georgina was surprised at the talk of shapeshifting she didn't let on, but stood silently beside Mary, the picture of restraint and dignity.

"They're going to take him to King's College Hospital," Mary told Ewen. "Do you know where that is?"

"I only arrived from Mumbai yesterday. I don't know where anything is, but I'll find it." Ewen was reluctant to part from this girl, who took his ability to shapeshift in stride. His reluctance was not like the feeling of leaving the Japanese girl at the temple during *Fifth Dimension*, which had felt like being parted from a piece of himself. This feeling was more like leaving a close friend, who one hadn't seen in a long time. He had to go. Tom would be wondering what happened to him. "Goodbye," he said, and then added, "see you soon."

Mary nodded, calm suddenly flooding her at the idea of knowing another person who could also do freakish things. And soon she would go to King's to visit Horus. A feeling of immense joy swept her being at the thought of this. Georgina noted the change in Mary's countenance.

"Let's go, darling. And maybe on the way home you can tell me what's going on," Georgina said.

Amisi was at Horus's side as they wheeled him toward the ambulance. He had regained consciousness and told her not to worry. She watched as they closed the ambulance doors, then turned to Adjo who had called their car. They followed the ambulance to the hospital, and paced the waiting room while Horus was taken off to be X-rayed. X-rays showed that both the tibia and fibula in Horus's right leg were not just broken, but shattered. There was no simple way to fix this damage and the danger of infection and consequently losing the leg were high. Horus needed surgery and would then have to remain in the hospital until the danger of infection had passed. From a corner of the room Darpith gloated as he listened to the doctor deliver this news to Horus and his parents. Now it only remained for Horus to develop that infection, lose his leg and become despairing and bitter that his career was over, and Darpith would swoop in and harvest him for the dark side.

Amisi insisted on spending the night at Horus's bedside, although both he and Adjo tried to convince her that it wasn't necessary and that she could return in the morning and see him before he went into surgery. Because of all the strange happenings in Horus's childhood and teenage years, Amisi was suspicious of foul play in this accident, and refused to leave Horus's bedside. Darpith, satisfied with his day's work, departed to turn his attention to the pleasure of sexually abusing several of his female minions. But first, he'd apparate to Washington, D.C. and swing by the White House to drop some divisive tweets into the head of the weak-minded American president as fodder for his theocratic fascist followers to gobble up and retweet. All in all, it had been a good day's work, feeding Tylor's greed, maiming Horus to create bitterness, and using the U.S. president to fan grievances, setting citizen against citizen. Soon he would shatter the U.S. democracy and turn it into a fascist state, where it would be easier to enslave more people for the dark side.

Chapter 12

Reunion

Yosiko was excited to be in London at King's College Medical School, beginning her journey to become a surgeon. Today the first-year medical students were invited to sit in the glassed-in gallery to observe the hospital's new surgeon operate on the player who had been brought in from the World Cup game yesterday with both his tibia and fibula in pieces. The surgeon had only arrived from New Delhi to join the hospital faculty the previous week. This was the first time students would see him operate. Yosiko rose early, showered and stopped in the dining room for a light breakfast before heading to the viewing gallery to get a good seat. The surgery was scheduled for eight AM.

Mary also rose early, dressed and went straight to the hospital for morning visiting hours. When she arrived, Ewen was already there standing at the front desk. He informed her that Horus was about to have surgery.

"Shall we go to the cafeteria to wait?" Ewen asked.

Mary agreed. If she couldn't see Horus, Ewen certainly was second best. And there were many things she wanted to ask him.

Amisi bent over Horus as the gurney was about to carry him through the swinging doors to the operating theatre. Adjo took her hand to pull her away and guided her toward the waiting room.

"No. I won't be able to sit still. Let's go outside and walk," she said.

Adjo nodded. "I'll tell the desk they can reach us on my cell if need be."

It was a gray day in London, but neither Amisi nor Adjo noticed as they walked the streets around the hospital for the next several hours. Once, they went back to check if Horus was still in surgery. And once they stopped at a cafe for tea and biscuits, but neither of them ate the biscuits.

Yosiko, who was seated in the front of the gallery, watched as they wheeled the patient in. The anesthesiologist and surgeon stepped up to either side of the operating table blocking her view of the patient's face. Her view of his leg was, thankfully, unobstructed. When the anesthesiologist nodded that the patient was under, the surgeon sliced open Horus's leg laying bare the shattered bones. As he worked to piece together the bits of bone, sweat formed on his brow. The damage was worse than the X-ray had shown. After three hours of painstaking work, the leg was still a mess of splintered bone. Yosiko sensed the tense atmosphere in the operating room right through the glass and began, almost without realizing it, to call on Lord Sananda and Lady Nada, Chohans of the Resurrection Flame, the golden flame she had used as a little girl to regenerate Hoshi's paw. She visualized the two pyramids around Horus, one facing up and one facing down, intersecting at his heart to form a star tetrahedron. She filled it with violet light and requesting permission of Horus's higher self, directed the two pyramids comprising the star tetrahedron to spin in opposite directions at nine tenths the speed of light, which is the speed at which the human merkabas rotate. She then directed the gold Resurrection Flame to work through the surgeon's hands to regenerate the bones in Horus's leg. As she did this the surgeon's hands took on a new assurance, moving quickly and deftly to reorder the pieces of bone. Under what appeared to be the surgeon's skill, the bones fairly jumped back into alignment and began knitting together. No one was more astounded than the surgeon himself. He did not understand the current of energy moving through him and directing his hands. But as a practicing Hindu, he thanked God as he continued to work and didn't stop thanking him until the last stitch was in place to close the long incision in Horus's leg. As Yosiko watched she held the vibration of love as the source of all healing.

While this was happening in the operating room, Ewen and Mary sat across from one another over tea, recounting the strange events of their lives, and how their calls for help had been answered by light beings. Mary shared how she had been dying of an unknown and untreatable infection in college, and how she believed that it was only the Chohans of the Blue Ray, Master El Morya and Amerissis, who had saved her. Ewen told her about Lord Sananda and Lady Nada answering his mother's prayers and resurrecting him after he'd been possessed by a dark force while playing a game called *Orion* at a gaming center in Mumbai. None of this surprised either of them. They talked easily like very old friends, which they, in fact, were. Ewen asked her how she happened to be at the game yesterday. She explained that she was there because she felt drawn to the Egyptian player on the Iranian team, and how she'd been to Cairo and stood at the pyramids and seen a young Egyptian boy with his mother, but they weren't actually there. When she described the scene in front of the pyramids, Ewen recognized it as the very image he'd seen when his roommate offered him the ticket to the World Cup. It was a relief to acknowledge that all their lives they had been different from other people. The longer they talked the more both felt that they had been friends before, in some other life, maybe even in some other world, and not just friends, but close friends.

Mary had never been to a gaming center and she wanted to know more about them and how Ewen had happened to be playing a game called *Orion*.

Ewen recounted the events, then began to tell her about his favorite game, *Fifth Dimension*. He grew excited as he talked.

"You team up with other players online to answer distress calls from people under attack by the dark lords. You have superpowers while you're playing. The game always feels more real to me than real life."

"Do we have this game in London?"

"We can check out the gaming centers."

"Do you think Horus is one of us too?" Mary asked, suddenly interrupting him.

"I suspect he is," Ewen answered. "And I think Arjuna, who is the guy I played *Fifth Dimension* with in Mumbai, may be, too, but he's in New York now. And there was another player who worked with us in the game, a girl called Ederah of Venus."

Mary started at the name Ederah.

"What?" Ewen asked.

That name, Ederah, I know it from somewhere. Who is she?"

"I don't know. She just appeared in the game and helped Arjuna and I save a plane which was under attack from the dark side and about to crash. She has the power to make things invisible."

"I definitely want to play this game." Mary glanced at the wall clock in the cafeteria. "Do you think Horus is out of surgery yet? And how do we meet him without it being too weird?"

"We need to see him the first time with no one else in the room," Ewen said.

"Won't his parents always be there during visiting hours? I wish I could make us invisible so we could sneak in after visiting hours are over," Mary said.

"Ederah of Venus has that power. Maybe we can contact her through the game?" Ewen answered.

"Let's check on the surgery first then go to a gaming center and see if we can get her to help us," Mary said.

Amisi and Adjo were just outside the hospital when Adjo's cell rang and a voice informed them that Horus was in the recovery room and that the surgery had gone better than expected. Amisi burst into tears at the news. They walked back inside and waited in Horus's room for him to come back from the recovery room. Amisi sat by Horus's bedside the rest of the day, holding his hand without once letting go except to go to the bathroom. But only after placing Horus's hand in Adjo's. She believed in the protection of love and touch. And she was right to, because Darpith was not far off brooding in a corner of the room over the interference by the Japanese medical student in the operating room. She'd escaped him before but it wouldn't happen again. He'd find a way to punish her once and for all, before she discovered she was a light being.

That evening Yosiko came by to check on Horus, who was asleep. She explained to Amisi and Adjo that she was a medical student and that she had observed the surgery. She assured them that all would be well with Horus's leg. Amisi thought the girl looked familiar. Yosiko had the same feeling, but couldn't remember where she had seen this lovely Egyptian woman before until she turned her gaze from Amisi to Horus, and her heart stopped. She had seen him and his mother in Tokyo, in a tea house, when she was a teenager. Now, as then, an electric current went through her at the sight of Horus's face. She knew this boy from somewhere beyond this world. She was sure of it. Yosiko turned to look again at Amisi. Yes, she was definitely the woman she had seen in the tea house. As Amisi talked to her, thanking her for the information about the surgery, Yosiko tried to concentrate, but the rush of emotions made it difficult. Amisi, too, felt something and was on the point of saying more but stopped herself. Yosiko wished them goodnight and left. She had to see Horus alone before he left the hospital.

Mary and Ewen learned from the desk that Horus was in his room with his parents. It was hard for Mary to wait. She wanted to rush to him but controlled herself and stuck to their plan. They found a gaming center and it did have *Fifth Dimension*. A new element had recently been added to the game. You no longer played using your own name, but instead, were assigned a name by those running the game. Tonight, it was Amerissis and El Morya, Chohans of the Blue Ray, who were guiding the game. Mary was surprised and delighted that they were in charge and smiled when she saw them. They had often answered her call in times of trouble, wielding the Blue Ray to heal her. She had not questioned this as a child but had grown accustomed to them, keeping them as her secret. But what did they have to do with virtual reality games? They assigned her the name *Maepleida*. She shivered when she heard it. Amerissis told Ewen he would be called *Toomeh* in the game. Ewen felt his mind open at the sound of it. He stretched out inside the vibration of the word and felt suddenly more at home in his own skin. Toomeh looked to see if Ederah of Venus was playing. She wasn't. He asked if you could request a player that you'd previously worked with. You could. Before they donned their gear Maepleida asked Toomeh if he really thought it was the dark side that caused Horus's injury?

"Didn't you see the black shadow around that player who took Horus down?" Toomeh answered.

"Right. I did. I guess I didn't want it to be true."

"OK, then. Let's see if Ederah of Venus will show up."

They sat in their gaming gear for only a few minutes before the screen lit up and Ederah appeared. They explained to her the problem of needing to be invisible to get into the hospital after hours to meet alone with someone they felt was connected to them. Ederah remembered working with Ewen and Arjuna to rescue the plane from Moscow and agreed to help them. Since they had learned from the nurse at the desk that Horus's parents were staying the night with him in the hospital, they made their plans for the following night. They thanked Ederah and agreed to meet in the game in twenty-four hours. The delay was becoming unbearable for Mary. Obsessed with thoughts of Horus, she neither slept nor ate. Occasionally a vision of Ederah drifted across her mind and she wondered why she seemed so familiar.

The next evening, when visiting hours ended, an invisible trio, Toomeh, Maepleida and Ederah, working through *Fifth Dimension,* transported to the hospital and entered unobserved.

They watched Horus's parents leave and waited for the nurse to make her rounds. When they walked into his room, Horus immediately felt their presence and opened his eyes, and although they were invisible to everyone else, he saw them, and as if racing towards joy, he turned his gaze from Toomeh to Ederah to Maepleida.

"Maepleida!" he said out loud, tears pouring from his eyes. When his eyes locked on hers, her heart stopped.

"You can see me," she said, "and you know me."

"I can and I do." Let this be real, he thought, losing himself in the deep green of her eyes, awash in a feeling like walking into a forest and being surrounded by the emerald silence of the trees.

"I am real," she assured him, reading his mind as she went to his bedside and took his hand. A bolt of energy shot through them both when they touched, setting bells ringing in their bodies. Looking back into Horus's own emerald eyes, she called him by his true name, "Heipleido."

The shock of being called by his soul's name pierced his heart. "You know my soul name."

"When I touched you, it came to me."

Heipleido watched light fall out of her mouth when she spoke to him. Like Attivio, he, too, had been walking over the Earth searching without knowing who it was he sought.

"Do you recognize Toomeh and Ederah?" Maepleida asked him.

"I do," he said smiling at them. "And I've never been happier to see anyone in my life than I am the three of you. But how did you find me?"

"Maepleida and I were at the World Cup game," Toomeh said. "We saw the attack on you. We called Ederah through a game called *Fifth Dimension* and asked her to make us invisible so we could slip in here after hours and see you alone."

"And on that note, I better get back to Natasha, my human body," Ederah said. "Natasha suspects that she's from another dimension, but she's not yet fully awakened. The trauma of the near plane crash awoke me as Ederah and split me off from Natasha. I'm working to mend the split so Natasha can awaken to her true identity. But for now, I better get back to her body, which is asleep in an apartment in New York City."

They all basked for another moment in the joy of being with kindred spirits, though as yet, they knew not why they were here or where they had come from. Ederah hugged them all goodbye and said, "Let's meet through the game soon. I have a million questions for all of you. Oh, and your invisibility will hold for another few hours."

"What's this game she's talking about? Heipleido asked.

Toomeh explained about *Fifth Dimension*. Then he saw the way Maepleida and Heipleido were looking at one another and decided to give them a moment, so, still invisible, he walked out into the hall. Yosiko was just coming around the corner stealthily, hoping to have a conversation alone with Horus. Toomeh's mouth dropped open when he saw her. She was the Japanese girl he'd rescued while playing from *Fifth Dimension*. She jumped when she saw him.

"You can see me?" he said.

"Of course."

"But I'm supposed to be under an invisibility charm."

"Nevertheless, I see you, and I have seen you before in my dreams. You and your friend rescued me from an evil guy and turned me into a kitten and took me to a healing temple."

"But what are you doing here?" Toomeh asked, his heart pounding.

"I'm a medical student and I wanted to check on the injured player." The calmness of her voice belied the joy coursing through her body at the sight of this man as she asked him what he was doing at the hospital in the middle of the night. Toomeh struggled to answer. He wanted to pull her to his heart and fold her in his arms. "I was at the World Cup and I saw the accident and felt drawn to the injured player, as did another who witnessed it, and she is with him now. But I have to ask you, do you know me, beyond the rescue, I mean?"

"I don't know from where or how, but I do – more than know you. But now we better get out of this hall, because I'm not invisible."

"Come into his room."

Toomeh and Yosiko entered Heipleido's room to find him and Maepleida in a state of sublime ecstasy at having reunited, and not only reunited but also remembered, that they were supposed to reunite on Earth, and that they were in fact on a mission from another dimension. Despite having passed through the veil of forgetting Maepleida had retained, embedded in a deep recess of her unconscious mind, some of her memories from the place with the pink-gold sky, and seeing Heipleido had sparked those memories. And she now knew beyond a doubt that that place was the planet Venus in the fifth dimension. When she told Heipleido what she remembered, he also began to recall snippets of scenes from Venus, but most of all he knew she was his twin flame, his one, and he never wanted to be parted from her again.

Heipleido recognized Toomeh as his old friend, and Yosiko as Laaroos, Toomeh's partner. On hearing the name *Laaroos*, Yosiko knew it to be her soul name. She and Toomeh turned to one another, the power of their true names allowing them to see one another in their totality as who they really were. Laaroos's orange-gold eyes filled with tears which flowed down her cheeks. Toomeh touched her face and felt all the warmth and sweetness of the sea. Maepleida remembered that Laaroos had the power to regenerate and asked her to work on Heipleido's bones. Laaroos explained that she already had, in the operating room, by calling on the Resurrection Flame, and sending it through the surgeon's hands. Heipleido testified that he was pain free and could most likely even walk. He thanked Laaroos. Toomeh beamed at her. After twenty-one years of being apart, and being confused about the strange happenings in their lives, they were all ecstatic to be together and to once again know who they were. The four old friends sat on Horus's bed and pieced together all they could remember of their last lifetime and training on Venus. It was a relief to finally know that the place with the pink-gold sky that each of them had seen so often in their dreams was real.

They talked all through the night, recounting the many strange events in each of their lives since they'd last been together as well as all that they could remember of their training on Venus and life in the fifth dimension. When the sky began to turn rosy and day was about to break, Toomeh and Maepleida were fully visible. Laaroos said she could lead them out a side door and they could come back later during visiting hours. None of them wanted to part. Maepleida bent down and kissed Heipleido's lips, promising to return soon. At the exit, Toomeh pulled Laaroos to him and embraced her as if he'd never let her go. He only released her when she agreed to move in with him as soon as he found an apartment, which he intended to do that day.

On exiting the hospital, Maepleida and Toomeh found themselves back at the gaming center, where, before they took off their gear, Master El Morya appeared on the screen and spoke to them.

"Light beings, you have done well. You have managed to wake up in the third dimension, and remember that you are here on Earth on a mission from the fifth dimension to help all beings awaken. But know this, the dark side will hound you now as never before in this lifetime. Be ever vigilant."

Then Amerissis added, "We are always with you. Call on us. Work through the game when you can as it affords a level of protection. Find your fellow wanderers and help them to awaken. We have much to do to save the humans from the dark side. Go now with our blessing. All is well."

Maepleida and Toomeh removed their gaming gear and

stared at one another. They could find no words, but hugged goodbye and agreed to meet in third dimensional reality, in the hospital, at eleven a.m. Maepleida fairly floated home and lay on her bed, bells still sounding in her body. With her eyes open she saw nothing of her surroundings, but only the face of one being.

In the few hours they had to sleep, Toomeh and Laaroos, in their separate beds, both dreamt the same blissful dream.

They lay together on cushions in a vaulted temple, open on all four sides to beautiful gardens and orchards, with trees bearing golden fruit under a pink sky.

But there was one who was far from feeling blissful. Darpith, enraged that the four light beings had awakened and reunited, fumed on Orion. He summoned his thousands of minions, and displaying his full demonic summa of hatred, arrogance, jealousy, malice and greed, ordered them to prepare for all-out war on planet Earth.

"The time has come to instill divisiveness within nations on every continent. I will install despots in all countries on Earth, even as I simultaneously pursue the light beings and all others who favor unity and brotherhood. In the United States, I order you to create divisiveness using the current polyamorous puppet I have installed as president, egg him on to create rage and hatred through his rallies which set citizen against citizen. It gives me pleasure to see the unrest he has already created as he uses the government to fill his own pockets, and aids the wealthy and the greedy with his lies so they can continue to manipulate the poor for their own ends. I order you to fuel right wing hate groups and bomb throwers in the Unites States. Stop at nothing to create disharmony and hatred. Likewise, in Russia, support the despot who is destroying democracies wherever they still exist. Praise him and feed his ego. He is still useful to me as he is helping me in completing the take down of democracy in the United States. In Brazil, I have installed a criminal as head of the government.

He shares my value of self-interest above all else. Keep him in power. I will starve, dishearten and enslave the populace through him. Enter the theocratic fascist state of Saudi Arabia, feed the cruel bullying prince with the belief that he has unlimited power to murder children, wage unjust war, torture and kill journalists to suppress free speech, starve whole populations at will, and crush women without retribution. There shall be no free speech anywhere on the planet when I am finished. In China, sow fear through torture and imprisonment of any who try to speak out against the dictator. Aid the Chinese in listening in to the phone conversations of my puppet in the White House, who is so stupidly lax that he refuses to use a secure phone. In the Sudan, assist the dictator in starving his people and setting them against one another. Continue to encourage the Saudi's to bomb the people of Yemen with American bombs. Use that U.S. solipsistic national security advisor to start a war between the U.S. and Iran. I have made progress for the dark side on every continent and I will not have the light beings undo all the chaos, hatred and misery which I have created by giving people hope, or any idea of their own divinity and power. Death to all light beings. You will be rewarded or punished according to your success in the goals I have laid out. Now make your plans to commence what I am calling: 'Operation Misery'. Do not fail me." When he finished speaking, to make his point, Darpith grabbed two of his minions and tortured them publically. Their screams were heard for three days before there was nothing but a terror filled silence on Orion.

Chapter 13

A Contest

Hunter returned from his business trip to London to discover that Rose had a boyfriend, and not only that, he had moved in with them. And furthermore, she had changed her name to Soonam. Hunter agreed to all this because he had never seen Rose happier. It seemed to him like she had suddenly blossomed into the woman she was always meant to be. There was a new wholeness to her and a new joy, which pleased Hunter very much. Calling her Soonam was a small price to pay for his daughter's happiness. As for her new boyfriend, Attivio, who had recently arrived in New York from Jerusalem to study writing at NYU, Hunter took an immediate liking to him, not only because of Rose's happiness, but because Attivio was himself such a decent and interesting fellow. If they sometimes seemed to inhabit a secret world, it was fine with Hunter, who frequently heard snippets of their conversation about Venus and The Violet Planet and a group of people called wanderers. Rose had always talked about these things, but this was the first time she'd had anyone who shared her ideas, and Hunter, far from being troubled by this, was happy for her.

Among the first things Soonam and Attivio planned to do, was to make contact with other wanderers. They remembered that they'd come as part of a group and they wanted to help other wanderers wake up in the third dimension and reunite with their twin flames. But how? There must be other wanderers in a place as populated as New York. They would have to do something to draw them out. Maybe they could use social media to float some information about the Chohans and the seven rays and wanderers, then check out who chose to follow them.

The sun was warm on their skin as they sat eating lunch on the back porch, brainstorming. Soonam looked out at the grass beyond the porch and saw that it was peppered with dandelions. When she was little her mother had called them weeds. But Soonam thought of them as little suns warming the grass. As she gazed at them, a thought struck her. "Attivio, do you remember that day on Venus when we learned where we'd be incarnating? Envelopes were delivered to our laps by colorful birds. Inside were holographic-like scenes of our future Earth parents. What if we posted pictures from those holograms?"

"But do you remember enough about those scenes?"

"I think so. I remember a Japanese couple on a bench under a plum tree."

"Yes, me too. It started to rain through the plum blossoms and the couple gazed up and let the raindrops fall on their faces," Attivio added. "That was Laaroos's parents, I think."

"Whose parents was it walking on the heath by the Irish Sea?" Soonam asked. "The young woman had lovely curly brown hair blowing in the wind."

"And the guy stopped to tie his hiking boot and to look up at her and smile. I think they were Toomeh's parents."

"Remember the Russian family ice skating on the ice with the colored lights under it?"

"Yes, yes, Ederah's family, and there was the Indian couple walking to the boat with all the monkeys jumping around them trying to get a bit of their food," Soonam said.

"Bereh's parents. We saw eight holograms, so there should be eight sets of parents. Who are we missing out?" Attivio asked.

"The Egyptian couple, Heipleido's parents," Soonam said. "They were sitting across from one another on love seats, with a large vase of orange poppies between them."

"And we saw Maepleida's mother, the English lady standing by the statue of Peter Pan when she started to bleed," Attivio said.

"How do we convey these scenes on Instagram to trigger memories for our friends? We don't even know if our friends are still in the countries they were born into."

"We need a good artist to create the scenes as we remember them."

"We could contact art schools in all the cities we just mentioned and set up a contest with a reward," Soonam said. "We could even post more than one entry for each brief we present and have multiple winners."

They spent the next several hours researching art schools in Tokyo, Dublin, Moscow, Mumbai, London and Cairo and posting ads describing the scenes they wanted created for their contest.

"I don't like the idea of judging," Soonam said.

"At least the criteria will be clear in our minds. The winner will be the work that looks most like the actual images we were shown of our future parents," Attivio said.

"What if someone gets it exactly? Does that mean they actually saw it the day we did on Venus? Does it mean they are a wanderer?" Soonam asked.

"I think so."

Pleased with their plan, Soonam and Attivio strolled to nearby Washington Park and sat together on the rim of the fountain in the afternoon sun. The wind blew the spray in their direction and wet their faces. Attivio reached for Soonam's hand. "I remember the first time we were here at this fountain, during an exercise El Morya gave us to find someone stuck in the third dimension and tell them they were a wanderer."

"And he instructed us to use our intuition, that it would be our most powerful tool when we incarnated."

"Laaroos met her Arcturian mother under that arch right there," Soonam said pointing to it.

"Our whole group was here, Heipleido and Maepleida, Ederah and Bereh, and Toomeh and Laaroos," Attivio said.

His voice sounded nostalgic. Soonam squeezed his hand. "We'll find them. And we'll all be here together again."

When she said this, their violet eyes met and locked. Attivio thought of the first moment his eyes had ever looked into hers, eons ago, across a crowded table on the Violet Planet, thousands of years before their training on Venus. Their passion for one another had never diminished. As it rushed through them now, they jumped over the rim of the fountain, ran home and burst through the front door. Attivio pressed her up against the wall in the foyer and covered her with kisses as he lifted her by the hips, pulled up her skirt, and entered her. Making love with third dimensional human bodies was still relatively new to them. Orgasm was the closest they could feel to Divine consciousness while in human bodies. Making love in the fifth dimension was a different order of experience as body and soul they hooked into the divine energy of the universe to experience a prolonged sublime orgasm. But human orgasms were quite divine in their own right, even though they couldn't be sustained continually as a state of consciousness like in the fifth dimension. After making love as third dimensional beings, they went upstairs to their room, shut the door and shifted into their fifth dimensional light bodies by opening all five of their extrinsic chakras one by one, as they had once done on Venus during an exercise with Lord Lanto. Once all five extrinsic chakras were open they were fully fifth dimensional and their love making became a continuous orgasmic state, an oceanic song filling their souls.

Within a week they had several hundred replies to their contest and they chose forty to post on Instagram. One set of drawings, done by a student at The Royal College of Art in London, looked identical to their own memories of the holograms. Several of the six water colors the artist submitted were so otherworldly, so filled with light, and so beautifully rendered, that no judging was necessary. He was the clear winner. They sent him an email telling him he'd won, and inviting him to come to New York at their, or rather Hunter's expense, to stay with them for a week, and receive his prize of a thousand dollars, which Hunter had graciously agreed to provide.

Not wanting to be parted from Laaroos for even a week, Toomeh had originally planned to turn down the trip if he won. He'd only taken the challenge because the briefs struck a chord in him. But as he began painting them, he saw them so clearly in his mind's eye that he felt sure he'd witnessed these scenes somewhere before. He read the briefs to Laaroos who agreed they were eerily familiar, but she couldn't place where she'd seen them until her dream that night.

She was standing beneath an ancient tree under a pink-gold sky with a group of friends. Each held a paper envelope. Hers was open and they were all watching a sort of holographic scene in which a young Japanese couple sat in a garden talking under a plum tree.

The dream woke her up. It was her parents in the dream. She was sure of it. And she'd viewed this scene before. That pink-gold sky was unmistakably Venus. And this very scene from her dream was one of the briefs Toomeh was painting. Whoever had created this contest had also witnessed this scene. Laaroos rubbed her eyes to be sure she wasn't still dreaming. She woke Toomeh up. "You have to go to New York. The people who set up this contest have to be wanderers like us. How else would they have created these exact scenes? They're looking for us."

"In that case, whether I win or not, we're both going to meet them," Toomeh said, with his eyes still closed. "Now come here," he whispered pulling her into his arms.

"But we have to tell Maepleida and Heipleido," she protested.

"Yes, but not tonight." And he kissed her eyelids and the corners of her lips and her earlobes.

Soonam was on her computer when Attivio woke up. He stared at the back of her blonde head bent over the keyboard. He wouldn't change anything about her, not a single hair on that head. Ribbons of wheat and gold, he called it. Soonam felt his eyes on her back and turned to meet his gaze.

"I'm arranging the tickets for the winner and his partner. Just three weeks until they arrive. He has given me what he refers to as the names on their passports, Ewen and Yosiko. He's from Ireland and she's from Japan, but they're both in London studying. Strange that he would refer to them as 'the names on their passports,' like they might have other names."

"Well, we had other names. I think that's a hopeful sign," Attivio said stretching in bed. "Can you take a break and come over here and kiss me good morning?"

"Maybe she's the Japanese girl whose parents were under the plum trees and he's the Irish guy whose parents were walking on the heath," Soonam said.

"Yes, yes, but come over here now."

Soonam jumped up and in one sprint was on top of him on the bed, kissing his neck, his eyelids, his chin, until he rolled her on her back, and gazing into her deep violet eyes told her he would gladly be a human for a thousand lifetimes just to be with her.

After a breakfast of warm oatmeal with bananas, strawberries, cream and maple syrup, Soonam opened her laptop to check that her email to Ewen had sent, and found a late entry to their contest. It was from a girl in New York called Natasha. She had entered only one painting, the scene of the family ice skating in Gorky Park. Soonam gasped when she saw it and carried her laptop over to show Attivio, who had climbed back into bed.

"She has to win too," Soonam said.

"Absolutely," Attivio said taking the laptop from her hands and putting it on the floor before again pulling her into his arms.

Chapter 14

Paintings

Natasha was settling into the apartment provided for her by the Ralph Lauren Company. It was in a new building on the Highline, overlooking the Hudson River. When she'd first seen the river, Natasha wondered if it froze in the winter and she'd imagined the joy of ice skating on it. In the few weeks she'd been in New York she'd formed a relationship with the river, and was posting photos of the light shimmering on the water on Instagram when she came across a painting contest. One of the briefs especially appealed to her because it was about a family ice skating in Gorky Park. Feeling a little homesick, she took out her watercolors and began painting the scene described in the contest. Though she'd been chosen as a model, she was still an artist and graphic designer at heart. After spending the whole day on the painting, imagining herself back in Moscow skating with her family, she debated whether or not to enter it in the contest and decided to sleep on it. Her dream made the decision for her.

She was in a gaming center watching herself and a young man called Ewen on a screen. He was requesting her screen self to use her power to make him and his friend, Mary, invisible, so they could slip into a London hospital after hours to visit a friend who had been a victim of the dark side. Natasha watched as her screen self actually made them invisible, then accompanied them to the hospital to meet their friend, Horus. As she watched, she felt that all of them were achingly familiar and she wanted to talk to them but they could only hear her screen self, who they called Ederah.

When Natasha woke up, she was lonely for these dream people, but more than that, she wanted to know more about this screen version of herself who seemed to be a character called

Ederah of Venus. Why was that name so hauntingly familiar? Still full of the dream, she opened her laptop, pulled up her painting of her family ice skating in Gorky Park and hit send.

A few hours after Natasha hit send, another new comer to New York sat uptown eating pea soup. Arjuna looked up from his soup and glanced out the window at 114th Street. Never having heard of pea soup before, he'd discovered it the first day he arrived in New York to study astrophysics at Columbia University, when he'd overheard a group of students sitting near him in the café talking about how good the pea soup was. It came with a thick slice of homemade bread and sweet butter and it was cheap as meals go. Arjuna finished his soup, paid the check and headed back to the physics lab. He'd been in New York for three weeks but his mind was still working overtime trying to sort out all the strange events of the previous month, meeting Ewen at the gaming center in Mumbai, rescuing the Japanese girl from the dark lord, saving the plane which had been about to crash, and especially the Russian girl who had been on that plane. He still didn't know her name and considered looking for a gaming center to see if he could make contact with Ewen to play *Fifth Dimension*. Ewen would be in London by now at The Royal College of Art, and maybe that other character, Ederah of Venus, would show up to play, too, and they could find out the Russian girl's name.

Back in the lab, Arjuna opened his laptop to resume his research, but feeling lonely decided to check his Instagram first. That's when he saw that Ewen had posted a series of six paintings. One was of an Indian couple on what looked to Arjuna like Elephanta Island. The couple were surrounded by monkeys as they made their way toward a ferry. The woman in Ewen's painting looked like Arjuna's mother, Aastha. He examined the other five paintings. Every one of the scenes was familiar to him. Before he could make sense of why, his phone dinged and he glanced at the text. It was from Ewen. Arjuna smiled. He loved synchronicity. Ewen was coming to New York with his girlfriend in a couple of weeks because he'd won a painting contest. Girlfriend? When did he get a girlfriend? Last Arjuna knew, Ewen had been hung up on the Japanese girl in *Fifth Dimension*. Now he had a girlfriend. Excitement spread through Arjuna's mind lighting up all his circuits as he texted his delight over the upcoming visit. Then he took another look at Ewen's paintings. His eyes lingered on a young couple walking on the heath beside what looked like the Irish Sea. The woman's wild, curly, windblown hair, the man's brown hiking boots, where had he seen them before? In each of the six paintings Ewen had done, Arjuna found familiar elements, and throughout the afternoon he returned again and again to look at them, until finally he took screen shots, printed them and hung them up on the wall over his desk. The one he liked best was of a family ice skating in a park. It reminded him of the trip he and his mother had taken to Moscow when he was fifteen, and of the shimmering Russian girl ice skating toward him, the very sight of whom had momentarily turned him into a light being.

Arjuna texted Ewen again to ask how he'd heard about the contest and why he'd chosen to paint these particular scenes. Ewen emailed him the briefs which he'd gotten for the contest. They'd come from a couple in New York. It wasn't until a few days later that Arjuna came across another Instagram post which listed the two winners of the contest as Ewen and Natasha, and showed their paintings. When he saw Natasha's painting of her family skating in Gorky Park he stopped breathing. Where had he seen the little girl with the red mittens before and that woman in the full green coat swinging gracefully about her legs as she skated? This version was even more evocative than Ewen's depiction. He had to meet this Natasha. Could she be the girl from the airplane? Was she in New York?

Natasha received the email that she'd won without surprise. She knew her painting was good, and more than that, she sensed that there was something behind this contest that was meant to draw her out and connect her with something or someone. She didn't consider that it could connect her with herself. The email contained an invitation to meet the hosts of the contest and the other winner in Greenwich Village, at the home of the contest hosts: Soonam and Attivio. Their names struck a chord in Natasha which kept ringing the whole day as she repeated the names to herself. Just thinking the names Soonam and Attivio in her head felt like a mantra which made her feel happy and light. When she faced-timed very late that night with her mother, it was already morning in Moscow. At first, she hesitated to mention the contest or her painting to her mother, but she was too excited not to share the news. When Masha asked to see her painting, Natasha hesitated again, and wasn't sure why. Masha gasped when saw the painting. It depicted Clara and Alexei and Masha and Igor skating together in Gorky Park at a time before Natasha was born. There were Clara's red mittens and Masha's own long, full, green coat and Alexei's blue woolen hat and Igor's beard. All things which had passed out of their lives before Natasha could have seen or remembered them. Igor had worn a beard only for a brief period and given it up while Masha was still pregnant with Natasha. There had been so many strange things throughout Natasha's childhood and teen years that Masha shouldn't have been surprised at the details in the painting. She had come to accept that her daughter was from another time and place and was somehow at risk because of that. Nevertheless, the painting startled her. Had Natasha seen them before she was born? And where had she been watching from, the place with the pink-gold sky which Masha had so often seen in her own dreams during her pregnancy?

"Mama, why do you gasp?" Natasha asked.

"The details remind me so much of when Clara and Alexei

were little, before you were born."

"Are the details accurate then?"

"Yes, yes, they are, my darling girl."

Arjuna also faced-timed with his mother. Aastha had been intimidated by face-timing at first, but after her sister helped her and she'd written down the instructions in case she forgot how to do it, she quite enjoyed it, and it gave her peace of mind to actually see that Arjuna was alright. He had shown her the lab where he worked and his dorm room and walked around the campus pointing out various buildings and the beautiful lawns and trees. But what Aastha most wanted to see was his face. She was happy to hear that his friend Ewen had won a painting contest and was flying from London to New York for a visit. Arjuna had brought Ewen over a couple of times for Indian food before they'd both left Mumbai, and Aastha had liked him. She felt a connection between Arjuna and Ewen which she struggled to describe to herself. It seemed somehow almost spiritual. Arjuna showed her Ewen's painting of the couple and the monkeys, and asked her if she thought it was Elephanta Island. As Aastha stared at the painting tears began to trickle down her cheeks. It was her and Siddharth on the path to the ferry the day before he died. She recognized her sari, and her jewelry, and not only Siddharth's suit, but his expression as he fed the monkeys from a paper bag. How could this be? Ewen, like Arjuna hadn't been born then, and she'd never worn that sari again. Aastha decided that it was one more thing to tuck away with all the strange occurrences that had happened in Arjuna's life, and when they hung up, she went to do puja. Arjuna turned to his own solace, which was not doing puja, but astrophysics, today he was reconsidering the remnants of a lost planet. In 2008 an asteroid exploded in the Sudan over the Nubian Desert creating a flash of light which many witnessed because it happened just after morning prayers. Meteorites with diamonds inside were later found in the desert. Had they once been part of the planet Maldek? Not all astrophysicists even believed that Maldek had ever existed. Arjuna was one who did.

Chapter 15

Travel Plans

Two days after his surgery Heipleido was released from the hospital. That same day he told Adjo and Amisi that he wouldn't be flying back to Tehran with them but would stay in London with Maepleida. Never one to dilute her opinions, a trait she shared with Horus's new girlfriend, Amisi had at first objected but after meeting Maepleida and Toomeh and Laaroos, and sensing the connection among the four of them, she stopped arguing with Horus and voiced her concerns only to Adjo, who pointed out that Horus, as they still called him, was twenty-one.

"But he's planning on living with her, and he's never even dated. And he's changed his name. I don't know which upsets me more."

"It's high time he had a girlfriend," Adjo told her. "His life has been too one-sided with all the sports. Love is a good thing. Have you seen the way they look at one another?"

"How could I not. And what is this job her father is arranging for him?"

"Another good thing," Adjo said. "Her father is a member of the House of Lords. As a member of his staff, Horus will get a visa and learn about government. He may never be able to play soccer professionally again. And despite his love of music, he's not going to be a concert pianist. He needs a new path."

Amisi had no rebuttal. What she didn't say was that she was afraid for Horus's safety. Not just the kidnapping incident but so many accidents during his short life had left her always wanting to be close at hand for what might happen next. She knew that Horus had abilities unlike other humans and she lived in fear of the snake beneath the flower.

Maepleida had planned on getting a small apartment just for herself, but now that she was reunited with Heipleido, and Toomeh and Laaroos, she started looking for a place big enough for all four of them. She found two carriage houses, which had been joined together to make one big place, in a mews in Notting Hill Gate. They all decided it was perfect and planned to split the rent four ways. Since Laaroos and Toomeh were students, their parents paid. Heipleido would be earning something, and Adjo agreed to supplement it. Maepleida was getting help from her parents while she looked for a job. As the one who had the most time, it fell to her to organize the place, a task she relished. Amisi offered to help for the two weeks until she and Adjo left London. She, too, had plenty of time since she wasn't going to attend any more World Cup Games now that Heipleido was out of it. The two women shopped and planned and talked. All was well until one morning when they were sitting together on some boxes in the carriage house waiting for a furniture delivery. Out of nowhere a heavy beam suddenly fell from the ceiling directly over Maepleida's head. It would have crushed her had not Amisi with her second sense, developed during Horus's childhood, of always watching out for danger heard the creaking, leapt up and pulled Maepleida out of the way. Both women knew this was no accident. They walked outside to get away from the dust and debris. Maepleida called the landlord to schedule a repair, though truth be told, all their powers were returning, and between Heipleido's strength and agility, Laaroos' power of regeneration and Toomeh's ability to shapeshift anything, they could have repaired it themselves. Amazed at Maepleida's calm over the incident, Amisi felt sure that she'd been attacked before, and, like Horus, must have some unusual power that caused someone to want to menace her.

Two weeks later when Amisi and Adjo left to return to Tehran, the carriage house was not only habitable, but thanks to Amisi's exquisite taste and Maepleida's knowledge of London shops and the best dealers on Portobello Road, it was beautiful as well as functional. Amisi was thrilled at the imported goods available in London. She added Egyptian and Persian touches to the decor using silk and wool carpets from Isfahan and exquisite textiles from Cairo. Both women had exhibited a lavishness and confidence in their decorating, together achieving a kind of utilitarian domestic elegance. Although the four wanderers were regaining more and more of their superpowers each day, they still wore human bodies most of the time, and still slept and ate food. So there were bedrooms and a kitchen and a living room and what they called their war room, where they made plans for their mission to awaken the populace to the knowledge of their Divinity, and the truth that we are all one. The more people who understood that they were Divine beings, and that we are all connected, the fewer would fall under the illusions of promised power, wealth and elitism created by the dark side.

At their first meeting in the war room, seated around their large wooden table, they discussed whether entering politics would be a good way to combat the greed of the wealthy and their suppression of the voices of the poor. There was general agreement among the four of them that this approach could prove fruitful as they suspected the dark side of controlling certain world leaders, even to the extent of dictating their divisive tweets. In addition to getting involved in politics, they were considering movies, books, art, rap and other pop music as ways to open peoples' minds. These were all big ideas which they would need to operationalize. Then there was the question of how to use the game *Fifth Dimension*, which the Chohans of the Seven Rays had created to help wanderers awaken and to bring them together, as well as to battle the Dark Lords of Orion. Now that they knew they were wanderers they could use their powers without the game, but there was more protection in working through *Fifth Dimension* as one of the Chohans was always overseeing it.

At that same meeting, Toomeh announced that he'd won the painting contest and that he and Laaroos would be traveling to New York in a few weeks. They'd all seen the briefs as well as Toomeh's paintings. Maepleida felt that whoever had written the briefs for the contest must have been on Venus with them and viewed the holograms described in the briefs. Heipleido wondered if it could even have been their old friends, either Soonam and Attivio, or Ederah and Bereh who had created the contest? All four of them were ecstatic when Toomeh won and hoped that it was in fact Soonam and Attivio who had written the briefs for the contest. That would mean that they, too, had found one another and were reunited. Then of their group of eight, only Ederah and Bereh would still be unaccounted. But Toomeh knew how to contact Ederah through the game, and he suspected that his gaming friend, Arjuna, was in fact Bereh.

"Where is Arjuna now?" Heipleido asked.

"In New York, studying astrophysics at Columbia."

"So, you can see him when you go."

"Why don't all four of us go to New York?" Maepleida said to the general excitement of all of them.

And so, it was agreed. After twenty-one years of not seeing one another, at least six of them might be reunited. Then they could awaken others. It would be full time work. Laaroos wondered how they would manage their other commitments? For now, Toomeh would continue in art school, and Laaroos in medical school, and Heipleido in Maepleida's father's office.

Before bed, Maepleida and Heipleido sat together at the computer and booked their tickets on the same flight to New York that Toomeh and Laaroos were taking. For a minute Toomeh considered telling them to book a different flight, in case Darpith or his minions tried the same thing again and attempted to bring down the plan. But then he decided the four of them with their fifth dimensional superpowers returning, and the ability to call on the Chohans of the Seven Rays, would be more than a match for anything Darpith could dream up. So he said only, "Goodnight," and left them to schedule their flights.

"Goodnight, Toomeh," Maepleida said, before turning back to Heipleido to ask him what he remembered of the time when Master El Morya, during their training on Venus, sent them to New York City and told them to use their intuition to find other wanderers and awaken them.

"My memory isn't yet complete but every day I recall more of our training on Venus, and also many of our other experiences around the galaxy over the last few thousand years. But I do remember that day in New York, first at a fountain in a park near an arch, then up at the sports arena called Yankee Stadium, where we saw the Reptilians."

"I wonder if New York will feel the same this time?" Maepleida said.

"We'll soon see. Now let's go to bed," Heipleido said, leading her toward their bedroom. Although they'd both gotten used to being human, and to having white skin in this earthly incarnation, Heipleido missed Maepleida's ebony color so after looking into her emerald eyes and kissing her lips, he closed his eyes and for a moment imagined her in her Pleiadian form, fourteen feet tall, with black skin, emerald eyes, a long slender neck and black hair down to her waist. She knew what he was doing and smiled to herself.

"Do you want to make love tonight as humans, or as our fifth dimensional selves," she asked him, even though she already knew the answer.

Toomeh and Laaroos also chose to unite that night as their fifth dimensional Arcturian selves. When he entered their bedroom, Toomeh beheld Laaroos as a goddess with orange-gold eyes, brighter than orange diamonds, hair like ribbons of spun copper and gold, and her whole being shimmering with light. She took his breath away. But he assured her that he did also love her adorable, human, Japanese form. But seeing her made of orange and gold light, that was coming home to her in her eternal form.

Chapter16

Reunion in Greenwich Village

Over a dinner of chili and rice with cheddar cheese melted on top, Soonam told Attivio that while he was in class she'd had another email from Ewen. Not only would Ewen be bringing his girlfriend with him from London, but two other friends as well. Soonam was sure the friends must be two more wanderers but Attivio, who was more cautious, didn't want her to get her hopes up. He wasn't convinced that even Ewen was a wanderer.

"Well, we'll know soon enough. They'll be here next week," Soonam told him as she carried their dishes to the kitchen sink.

"Did we hear back from the other winner yet, the girl who painted the ice skating scene?" Attivio asked as he tried to untangle the saran wrap so he could cover the leftovers. Soonam smiled at his fumbling attempts, and made a mental note not to buy any more saran wrap because it was a single use plastic.

"Yes, Natasha emailed that she'd like to come. So we'll be seven for dinner and we'll have four house guests. I'm jumping out of my skin with excitement. But I do have the feeling that someone's still missing, that we should be eight."

"Darling, Soonam," Attivio said coming up behind her and putting his arms around her, "remember we're just at the beginning and these people may or may not be our group, but either way we'll find them."

"Yes, yes, you're right, but I have a feeling they are," Soonam insisted as she rinsed a plate and set it in the drainer. Attivio gave her a kiss and picked up the dish towel. She was, and always had been, relentlessly positive and hopeful, not to mention enchanting. He stood beside her holding the dish towel and watching her.

"Do we really have to go on cooking and cleaning up when

we could manage it all effortlessly with our fifth dimensional powers?" Attivio said.

"When we're alone we can use our power, but the danger is that if we get in the habit we might forget and do it when someone could notice," Soonam said. "Oh, what the heck," she said, and with a simple command the kitchen was sparkling and all the leftovers were put away and the tangled saran wrap perfectly untangled.

Attivio summoned a fire and they curled up in front of it. Soonam said she could hardly bear the two-week wait until everyone was together so Attivio sped up time for her until it was the very day for their London visitors to arrive, and for Natasha to join them. Not wanting to meet their guests in a public place, in case they were wanderers and something unusual happened when so many fifth dimensional beings reunited at once, Soonam and Attivio sent a car to collect their guests at the airport. When the doorbell rang Soonam was upstairs arranging bouquets of fragrant multi-colored roses next to each bed. She raced down the stairs, with her full skirt floating up around her legs like a ball gown, to meet Attivio who was standing in the foyer waiting for her.

"This is it," she said, her violet eyes glistening with anticipation.

Attivio opened the door to find four human looking beings standing face to face with him. Light beams shot out of four pairs of luminescent eyes, two of deep emerald and two the color of orange diamonds, to be met with the four violet rays streaming from their hosts.

Maepleida spoke first. "Attivio! Soonam! It really is you."

"Yes, yes," Soonam gushed, rushing forward and trying to embrace all four of them at once. "Come in, please, come in," she said through violet tears of joy at seeing her old friends after a twenty-one-year separation. A gust of October wind blew maple leaves up the steps and swirled them about the feet of the four wanderers standing on the steps. Laaroos shivered.

"It's chilly, come inside," Soonam urged.

Attivio, regaining himself after the shock of recognition, stepped forward to help with their bags. Somehow, they all made it into the foyer and dropped the bags to have proper hugs all around. If the light rays streaming from their eyes hadn't made it clear to each of them just who they were, the electricity rocketing through them when they touched left no doubt. The intensity and joy the hugs conveyed into each of their hearts and souls made it impossible to even speak.

Once they were all gathered around a roaring fire, Soonam fairly floated into the room carrying a tray with mugs of hot cider and a plate of warm cinnamon donuts and set it on the large ottoman between the two yellow sofas flanking the fireplace. Heipleido and Maepleida were on one, and across from them, on the other, Laaroos was snuggled against Toomeh. Attivio sat on a large cushion next to fire.

"What a sight you all are," Soonam said, her voice bubbling over and her violet eyes dancing. "I am over the moon just to look at you."

"Soonam you are still so much yourself, I see," Maepleida said, laughing and helping her hand around the mugs of cider. Soonam beamed in response and settled herself on a cushion next to Attivio. Toomeh passed around the plate of donuts. As he looked at each of them in turn, he thought of the last time they'd all been together on Venus, about to descend the golden staircase and step off to incarnate into the third dimension. Having been torn from every near tie, alone, each of them had arrived on Earth and survived for twenty-one confusing years. Together again at last, they luxuriated in the sensation of their current propinquity, and like dry sponges, they drank one another in, not only with their resonant and porous minds, but with their hearts and souls.

"I have a million questions," Attivio said. "For a start, how did the four of you find one another?"

Heipleido began the explanation with how Darpith had tried to cripple him during the World Cup. The others jumped in to add their parts of the story. Then Toomeh told them about Arjuna and the game *Fifth Dimension,* and about Natasha and Ederah of Venus. Maepleida asked how Soonam and Attivio had found one another. After that, questions flew back and forth as they shared a kaleidoscope of childhood experiences with the dark side, and how each of them had been helped by the Chohans of the Seven Rays. Several hours passed and the fire was glowing with red heat by the time the conversation slowed down. Attivio put another couple of logs on the fire and returned to something Toomeh had said about his gaming friend, Arjuna, and the girl they had worked with to save the plane. "Do you think those two could be our Ederah and Bereh?"

"I've had that thought," Toomeh said.

Then Soonam piped in to explain about the other winner, a girl called Natasha, who had painted a picture of a family ice skating in Gorky Park.

"Didn't you say the girl that your friend Arjuna wanted to save from the plane crash was named Natasha?" Attivio asked.

"Yes, I had to keep reminding him it was just a game, but he was smitten with her. We didn't know at that point that it was more than a game or that it had been created by the Chohans to help awaken us and to fight the dark lords," Toomeh explained.

"So Natasha could be Ederah, and not yet realize it, and Arjuna could be Bereh, and not yet know it," Maepleida said.

"Natasha is coming for dinner tomorrow," Soonam said.

"Should I invite Arjuna?" Toomeh asked the group. "He's right up at Columbia University."

"Absolutely!" Soonam said.

Everyone smiled at the unbridled enthusiasm so typical of her, and agreed that Arjuna should definitely be included.

"OK, who's hungry? How's Chinese?" Attivio asked, taking

out his cell phone to order.

"Do they have sesame noodles in New York," Laaroos asked.

"And scallion pancakes?" Heipleido added.

"I love those," Laaroos said, "eating food has been part of the fun of being in a human body."

"Do we actually need to order?" Maepleida asked. "We just use a command when we're alone."

"Alright then, command what you will," Attivio said.

Immediately all their favorite Chinese food appeared on the ottoman, along with plates and cutlery.

After much eating, laughing and reminiscing, Toomeh gave the command for all the leftovers and dishes to be cleared away, and Soonam offered to show them to their rooms.

As they all trooped up the stairs, Maepleida remembered them all climbing a grand staircase in another home, on Venus, the day they visited Ederah's parents and swam under the waterfall. Heipleido saw her smile as if at some private satisfaction, and reading her mind caught her hand and brought it to his lips.

The next day dawned cool and crisp and Attivio was up early conjuring coffee, bacon and eggs. Soonam came downstairs, hugged him around the waist from behind as he stood at the stove and rested her cheek on his back for a moment breathing in the scent of him. Reluctantly she released him and commanded the large, round, wooden kitchen table to set itself with her colorful fiesta ware and multi-colored striped napkins. It struck her for the first time why she loved fiesta ware. Of course, it was the color of all Seven Rays belonging to the Chohans responsible for guiding Earth safely into the next dimension. Today she chose yellow-orange plates for Laaroos and Toomeh, green for Maepleida and Heipleido, and violet for herself and Attivio. Toomeh was next down and he conjured the toast, butter and jam.

"I still can't believe we're under one roof," Toomeh said. "I haven't slept so well my whole time on Earth as I did last night with all of you nearby."

Soonam danced over to him and gave him a hug and a kiss.

Over breakfast they planned the dinner for Natasha and Arjuna who would be joining them that evening. In case the two guests were not Ederah and Bereh but simply humans, they decided to do everything in preparation for the dinner without using fifth dimensional power, just to make sure they stayed in the human mode until they knew for sure who their guests were. Soonam said she would bake a pineapple upside down cake, and Toomeh and Laaroos offered to make Indian food. During his time in Mumbai Toomeh had learned a few of the recipes which Caitlin had put in her cookbook, but they'd need a few things so Soonam said she'd take them to Trader Joe's. When breakfast was over and they'd all cleaned up amid much laughter, they set off in different directions. As Halloween was in two days and they'd never before celebrated it, Maepleida and Heipleido thought it might be fun to carve scary faces on pumpkins. Attivio took them to get eight carve worthy pumpkins at the Union Square Farmers' market. Soonam offered them a cart, but Heipleido gave her one of his smiles and she burst out laughing at herself. Did superman really need a cart to carry eight pumpkins?

The previous evening Toomeh had texted Arjuna who happily accepted the invitation to come to dinner in Greenwich Village. He'd been more than lonely since arriving in New York and relished the idea of seeing Ewen again. Arjuna felt a strange sensation in his heart when he heard Ewen say the names of their hosts, Soonam and Attivio. Ewen sensed that the names had affected Arjuna, but didn't mention it. When Arjuna asked who else would be there, Ewen told him that another couple, Maepleida and Heipleido, had also come from London with him and his partner. Again, Ewen sensed a reaction in Arjuna when he heard the names.

"And there's another thing I want to tell you. I now go by the name Toomeh and my partner is known as Laaroos."

Arjuna felt his heart pounding at the mention of these names, Soonam and Attivio, Maepleida and Heipleido, Laaroos and Toomeh. He knew these names from somewhere. But all he said was, "I shall happily call you Toomeh from now on."

All his life Arjuna had known he was different, but it wasn't until he met Ewen, now Toomeh, at the gaming center in Mumbai, that he'd ever met anyone else who had had as many strange experiences as himself. He'd loved playing *Fifth Dimension* with Ewen, and fighting the dark lords, and trying to rescue the Russian girl on the plane. It felt more real to him than his real life. Since coming to New York he'd tried to bury himself in astrophysics to escape his loneliness, but now, here was his friend, and he was with a group of people whose very names stirred Arjuna's heart. Toomeh had also said a girl named Natasha would be there, and that she'd won the same contest as he had by painting a scene of a family ice skating in Gorky Park. Arjuna was afraid to hope too much that this Natasha was the very same girl he'd seen skating in Gorky Park when he was fifteen. But the painting of Gorky Park, that would be too much of a coincidence. It must be her. Arjuna paced up and down, then finally, unable to contain himself, went out to walk beneath the vastness of starry heavens. As he walked, Arjuna reviewed all the strange near-death accidents he'd had in his life, as well as the healing he'd received from Master Hilarion. He smiled at the thought of his mother, Aastha, including Hilarion who was, after all, a higher dimensional light being, in her prayers every day when she performed puja.

Before going to bed the night that her guests arrived from London, Soonam sent an email reminding Natasha that tomorrow was the day of the prize winners' dinner. She also told her that the other winner had arrived from London with a group of three more people, and that she might have a lot in common with all of them. At first Natasha doubted this. She'd never had much in common with anyone. In fact, before she left Moscow, Igor had tried to impress upon her the need to act like everyone else and not to get up to any funny business. She despaired of her father ever understanding that she didn't get up to funny business, it just happened to her. Masha, on the other hand, had always understood this about her daughter, and it comforted Natasha to think of her, and to remember Masha telling her stories of seeing her in a place with a pink sky, walking with a group of tall light beings. When Natasha asked her mother if she thought these dreams were just caused by the pregnancy hormones, Masha had been definitive in her answer.

"No, I was seeing into the world you would leave to come to Earth."

As Natasha recalled this conversation with her mother she felt fragments of feeling which seemed to belong to another world. She wondered if the people she was about to meet came from a far-off place, too, and if they had ever called on light beings to help them. Then she sent a silent thanks to Paul the Venetian and Lady Ruth, Chohans of the Pink Ray, her own childhood saviors. To her surprise, they appeared before her.

"We have a message for you," Lady Ruth began, "the beings you will meet tomorrow will be very important to you. Do not fear them. They are old friends from a different dimension and you will all be of great service to one another, and to the Earth and her surface dwellers."

Paul the Venetian then showered her in pink ray light. Natasha bowed to them in gratitude and then, before she could ask them the many questions about the beings she would meet the next day, they vanished. Sleep now being impossible, Natasha, with her heart full of anticipation, sat by the window staring out at the city lights from both New York and New Jersey, shining on the Hudson River. Communing with the river she grew calm and memories of her Earth life began floating downstream into consciousness, first her childhood and then her teen years and that remarkable event in Gorky Park when she'd seen a boy turn into light, and most recently her strange dreams of working with others to save a plane from crashing and of making two beings invisible so they could slip into a hospital unseen. Natasha observed all these scenes until finally the sky grew light, becoming lavender, then a soft rosy-pink. At daybreak she looked up into the sky and asked her Higher Self to guide her through the day. Then she drew a hot bath, scented it with rose oil and sank into its warmth.

The dinner was arranged for eight. At five of eight Attivio was zipping up Soonam's rose colored dress while at the same time she was trying to fix her unruly golden hair.

"Hold still a minute."

"I can't possibly, I'm too excited."

"Oh bugger," Attivio said, "I know we said we wouldn't today, but I'm just going to will it to be zipped." The dress zipped itself. They were still testing out their powers, which had been mostly latent for the past twenty-one years. Careful to use their superpowers only in private, it thrilled them each time they successfully managed them.

While Soonam's dress was zipping itself up, Maepleida and Heipleido were standing before the full-length mirror in their room checking themselves out.

"I don't know about the blue," Maepleida said, turning sideways for a different view of her dress.

"Change to the color emerald," Heipleido commanded, forgetting their agreement not to use fifth dimensional power until they knew who their guests actually were. The dress instantly matched Maepleida's emerald eyes. "Better?"

"Much," she answered, "I don't know why I'm anxious."

"Yes, you do," he said with his characteristic directness and strength, which had always matched her own, "you're afraid to hope it's really Ederah and Bereh coming tonight, so you're finding fault with your appearance. It's very human of you," he teased.

She gave him a withering look which didn't wither him but drew him to her, and he pulled her into his arms, tilted her head back, brushed her long black hair from her forehead and kissed it as one would do to soothe a child.

"It's tricky being both fifth dimensional and human," he said kissing her again, "we're not used to the constant anxiety most humans experience."

The aroma of Indian food wafting up the stairs greeted them when they opened their bedroom door. "Intoxicating," Maepleida said breathing in the scent.

Toomeh glanced around the kitchen to check that all was ready. Laaroos followed his eyes and said, "All set except the nan, which we can do once we're about to eat so it'll be hot."

"OK, aprons off then," he said, turning her around to untie hers and slip it over her head before undoing his own. She looked down at her orange-gold dress. There was a small spot of spinach on the skirt. "Spot be gone," she whispered, and it disappeared. "Oh damn, I forgot."

"Let it go, it's good it comes so naturally."

"Yes, but I don't yet feel battle ready, do you?" Their conversation was cut short by the doorbell.

The little scenes inside the house were playing out as a taxi pulled up outside. A young woman, intent on paying the driver, didn't notice the man walking toward her cab checking out the numbers on the houses, but he saw her, and quickened his pace until he was only a few feet away. As he drew closer she finally sensed someone approaching her. For a moment she was frightened, until her intuition told her this was a good guy, not some minion from the dark side. She turned and looked directly at the man, who returned her gaze. In the pool of yellow light streaming from the house's large parlor floor windows, Natasha saw that she was face to face in physical reality with the man she had dreamed of many times standing on a cliff looking down at the Arabian Sea. And Arjuna knew instantly by the thumping of his heart that this was the girl he had seen skating in Gorky Park. The two of them stood, neither moving nor speaking, their eyes locked on one another. His grey-gold eyes, so like her own, poured out a warmth hitherto unknown to her in this lifetime. Arjuna felt such rapture that he never wanted the moment to end. But she was speaking now. "I've seen you before."

He struggled to comprehend her words through the maze of feelings rushing through him. She watched him as he tried to speak.

Finally he managed to say, "Yes, once, ice skating in Gorky Park."

"You were the boy who turned to light?" She gasped. "How is it that you are here?"

"I'm going to dinner. In this house," he said pointing.

Natasha looked up at the number on the house and saw that it was her destination as well.

She wanted to pour out the story of all the dreams she'd had of him, especially the most recent one where he'd been rescuing an airplane from the dark side. For his part, he wanted to take her hand, to kiss her and never let her go. But they did nothing except gaze at one another until a strong wind blew up the street, rippled through the trees, shaking the branches and raining leaves down on them.

"Shall we go in?" Natasha ventured.

Arjuna offered his arm to escort her up the steps. When she put her arm through his, her heart exploded with recognition. She had held this arm before, many, many times. Fire shot through them both and tears sprang to their eyes.

"Bereh," she heard herself say out loud, not knowing from where the word came.

At the sound of her voice saying his name a spring opened deep inside him and poured forth a radiant light turning him once again into that light being she had seen in Gorky Park.

"Ederah," he answered as he embraced her and she, too, turned to light.

Had anyone been on the street to see, they would have witnessed a shower of pink-gold sparks shoot up out of the crowns of two beings made of clear light. Fortunately, this was a small, quiet, winding street in the West Village. A second later they were once again in human form. But the two natives of Venus who had come to Earth as wanderers had reunited.

When she could speak, Ederah said, "I don't know if I can face a group of strangers at this moment."

"Maybe they're not strangers," Bereh said.

Taking strength in Bereh's presence Ederah agreed to go in.

Together they climbed the eight stairs and rang the bell.

It was Toomeh and Laaroos who answered the door. Toomeh saw at once that Arjuna was changed.

"You've met," Toomeh said looking at Ederah and Bereh.

"Just this moment," Ederah said, "on these steps." She turned and smiled at Bereh as she spoke, unable to take her eyes off him for long and unwilling to let go of his arm.

"So, do you remember us as well?" Laaroos asked.

"We do," they said together. "We absolutely do."

"Prepare yourselves, because the rest of our group is here too," Toomeh warned them.

As he spoke Soonam came bounding down the stairs followed by Attivio. Maepleida and Heipleido, who had been sitting by the fire, hearing the commotion came into the foyer too. Amid the bursts of joy, someone managed to shut the front door and lead the way to the fire, where Toomeh passed around a tray laden with mango drinks. Maepleida proposed a toast to their reunion.

"We did it. We awakened in the third dimension and we are together and will fulfill our mission."

Ederah and Bereh had a million questions and so it was a while before they were able to leave the fire to gather around the big wooden table for dinner. For that night, at least, they spared themselves the discussion of all their run-ins with Darpith, and concentrated instead on reminiscing, and rejoicing at how they had all found one another again on Earth. The night was already far gone by the time Soonam led Ederah and Bereh to the last guest room, a cozy place up on the third floor under the eaves, its windows overlooking the autumn garden. To please Ederah, Bereh transformed it to look like the cottage they had stayed in during their training on Venus. In response Ederah changed herself so she looked like the girl she had been skating in Gorky Park the day he first saw her on Earth. Bereh scooped her up in his arms and carried her over the threshold.

Chapter 17

Halloween

For the next few days they talked for hours about how best to awaken humans to the knowledge of their own divinity, and how to prepare them for ascension so they wouldn't get stuck in the third dimension for another 75,000 years, maybe not even on Earth, but on some other third dimensional planet. Besides these serious discussions, they had fun thinking up costumes for the Halloween parade. For the joy of it, they had all decided to dress up and walk in the parade through Greenwich Village. There was no need to buy or sew anything as now that they were together their united energy opened up the rest of their fifth dimensional powers so they could create anything they desired simply by commanding it.

Ederah and Bereh were up in their room planning their costumes when he paused and looked at her thoughtfully. "It's strange," he said, "how involved we've all become in life on Earth, on this little blue dot of a planet on the edge of an ordinary galaxy which has billions of other suns in it, and is only one galaxy among a hundred billion other galaxies in this universe, and this universe is but one of an infinite number of universes."

"Is that the astrophysicist in you speaking or the fifth dimensional being?" Ederah asked.

"Both. But being human for the past twenty-one years, I've lost some of my perspective on infinitude."

"It is wild," Ederah agreed, "that as human, we feel we have some special cosmic importance, when as fifth dimensional beings we know everything and everyone is part of the one and no one is more important than another."

"Of all the missions which we've undertaken in different

universes, this has been the strangest in some ways," Bereh said. "Even though the human vehicle is a similar shape to our own because we evolved in the same solar system, having a human ego has been one of the greatest challenges I've faced on any mission."

"I agree. It's painful to witness the extent of human and animal suffering on Earth. The genocide. The slaughter. The starvation. And on the personal level there's the heartbreak of the death of a child, a parent, a husband, a wife, a friend, the ravages of cancer, the shock of a heart attack or an accident. And humans don't understand why."

"The third dimension is the most exacting of all the dimensions on any planet," Bereh reminded her, "because suffering is the catalyst for growth. Thankfully, eventually everyone evolves to the fourth dimension and beyond."

"That human suffering is so intense makes our mission all the more urgent to me," Ederah said.

"You've always had the softest heart," he said.

"OK, now let's make a decision about our costumes for the Halloween parade," she said.

As the hour grew near to leave for the parade, Soonam suggested they ground themselves by eating some human food. She commanded the table to be set for eight with a delicious pasta primavera, warm garlic bread and a Caesar salad. Attivio added a Chianti, though none of them were drinkers, but a little taste wouldn't dim their powers and it would be warming to their human bodies. During dinner, everyone was playfully mysterious about their costumes. When they finished eating, the kitchen cleaned itself up after one command from Attivio and they all went upstairs to get ready for the parade.

The plan was to assemble in the foyer at 7:00 p.m. Soonam and Attivio, dressed as Beauty and the Beast, were standing by the front door waiting for the others when Heipleido and Maepleida came down the stairs as Batman and Cat Woman.

Attivio whistled at them.

"You're perfect," Soonam gushed.

With his extraordinary strength and agility, Heipleido was the quintessential Batman. And Maepleida, brandishing her whip, made a fearsome Cat Woman. Behind them were Toomeh and Laaroos dressed as frightening-looking, baby-gobbling ogres. The six of them stood there enjoying the fun, awaiting Ederah and Bereh, who moments later appeared at the top of the stairs as Mr. Fantastic and the Invisible Woman. It wasn't lost on any of them how closely Edereh resembled her choice. She did have the power to become invisible and to make others invisible as well. The two descended the stairs to the approval of the group at the door. They all filed out of the house and down the front steps between the eight pumpkins they'd carved earlier in the day. Maepleida pointed to the pumpkins, all of which had scary faces meant to ward off evil. "Do we leave them burning?"

Attivio looked at Soonam for an answer.

"We better not while we're out," she said, thinking of the possible opportunity for the dark lords to burn the house down and make it look like an accident, but then she supposed they could do that anyway. Still, no sense giving them the idea. At her command, all eight candles extinguished themselves at once, leaving the steps in darkness as the eight wanderers made their way over to Sixth Avenue to join the parade.

They did not walk unobserved. Darpith watched them leave the house, and then quickly transformed himself into Mr. Fantastic so he looked exactly like Bereh. Now he just had to get rid of Bereh, infiltrate the group, and it would be child's play to bump them off one at a time, ending their mission before it got off the ground. It didn't occur to him that this might be stupidly confident. Evil can be dumb. Foolish of them to dress up for Halloween, he thought. The group joined the parade at Houston Street and made their way up Sixth Avenue with the throng.

Enjoying the feeling of Hallows' Eve, the pleasure of those cross-dressed to kill, and the many other creative costumes surrounding them, the couples lost track of one another in the crowd. When Edereh turned to look at a huge balloon puppet of the U.S. president dressed in a diaper, Darpith closed in on Bereh and hit him with a bolt of dark energy. As Bereh crumpled to the ground Darpith stepped into his place beside Edereh. When she turned back to say something to him, it was not Bereh but Darpith to whom she spoke. He cut her off and suggested they leave the parade and take a break. She was surprised at his sudden suggestion, but agreed. However, before they could make their way out of the crowd, Soonam rushed up saying, "Come with me, you have to see something," and she reached out to pull Bereh along; however, gifted with psychometry, the moment she touched him, she knew it wasn't Bereh. Her veins turned to ice at the horror she saw at the moment of contact and she immediately let go. Without giving away her discovery, she turned to touch Edereh. When her touch verified that it was really Edereh, Soonam kept up the pretense of wanting to show them something, and pulling Ederah forward whispered in her ear, "Make yourself and me invisible at once, this isn't Bereh beside us."

A second later they were invisible and back-tracking to find the real Bereh. A few people had seen him fall and carried him to the curb where they were trying unsuccessfully to revive him when Soonam and Edereh reappeared beside him. Attivio walked up a few minutes later looking for Soonam.

"We need Laaroos," Soonam said. "We don't know what the dark lord has done to him. He may need regeneration," she whispered to Attivio who knelt beside her.

Their group had planned to meet up at Tenth Street and Sixth Avenue for a check-in. That was just two blocks away. Attivio made his way, as fast as he could in his beast costume, through the crowds to get there. Heipleido and Maepleida were already there and Toomeh and Laaroos were just approaching when Attivio arrived. He told them what had happened to Bereh and warned them to be on the lookout for a Mr. Fantastic double as they made their way back to the others.

Maepleida was the first to spot the fake Mr. Fantastic, standing with his back to them, scanning the crowd. She tightened her grip on her whip and doubled herself. When they saw what Maepleida was about, Toomeh and Laaroos, dressed as two chunky, hideous ogres, began leaping into the air and performing back flips to create a distraction. Heipleido looked at Maepleida and nodded. She cracked her first whip and got Darpith's Mr. Fantastic around the neck. Using her second whip as a lasso she wrapped it around his ankles causing him to fall over. She was tightening the one around his neck to choking point when he apparated out of the third dimension. Heipleido smiled at Maepleida. "Well done."

"Come on now," Attivio said, "we have to get Bereh home so Laaroos can work on him."

When they reached the others, Bereh was still lying unconscious in the street, his head in Ederah's lap with Soonam beside them. Heipleido effortlessly picked up Bereh, carried him home and laid him on the sofa. As Laaroos bent over Bereh, Attivio commanded a fire to light in the fireplace. Toomeh told them how when the dark lord had taken control of his body through the game, *Orion,* Lord Sananda and Lady Nada had wielded the Resurrection Flame to save him. "He poisoned my pineal gland and the poison spread slowing my merkaba almost to a standstill, which would have been fatal. My skin had turned grey, like Bereh's is now. I was no longer in my body but watching from above as they moved the flame upward through my body from the soles of my feet to neutralize the poison."

"Everyone place your hands on Bereh," Laaroos commanded, "and together we'll call on the Resurrection Flame and envision its gold light moving into Bereh's central tube to balance the polarities in his electrical circuits. As you envision the light coming up the central tube from six inches below his feet, also envision it coming down the tube from six inches above his head," Laaroos directed. "See the two streams of light meeting at his heart then drop the two streams all the way down and out the bottom of the tube into Mother Earth. Next bring the two streams of light energy to Bereh's pineal gland. Bathe it in the Resurrection Flame and then drop the flame down the central tube and into the Earth. This will pull the dark energy out of his body and down into the earth to be neutralized.

"Courage, Ederah," Soonam whispered to her, squeezing her hand before they both placed their palms on Bereh's limp grey body.

"Focus everyone," Laaroos said.

The seven of them watched as the Resurrection Flame responded to their call. Using their will and love, they drew the gold light energy up through Bereh's body into his heart and then to his pineal gland. When the golden flame hit the gland, Bereh stirred for the first time since Darpith had attacked him, but did not open his eyes.

"What was the mantra Lord Sananda gave us during our training on Venus?" Ederah asked.

"I am the resurrection and the life," Toomeh answered.

"Everybody keep up the mantra, 'Bereh is the resurrection and the life of his restored body and mind'," Laaroos said.

After several minutes of this, Bereh's color started to return and he opened his eyes, but he was disoriented, until Ederah leaned over him. At the sight of her face he smiled. Everyone breathed a sigh of relief. Bereh sat up.

Soonam conjured hot cider with cinnamon sticks and they drank silently, each sinking into their own thoughts until Maepleida broke the silence.

"We have to be on guard more than ever now. The dark lords know we're awake in the third dimension and that we've reunited. They'll be more desperate than ever to stop us, and they'll probably be reckless like Darpith was tonight, for I'm sure it was him. His vileness has a particular feel I'm familiar with."

"Maepleida's right, whether we're ready for battle or not, it is upon us," Ederah said. "We need all our fifth dimensional powers awakened and sharp and we're not there yet."

"Let's try to remember every healing mantra we were given during our training on Venus," Laaroos added.

"Yes, we can't defeat the dark lords and all their minions immediately, "Toomeh said, "so we'll have to spread our message even while we're under attack, and we may incur injury and need healing."

"Tomorrow we can make our plans," Laaroos said, "Bereh needs rest now for his adrenals to recover. Thankfully his pineal gland is unharmed. The dark energy wasn't in his body long enough to damage it."

Ederah and Bereh said "goodnight," and climbed the stairs to their Venusian-like room under the eaves. Soonam put a charm round the house so no one from any dimension could enter. And before falling asleep, Edereh also put a charm around the house making it invisible.

Chapter 18

Battle Plans

The next morning the eight of them gathered at the big wooden table in the kitchen.

"Anyone hungry?" Soonam asked, as she conjured blueberry pancakes with sweet butter and maple syrup. Seven heads nodded yes. Maepleida added hot tea and Heipleido fresh squeezed orange juice. While they were still enjoying breakfast, Bereh brought up the attack from the night before. "Darpith isn't wasting any time. Without the quick action by all of you my human body would no longer be viable."

"How does Darpith decide whether to send his minions after us or to act himself?" Ederah asked. "Most of the attacks on me during these past years were by him, not his minions, except for the attempt to crash the plane."

"It's been mixed for me, sometimes him, sometimes his minions," Heipleido said. "It's a different feeling when it's him. There's a crude heavy-handedness to him, nothing elegant or brilliant like some dark lords."

"Speaking of elegant and brilliant, have any of you been attacked by Veldemiron?" Maepleida asked. When no one spoke Maepleida continued. "Once when Master El Morya came to my rescue during college, I heard him tell Amerissis that for the time being it seemed like Veldemiron was leaving it all to Darpith, who is nowhere near as subtle in the use of evil as himself.

"Amerissis then said, "Perhaps Veldemiron plans to see how far Darpith gets before he sweeps in, enslaves him, and takes over.""

"I've not heard of Veldemiron. I don't think he was involved in the battle for the Violet Planet," Soonam said. "Is he also from Orion?"

"I believe so," Maepleida answered, "I think most of the current enemies of Earth hoping to turn her to the dark side are fourth and fifth dimensional entities from Orion and Draco."

"The more humans who are awake, the more difficult it will be for the dark lords," Heipleido said, "we need to plan how to get the message out that we are all one, and all Divine."

"The menacing orange overlord in the White House is an evil genius at getting his lying message out," Soonam said.

"Why is it people believe his lies?" Maepleida asked.

"Some people do want to return to a more racist past because it makes them feel powerful. But for some, I think it's hope of escaping their poverty which makes them vulnerable to his false promises. And the rich are motivated by self-interest. They benefit from his fascist policies and capitalist greed," Soonam said.

"This is indeed an unpropitious time for the United States," Maepleida said, "as it is for Britain."

"We must take a page from his book to get our own message out," Attivio said.

"His name calling, lying, racist solipsism or schoolyard bullying?" Heipleido asked, hoping to lighten the mood.

But Toomeh answered him seriously. "Many of the actual people in power in every country are not the politicians or the elected leaders but the super wealthy, who are already firmly in the hands of the dark side."

"True, but there is a movement here in the U.S. among minority candidates, some quite young, to correct the imbalance of wealth, and to stop the persecution of minorities who are unjustly shot or incarcerated in the for-profit prison system," Soonam said.

"We could start by supporting smart, courageous, energetic young candidates who are not afraid to speak truth to power," Maepleida said.

"These young leaders will need not only support, but

protection," Soonam said. "If they try to upset the status quo where the greedy, who are in service only to themselves, are in control, they'll be targets of the dark side. Fostering greed and self-interest at the expense of others is one of the major paths to becoming a dark lord. They won't want that messed with."

"Look, there are four of us in New York and four of us in London," Bereh said, "and four together is formidable. And if necessary, we can be eight for some missions. And other wanderers may also be waking up. There's an election for an American president in less than a year. Let's throw our weight with a progressive candidate who can defeat the current orange overlord."

"I would like to work on a political campaign," Soonam said.

"Britain, too, has gone down a dark, backward road with the intention of Brexit being to exclude certain minorities," Toomeh said.

Maepleida and Heipleido said they'd work in politics in London, supporting progressive candidates. "Maybe I'll even run for office myself," Maepleida said.

"We're all agreed then that politics is one path we can employ to spread the message that we're all one, and wealth should be redistributed fairly. But how do we deliver the second part of the message, that not only are we all one, but we're all Divine?" Attivio asked.

Soonam got an inspiration. "We need a best seller translated into every language to deliver this message."

"You're right!" Ederah said. "And probably it should be a novel which can be made into a film to reach more people."

"What kind of novel would have mass appeal?" Bereh asked.

"Fantasy fiction often gets made into movies," Soonam said. "Why not our own story? It's fantasy fiction to most humans, who don't believe in extraterrestrials incarnating on Earth and getting attacked by the dark lords from Orion."

"I can write it," Attivio said. "I need a big writing project for school this semester anyway."

"We also have the game, *Fifth Dimension,* to let humans know what's happening on the planet," Toomeh said. "We'll need to popularize it so people will get it that there is a battle going on between light and dark for the future of not only the planet, but for the humans themselves."

"A contest could popularize the game," Ederah said. "Bereh could start it among students at Columbia University here in New York, and Toomeh could do it at The Royal College of Art in London. Then the two schools could challenge one another."

Toomeh agreed. "We'll set it up between our two schools to start, and invite other universities and even high schools to join. The winner will be the player who wins the most battles against the dark lords."

"How do we include players who aren't in school?" Laaroos asked.

"Gaming centers could form teams," Soonam suggested.

"I could organize the gaming centers in New York using social media," Ederah said.

"And I could do it in London," Laaroos said. "And once it catches on, gaming centers in other places could organize themselves and join through an online registration we set up."

"OK, so here's the list of assignments," Maepleida said.

"Soonam works with progressive political candidates in America, and Heipleido and I enter politics in Britain.

"Attivio writes our story as fantasy fiction with an eye to having it made into a movie.

"Toomeh and Laaroos promote *Fifth Dimension* in Britain, and Ederah and Bereh do the same in America."

"I'd like to add a reminder," Laaroos said.

But before she could say it Soonam's cell phone rang. It was her father, Hunter.

"Rose, I mean, Soonam, I'm in the street, but our house seems to have gone missing."

Soonam looked at the others. "It's my father, he says the house isn't where it's supposed to be."

"Oh," Ederah said. "That would be me. I placed an invisibility charm around it last night."

She lifted it at once and Soonam ran to the front door to welcome Hunter home and introduce him to everyone.

"What were you about to say, Laaroos?" Toomeh asked.

"Just that we should remember to call on the Chohans of all the rays for help. Once asked, they will come to our assistance."

"Right. They're probably watching from Saturn's rings even as we speak."

Everyone needed a stretch after the meeting. And once Soonam had introduced Hunter all around, and he'd gone upstairs to unpack, she suggested they take a stroll to Washington Square Park and revisit the scene of their first time together in New York, when they'd come as part of El Morya's training exercise. Even though it was November first, the fountain in the center of the park was still on and blowing in the wind. They were quiet as they walked across the big lawn through the fallen leaves toward the fountain. Attivio slipped his hand into Soonam's. She stopped under a large oak tree on the lawn. "Did you hear that?" she asked looking up into the branches.

"What?"

"The tree. It's saying something." Soonam walked close to the trunk but stopped short of touching it. Immediately she heard the words, "Don't go near the fountain. He's in there."

"Who's in there?" Soonam asked.

"The dark lord. Look at the trees. We're all leaning away from the fountain."

"You're right," Soonam said, turning quickly to Attivio and asking him to warn the others about the fountain. Then turning back to the tree, she asked, "Who are you?"

"I'm Theodora, but you can call me Thea," the tree answered.

"Thank you, Thea. Do you know what the dark lord was

planning?"

"He created a vortex to suck you into the center of the fountain and pull you through the bottom into a merkaba bound for Orion, where he would enslave you. I believe it was he who put the idea into your head to walk to the park today. Very tricky to use something you often do in order to ensnare you."

"But how did you know what he was up to?" Soonam asked.

"On Earth, third dimensional humans are the only ones who can't see and hear the other dimensions, but trees are second dimensional beings and we perceive all dimensions both above and below us."

By now the others were all gathered around Thea, too, thanking her. Soonam gave Thea a hug and immediately saw the wealth of lifetimes which Thea had lived as a first, then as a second dimensional being.

"What a journey you've had," Soonam told her. "Can I visit you again and call on you for help?"

"Yes. Trees don't like the dark lords," Thea told her, "they have no regard for us."

Once home again and gathered around the fire, sipping hot chocolate, Heipleido cleared his throat. "Much as I don't want to part from any of you, I think we should return to London immediately. It'll be harder for the dark side if we're spread out. Today's attempt is proof of that."

"Sadly, I agree," Maepleida said.

"The four of us can travel by merkaba and be there instantly," Toomeh added.

What none of them knew was that an enraged Darpith, unable to get past Soonam's charm around the house, had made himself invisible and was looking in the window and listening. He especially had it in for that cat woman, Maepleida.

"I'm not ready to let you go," Soonam said.

"But now that we're awake we can travel easily and meet for progress reports," Laaroos reminded her.

"The sooner we depart the better," Toomeh said.

But before they could stir, seven ovals of different colored light appeared and materialized into the Chohans of the Seven Rays and their twin flames. Out of the Blue Ray, wearing long robes of cobalt blue, emerged Master El Morya and Amerissis, from the Pink Ray, dressed in pink and aquamarine, came Paul the Venetian and Lady Ruth, from the Green Ray, in a cloak of many shades of green, Master Hilarion became visible, from the Gold Ray, Lord Sananda and Lady Nada emerged, glowing with gold and purple light, from the White Ray, Lord Serapis Bay and Amutreya were the next to materialize in flowing robes of white and gold, then, from the Violet Ray, Saint Germain and Portia, wearing shimmering robes of violet, stepped forward to greet them, and finally, from the Yellow Ray, with a beam of light glowing in his heart like a lantern, emerged Lord Lanto with Shoshimi beside him. Not since descending the golden staircase on Venus had the wanderers seen all the Chohans together, and they were struck dumb at the sight. Outside the window Darpith shrieked in pain. The energy of love and light was so intense that he felt as if he was being burned alive. Reeling in agony, he fled.

The wanderers felt whole and completely restored to their fifth dimensional powers in the presence of the Chohans. Saint Germain bowed his head in acknowledgment of the divine resting within each of them. "We've come to offer you our congratulations on completing the first major task of your mission, awakening in the third dimension. Well done, all of you. And we see that you have come up with plans for awakening the Earth beings. Again, well done. Your powers are restored, but we would like to give you an infusion of each of the rays which will further strengthen and protect you."

El Morya and Amerissis went first and surrounded each of the wanderers with the Blue Ray, adding a layer of protection to their auras and aligning them even more closely with the Will of the Divine. Next, Paul the Venetian and Lady Ruth filled the room with the Pink Ray, creating an intoxicating infusion of love as it penetrated each of them. Hilarion wielded the Green Ray imbuing them with a greater power to heal. Then the golden Resurrection Flame shot out from the hearts of Lady Nada and Lord Sananda, and pierced the heart of each wanderer strengthening its sinews. The White Flame of Ascension was delivered by Serapis Bay and Amutreya to ensure that the wanderers would ascend at the end of their mission. After that, the Violet Ray of Transmutation, wielded by Portia and Saint Germain, saturated them in violet light which seeped into each wanderer empowering him with the ability to transmute energy. And finally, Lord Lanto and Shoshimi bestowed the Yellow Ray of Illumination and Wisdom which could illuminate any situation and make clear the right decision and course of action.

The eight wanderers bowed to the Chohans. They had so many questions they wanted to ask, but Lord Serapis Bay addressed them before they could speak. "As you know this solar system is governed by the Council of Nine who meet in Saturn's rings. In view of accelerated efforts by the dark lords of Orion to wage a hostile takeover of Earth, we have set up an additional tracking center on Titan, Saturn's largest moon, to monitor them. We will also oversee the playing of *Fifth Dimension* from Titan. One of the Chohans will always be on hand when any of you are working through the game. In addition to your other gaming gear we now request that all wanderers wear a coverall made of the element molybdenum while playing. Molybdenum has a melting point of four thousand seven hundred fifty-three degrees Fahrenheit, and a boiling point of eight thousand three hundred eighty-two degrees Fahrenheit. We have information that Darpith is developing new weapons to target both the body and the brain. A molybdenum suit will afford some protection for your human aspect. As sometimes you will be in human form during the game, we request that you use the suit. The battle for Earth has begun. Work always from your hearts. And remember, all beings serve the creator in their own way. We will leave you now. All is well." And they were gone.

Maepleida was the first to speak. "How I have longed for them during these years on Earth. Even though El Morya came when I was desperate, to see them all together with all of you is a different order of experience."

"At this moment, I feel ready for anything the dark lords can throw at us," Heipleido said.

"We should be off," Toomeh said.

"So suddenly?" Soonam asked.

Attivio took her hand, "Soonam you know it's best."

Soonam hugged each of them and stepped back.

"Until we meet again, many blessings," Laaroos said.

They each bowed to the Divine in one another. Then, Laaroos, Toomeh, Maepleida and Heipleido joined hands, created the energy for a group merkaba, and vanished.

To ward off the feeling of sadness, Attivio directed the fire to burn more brightly and manifested warm salted popcorn covered with caramel. Soonam put a piece in her mouth and savored the sweetness as she snuggled into Attivio on the sofa. Across from them on the other sofa, Ederah and Bereh were discussing their living arrangements.

"Why don't you just move in with me and commute uptown to Columbia," Ederah said.

"Or, you could both live here," Soonam said, "my father is in London half the time for work, but he wouldn't mind anyway."

"Nice as that would be, it might be safer if we weren't all under one roof," Bereh said.

"I think you're right," Attivio agreed.

"But you'll at least stay tonight," Soonam said.

Hunter, on his way out for the evening, dressed in a tux, appeared in the doorway to say good evening. Soonam jumped up when she saw him and gave him a kiss on the cheek. It made him happy to see Rose sitting with friends, eating popcorn by the fire. Although he called her Soonam now, he still thought of her as Rose. They all wished him a good evening and returned to their conversation. To delight Ederah, Bereh turned some of the popcorn into chocolate covered caramels.

"Delicious," she said giving him a kiss on the nose.

"God I've missed you," Bereh said. "All the longing in my heart is answered by your touch."

The four of them sat up late sharing more of the stories of their earth journey so far. Bereh loved hearing Ederah's description of Igor telling her not to get up to any "funny business".

"If he only knew," Soonam said.

"He probably suspects more than he admits," Ederah said, "my mother certainly surmises the truth."

"What about your mother, Bereh?" Attivio asked.

"She's a Hindu, so reincarnation is a fact for her, as is enlightenment, but her son being a fifth dimensional being, here on a mission, might be a stretch even for her."

Attivio shared that his mother had always been sympathetic to him when strange things happened but his father reacted with frustration, like when they were sailing off Corfu and suddenly Attivio fell overboard and almost drowned.

"Did your parents ever get frustrated when weird things happened to you?"

"My father, never," Soonam said, "and I don't remember my mother, other than that she often seemed to be annoyed at me."

Their conversation was interrupted by a bubble arriving in Toomeh's voice.

"We arrived back in London with no interference on the journey. Love you all."

Ederah sent back a bubble acknowledging receipt of their message. Soonam yawned.

"Let's go to bed," Attivio said, pulling her up off the sofa.

"Goodnight," Soonam half whispered to Ederah and Bereh.

As the fire glowed red, Ederah lay her head on Bereh's chest and rested in the comfort of his arms.

Chapter 19

Ambush

So much had happened in the few days they'd been away in New York, and so changed were they by reconnecting with their fellow wanderers and seeing the Chohans all together again, that everything once familiar, now felt unfamiliar. Even their carriage house looked different. As they adjusted to the new reality, they began following through on their plans. In frequent contact with Ederah and Bereh, Toomeh and Laaroos created announcements for the gaming contest. Their aim was to get as many people as possible playing *Fifth Dimension*. Laaroos found several gaming centers in London which agreed to sponsor the contest, and Ederah did the same in New York. Toomeh and Bereh organized the contest at their respective schools and began to spread the word to other institutions. Once the U.S. and the U.K. were engaged, they would spread the game throughout Europe and North and South America. Finally, they would try to get footholds for it in the Middle East, Far East and Africa.

On the political front, Heipleido, still using the name Horus at work, formed a group of progressives from those like himself who worked as assistants to members of the House of Lords. Their first goal was to write legislation to help the poor, and then to present it to their members.

Maepleida decided to run for the House of Commons. To further this end, she needed her fraternal grandmother's help. A notorious extrovert who knew everyone, Maggie would be invaluable if she signed on. While her family no longer had a country seat, they still maintained a small property and the comfortable dowager house, and their name was still well known in the district. Once her grandmother was on board, Maepleida would begin canvassing to secure one of the six hundred and fifty seats in the House of Commons. She would have to run using the name Mary, but that was OK. In fact, all eight of them decided to use the names their human parents had given them, and to only use their eternal names among themselves. Hunter had been particularly happy to be able to once again call his daughter Rose.

To run for office, Maepleida would need to establish a brand. For this she consulted Toomeh, who had several new friends at the Royal College of Art who could help. After discussion with the others, Maepleida chose the issues she wanted to work on: affordable housing, transport infrastructure, and broadband service for rural areas. Since she would be running in a rural district these causes, as well as being worthy of her effort, made the most sense. She sent a bubble to New York to run them by Soonam, who was also deciding what issues to work on.

Soonam sent a bubble back to Maepleida supporting her choices, and adding her own current thinking. "There are so many things that need changing in the U.S. that I'm bursting with ideas. Do I focus on global warming, immigration policy, campaign finance reform, ending for profit prisons, clean energy, health care for everybody, lower drug prices, higher education or trade school for all?"

"Find the candidate who supports your position in each of these issues and get on the campaign staff," Maepleida bubbled back.

"Yes, brilliant. The Democratic field is shaping up now. Soon I'll be able to choose a candidate to go up against our current racist overlord whose presidency is already a total dumpster fire."

While Soonam and Maepleida talked strategy, Heipleido's progressive group met to discuss which issue they would tackle first. It had to be something which a number of their bosses would be willing to take to the House of Lords. Heipleido wanted it to be something which would help the poor and homeless. He tested the water with Maepleida's father, Lord Merton.

"Yes, yes, all well and good, Horus, but it's a long process to bring legislation to the floor. It has to be step by step."

Heipleido wasn't deterred. "Is the first step writing a bill to present to the appropriate committee?"

"Yes, but know that it will go through many changes, should the committee even take it up. You'll have to garner support to even get it to committee."

Never the less, Heipleido took encouragement from Lord Merton's words and met with his progressive colleagues to begin the process. It's true that none of the other committee members were fifth dimensional but as humans, each of them had a great deal of love for his fellow man. And each of them seemed to know already that we're all connected, all one. What they didn't yet understand, was their own divinity and that of all beings.

Maepleida was on the computer, with Toomeh looking over her shoulder, when Heipleido arrived back at the carriage house after his meeting with her father.

"Come have a look at my new website."

"It's very green and blue," Heipleido said.

"Yes, the green is for the Green Ray of Healing and to enlist Master Hilarion's aid, and the blue is for the Blue Ray of Aligning with the Will of the Divine, and its Chohans, El Morya and Amerissis."

"I like the photo of you," Heipleido said bending down to kiss her.

"The problem is that many of the people in the rural district where she's running don't have internet," Toomeh said, "so we've also designed these buttons and fliers using the same color palate." He leaned over and clicked to a different page on the computer to show Heipleido. After he admired their work, Heipleido asked where Laaroos was.

"She should have been here by now," Toomeh said. "We were planning to conjure up some New York pizza for dinner."

After an hour passed and Laaroos still hadn't returned, Toomeh felt something was wrong.

"Could she have stopped at one of the gaming centers to check on the contest?" Maepleida asked.

"Isn't there a center on her way home from the hospital?"

"Let's go," Heipleido said, holding out his hands so they could create a group merkaba and be there instantly. The next moment they materialized inside the gaming center. Maepleida was the first to spot Laaroos, slumped over in her chair, partly obscured under a black cloud. None of the other gamers around seemed to have noticed, so intent were they on their own playing. Toomeh read the word Orion as it moved across Laaroos's screen. He removed her gear, pulled her out of the chair and lifted her in his arms. Heipleido disabled the game with a command. The four of them moved to a corner, created a group merkaba and departed. Back at the carriage house Toomeh laid Laaroos across their bed and the three of them placed their hands on her as they called on the purple-gold Resurrection Flame and pulled it up her central tube from below her feet, directing it up through her body all the way up to her head and into her pineal gland. Once the flame reached her pineal gland they directed it to form a figure eight around her pineal and pituitary glands and to keep moving in the shape of the infinity symbol. After several minutes, Laaroos's limp body and grey skin began to show signs of recovery, her color returned and she opened her eyes.

"Where am I?" she asked in a confused voice.

"You're safe now," Toomeh told her. "Do you remember what happened?"

Laaroos struggled to sit up but three pairs of hands pushed her back down.

"I stopped at the gaming center to see how the contest was going, and a young guy asked me to teach him how the game worked because he wanted to join the contest. I sat down at his station to show him and I put in the code, but *Fifth Dimension* didn't come up. Something strange came on the screen, so I thought I'd put in the wrong code. I tried again, but the same thing happened. I thought someone might have tampered with the code, but before I could try to fix it, a person in distress came on the screen calling for help and I entered whatever game it was to rescue her. The person calling for help was you, Maepleida. I went deeper and deeper into the matrix but you were always just out of reach, and I knew they were taking you to Orion. Then I must have blacked out."

"So, the dark side has breached the game and can replicate images of us," Toomeh said, "we'll need stronger protection around it."

"And, we'll need a way of proving to one another that's it's really us calling for help and not an imposter created by the dark lords," Maepleida said.

"Do you think the young guy was on the up and up?" Toomeh asked.

"Now that I think about it, no. Even in the first moment I felt a dark vibe from him, but I thought maybe he wanted to move toward the light and *Fifth Dimension* could help him."

"You can't take risks like that, Laaroos," Toomeh said. "Trust your intuition. If a being feels dark, don't engage alone. Wait for one of us."

"Are we to awaken only those who aren't dark?" Laaroos said with a hint of disapproval.

"Of course not," Toomeh answered, "but no one can try that on her own. We must at least be in pairs to attempt it."

Hoping to dispel the tension Maepleida said, "Eating will ground us all. Shall it be human food, mana, or light?"

"I'm still up for that New York pizza," Heipleido said, and conjured it up.

"Smells delicious," Laaroos said, finally being permitted to sit up.

After several slices of pizza, Laaroos said she wanted to warn

Ederah about the attempt to disrupt the contest by tampering with the codes, and she sent her a long bubble explaining what had happened and suggesting they place more protection around the game to make it more tamper proof. Ederah sent a bubble back saying she thought the Yellow Ray of Illumination would be a strong deterrent as it would immediately illuminate any attempt at tampering. Both groups agreed to call on Lord Lanto and Shoshimi, Chohans of the Ray of Illumination, to ask for their assistance in protecting *Fifth Dimension* wherever it was played.

"But before we protect it we'll have to check every gaming site to make sure nothing else has been tampered with. I'll send word to shut down *Fifth Dimension* everywhere until we check. And Ederah and Bereh should do the same in New York," Laaroos said.

After directing their leftover dinner to put itself away, Toomeh said, "You need to rest now, Laaroos."

Laaroos went back to their bedroom while Toomeh spoke to Heipleido for a minute. When Toomeh entered their room a few minutes later and walked toward the bed where Laaroos lay propped up on several pillows, he looked so strong and virile that she felt her heart pounding just looking at him. She smiled to herself thinking how happy it made her that her heart beat faster at the very sight of him approaching her. He sat down on the bed beside her.

"Your heart and my heart are very old friends," he telegraphed to her. Tonight, had been too close a call. Darpith nearly had her, and what that meant, he couldn't think about. Death was easy compared to being captured and turned to the dark path for hundreds of thousands of years. Laaroos knew his thoughts and took him in her arms, whispering, "You are my heart's shelter."

Maepleida and Heipleido lay side by side in their own bed communicating telepathically about Maggie, Maepleida's grandmother, who had agreed to canvas with her. After imagining several amusing scenarios about this, Heipleido cut it off and rolled onto his side to look at Maepleida. Her emerald eyes and black hair, even in her third dimensional body, stunned him with their beauty. Thirsty for her he gathered her long hair in his hands, felt its thickness, let it drop, and moved his hands to her temples, turning her face to his to kiss first her eyes and then her cheeks, before finally reaching the softness of her lips. Her response was full and warm, and for a long time they luxuriated in the joys of a third dimensional body before leaving the rushing world and becoming fifth dimensional to travel to a place beyond thought. As they moved into the Violet Ray and connected with the Divine, they experienced Unity in a sweeping cosmic orgasm. Renewed, they drifted to the borders of sleep, his head pillowed on her heart.

Chapter 20

Death at the Border

Ederah and Bereh were looking out the window of their apartment, watching boats on the Hudson River, when the bubble arrived from Laaroos telling them that *Fifth Dimension* had been hacked in London. "We'll have to shut it down here, too, until we can check every gaming center," Ederah said. "Then once we're sure it's clear we can add more protection."

"Can you send out a command now to shut it down, until we can get around to all the sites?" Bereh asked. "I can take all the schools and you can handle the gaming venues. Or, should we check all of them together?"

"Let's work together. It's only four o'clock. We can still get a lot done today," Ederah said, as she typed the command to shut the game down everywhere in New York. They grabbed their backpacks and jackets and headed out to the closest gaming place first.

Seven hours later, they'd checked every place and found that there had as yet been no hacks. But they'd have to settle on the increased protections soon, as all eight of them were scheduled to play *Fifth Dimension* the next night. The idea was to increase interest in the game by letting gamers watch the wanderers play. As they walked toward home along the Highline, Ederah stopped and looked out over the river. "When I first arrived in New York, I imagined ice skating on this."

Bereh stood still beside her remembering the first time he'd seen her in this lifetime, ice skating in Gorky Park in Moscow. He reached for her hand. "I've longed to ice skate with you since I first saw you," he said.

"I wish I could freeze the Hudson River and skate the length of it with you, but that would draw too much attention, so will you settle for the rink in Central Park?" Ederah asked.

Bereh gave her a look that made her smile.

"Oh, you have in mind to do it now, this moment, in the middle of the night."

"I do," he said pulling her into the circle of his arms and creating a merkaba which moments later landed them right on the ice in the Central Park rink. Ederah manifested skates on their feet and they glided over the ice hand in hand, two halves of one soul.

"Do we risk putting colored lights under the ice for a minute?" Bereh said.

Instantly Ederah commanded it, and together they flew across the ice under the stars, the colored lights shining up on their moving figures. Bereh had at last fulfilled his longing to skate with the girl from Gorky Park. He even managed a few leaps and turns to delight her before kneeling at her feet to untie her skates. "You are my queen, and I, but a lucky servant."

Despite the late night they were up early the next day, working on enhanced security for *Fifth Dimension*. Ederah made a case for Blue Ray protection, as that would align the game with the Will of the Divine so that it could not be used for any purpose contrary to the Divine Will. Bereh suggested adding the Pink Ray of Cosmic Love, as love is the strongest protection in all worlds. And they included the Yellow Ray of Illumination so they would be alerted immediately to any breaching of the rules of the game. In order to initiate these measures, they called on the Chohans of each of the rays and asked for guidance and permission. El Morya and Amerissis granted permission for them to use the Blue Ray, and instructed them to not only protect the game itself, but to have the ray enter any player who logged on to play so that he could act only in consort with the Will of the Divine. The dark side could still play the game, because even those on the dark path serve the Divine in their own way, but they could not hack the game and change the rules.

Paul the Venetian and Lady Ruth gave permission for the Pink Ray of Cosmic Love to be employed as a protection, and said this could be further facilitated by using a background screen of pink during logging in. Each player would then be bathed in the Pink Ray before they commenced play. Lord Lanto and Shoshimi also granted permission for the use of the Yellow Ray of Illumination as an alert to pick up any attempted breach of the game's security. Ederah sent a bubble to Laaroos about their plan. She and Toomeh agreed to use the same rays so protection would be universal and identical in both countries and in all other countries going forward.

While Ederah, Bereh, Laaroos and Toomeh spread the word about *Fifth Dimension* and set up protections around it, Attivio was writing the story of their training on Venus and their incarnation as human. And Soonam was checking out presidential candidates for the next election. The Democratic field was broad, twenty-three candidates in all. She began sifting through each of their positions on every issue to discover who could best restore the country for the benefit of every citizen and every aspiring citizen. Soonam was telling Attivio about her favorite candidates over a breakfast of French toast with blueberries and real maple syrup when Ederah's bubble arrived informing them about the breach, the attack on Laaroos in London, and the new protections around the game.

"That's the first attack on our group by the dark lords since Halloween, nearly three weeks ago," Attivio said.

"Now that we're beginning to advance our mission to awaken the humans, the dark lords are bound to rev up their attacks on us," Soonam said. "We'll have to take extra care tonight if we go ahead with the plan for all eight of us to play *Fifth Dimension*. I better check if the game is still on."

Soonam sent a bubble back to Ederah asking, and received a reply confirming that the game was on for seven p.m. London time, twelve midnight New York time.

At the agreed upon hour, Ederah and Bereh joined Soonam and Attivio at a gaming center in the East Village, while across the Atlantic in London, Toomeh, Laaroos, Maepleida and Heipleido went to a gaming center in Notting Hill Gate. They all signed in to play together, put on their gear, bathed in the Pink Ray, then felt the Blue Ray pass through them. Lord Lanto and Shoshimi appeared on the screen and instructed them that only wanderers could participate in this round, but all gamers were free to watch. They each set the controls to follow this instruction, and then immediately found themselves at the United States/ Mexico border. All eight of them were in their fifth dimensional bodies, and therefore invisible to the third dimensional border guards. The first thing they saw were cages where thousands of small children who had been taken from their parents were being held. There were toddlers with no diapers, five-month old babies uncared for, children with lice, and children sick with pneumonia. The agony on the faces of the children tore at the hearts of the wanderers. There were no beds, no blankets, there was no soap, no comfort or care of any kind. One small girl lay dead on the cement floor. Her little dehydrated body had not even been removed from the cage. Some of the children and babies were crying, but most were mute. All were suffering and their misery was palpable.

"I will attend to the Soul of the dead child," Soonam said. As she approached the child's body, Soonam could see the Soul hovering over it in a state of confusion. She spoke gently to the Soul, who now, disembodied, could see Soonam as she telepathically explained to her that her human body was no longer habitable and she must return to the light. Leading the way, Soonam drew the Soul out of the cage and looked around to see who might have come for it. Above them, and a little way off, she saw two golden angels waiting, and she took the Soul to them and gave her into their care. Soonam was grateful to see the angels. While angels were often encountered in the fifth dimension, one rarely met them in the third dimension and Soonam had missed their presence which always filled her being with joy. The angels told Soonam that this Soul was a fourth dimensional being who had come alone as a wanderer to help humans, and she would now return to the fourth dimension. But the Soul was concerned for those who had been her human parents and she didn't want to leave without reassuring them that she was free and thanking them for their service to her.

While this was happening Maepleida and Laaroos began channeling light energy into the children in all the cages to comfort them and reduce their fear. Laaroos eliminated the lice while Maepleida manifested diapers, clean clothes and soft blankets for all the children. Next they provided the food of their native countries. The desperate children accepted all this without question, whether because they were in shock or because children still believe in magic, Maepleida didn't know. Meanwhile, Toomeh and Heipleido went into the guard station to see who was controlling the guards. The guards were playing cards. Toomeh froze them in place with a trance ray. Attivio, Ederah and Bereh headed for the records office and pulled all the records they could find for the children's parents. Ederah also used a deep trance to immobilize the man in charge of the records before he even realized they were there.

Soonam left the child's Soul with the angels and joined Attivio, Ederah and Bereh in the records office to see if she could find out where the child's parents had been sent. Toomeh told her the records were incomplete and mixed up, and it would be impossible to find the parents using the records as they were. Heipleido suggested to Attivio that he turn back time to when the families had been separated and learn where the little girl's parents had been sent. Since the space-time field on Earth is associated with the force of gravity, Attivio manipulated the force of gravity on the space-time field and shifted them back to the earlier time. While they were back in time they began straightening out the records, inducing those in charge to assign all family members the same number, with only a different letter attached for each family member's name. That way they could reunite families no matter where they were sent.

After immobilizing the guards Toomeh and Bereh had joined the others in the records room and reported that the guards were definitely under the control of the dark side, and that the control was coming down the chain of command from the Secretary of Homeland Security and the President, who were both traveling the dark path of service only to themselves, and whose aim it was to create fear, hate and separation. Attivio had succeeded in turning back the clock to the precise time the little girl had been taken from her parents, and Soonam was able to see that the child's mother and father had been sent to different camps, both hundreds of miles from here.

While the others worked to set up a system so families could be tracked and reunited, Soonam returned to the angels and the child's Soul with the information about her parents' locations. The angels agreed to accompany the child's Soul to each of her parents and explained to the Soul that her parents would experience her visit as a dream telling them that she loved them and that she had died and was free and returning to the light, where she would watch over them. Although they would be anguished, they would at least see that she was no longer suffering in a cage, and they would be free from the torture of worrying about what was happening to her. Soonam reluctantly said goodbye to the angels and the little girl's Soul.

Maepleida and Laaroos were still with the children, soothing and nourishing them. Laaroos was thinking about what to do about the long-term effects of the trauma caused by separation from their families. Would wiping their memories of the separation from their parents even help since by now the trauma was downloaded into blood and bone?

Back in the records room as they were finishing their work of setting up traceable records for all the families, Attivio sensed a malignant presence. He swung around to face Darpith who stood on his hind legs wearing his intimidating reptilian form. Covered with black scales, his long tail stretched out behind him. He bared his ugly yellow teeth and shot daggers from his beady eyes. Heipleido cast a shield of light protection around Attivio as soon as Darpith began to speak to him.

"You will not interfere with my plans for Earth," he bellowed. "I will enslave all beings here for the dark side. Even now I am feeding the racists in the white population with hatred so they will cage, jail, humiliate and torture black and brown people. The racists among the whites walk right onto the dark path when they abuse others. You wanderers are in my way but I will stop you with my new weapon, created especially to destroy fifth dimensional beings."

With these words, he let out a hideous laugh and raised his large front claws. Out of his claws shot jets of poison rays targeted on Attivio's pineal gland. Attivio instantly deflected the rays back at Darpith who couldn't move quickly enough in his reptilian form to avoid them and screamed in pain as the rays rebounded on him, momentarily blinding him.

Soonam, who had come back in, took the opportunity to touch Darpith's tail, and using her talent for psychometry, to read his past. She shuddered at what she saw. He had had several lifetimes on Earth when he was a third dimensional being. In his last lifetime on Earth he had been a cruel slave owner in Mississippi where he raped the female slaves, flogged both men and women for pleasure, and sold children away from their parents. Soonam saw that Darpith's lifetimes on planets in other galaxies were equally dark. If she had been hoping for a clue as to how to find the light in him, she was disappointed. He reeled on her and having partially regained his sight attempted to shoot poison rays from his claws into her pineal gland, but Ederah instantly made Soonam invisible. Furious, Darpith turned on Ederah and directed his rays at her. Expecting this, she ducked, and Bereh multiplied her ten times. Still in pain from the rebounding rays of his own poison rays and enraged at not knowing who the real Ederah was, Darpith bellowed and roared but to no avail. Attivio hit him with a diamond ray to weaken and depolarize him, and continued to hold him captive with the ray until all the children, along with their records, had been rescued. Then too weakened by the diamond ray to fight on for the moment, Darpith fled back to Orion.

Heipleido created a giant group Merkaba to hold all the children. The wanderers divided into pairs and spent the whole night transporting the children to the facilities where their parents were held, uniting them with their parents, freeing the parents and taking the reunited families via merkaba to sanctuary cities around the country where they had relatives. The only memory adjustment was to make the families feel as if they were traveling by plane rather than merkaba. Those who had no relatives were welcomed by those who had people.

The cruelty of what they had witnessed shook them all. Soonam, who usually found the light in any darkness, was gutted. Tearing nursing babies from their mothers' arms and the unspeakable harm it would forever cause them was too much, and when she arrived back at the gaming center in the East Village she looked half dead. Attivio reached for her as she nearly toppled from her chair.

Ederah took off her goggles and mask and looked to her right to find Bereh. Lord Lanto and Shoshimi came on the screen to tell them not to loss heart. Many gamers had viewed what happened at the border and learned more about how the dark side works. Several thousand gamers in New York alone had watched. Word of the game was spreading. Before they signed off, Shoshimi reminded them that one does not defeat the dark with weapons or hatred and cruelty, rather, one finds the light in it. The four New York wanderers signed off. Attivio helped Soonam up.

When they had readjusted to their third dimensional bodies they left the gaming center.

"We could all use a little time by a warm fire," Attivio said.

"Join us for a bit, won't you," Soonam said to Ederah and Bereh, who readily agreed. They walked home through the Village without talking. Each reviewing the events of the game. When the four of them were settled by the fire, Bereh manifested a fragrant sag panir and warm garlic nan. They all tucked in, relishing the warm spicy food. After they'd eaten they discussed Darpith's new weapon. It was clear that he was again targeting the pineal gland, like on Halloween, but with what he hoped would be something so powerful that they wouldn't be able to heal from it as they had done before. They would all need special protection for both their pineal and pituitary glands.

"Evil is dumb," Attivio said. "Didn't he know we would deflect his attempt?"

"Next time we meet Darpith, he will no doubt take a form where he can react more quickly than he can in his reptilian body, or he'll make a sneak attack. He'll have to let go of his ego desire to intimidate us with that clumsy reptilian form," Ederah said.

"In the end, I believe his ego will be what defeats him," Soonam said.

Bereh had been silent, thinking about how to protect their most spiritual gland, the pineal. Finally, he spoke. "I think we should consult Master Saint Germain and Lady Portia about how to protect ourselves from this new weapon. As Chohans of the Violet Ray, they might have the best idea as the pineal falls in the Violet Ray range."

"Let's send a bubble to London and suggest this. I'd also like to know how they're doing after the game," Ederah said.

Within minutes Heipleido send a bubble back. "We agree about consulting Master Saint Germain and Lady Portia. Will you go ahead and inform us of what they advise? We had several thousand gamers watching here in London too. Time to expand outside London and New York. We want to meet with the four of you in person soon, in the third dimension, either in New York or London, maybe over Christmas. I have an idea for how to get out the message that everyone is Divine. All is well. Heipleido."

Via bubble, Bereh consulted with Saint Germain and Lady Portia, Chohans of the Violet Ray of Transmutation, about how to protect their pineal and pituitary glands from Darpith's new weapon. They instructed Bereh in the use of the silver and gold Infinity Ray, which was to be drawn up through the base of the spine into the brain and run in a figure eight around the two master glands eight times. This was to be done daily, and again before each time they played *Fifth Dimension*.

"This practice will protect the electron fields streaming through your glands," Saint Germain explained.

"In his attack on Attivio at the border," Lady Portia added, "Darpith attempted to alter the particle stream flowing through Attivio's pineal gland to cause the electrons moving through his pineal to slow down and reverse the direction of their spin from clockwise to counter clockwise. If the movement of the electrons in your pineal is sufficiently altered it can cause death."

"How was Attivio saved then?" Bereh asked.

"The light shield Heipleido put up around Attivio allowed him the time to deflect the rays and protect his electron field, but one of you alone might not have been able to repel the force of Darpith's attack," Saint Germain said. "The Infinity Ray, however, will create a photon shield strong enough to protect the fields of particles streaming through your glands whether they are moving through you from outer space or up from the Earth."

Bereh immediately passed this information on to all the other wanderers.

Soonam couldn't fall asleep. She kept seeing the agony on the little faces in the cages and trying to comprehend a consciousness capable of such cruelty. Attivio picked up his guitar, sat on the bed beside her and made up a song about all the children they had rescued, now sleeping in the cradle of their parents' arms.

Chapter 21

Heipleido's Idea

Maepleida returned late on a chilly December evening from a week of canvasing in the country with her grandmother, Maggie, to find Toomeh and Laaroos bent over the computer working on plans to introduce *Fifth Dimension* to Ireland and most of Europe. But when Maepleida walked into the carriage house, the human way, through the front door, the first person she saw was Heipleido, at the piano. He jumped up and embraced her. Laaroos and Toomeh, too, stopped their work to look up and inquire how the canvasing had gone.

"With a few more trips over the coming months, Granny thinks I should be able to secure the votes I need to stand for the election," Maepleida said. "But I've spent so much time as only a human this past week that I'm wiped out. Were you writing a song on the piano?"

"Just noodling to help me think, but never mind that now," Heipleido said kissing her.

Maepleida had been careful not use any of her fifth dimensional powers while she was under her grandmother's eagle eyes, so she had only been in internet and phone touch with Heipleido, and she'd missed the physical contact. Reconnecting with him tonight would rejuvenate them both. He lifted her easily in his strong arms and carried her to their bedroom. Laaroos and Toomeh smiled at one another as they called goodnight to the retreating pair. Heipleido laid her down on their bed on the exotic Egyptian fabric which covered it, and gazed at the beauty of her emerald eyes and her long black hair spread out over the gold woven into the cloth. He lowered his eyes to her lips and watched as she formed the words, "Come here, my Soul, my heart's shelter."

Hours later they fell asleep with Heipleido curled around her.

The early morning light was peeping through a narrow opening between the drapes when Heipleido opened his eyes. "Maepleida, are you awake?" he whispered to her, turning on his side to look at her.

"No, I'm asleep." She sighed.

"Sorry," he said kissing her shoulder and laying back down. "OK, what?"

"I want to run something by you."

"Go on then," she said leaning up on one elbow and turning to face him wearing nothing but a half-smile.

"It's great that you're getting enough support to run for MP in your family's old borough, but I believe we can also reach a big group of humans with a holiday message but I need your help to craft it. I don't know much about Lord Sananda's life as Jesus since I was raised in a Moslem household, but I think by taking a human birth he was enacting the truth that all humans are divine beings, that God lives within them as them. You were raised Christian. Am I interpreting his message correctly? And isn't that what part of our mission is, too, to bring the message to humans that they each carry a spark of the Divine within?"

"Yes, that is part of it," she said. "The human Jesus was the Divine incarnate. And Jesus did teach that every person could perform the same miracles that he did. You could say that one lesson of Jesus is that the Divine resides in every human."

"That's the message we're supposed to pass on to humans," Heipleido said, "that they are divine. God, by whatever name each faith calls her, isn't out there somewhere in the sky, but within each being. Imagine if everyone knew they were Divine, what that could do for the Earth and all her creatures. The dark side would pale before them."

"Do you have an idea for spreading this message?" Maepleida asked. "I can't imagine just walking up to people, as we once did in New York when we went there for an afternoon from Venus, and telling them."

"I haven't worked out how, but I know that during Christmas and Hanukkah and Kwanza and all the celebrations of light is the time for us to share the message with all humans that 'God dwells within you as you'."

"What about this," Maepleida said. "You know how the Chohans meet with un-awakened wanderers during their sleep time. I first saw such a gathering when I visited El Morya and Amerissis in their temple above the Himalayas before we incarnated. We could ask them, and all the Chohans, to make this part of their message this season of light. Then all the wanderers can download it into their humans when they go back into their human bodies after the meeting in the Chohans' fifth dimensional temples. It won't reach all humans, but it's a start."

"Yes. And I think this request demands to be made in person," Heipleido said. "We'll need to visit all the temples. Dividing up the task among the eight of us will make it easier."

"I'd like to go to the Blue Flame Temple of the Will of the Divine and see El Morya and Amerissis," Maepleida said.

"I want to go there with you, to see where you were when you left Venus. Let's go ask Toomeh and Laaroos and see what they think," Heipleido said, pulling her out of bed.

Maepleida picked up her pale-blue, silk Japanese kimono with a pattern of cranes on it, slipped her arms through it, and tied it around her waist. Heipleido put on his dark-blue wool robe with the white piping, and still tying it, opened the door.

Toomeh and Laaroos were already up and manifesting a delicious breakfast to welcome Maepleida home. The big wooden table was set with red and white dishes of blueberry waffles, poached eggs and buttered toast, orange marmalade, steaming cappuccino and pots of fragrant tea from around the world.

"Wonderful," Maepleida said on seeing it. "I love eating human food."

After a few mouthfuls of eggs and toast Heipleido couldn't

wait any longer to share his idea.

"I think it's the perfect message," Toomeh said setting down his teacup and smiling his open, honest smile. Toomeh's directness always reminded Maepleida what a good friend he was and how much she liked him. Toomeh looked at her and added, "This is the message we came to Earth to bring. I'll take the Temple of the Sun over the Statue of Liberty and speak with Paul the Venetian, and Lady Ruth, Chohans of the Pink Ray of Cosmic Love."

"I'll go to Master Hilarion in his retreat, the Temple of Truth, above Crete," Laaroos offered. "There are some things I want to ask him about the emerald healing flame."

"Then let's ask Soonam and Attivio and Ederah and Bereh to visit the Chohans of the other four rays," Maepleida suggested.

Less than an hour later they received a bubble back. Soonam would visit Lord Sananda and Lady Nada, Chohans of the gold and purple Resurrection Flame, in their temple near Jerusalem. Attivio would accompany her, then they would visit Master Saint Germain and Portia, Chohans of the Violet Flame of Transformation, in their retreat in Romania. Ederah and Bereh would visit Lord Lanto and Shoshimi, Chohans of the Yellow Flame of Illumination, in their temple above the Grand Teton Mountains in Wyoming, and then proceed to the Temple at Luxor, over Egypt, to visit Lord Serapis Bey and Amutreya, Chohans of the White Flame of Ascension. After several more bubbles back and forth they decided to make these visits on the Winter Solstice and then gather in London for an English Christmas as the guests of Maepleida's parents, Lord and Lady Merton, who had invited Soonam's father, Hunter, to join them as well.

In the few days remaining before the Solstice they continued their work as wanderers, as well as their human obligations. Laaroos, who was in medical school, had the most intense demands upon her time. The programs of the others had a lot of space in them and were more flexible. Although Ederah didn't enjoy the modeling assignments much, she had to keep her commitment for her visa.

Maepleida offered to double both Laaroos and Ederah, and they both took her up on the offer. Ederah loved sending her double to do the modeling in her place and Laaroos was able to skip medical school whenever she needed to for her work with *Fifth Dimension*. Her double could download the whole hospital day into her in a few minutes, and she found she was resorting to this more and more often.

They were all excited when the night of the Solstice arrived. The four wanderers in New York and the four in London all shifted into their fifth dimensional bodies, and set their frequencies to match their destinations. They understood that beings who see the universe as One can move from place to place at will with no time elapsing. Heipleido and Maepleida instantly found themselves high above the Himalayas, standing on the white steps of the Temple of the Blue Ray of Divine Will. They paused to take in the beauty of the majestic Himalayas before ascending the steps to the arched entrance of the huge white temple. At the entrance, they were greeted by two blue flame angels. The angels led them through the large entrance hall past the hundred-foot high Blue Flame, to a smaller chamber where Master El Morya and Lady Amerissis were discussing that evening's program. Wanderers from all over the Earth who had not yet awakened would soon be arriving in their light bodies, not only here, but at each of the Temples of the Seven Rays. The Chohans in every temple would speak to the light beings in the hope that they could carry the message back to their sleeping human bodies and stir them to the realization of who they truly are, wanderers from a higher dimension.

El Morya and Amerissis welcomed Maepleida and Heipleido with the joy and ease that flows between kindred spirits. Heipleido explained the reason for their visit and El Morya invited them to speak at the meeting which would begin in a few minutes. Already the great hall was filling with unawakened wanderers in their light bodies. When Maepleida looked in she remembered that earlier time when she'd come from Venus, unsure about the mission to Earth. The great hall felt now as it had then, like a village ringing with anticipation.

El Morya and Amerissis swept into the hall with their royal-blue, sapphire studded cloaks trailing behind them. El Morya carried a staff with a diamond as large as an orange on top. Maepleida and Heipleido, also in long, sweeping, blue cloaks, but bearing the emblem of the Pleiades, stood to their full fourteen-foot height, waiting at the entrance until El Morya and Amerissis reached the center of the group, turned and summoned them. Several thousand light beings fixed their eyes on the foursome standing in the middle of the throng. Amerissis welcomed them all and introduced Heipleido who would be the first to speak.

"Greetings, my fellow wanderers. I have come with a special message for each of you. Take it into your heart this evening of the Winter Solstice and carry it back to your sleeping human. In this season of light when we remember the birth of the great avatar, Jesus of Nazareth, know this: you are no less divine than Jesus. Remember his message: God is in man. Yes. Within each of you rests the Divine in all of her wonder. Step into your divinity, embrace it. That is the message of this season of light. You are the savior. God lives within you as you. Awaken wanderers and know that you are God."

Heipleido looked around at the light beings before him then turned to face those who were behind him and bowed to them as well. As he rested in a momentary silence, he felt the wanderers absorbing his words. He turned to Maepleida.

"I was asleep in my human body," she began. "I lived twenty-one years on Earth feeling that I was here to do something, but I couldn't remember what. The memory was just beyond consciousness. I know now that I am a wanderer from the fifth

dimension, but more importantly, I know I am a divine being."
Here Maepleida paused and looked toward Heipleido. "My twin
flame and I walk the path of service to others. When necessary
we battle those on the dark path who also serve the Divine, but
in their own way. Fear not what you perceive as evil. Evil is
necessary for the growth of consciousness. Awaken now to your
true identity and join us in bringing the truth to all humans that
they are divine. Join us in bringing the Earth into the group of
light planets." Maepleida bowed to the listeners in front of her,
then turned and bowed to those who were behind her.

El Morya addressed the gathering next. He suggested things
the wanderers might try to help their sleeping humans awaken,
emphasizing dreams as the most effective tool. "Dreams can
pierce the veil of forgetting," he explained to them, "and present
symbols which work directly on the psyche."

Finally, Amerissis again addressed the throng, thanking them
all for coming and offering a prayer that each might help their
human discover the Divine within during this joyous season of
light. As she spoke, Archangels Michael and Faith flew over the
heads of all present, blessing them. The archangels filled the
temple with a fragrance so beautiful it seemed they must all be
standing in a garden among thousands of summer roses in full
bloom. There are few more exquisite feelings than that moment
of receiving a blessing from an archangel. Even Maepleida, in
whom restraint and dignity generally reigned, melted a little.

While these events were unfolding above the Himalayas, a
similar scene was taking place in the Temple of Resurrection
above Jerusalem. Soonam and Attivio were with Lord Sananda
and Lady Nada making the request that the message that all
are divine be delivered to the wanderers gathering that night
in their temple. Bursting with joy to be with the Chohans,
Soonam exclaimed, "And who better to remind the un-awakened
wanderers than you, Lord Sananda, you who incarnated as

Jesus."

Lord Sananda smiled at Soonam and then glanced at Lady Nada, who during Sananda's lifetime as Jesus had herself been incarnate as Mary Magdalene.

"During this season, many humans celebrate your birth as Jesus, bearer of light and hope," Soonam continued, "it's your very own message that all men are divine. But why do you smile so?"

"He smiles at your enthusiasm, Soonam," Lady Nada said. "We both applaud it. And of course, this will be our message to the light beings tonight. And you both shall help us deliver it."

The great hall of the temple was already lit with thousands of gold and purple flames burning in golden sconces every few feet along the walls of the huge circular room when the four of them entered. Lord Sananda wore a long white robe, and Lady Nada a Grecian style gown of deep purple and burnished gold. Soonam and Attivio walked beside them wearing the violet robes of their own home planet. Anticipation filled the temple as they made their way to the center of the throng of several thousand light beings. Lady Nada welcomed them all, then turned to Soonam and invited her to speak, which she did with enthusiasm, pausing only now and then to see if the other three wished to add a word. Soonam's gentle, casual approach enchanted her listeners creating ripples of approval and delight. Despite her light-heartedness, the seriousness of her message entered the hearts of all present, much as softly falling snow sinks more deeply into the ground than a heavy downfall.

When Soonam finished speaking, the Archangels Uriel and Aurora flew into the hall, and circling above all those present, released golden doves. The birds flew low over the light beings and one dove landed on each breast, transforming itself into liquid gold and flowing into the heart, sealing in the message of divinity. Soonam was nearly overcome when a golden dove landed on her. Attivio saw her falter and caught her around the waist. When the meeting ended and the light beings had all returned to their sleeping human bodies, Soonam still did not want to leave the temple. Attivio reminded her that they must be off to visit Saint Germain and Lady Portia, Chohans of the Violet Ray of Transmutation. When she again asked to stay for a little longer, Sananda told her that although she would have to part from Archangels Uriel and Aurora, the Archangels Zadkiel and Amethyst would be present at her next stop. Sananda smiled at Soonam and telegraphed to Nada. "Soonam will always be happiest among angels, for she is part Nephilim."

While Soonam and Attivio were saying good bye to Lord Sananda and Lady Nada, Toomeh was arriving high above the Statute of Liberty in the Fifth Dimension at the Temple of the Sun. Standing at the temple entrance to greet him, the Chohans of the Pink Flame of Cosmic Love, Paul the Venetian and Lady Ruth, were resplendent in flowing rose colored robes with jewel clasps at the throat. On either side of them at shoulder height, hovered the golden Archangels Chamuel and Charity. Together the group entered the temple, which was one of the most beautiful places Toomeh had ever seen. Rose colored flames and flowers of every shade of pink, rose and ruby lined the temple walls. Angel voices filled the space. A feeling of love without end pervaded every atom in the temple. On hearing Toomeh's request, the Chohans readily agreed and invited Toomeh to speak to the gathered wanderers.

As Toomeh addressed the throng at the Temple of the Sun, Laaroos was arriving at the Temple of Truth above the island of Crete, to be welcomed by Master Hilarion, Chohan of the Flame of Healing. Archangel Raphael and Mother Mary were with Hilarion to greet her. After she delivered her request, and Hilarion agreed to give this message to all wanderers to his temple, Laaroos asked Hilarion about any method he could share with her for healing third dimensional humans of heart disease and cancer. He instructed her again, as he had on Venus, in the use of the Emerald Flame, but added a new detail.

"Not only must the flame pass through every atom, electron, proton, neutrino and quark in the being to be healed, it must also be directed to the field streaming through the being, and to the force which interacts with that field. In the case of humans, it is the force of gravity which interacts with the space-time field on Earth. To heal a human, you must simultaneously direct the emerald light to the field streaming through them, while also enlisting the co-operation of the force of gravity. A simple request of gravity should do it, as gravity is a most gracious and helpful force. Use the central tube running through the body and direct the flame out from there by encircling the tube with a sphere whose diameter is the width of the beings outstretched arms from the fingertips of one hand to the fingertips of the other hand. Fill the sphere with the flame you are using."

Laaroos thanked Hilarion and together they, along with Mother Mary and Archangel Raphael, entered the emerald hall to address the gathered wanderers. Hilarion introduced each of them to all those gathered, beginning with the Mother Mary.

"The Virgin Mary, also known as Mother Mary, stands beside me tonight to remind you that it is only in the soul of each of you that God can be born. The Virgin Mary is not just a blessed light being and the mother of Jesus, she is also the archetypal symbol of the soul of man. Wanderers, enlist Mother Mary's aid in awakening your humans to their own divinity."

While Hilarion was speaking, far away across the Atlantic, another group of wanderers was also receiving a message reminding them of their divinity. Ederah and Bereh addressed the throng gathered at Lord Lanto and Shoshimi's temple, the Great Hall of Illumination above the Grand Teton Mountains in Wyoming. When they had spoken they reluctantly took their leave, and accompanied by Archangels Jophiel and Christine, they apparated to the Temple at Luxor above Egypt, where Lord Serapis Bey and Amutreya, Chohans of the White Flame of Ascension were about to enter their own great hall. Inside the Great Hall of Ascension, Archangels Jophiel and Christine joined Archangel Gabriel and Archangel Hope to bless the gathering. The four archangels used their voices to bestow the blessing. Angel voices have the power to heal and awaken even those in the darkest places. The great hall at Luxor transformed at the sound of the archangel voices, inducing in the wanderers a state of joyous peace. Amutreya welcomed everyone and introduced Ederah, who reminded all present of their divinity and directed them in the use of the Ascension Flame to hold that consciousness, asking each of them carry the flame back to the heart of their sleeping human.

All their messages delivered on this night of the winter solstice, the eight wanderers met at the carriage house in Notting Hill Gate to exchange stories of their temple visits. This was accomplished with great fun. Laaroos and Toomeh manifested a feast of nectar and mana, and Maepleida added two more bedrooms in sumptuous Egyptian style inside the carriage house for their guests from New York.

No one detected the fuming presence of Darpith outside the house, unable to break through the seal around it to disturb their happiness. No one, that is, except Veldemiron, who was now having Darpith continually monitored. There are no friendships or collaborations on the dark path of service to self. There are only master/slave relationships. Veldemiron, like Darpith, was a fifth dimensional entity traveling the dark path. They were known to each other and had about an equal number of minions. However, their styles were very different. Darpith was crude and violent. Veldemiron was subtle and serpentine. Unlike Darpith, Veldemiron would not provoke a nuclear war. No, he'd let the humans come to the brink of destroying their atmosphere with carbon emissions and ozone holes, choking their oceans with plastic and burning and flooding their land. Then, when California, the Pacific Northwest, the Amazon and Africa were on fire, New Orleans completely under water, flooding swamping India and most of the world's rain forests destroyed, he would step into the chaos and take command. Although he had been fifth dimensional for a few thousand years less than Darpith, he was on the verge of surpassing him in power. His plan was to enslave Darpith and bring all Darpith's minions into his own army. To accomplish this, he would have to outdo Darpith in evil acts. For on the dark path, the more selfish and cruel you are, the more you polarize to the negative and the more power you amass.

Chapter 22

Christmas Eve

Charlotte was adjusting an ornament here and there on the twelve-foot Christmas tree, when her mother-in-law, Maggie, rustled into the drawing room, in her navy-blue silk and lace evening gown.

"Who's coming this evening? I see the dining table is set for thirteen, an unlucky number."

Charlotte ignored the editorial comment in the question and answered simply. "Mary and seven friends, the father of one of them, and my mother."

"A dinner for thirteen and no butler, it isn't done."

"Well, I'm doing it. You know we don't keep a butler. Mrs. McQuade has hired the usual two young men for the evening."

"And where is your maid?"

"It's Christmas Eve. She has the night off."

Maggie harrumphed.

"Good evening, Mother," Robert said, entering the drawing room and seeing Maggie. "Can I get you a drink?"

"No, no. I want to have my wits about me this evening."

"Why particularly?"

"I want to see if any of Mary's friends can be helpful with the canvassing. It takes a certain type."

"If you two will excuse me," Charlotte said, "I'll check on the dinner preparations."

As she passed through the dining room, Charlotte shook off all thoughts of the exchange with her mother-in-law, much like a dog shakes off a troublesome encounter. She turned her attention instead to the Christmas Eve table set with gleaming silver candelabras, white napkins, and pine boughs running down the center. The wine was breathing on the sideboard and a tree shaped pat of butter was already softening on each bread and butter plate. Descending the stairs to the kitchen, she found the sight and scent no less pleasing. Her cook, Mrs. McQuade, was just checking on the roast. The potatoes were in the warmer, waiting to be mashed. The rolls were rising in preparation for baking, the Brussels sprouts and bacon were cooking, and the gravy was thickening. Charlotte glanced at the desert table. There were jeweled coconut drops, a dark chocolate soufflé, and of course, the brandy soaked Christmas cake ready to be lit. Next to the cake was a tray of cookies shaped like bells and Christmas trees and reindeer, all iced in red and green and white and decorated with candy pearls. Before thanking Mrs. McQuade, Charlotte paused a moment over the cookies to offer a prayer that all over the world people might enjoy the food they loved and that no one should go hungry. She knew it wasn't so, but it helped her for a moment to wish it, and maybe intentions had some effect. Prayer, donations and volunteer work were more and more becoming her solace.

Over at the carriage house, before they went off to dress for the festivities, Maepleida reminded them all that they would be known this evening by the names their human parents had given them at birth.

"I like calling you Mary," Heipleido told her, "and we'd all better get used to it if you win the election to the House of Commons. Mary Merton, MP."

"Don't tease me, *Horus*," she said, emphasizing the Horus.

"Come here," he said pulling her into his arms. "I've got a little present for you."

He reached into the pocket of his tux and pulled out a delicate gold necklace with the name Mary worked into a repeating pattern. The workmanship was so fine that one didn't immediately notice that it was the name Mary repeated again and again to create the golden links in the chain.

Maepleida lifted her long black hair so that Heipleido could fasten the necklace. The gold looked perfect against her red, silk dress and she turned to the full-length mirror to admire the effect before telling him to look at the cufflinks he was wearing.

"When did you do that?" Horus asked, seeing his name inscribed in small block print on the oval face of each of his silver cufflinks.

"I timed your name to appear just after you'd put them in." Mary smiled, with that smile which she reserved only for him.

Similar scenes were also taking place in the other three bedrooms as they all dressed for the evening.

"I have to practice calling you Yosiko," Toomeh said as he tied his black evening shoes.

"Yes, you do, *Ewen*." Laaroos laughed, sitting down beside him on the bottom of the bed.

He took a moment to breathe in the warmth and sweetness of her human body before opening his palm. In his cupped hand, he held a bracelet.

"Orange diamonds," she said, "you do remember we're only students in the third dimension."

"Not just diamonds," he said, fastening the bracelet on her wrist.

Laaroos looked closer and saw that the little orange diamonds spelled *Yosiko*. She raised her eyes to meet his and for a moment their orange–gold eyes locked and an orange ray passed between them reminding them of their home planet, Arcturus. On some gifts there is no improving, she thought. Then it was her turn. And she presented him with a gold pinky ring with the name Ewen engraved on its oval face.

"This is to remind us of your earthly life before we met," Yosiko said, "when we walked over the earth as only half ourselves, so we will always be grateful for our reunion."

Toomeh slipped his "Ewen" ring over his finger and held out

his hand to show her. She reached for his hand and kissed the tips of his fingers.

"Now I better finish dressing," she said, and standing up she manifested a kimono, complete with obi and Japanese socks with the big toe separated by fabric. Ewen caught his breath. He'd never before seen her in a kimono and this one was spectacular, pale green with a pattern of white poinsettias and a black obi.

"Now I feel like Yosiko." She smiled at him.

In the adjoining room Attivio was zipping up Soonam's rose colored, full skirted evening dress. She twirled to show him the effect.

"Close your eyes," he told her, "and hold out your palm."

He dropped two rose-violet ruby earrings into her upturned hand. Soonam opened her eyes and squealed with delight.

"Let me, darling, *Rose,*" he said, placing one ruby earring on each of her soft earlobes, then looking at the violet of her eyes and back again to the rubies.

"Yes, perfect," he said.

"Thank you, *Ephraim,*" she said, wrapping the word Ephraim in love. Then facing him she placed the tip of her index finger on his cravat and when she lifted it, where her finger had been, was a small golden cravat pin bearing the initial E. He glanced down at the pin then up into her eyes before pulling her into his heart, kissing her soft lips and breathing in the scent of her hair, which always seemed to be made of light and wheat and ribbons.

Ederah and Bereh, aka, Natasha and Arjuna, were no less inventive than their friends. To honor Bereh's human life as Arjuna, Ederah chose to wear a sari in deep blues and burnt orange. Arjuna completed her outfit with a gift of the eight golden bangles which had been given to his mother the day he was born by her parents. Natasha held her arm up to admire them.

"Was your mother wearing these the day you saw me in Gorky Park when we were teenagers?"

"No doubt, as she never took them off until she gave them to me."

"I will treasure them. Now look in the pocket of your tux," Natasha told him.

When he reached into his jacket pocket Arjuna felt a flat square box.

"Open it," Natasha urged.

"A flask."

"Not just any flask. It contains a Venusian elixir which, when you are most in need, will rejuvenate you."

Arjuna turned the flask over and saw etched into the silver on one side two ice skaters, and on the other side a heart containing their human names, Arjuna and Natasha. He tried to unscrew the top to smell the elixir, but Natasha stopped him.

"It won't open until the moment you need it."

Arjuna slipped the silver flask into the pocket of his tux, patted it, and said, "I will treasure this."

He was quiet for a moment before he added, "But don't you know that it is *you*, who makes me invincible."

Christmas carolers were singing "Oh Come All Ye Faithful" in the mews when the wanderers came out of the carriage house. They stood and listened a few minutes before setting off for dinner at Lord and Lady Merton's. When they arrived, Mary's other grandmother, Georgina, looking lovely in a gown of deep blue-green velvet, and Rose's father, Hunter, were already standing before a crackling fire with champagne flutes in hand. Rose approached her father who kissed her on both cheeks. Mary introduced them all to her parents and grandmothers. As greetings were exchanged, Charlotte's tree, Yosiko's kimono and Natasha's sari were much admired. Conversation broke up into various pairs and threesomes, gathered by the fire or near the tree. Two young men with trays of baked goat cheese with honey on crostini, warm vegetable bruschetta, and maple-caramelized figs topped with smoky bacon walked among them offering the delights. The gay jingling of Natasha's gold bangles punctuated the conversation as the concert of voices rose and fell. Charlotte announced that she, Robert, Maggie and Georgina would be attending church service that evening, and invited anyone who'd like to join them. "The service begins at eleven. We can leave about quarter to and make it easily."

The wanderers found the idea of celebrating the birth of Jesus very appealing. None of them mentioned that they actually knew Lord Sananda, formerly Jesus. It was agreed that everyone would attend the Christmastide service after dinner, a tradition among Christians since the twelfth century. By the time the five humans and the eight wanderers sat down to dinner everyone was in high spirits. In a stroke of genius, Charlotte placed her mother-in-law between Arjuna and Ewen. Maggie had spent several years in India as a young bride when her husband was posted there in the diplomatic corps, and she was delighted to share her knowledge of India with the young men and tickled to learn that they had met in a gaming center in Mumbai, whatever a gaming center was. Georgina found herself next to Horus, whom she hadn't seen since the World Cup. This was again a happy pairing. On Georgina's other side was Hunter. And she was no less eager to speak with him than with Horus. The dinner moved along with many thoughtful exchanges between various dinner partners to the left and right. When the Christmas pudding, all aflame, was placed before her to be cut, Charlotte's voice rang out, "And a Happy Christmas to us all." It will be noted that Maggie did manage over the course of the evening to corner each of Mary's friends for a cursory assessment as to whether they would be useful for canvassing and found them all hopelessly wanting.

At ten forty-five the entire group donned their coats, hats and gloves and stepped out of the elegant townhouse to walk the short distance to the Anglican church. As they entered the church the smell of wax candles, pine boughs, frankincense and myrrh wafted over them. Soft candle light lit up the crèche where the infant Jesus lay in the hay surrounded by lambs. Rose wanted a closer look but the service was about to begin and the church choir and the entire congregation began to sing Vivaldi's "Gloria." Ephraim thought for a moment of all the misery humans had created in the name of religion over the centuries. Then he reminded himself of their mission. Once all humans knew themselves to be divine beings all war over religion would end forever on Earth. Comforted by this thought he allowed himself to rejoice in the birth of Jesus and in all light beings. Had he tuned in, he would have picked up similar thoughts running through the hearts and minds of his fellow wanderers. He reached for Rose's hand and felt her fingers squeeze his in response as she raised her voice in song.

Christmas day the eight wanderers were up early and heading to the hospital where Laaroos was training. Toomeh, dressed as Santa, carried a bottomless pack of gifts. Laaroos was Rudolph and the other wanderers were Dasher, Dancer, Prancer, Vixen, Comet and Cupid. Rudolph led them first to the children's cancer ward where the reindeer spread out and visited each child to see what he most wanted. Then Santa came around and pulled just that exact gift from his bag. There were remote controlled cars, Lego sets of Hogwarts Castle, baby dolls that drank and wet their diapers, airplane models and glue, stuffed unicorns and teddy bears, chocolate Santas, candy canes and gingerbread people. Before they left, they all sang "Rudolph the Red-Nosed Reindeer" together. One little boy asked if Donner and Blitzen were on the hospital roof guarding the sleigh.

Next Rudolph led them to the geriatric unit. They entered singing "Silent Night" and were greeted with a few surprised smiles and some patients even joining in. As they made their way around from bed to bed Santa seemed to know just who wanted a box of chocolates and who wanted a book of crossword puzzles or a mystery novel or a soft shawl or new slippers.

Some patients reached out to hold the hand of the reindeer and look into her eyes with gratitude. Laaroos led Santa and the reindeer from ward to ward until every patient had been visited and received a cherished gift. For with each gift bestowed, the reindeer implanted the idea of love in each heart, love, that is, of self as a divine being. Happy in their souls for a day well spent, Santa and the reindeer made their way back to the carriage house in the growing dusk of Christmas evening and gathered around a blazing fire.

Chapter 23

A Visit

The day after Christmas the eight wanderers were discussing the next gaming session of *Fifth Dimension*, which would be on New Year's Eve, when two ovals of white light appeared and materialized into Amutreya and Lord Serapis Bey. Standing before them, shimmering in long robes of gold and white, a simple gold crown encircling each of their heads, they were luminescent and imposing.

"Greetings," Amutreya began, bowing to the Divine in them. "We've come to give you some updates on your fellow wanderers and on the operations of the dark side."

The wanderers returned the courtesy, bowing their heads to the divinity residing in the two Chohans of the Ascension Flame.

"We're happy to report that more than half of the wanderers you incarnated with are now awake, and know themselves to be travelers from a higher dimension who are here on Earth on a mission," Amutreya announced. "Your fellow awakened wanderers are working in countries like Brazil and Venezuela to stem the tide of right leaning leaders and outright dictators who go against the truth that we are all one. Many are also working in Syria and Yemen to offer aid to the starving and to support the Kurds. There is also a contingent of wanderers living among the Palestinians and Israelis, trying to foster an agreement. A special group of wanderers has also volunteered to work in Saudi Arabia to either bring the dark crown prince to unity consciousness or to replace him. Wanderers in Afghanistan, Iraq, and Iran, carry the message that we are all one and all divine. Another group is focused on Somalia, and another on the crisis in Sudan. These wanderers are attempting to instill the idea of unity consciousness in all African nations. In addition, both Russia and China each have about a hundred awakened wanderers whose task it is to mitigate the forces of separation and tyranny in their governments and to foster the knowledge that we are all one, all *star stuff* as the astronomer Carl Sagan said. Despite this, thousands of your group remain asleep and are being targeted by the dark side. Until they awaken they are especially vulnerable. All the Chohans continue to hold meetings for un-awakened wanderers to attend in their light bodies during their humans' sleep time in the hope that they will be able to spark their humans to awaken to their true identity. Your group has done well in the Americas and the United Kingdom. But we'd like all of the wanderers to awaken. We hope the game, *Fifth Dimension,* will ignite the memory of many more of them so they will remember who they are and why they incarnated. Continue to spread word of *Fifth Dimension*. It has the power to awaken both wanderer and human alike to the purpose of human incarnation. For truly, Earth is moving quickly now into the Fourth Dimension. Bringing as many people as possible to the awareness that we are all one is urgent. Unity consciousness must sweep the planet for humanity's successful ascension on the path of light."

Here Amutreya stopped and turned to Serapis Bey.

He began, "As the Chohans responsible for the Ascension Flame, Amutreya and I hope that as many humans as possible will ascend and make the jump to the Fourth Dimension with the planet. This is the moment when all will be decided. It is time for action, but know that the way is not clear. For the dark side also knows this is the moment, and they are mobilizing. The advantage we have is that those on the negative path of service to self do not work together. They attempt to enslave one another. For most of the twenty-one years you have been on Earth, the attacks on you by the dark side have come from Darpith or his slaves. He himself is now under siege by Veldemiron, who is more subtle, sophisticated and elegant in his approach. It is his plan to enslave Darpith and seize his minions, then he will come after you. The prize he seeks is complete control of all beings on Earth and the capture of Earth herself for the dark side. Continued attempts by Veldemiron to promote the idea that climate change is a hoax have hurt attempts to address it. More holes in the ozone layer are appearing. The level of carbon dioxide in Earth's atmosphere is rising. Without the protection of the ozone layer all life on Earth will be fried. Greenhouse gases are building toward a greenhouse effect which could raise the temperature on Earth to over eight hundred degrees Celsius, hot enough to melt lead. An Earth heading toward disaster, with its inhabitants in chaos is easier for the dark lords to control. Veldemiron and all the dark lords must be stopped. They must not win. But even the dark side is subject to cosmic law. If more than sixty percent of the beings on Earth are on the positive path of service to others, the dark side will have to concede defeat. They may then only harvest those beings who are more than ninety percent in service only to self. Should Veldemiron fail to subdue Darpith, and Darpith defeat him instead, a nuclear war could result. For Darpith, neither humans nor the planet have any value other than as a means to greater polarization to the dark side for himself."

Serapis Bey looked around at each of them to see if there were questions. Ederah spoke first.

"Would you have us then concentrate on *Fifth Dimension* to the exclusion of other avenues of pursuing our mission?"

It was Amutreya who answered. "Not to the exclusion, but concentrate on the game and be flexible as to what else is working. Attivio's book telling the story of wanderers could awaken thousands, millions, even. And elections do matter. They have consequences. Follow through with writing, creating legislation and helping candidates, but prioritize the game because it can address real time crises and open the minds of gamers who watch you work."

Maepleida returned to the subject of Veldemiron. "How are we to recognize so subtle a purveyor of evil?"

Serapis Bey smiled at her. "Veldemiron seldom shows himself or takes a physical form which can be perceived with the eyes. You must learn to sense him. His presence will sicken you, make you feel hopeless. You must resist this. Use the light of your home planet, or any of the seven rays to protect yourself. He will be cold, colder even than Darpith. At most, you may see him as a black shapeless fog. Flowers, plants and trees turn their faces from him. Animals shiver in his presence. Notice what's going on in the plant and animal kingdoms. Flowers will tell the bees if he is near and they will spread the word. He has not yet defeated Darpith, but it is likely that he will. Then Darpith will be his slave and may be given orders to continue his attacks on you. Or Veldemiron may send Darpith on some other business to another solar system or even to another galaxy."

"Will we know when this happens?" Attivio asked.

"The Council of Nine responsible for this solar system is watching closely from their headquarters in Saturn's rings, and they will get word to the Chohans on Titan who will inform you, but you may perceive it yourselves, depending on how Veldermiron carries it out. We leave you now, beloveds."

Bowing again to the wanderers, the two Chohans turned into white light and disappeared.

"We'll have to be especially on guard New Year's Eve when we play *Fifth Dimension*. We may be facing not only Darpith, but Veldemiron as well," Laaroos said.

The others all agreed, then Soonam chimed in about the news of the other awakened wanderers. "I'm so happy to hear that more than half of our group is awake and working on the mission."

"Yes," Maepleida agreed, "that is good news, but Veldemiron is going to be a new challenge."

"I wonder which Chohans will be overseeing the game on

New Year's Eve," Heipleido said.

"We won't know until we log in," Toomeh said, getting up and heading to the kitchen. "Anybody want rye bread with peanut butter and bananas?"

"I do." Laaroos smiled before turning back to the group to ask if the Chohans could enter the game to assist them.

"Only if we request them," Ederah said.

"Then we must remember to call on them," Soonam added with a note of positive energy in her voice.

Attivio caught her eye and held it, the immense deep violet of her eyes calling to his mind the oceans of their home planet. Like those waters, her eyes sang to him, a soft concerto.

Maepleida and Heipleido were the first to say goodnight. Heipleido followed her into their room, closed the door and pulled her toward him. Taking her face in his hands, he tilted it up and whispered close to her lips, "After all these eons I am still bewitched by you."

Chapter 24

Veldemiron

On New Year's Eve the eight wanderers made their way to the gaming center in Notting Hill Gate, activated their protections, donned their gaming gear and logged in to *Fifth Dimension*. When their screens filled with violet light they knew at once that Portia and Saint Germain, Chohans of the Violet Ray of Transmutation, would be overseeing the state of play. As the deep violet light washed over the wanderers, out of the deep color, Saint Germain and Portia emerged, bowed in recognition of the divinity of all watching, then announced that only awakened wanderers around the world would be able to participate in the game that night, but all gamers could log in to watch.

"Before you begin we want to give you a little background," Portia told them. She then explained that Russian trolls, working for the Russian president, had menaced British voters by spreading misinformation about the benefits of Brexit, inducing them to vote to leave the European Union. "Destroying the EU and NATO are currently the top two goals of the Russian president. To accomplish these aims he interferes in elections in both Britain and the U.S. fostering divisiveness in their populations and dysfunction in their governments. Less unity in western nations and less co-operation among western powers eases his way to world dominance. The Russian president already has the American president in his power and is demanding that he withdraw the United States from NATO. NATO has prevented a third world war ever since World War II ended. It is the alliance which keeps the Russian president in check. However, it is now threatened as he has successfully installed his puppet as the U.S. president, a man who is being investigated by the FBI in his own country to determine whether or not he, the president of the United States, is in fact, a Russian agent. In addition, having succeeded in influencing the Brexit vote, the Russian president is well on his way to achieving his goals. The Prime Minister's exit plan from the EU has been soundly defeated, unrest is brewing and the reality has begun to sink in for the British people that leaving the EU may not be the best thing for Britain, especially without a plan. But it is definitely the best thing for the Russian president. The British people, the American people and their governments have both been duped by Russian trolls and bots. Both governments are in disarray. The U.S. government is shut down and Britain is reeling toward Brexit without a plan. This has created fear of food shortages and failing businesses. The British people have begun to riot. It is not clear if the riots have been incited by the Russians working on their own or if the Russians are under the control of dark forces from Orion, including Darpith, and possibly Veldemiron. In any case, the riots must be stopped and the British people reassured."

Here Portia turned to Saint Germain who addressed them next.

"When you enter the game tonight your human, third dimensional body will remain here in your seat at the gaming center. Please refrain from shifting into it during tonight's play. While playing the game as your fifth dimensional beings, you will appear as human to actual humans. If you are observed using your fifth dimensional powers, wipe the memory of that human so as not to confuse or frighten him. Good luck."

After delivering this information, the Chohans disappeared from the screen and the wanderers found themselves in the middle of a London riot. The police had not yet arrived. Fires had been lit in several places and people were throwing bricks through store windows, smashing them and carrying off food, medicine and supplies. A nearby twelve story high-rise apartment building was on fire. The exits from the building appeared to be locked and sealed. People were piling up behind the glass doors unable to escape. Screams were coming from the burning high rise. Maepleida was the first to see the problem. She immediately blew out the locked exits with a single command and people poured out of the building. Heipleido employed his agility and strength to leap up four stories to rescue two small children and their dog who were leaning out of a window. His only wish to make all creatures safe. Heipleido repeated this feat many times saving children, the elderly, dogs and cats. One clutch of old people frozen with fear clung together at a third story window. Coaxing them from the edge of terror, Heipleido carried them to safety. Maepleida doubled herself, and both selves levitated to the highest floors bringing down as many as six people at a time in her merkaba, which appeared to them only as a moving platform. She also created shoots with slides inside of them for others to slide down. Laaroos worked to control the blaze while she waited on the ground to treat burns and smoke inhalation. Heipleido made certain that every person, dog, cat, hamster, turtle and gold fish was saved.

While this was happening, Soonam, Attivio and Toomeh searched the crowd looking for Darpith and Veldemiron. Ederah and Bereh used violet light on the pineal glands of the rioters in an attempt to subdue and calm them. Within moments Soonam spotted Darpith writhing on the ground with a dark shape bending over him. She alerted Attivio and Toomeh. The three of them watched as Darpith refused to kneel in surrender to Veldemiron even as he delivered another exquisite dose of pain which appeared to be at the same time both emotional and physical. Darpith, with a permanently engraved shriek on his face, howled in agony. Veldemiron pressed on, torturing Darpith to the point where pain becomes art. Soonam, unable to watch any longer, stepped forward to intervene. Veldemiron shot her with a paralyzing ray. Seeing the attack on Soonam, Attivio reeled on Veldemiron. Ready to rip his head off, Attivio held out his hand and released the light rays from his fingers, aiming them at Veldemiron. The two dueled ferociously, their light rays clashing and locking and clashing again. Meanwhile Toomeh held Darpith in check with a powerful diamond ray in order to protect Soonam, who lay on the ground paralyzed. Toomeh knew that if Darpith could kill either him or Soonam, he would regain some power and could possibly defeat Veldemiron. On the dark path of service to self, power comes from subjugating others. The more pain you inflict, the more you polarize to the negative and the more powerful you become. The ultimate power over another is to take his life. So Toomeh continued to focus diamond ray on Darpith, pining him to the ground until two of Veldemiron's minions arrived and took on Attivio freeing Veldemiron to turn his attention back to torturing Darpith. Toomeh joined Attivio in the battle against the two minions. The female, Koultar, was a tall skinny being with a mouth which occupied the whole lower half of her very long face. She resembled nothing so much as a praying mantis. The other, Limbat, looked like a chunky bratwurst, with arms sticking out the sides and legs coming off the bottom. He had a huge gaping hole for a mouth. While Attivio and Toomeh engaged with these two creatures, Veldemiron continued to torture Darpith who mutated into his reptilian form hoping to better withstand the pain. Veldemiron laughed at this feeble attempt and picnicked on Darpith's suffering, growing even stronger. He thanked Darpith for inciting the riot before assuring him it would be his last independent act, weak as it was compared to Veldemiron's own treacherous act of trapping hundreds of families and animals in the high rise apartment building, preventing every means of escape before setting fire to it, thus ensuring their death. This action had provided enough power on the dark path for him to defeat Darpith who was now unable to even get to his feet, let alone escape or strike back. Darpith endured several more minutes of torture before dragging himself up to his knees.

"Crawl to me, you vermin," Veldemiron ordered.

Darpith crawled forward to Veldemiron's feet.

"Swear allegiance to me, slave."

While Veldemiron's ego was caught up in receiving allegiance, Attivio and Toomeh succeeded in driving off Koultar and Limbat who, unlike Veldemiron, showed themselves to be not only inelegant fighters, but also only semi-reliable minions.

Flying to Soonam's side, Attivio picked her up in his arms and telegraphed to Toomeh, "We need to find Laaroos to help Soonam."

It was then that Veldemiron gave Darpith an order.

"Destroy those three wanderers before they get away."

But Toomeh was quicker and shapeshifted the three of them into birds. Weak and confused, Darpith lifted his trembling claws to strike but he was too slow and they flew away. They found Laaroos working by the burning high rise. She freed Soonam from the paralysis, and using Hilarion's recent instructions, counteracted the poison Veldemiron had shot into her system. Attivio took Soonam back to the gaming center. Toomeh shapeshifted himself and Laaroos into English police. In this disguise they helped to subdue the crowd using violet light, invisible to humans.

To punish Darpith for his failure to destroy the wanderers, Veldemiron bound him in chains and returned with him to the Fifth Dimension on Orion where he displayed Darpith to all his former slaves, informing them that they no longer belonged to Darpith but to him. And for once, appearing to understand nothing of nuance, he bellowed, "Bow down, slaves."

Back on Earth, in London, the riot subdued and all the fires put out, the wanderers returned to the gaming center to join Attivio and Soonam. Saint Germain came on the screen. "As you have just experienced, we now have a new challenge in an even stronger Veldemiron. Many wanderers and gamers watched tonight and increased their understanding of how the dark side feeds on pain to grow stronger. Our side grows stronger also by working together, creating unity and being in service to others. This has not been lost on our viewers. Well done all."

The wanderers removed their gaming equipment, stood up and stretched. Soonam was weak but unbowed. Attivio kept a protective arm around her as they walked back to the carriage house.

"Anybody besides me hungry?" Heipleido said. "My human body is always starving when I've been out of it."

After considering their options they manifested a feast of specialties from each of their human birth places. Ederah had a bowl of borscht filled with cooked cabbage, carrots, onions and potatoes, topped with sour cream, followed by a plate of cheese blintzes. Bereh created, in a single command, a delicious spicy curry with spinach and potatoes, and a warm garlic nan. Laaroos, feeling less hungry than the others, manifested only green tea and honey cake. But Toomeh, who was famished, called up a lovely vegetarian Irish stew with carrots, pearl onions and peas and a warm soda bread with melted butter. Soonam savored New York pizza from her favorite pizza place, Numero28. Attivio feasted on olives, humus, and fresh pita. Instead of Egyptian food, Heipleido created a Persian kabob, herb rice, cucumber yogurt and lavash. And Maepleida served herself an English tea complete with tiny cucumber sandwiches, hot scones with cream and jam, and a pot of fragrant Earl Grey tea with milk and honey. They lounged around the fire resting in the winter silence, enjoying the taste, texture and fragrance of their food, but also the memories that each dish evoked of their earthly lives with their human parents. Ederah felt a momentary sorrow realizing their group would soon breakup and four of them would return to New York. Bereh reached for her hand. As they relaxed under the effects of the food and the fire, they broke their silence and began to discuss the evening's game as well as the information the Chohans had given them about the Russian president's plans for world domination. Ederah voiced her concern for her human parents who were still living in Moscow. Would her father, a diplomat, go along with all that had been done if it came to light in Russia that the Russians had in fact interfered in the U.S. presidential election to put a fascist in the White House? Maepleida felt it was more urgent than ever to be elected to the House of Commons to be an honest voice for the people. Soonam felt ashamed of the American president and his crime family, and wanted the country purged of their darkness. Attivio pulled her toward him and kissed her forehead, banishing thoughts of that polyamorous orange monster. As the fire grew low, Heipleido mentally stoked it into a blaze again. The warmth and food made Laaroos drowsy and she leaned back on Toomeh and closed her eyes. His arms encircled her. Heipleido finished his kabob, wiped his fingers on a cloth napkin, and sensing Maepleida's urgency took her hand in his and pulled her to her feet.

"Come, let's have a look at your website. I have an idea for an event we can promote to move things along for your election."

"Now?" she asked. "It's nearly the New Year."

"Yes, now. Come on."

They went off leaving the others, who welcomed in the New Year then very soon drifted off to their own rooms calling "Happy New Year" as they went. Soonam was asleep, curled up in Attivio's arms in front of the fire. Attivio gazed at her, her clothes and hair in sweet disorder. Picking her up, he carried her to their bed, and pulling back the covers with one hand, laid her down and tucked the comforter around her sleeping body. Forgetting for a moment all else, he stood looking down at her sleeping form, and allowed himself the luxury of absorbing her loveliness.

Chapter 25

Laaroos's Dream

It was still dark out when Toomeh awoke to the sound of Laaroos talking to someone he couldn't see. "Laaroos, are you awake?"

When she didn't respond, he realized she was talking to someone in her dream. She smiled in her sleep and moved her hand as if she was petting an animal. Toomeh waited until she was still, then he called her name again until she awoke. "You were dreaming."

"Yes, Shoshimi and her black jaguar visited me in my dream. They brought a message. They want us all to have cats in our homes. Cats are protective and unafraid of either spirits or of beings from other dimensions. They can warn of a hostile presence. Shoshimi also reminded me that plants can serve as a warning and we should have them in every room."

"Did she suggest any special type of cat or plant?"

"No, all cats have the ability to protect and warn those they love, as do all plants. I want us to get two cats from an animal shelter."

"Kittens or cats?"

"Let's see who speaks to us."

Toomeh could hear the joy in her voice at the thought of having a cat again.

"Until this dream, I'd forgotten how much I missed Hoshi," she said.

Over a breakfast of blueberry pancakes and tea, Laaroos shared her dream. Everyone was delighted with the idea of plants and cats. Soonam, Attivio, Ederah and Bereh would be leaving the next day to return to New York, but today they would visit the animal shelter and help choose the cats for their London friends.

"You don't think we'll overwhelm them," Maepleida said, "all eight of us showing up at once at the shelter."

"We can make it fine with a few light rays if they seem troubled," Heipleido said.

"Can we go now?" Laaroos asked, more like an excited child than a light being from the Fifth Dimension.

Everyone laughed and agreed with pleasure.

The shelter was a lively place full of dogs being taken out for their morning walk by volunteers, and puppies, dogs, cats and kittens being considered for adoption. Laaroos wanted to meet the grown cats before visiting the kitten room, knowing how hard it would be to leave without a kitten or two once entering that room. The cages for the adult cats were lined up on shelves along the walls at about chest height so it was easy to converse with the cats. A couple of cats were facing away and seemed uninterested in communicating. Laaroos saw that they were depressed. The wanderers spread out and introduced themselves to the cats in hopes of making a connection. Soonam, who had grown up with a Labrador retriever, was enjoying her first intense meeting with the feline world. "They're all so beautiful in different ways," she telegraphed to Attivio.

Each of them had a favorite, but everyone deferred to Laaroos, who was the only one of them who had ever had a cat in this lifetime. She returned a few times to a cage with a light-ginger cat who was facing away, his back to the cage door. Was she sad for him, or was there a connection despite his facing away? The third time she went back to his cage he turned and walked forward, putting his paw through the bars. She could see now that he wasn't much more than a kitten himself, maybe nine months old. Without thinking, when she touched his paw with her finger, the name Kenji sprang from her lips. Toomeh walked up and she told him that Kenji means healthy son in Japanese. When the volunteer took Kenji out of his cage and handed him to Laaroos, the others gathered around to meet him.

In her arms, he tilted his little head into her palm to be petted. Then he submitted to pets from all of them, and to being held by both Maepleida and Heipleido, as well as Toomeh and Laaroos.

"OK, that's one," Toomeh said. "Now he needs a friend."

"Oh, do let's go to the kitten room," Soonam said, "just to look."

The kitten room was much smaller and cozier, with cages on three walls. There were one or two kittens in each cage. The volunteer offered to let any of them out on the floor to play, one or two at a time. Maepleida spotted a beautiful solid light-grey kitten with green eyes sitting alone in his cage, looking at them. When the volunteer placed him on the floor, Maepleida sat down on the floor cross legged. The kitten ran joyfully about the room, practically bouncing off the walls as he chased a tiny ball with a bell in it. After a few minutes of play he jumped into Maepleida's lap and purred.

"Should he meet Kenji to see if they'll get on?" Maepleida asked.

"There may be a little hissing at first but they'll work it out," the volunteer said. "I'll get Kenji for you."

But when she brought Kenji in there wasn't any hissing. The little grey kitten jumped off Maepleida's lap and the two cats chased the ball around the kitten room together.

"What shall we call you, little one?" Maepleida asked, scooping him up and kissing the top of his tiny head.

"Here, let me have a look," Heipleido said, taking him from Maepleida and looking into his kitten eyes. "He looks like an Albus to me," he said.

"Then Albus it is," Maepleida agreed.

A short while later the ten of them left with instruction papers, vaccination records, a litter box, litter, and more than a few toys, all purchased from the shelter store.

The rest of the day was spent at the carriage house relaxing, discussing the merits of various plants, and in delightful play with the lively young cats.

Soonam watched as Kenji climbed the drapes and hung there momentarily until Laaroos freed his tiny claws from the fabric. Albus jumped into a large urn of flowers and toppled it, frightening himself and speeding away. Finally, they both fell asleep, Kenji curled up in Toomeh's lap and Albus in Maepleida's. Heipleido summoned a warm fire and talk turned back to plants. Laaroos said she'd like a plum tree for their bedroom if they could create the right conditions for it.

"Of course we can," Toomeh assured her. "Did Shoshimi say to put a plant in every room?"

"Yes, and to always check their state when we come home to see if we've had any dark visitors. Around beings from Orion, all plants will shrivel and turn inward, only recovering hours later when the energy has cleared."

Maepleida fancied a tree hydrangea for their bedroom, a dragon tree for the living room and a red pepper plant for the kitchen.

"I'd like an orange tree for our kitchen," Soonam said to Attivio.

"Did Shoshimi say anything about dogs?" Attivio asked, knowing Soonam's love for them.

"She specifically said cats for protection, but I believe dogs carry the vibration of loyalty. I don't see why you couldn't have both dogs and cats."

"Then that's what we'll do," Attivio said to Soonam's delight.

"Our house has never been the same since my dog, Lucy, died. Having a puppy and kittens will fix that," Soonam fairly bubbled.

"What kind of dog will you get?" Maepleida asked.

Without hesitating, Soonam answered, "I adore Labrador retrievers, and they get along well with cats."

"How about you two?" Toomeh said to Ederah and Bereh. "You've been quiet on the subject of plants and pets."

"I was just remembering the lime tree in our garden in Mumbai, how fragrant it was when it flowered," Bereh said.

"We shall have a flowering lime tree then, Ederah said.

Bereh smiled in response and asked her what plants she liked.

"I love herbs, basil, chives, rosemary, thyme, mint. I'd like a window box in the kitchen, and maybe a large lavender plant for our bedroom, oh, and an olive tree in the living room to keep your lime tree company while they both watch the river flow by."

By the time dusk came many plans had been made regarding plants, cats, and at least one dog.

The next day Soonam, Attivio, Ederah and Bereh apparated to New York.

Chapter 26

Darpith's Fate

Veldemiron was considering several options as two minions dragged Darpith forward and threw him on the ground at Veldemiron's feet. Circling Darpith, and speaking out loud to create more fear in him, Veldemiron began. "Let me see. How would you enjoy exile on one of those Martian moons, Phobos or maybe Deimos? You couldn't get into much mischief there but life wouldn't be very exciting either, especially for someone like you who had such big plans for yourself."

Here Veldemiron stopped and looked down at the miserable heap he'd been circling. The more misery he caused, the more strongly he polarized to the dark side and the further he advanced. "You're very quiet, Darpith," he said, kicking him. "Perhaps you don't like the idea of exile on a potato shaped moon? I don't know, maybe a little farther away is a better idea. How would you feel about exile in the Tau Ceti solar system? I could find work for you on one of Tau Ceti's minor planets. Still, I don't really want you even that close. Let me consider further. Perhaps the Magellanic clouds, or better yet, some place in the Andromeda galaxy. That should keep you from trying to interfere here in the Milky Way, particularly on the Saggitarius spiral arm. I don't want you anywhere near Earth. She's mine. Bite on that reality, slave." Veldemiron gave Darpith a hard kick in his side as he lay on the floor, face down, before barking, "Take him away."

Veldemiron's minions dragged Darpith out of his sight and transported him to the furthest star among the trillion stars comprising the Andromeda galaxy. Circling this far away star was an isolated planet. This was to be Darpith's new home. Veldemiron didn't trust him enough to assign him tasks and settled for keeping him out of the way. But Darpith was making his own plans. He well understood there was no loyalty among those who traveled the dark path and at one point his captors, bored with this assignment, would drop their guard and he would be ready to make his move.

After ordering Darpith's exile, Veldemiron began making new plans for the takeover of Earth. He would bring Moscow and Beijing together against the United States by planting the idea of hacking United States utilities and working up the chain until the electrical grid could be brought down and the gas lines disrupted. The next time there was an Arctic blast in the United States he would have the Russians and Chinese cut the power, insuring the freezing to death of millions of Americans in the Midwest. This would further induce fear in the once democratic country. Democracies impeded Veldemiron's plans. Unity and equality, even as limited as they were in the United States, were intolerable to him. Pleased with his plan to create death in North America, Veldemiron turned his attention to Africa. An Ebola breakout, he thought, would create plenty of misery and help him polarize more strongly to the dark side. He might even move up to the Sixth Dimension on the dark path if he succeeded in creating enough despair to lead an entire nation to ruin. But where to start. Yes, the Democratic Republic of the Congo would do. The virus could spread out from there.

When he finished making plans, Veldemiron set his co-ordinates for Titan to spy on the Chohans in charge of Earth. When Veldemiron arrived, Lord Serapis Bey was remarking to Amutreya on the beauty of the universe.

"Yes, it's subtly and intricately constructed," she agreed. "The tessellated facets of creation are a stunning mosaic."

But Serapis Bey barely heard her answer for he'd picked up Veldemiron's energy, and rounding on him said, "You dare to come here, to Titan, Veldemiron?"

Veldemiron had underestimated the power and sensitivity

of the Chohans. He wasn't ready for an altercation with a sixth dimensional entity and fled, flinging a passing asteroid at Titan as he left. But Amutreya was quicker and deflected it before it could strike Titan. However, his action had given Veldemiron a new idea. He'd attempt to redirect a large asteroid onto a collision course with Earth. He'd have to wait until one was orbiting close enough. Nothing as big as a kilometer across. That size could possibly destroy all life on Earth. No, something a little smaller, just enough to arouse planetary fear.

Chapter 27

Arctic Blast

Soonam was out in the garden with their yellow Labrador Retriever puppy when Attivio got home from class. "It's hard training him without a name," she said, looking up and tossing a ball for the puppy, "but I want to get it right, so it suits him."

"He looks like a baby bear on roller skates chasing that ball, with his legs going in all four directions," Attivio said.

"What about calling him Shiva, after the Hindu god with four arms, signifying the four cardinal directions?"

"But isn't Shiva the god of destruction?" Attivio said.

"Well that fits. Have you seen my pumas? Anyway, Shiva is the god of destruction which leads to transformation."

"He definitely transformed your sneakers. And it looks like he's had a go at your sweater as well."

"I left it on the sofa when I went out to meet Ederah, and when I got back he'd chewed three holes in it."

"Naughty Shiva," Attivio teased setting down his backpack and scooping up the wriggly, soft body for a cuddle. "His skin is so loose."

"Room to grow," Soonam said leaning over and planting a kiss on Shiva's forehead.

"I like that we're giving him a Hindu name since we gave the kitten a Hindu name," Attivio said. "I still think a name meaning 'protector and fighter against evil' is a little heavy for a tiny kitten. Where is Ramona anyway?"

"Asleep on the radiator cover in our room," Soonam answered. "And she is a protector and fighter against evil."

"I'll just go and say hello," Attivio said setting Shiva on the ground and picking up his backpack. Soonam heard him calling "Mona, Mona," as he entered the kitchen through the back door.

Soonam and Shiva were still playing ball when Attivio appeared a few minutes later and sat on the steps holding a purring Mona inside his sweater, next to his heart.

"Did you and Ederah arrange everything for tonight's game?"

"We did, but let's go inside and have some tea."

Once they were seated at the kitchen table with mugs of hot tea, Mona still inside Attivio's sweater, and Shiva under the table chewing on a toy, Soonam told him the plan for the evening. "Ederah and Bereh will meet us here at 11:30 and we'll walk over to the gaming center in the East Village together. The game will begin at midnight, New York time. Ederah thinks we may be deployed to the Dakotas because of the polar vortex hitting there."

"Isn't it headed toward New York too?"

"It'll be a day or two before it reaches us," Soonam said, "and even when it gets here it'll be nothing like the sixty-five degrees below zero that they're experiencing," she said.

"They suffer in the cold because they're constrained by the belief that their provisional human body is them," Attivio reminded her. "One day they'll realize that the world is a mass projection and that they are the creators, not the film."

"True, one day they'll know that humans aren't just the result of what hydrogen atoms can do in fourteen billion years of cosmic evolution. But right now the cold is real for them and they could freeze to death."

That night the four wanderers walked though Washington Square Park on their way to the gaming center, and stopped by Thea to say hello. The tall tree acknowledged their greeting and told them it was being whispered from tree to tree across the whole country that there was danger from the dark lords coming to the middle of the United States that night. The wanderers thanked Thea, and Soonam gave her a hug before they left to make their way to the East Village. When they logged in to *Fifth Dimension,* it was Shoshimi and Lord Lanto who appeared on the screen, surrounded by bright yellow light. "The Russians and Chinese, directed by Vedemiron's minions, two of whom you've encountered before, Koultar and Limbat, moments ago breached the power grid and the gas lines in the Dakotas, Wyoming and Montana. The air temperature is too low for the human body to survive long," Shoshimi said. "Soonam and Attivio, you will go to Fargo, North Dakota. Ederah and Bereh you will deploy to Sioux Falls, South Dakota." Here Shoshimi turned to Lord Lanto who spoke next. "A dozen other wanderers are also heading to mid-western locations. You will all be in your fifth dimensional forms, though invisible to most humans you will be visible to one another, to watching gamers, and to the dark side. The breaches to the grid are not yet generally known, but the effects will soon be felt. It is our plan for the wanderers to restore power and gas before anyone freezes to death or mass hysteria arises. Some of the wanderers from Canada have expertise in repair and will oversee the restoration. Your group will engage the dark side if necessary so the Canadian wanderers can work, and you will, if possible, also tend to the human suffering and fear. Go now."

The wanderers set their co-ordinates for their locations, left their human bodies in their chairs at the gaming center in the East Village, and deployed. Soonam and Attivio instantly arrived in a dark, icy, windswept Fargo. It no longer felt like any place on Earth but like some cold, empty planet far distant from the sun. Although they saw no one, they immediately sensed the presence of the dark side. Placing their fifth dimensional sensors on high, they made their way to the electrical power station. The building was pitch black. Before entering the building, they sealed themselves inside an energy shield so it would be more difficult to pick up their presence. The main control center was in the center of the building. From the doorway of the control center they saw two wanderers working on computers, attempting to get the grid activated again. For the moment, at least, no one seemed to be interfering with their work. Communicating via telepathy Soonam told Attivio she thought they should stand guard for a time, unobserved, from a corner of the room. They moved into position unperceived and waited. Then suddenly the energy shifted. Attivio recognized Koultar and Limbat stealthily approaching the two light workers who were repairing the grid. As they were about to strike, Attivio sent a diamond ray into Limbat causing him to swing around looking for his attacker even as he recoiled in pain. Unused to the purity of the diamond ray, Limbat shrieked, which alerted the Canadian wanderers attempting to repair the grid. Koultar rounded on Attivio, but Soonam was ready for her and sent a diamond ray straight through her heart chakra. Before they could recover, Attivio and Soonam pinned them with a continuing stream of diamond ray energy so the Canadian wanderers could finish their repairs. If they completed the work quickly enough many deaths, as well as mass hysteria, would be averted. The power loss would appear to be just a temporary outage from overload and not a sabotage by a foreign government under the control of the dark lords, which could possibly ignite a war between the United States and Russia and China. With repairs nearly complete, and Limbat and Koultar so depleted from enduring the purity of the diamond ray that they no longer posed a threat, everything seemed under control, then seemingly out of nowhere a black ray hit Attivio. Soonam felt rather than saw him crumple. She reeled on Hannitor, another of Veldemiron's minons, and skewered him with a diamond ray. Limbat and Koultar, always concerned first with themselves, took the opportunity to make their escape, leaving Hannitor to suffer. While she continued to deliver diamond energy to Hannitor, Soonam called on Master Hilarion to send the emerald healing ray to Attivio. The effect on Attivio was immediate. As the emerald ray entered Attivio's light body a black fog flowed out of his mouth, nose, ears and eyes, and he sat up. Hannitor begged Soonam to stop the diamond energy. Receiving so much purity made him feel like he was being burned alive. In fact, what was being burned was the intensity of his polarization to the dark side. For a while at least, until he could repolarize by inflicting pain on another, he would be a little less polarized to the dark side. When Soonam released him, he apparated. The repairs complete, the Canadian wanderers stood guard while Soonam and Attivio went in search of those suffering from frostbite, exposure and fear. Working through the night, using light energy, they healed and calmed people all over North Dakota without ever being perceived by the humans.

While this was happening in Fargo, Ederah and Bereh were facing their own challenges in Sioux Falls. Like Fargo, it appeared to be a dark, desolate planet far from the sun. Nothing was moving and there wasn't a sound. The Big Sioux River looked like an ice sculpture. Even the falls were frozen solid, captured in place at the moment of tumbling over the rocks. Ederah and Bereh found themselves standing before a house. Entering, they found a family of six, all unconscious, huddled together in one bed, their fingers and toes already black and their vital organs beginning to fail. Ederah instantly directed the mitochondria in each of their bodies to generate heat by exchanging protons and electrons between molecules. Once all of their vital organs were out of danger Bereh directed the blood flow to their extremities, to save their fingers and toes. Then he sent the gold Resurrection Flame up through the bottom of all their feet and into every cell to restore the damaged tissue. Meanwhile Ederah canvassed the house to find a believable way to heat it until power was restored. She found a fireplace in the living room with a blocked flu. She unblocked it with a command and created a fire before manifesting a huge pile of neatly stacked logs against an adjacent wall. Bereh teleported the whole family and their mattress and set them down on the hearth before the fire. The parents regained consciousness first, but had amnesia about what had happened. The mother seemed to be hallucinating. Ederah increased the blood flow to her brain, restoring oxygen. Bereh watched as the father checked the children for signs that they were breathing. Color had returned to their skin and blood flow to their fingers and toes. Before leaving Ederah directed the fire to burn all night without additional wood. Working through the night, they went from house to house resurrecting the tissue in the unconscious bodies of one family after another. Apartment dwellers fared slightly better as they had fewer exterior walls, still fatalities would have been high had not the many teams of wanderers intervened. Sometime before morning power was restored. There had been no fatalities, even among the elderly and infants. Authorities later found this remarkable, as there had been no power for several hours while temperatures had been sixty-five degrees below zero. At that temperature, it takes less than twenty minutes for a human body to freeze to death.

Dawn was in the sky when the wanderers returned to the gaming center in the East Village. Shoshimi came on the screen and addressed them. "Disaster has been averted for the moment. Well done. Some of you have asked why you are working through the game when you could simply go to crisis areas in your light bodies. We first created the game to help awaken you, but now it serves to help humans gamers learn about higher dimensional powers as they watch wanderers battle the dark side. Most humans don't yet realize that evil is required for development. Evil offers an opportunity. It provides a choice. When gamers log in and observe your confrontations they are learning about the necessity of evil for growth. Will they choose the path of caring only for their own needs or will they choose the path of service to others?" Shoshimi let the question hang in the air and turned to Lord Lanto who picked up the thread of the conversation.

"Thousands of gamers watched tonight, and while they believe that they were only observing a game and that no one was in actual danger, they learned several things. Not only did they see the power of light, wielded with love, to heal, but perhaps more importantly, they saw that suspending judgment opens the door to that ultimate power, which is love. None of the dozens of wanderers working in the deep freeze tonight judged any being from either side. Yes, you discerned who had to be aided and who prevented from causing many deaths, but it was all done with love for all beings as one. Discernment is not judgement. The other thing the gamers saw, and which Shoshimi has already mentioned, is that evil is required for development because it forces a choice. Each of us must make choices. This is the way we create our reality. Accepting that we are all the creators of our lives through the choices we make helps humans to avoid the bitterness of feeling they are victims. There are those who are destroyed by what they perceive as unfairness, and those who are not. When human gamers watch wanderers play *Fifth Dimension* they experience hope, for their own lives and for the life of their planet. Hope is necessary for Earth to survive its current crises, particularly in the face of forces which would prevent humans from learning the truth – that they are divine beings in human form. All is well."

Ederah was the first to remove her gear and stand up to stretch her human body. "Did any of you see Toomeh or Laaroos or Maepleida and Heipleido tonight? I wonder if they were playing?"

"Shall we go home and send them a bubble?" Soonam asked.

"Why don't you come over to our apartment. You can meet our kittens," Bereh said

The four of them set off toward the Highline, which they had to themselves at this 5:00 a.m. hour. Light was beginning to caress the gray-blue surface of the Hudson River and they paused to admire it. A breeze ruffled Soonam's hair, bringing her a message. The wind had often carried messages from trees to Soonam, even before she was awakened. "Wait," she said. The other three turned to her. "Thea, my tree friend in Washington

Square Park, is sending me a warning of danger for New York City. The trees in Central Park picked it up first and sent it out to trees all over the city. She says that a meteor is heading for New York City. It was redirected out of its orbit and will hit midtown during morning rush hour, in three hours."

Attivio reacted first. "We have to alert the Chohans on Titan and ask for their help."

"And our friends in London," Laaroos added. "I'll send a bubble asking them all to come now."

"Let's go inside and make plans," Bereh said.

Two, lively, young, grey and black striped kittens, Tiger and Lily, greeted the four of them at the front door of the apartment. Soonam scooped them up and kissed them on their little heads. "Lovely to meet you two." Before she had even set the kittens on the floor again, Heipleido, Maepleida, Toomeh and Laaroos apparated into the living room. Moments after that, Portia and Saint Germain appeared, their violet robes flying out behind them. "The meteor is the work of Veldemiron and a large host of his minions," Portia began. "He's enraged at your intervention tonight which foiled his plan for the Russian and Chinese disruption of the power grid during the Arctic blast. He'd hoped to cause thousands of deaths and mass hysteria in the United States. It is in Veldemiron's interest for all democracies on Earth to fail. He is aligned with the Russians and the Chinese in this. He, like Darpith before him, has already succeeded in controlling the United States president, directing him to break with his European allies and to align himself instead with dictators and assassins around the world. The United States was once a beacon of hope, where many strove, though incompletely, to live the axiom that all humans are created equal. Under the current president, hope feels all but lost." Here Portia fell silent to allow this reality to sink in.

Master Saint Germain then addressed the eight wanderers. "Killing thousands of humans in midtown New York would be sweet revenge for Veldemiron, and at the same time allow the corrupt president another opportunity for a power grab while the people panic. We must make our plans quickly. The meteor is one hundred meters wide. We'll have to work together to return it to its original orbit. How do you want to proceed?"

"First, we have to get it away from New York, then we can reset its orbit," Maepleida said.

"Even if we move it away from New York, if we don't want it to crash into the ocean, we'll have to make it lighter than air," Laaroos said. "Bereh, you're an astrophysicist in the third dimension. What do we do?"

"Hydrogen, helium, neon, nitrogen, ammonia, methane and carbon monoxide are all lighter than air," Bereh said, "but in the third dimension it is only at the atomic level that one element can become another."

"Can you transmute this rocky meteor into one of these gases if we can move it to the fifth dimension for a few seconds?" Ederah asked him.

"If we combine our energy and shift it into the fifth dimension even for a few seconds, then the Violet Ray of Transmutation should work," Bereh said. "Nitrogen would probably be the best choice as there is considerable nitrogen in rock already."

"Once the meteor becomes lighter, I can push it away from New York," Heipleido said.

"The Chohans on Titan will transmute it back into a meteor and reset its orbit once it's floated far enough up and away from Earth," Master Saint Germain said. "For now, let's get up above the cloud deck and scan the sky for it. The further out in the atmosphere we meet it the better. It is currently moving at a speed of 25,000 miles per hour. Lock the Violet Ray onto it as soon as you sight it so that the ray moves with it. Bereh will have to transmute it to nitrogen while its moving. Moments later, the apartment was empty except for Tiger and Lily who busied themselves climbing Bereh's lime tree.

Bereh sighted the meteor first and alerted the others. At once, ten streams of powerful violet energy struck the meteor and pulled it into the fifth dimension, where Bereh began transmuting it into nitrogen even as the meteor continued speeding toward New York. Partly transmuted, it began to slow down. With a single purpose the Chohans and the wanderers held their focus. The meteor continued earthward until, at two miles out above New York City, it slowed enough for Heipleido to contact it and push it out over the ocean. The others kept up the Violet Ray and Bereh completed the transmutation. The meteor, now mostly nitrogen, was lighter than air and began to float upward over the ocean. When this happened, the Chohans took charge of it and the eight wanderers returned to Ederah and Bereh's apartment to find Lily and Tiger asleep together under the lime tree.

Once inside the apartment they powered down to their third dimensional bodies and collapsed on the sunflower colored sofas in Ederah and Bereh's living room. For a few minutes, no one spoke as they readjusted to their human bodies. Maepleida gazed out at the light on the Hudson River, Heipleido took off his runners and put his feet up on an ottoman, Laaroos pulled a soft cashmere throw over her body and snuggled into Toomeh. Soonam moved down onto the carpet and began petting the kittens. Attivio joined her on the floor and stretched out on his back. Tiger woke up, settled on his chest and began purring. Ederah curled her legs under her and Bereh closed his eyes and let his head rest on the back of the sofa. A peaceful quiet fell over the apartment until the buzzer jolted them all. "What could the doorman want?" Bereh asked Ederah, who uncurled her legs and got up to see.

"A Russian couple is here to see you, Miss."

"Oh, please send them up," Ederah said, recovering herself and turning to the group. "In all the excitement over the arctic freeze and the meteor, I forgot that my parents were arriving today for a week's visit. I was supposed to meet them at the airport and take them to their hotel. They've never been to New York before."

"We'll all welcome them," Soonam said.

"They're on their way up in the elevator now."

"Shall I manifest a Russian breakfast for all of us?" Bereh asked.

"My father would adore that," Ederah answered.

Two minutes later, when Ederah opened the apartment door, the large wooden table was already laden with syrniki, blintzes, sour cream, strawberries, powdered sugar, warm blinis with honey, hot tea and strong coffee. Seeing the food Igor forgot his annoyance that Natasha had not met their plane. She hugged them both as she apologized, then turned to introduce everyone beginning with Bereh. Soonam, used to taking care of her own father, showed Igor to a seat at the head of the table, poured his tea and made sure each dish made its way to him. Natasha's mother couldn't quite let go of her yet and stood next to her with her arm linked though her daughter's. The others joined Igor and Soonam at the table, and however much they ate, the serving platters, much to Igor's joy, were never empty, thanks to Maepleida's doubling skill. When breakfast was over, Natasha accompanied her parents to the Soho Grand so they could settle in. The other wanderers offered to clean up, which they accomplished with a single command as soon as the apartment door closed on Natasha, Masha and Igor. Then the Londoners said goodbye, created a merkaba and apparated, and Soonam and Attivio, hand in hand, walked down the Highline the short distance to the Village. Happily, they were home in twenty minutes, tucked in bed with Shiva and Mona. Soonam buried her face in Shiva's neck and kissed him again and again breathing in his doggie warmth as she curled up around him, almost longing to live his innocent life. Next to Soonam and Shiva, Mona settled on Attivio's chest, kneading and drooling and singing her soft song to him.

Chapter 28

Once on Venus

When the nitrogen bubble was safely away from Earth, Saint Germain and Portia transmuted it back into a meteor and reset its orbit. They then returned to Titan to meet with the other Chohans responsible for Earth. All the Chohans understood that Veldemiron's long game, should he fail to turn enough humans to the dark side, was not to provoke a nuclear war to destroy Earth, as Darpith had planned, but instead, to steadily increase carbon dioxide in the Earth's atmosphere to the point where the surface temperature of the planet would be so broiling it could no longer support life. It would be easy enough to do given the greed of corporate CEOs and their shareholders, the shrinking rain forest and the massive wild fires.

All of the Chohans responsible for Earth were assembled on Titan when Serapis Bey stepped forward to address them. "Even without Veldemiron's efforts to encourage greed, Earth is already far down the path toward a greenhouse effect with human beef consumption and reliance on coal, oil, and natural gas. Burning these fossil fuels has caused such dangerous levels of carbon dioxide in the Earth's atmosphere that there is now a mist of sulfuric acid in the stratosphere. Noxious molecules pollute the air in all the major cities on the planet, particularly in China. Corporate greed and the desire for political power have played the largest role in this pollution. Veldemiron continues to foster that greed, encouraging service only to self within oil company executives and the politicians whose votes they buy. Destroying life on Earth through the greenhouse effect is his backup plan if he cannot draw enough humans to the dark side. He will destroy the planet itself rather than let it move to the light, as all destruction helps him polarize more strongly to the dark side."

The Chohans considered Serapis Bey's words. El Morya was the first to speak. "Many world leaders, including some members of the Unites States House and Senate, as well as the current president and his cabinet, value their own careers over the welfare of the country and the planet. But many of the citizens do not share those values and more and more are becoming aware of the threat of global warming. We must enlist the wanderers to wake up the rest. China has the highest carbon dioxide emission levels on Earth. The European Union is second and the United States third. Wanderers can awaken humans in these areas first," El Morya said.

"How will the wanderers get humans to understand that climate change must be a priority?" Amerissis asked. Then she answered her own question. "There are several thousand new wanderers incarnate from our most recent group and over half of them are now awake. What if we organize a time travel back to when Venus was third dimensional, and show them the living hell of the greenhouse effect. We can do it through *Fifth Dimension* so that gamers all over the globe can observe the wanderers time travel and see firsthand what the greenhouse effect can do to a planet. They'll see exactly what could happen on Earth."

"Yes, let events from Venus's past serve as a warning to humans," Serapis Bey said.

"Are all the wanderers capable of time walking?" Shoshimi asked.

"They're all at least fifth dimensional, so yes," Lord Lanto said.

"Alright, we'll organize the time travel through the game so that hundreds of thousands of gamers around the world will get to see what happened to Venus when she was third dimensional, though the observers won't actually be time traveling themselves," Portia said.

"The sooner we set up this time travel back to third

dimensional Venus the better," Paul the Venetian said. He was a lover of all things Venusian and still felt the trauma of that period in Venusian history. Fortunately, the council had found a way to cool the surface temperature on Venus, heal her atmosphere, reduce the surface pressure, and restore her to her natural beauty, but it had taken over a million years to accomplish. Venus had had to be evacuated during all that time and many different life forms were lost forever. The Chohans would do all in their power to prevent this from happening on Earth.

"When is the next worldwide game scheduled for?" Lady Ruth asked.

"Six Earth days from now," Amutreya answered.

"That will give us time to prepare," Hilarion said. "Should we inform the wanderers beforehand or announce it when they log on for the game that night?"

"There are many natives of Venus among the wanderers and many others very fond of her. It will be a shock even for fifth dimensional beings to see what Venus went through in the third dimension. Let's notify them in advance," Lady Nada said, to the agreement of all present.

"I'll compose a wanderer-wide bubble after our meeting," Lord Sananda offered.

The Chohans of the Seven Rays bowed to one another and apparated to their various temples. Only Amutreya and Serapis Bey remained at the command center on Titan.

Back on Earth, Bereh spent most of the next week in his lab up at Columbia, while Ederah enjoyed the days with her parents, principally by taking them to museums, her mother shopping, and her father to restaurants. The favorite museum of all three of them turned out to be the nearby Whitney, which overlooked the Highline and Greenwich Village. Igor surprised them by enjoying Andy Warhol's work more than Edward Hopper's. Masha preferred the Georgia O'Keeffe's to both male artists. As for the shopping, Masha was interested in everything from the unusual fashion at Jeffrey, in the Meat Packing district, to the simple household items on offer at Pearl River Mart, and Igor found a home away from home in the rare books room at The Strand. Still, the highlight of each day for him was sitting down to dine with his wife and daughter and eating to his heart's content. From the Champagne Bar at the Plaza, where he enjoyed the people watching almost as much as the caviar, to tucking into pizza in the Village at Numero28, Igor relished it all. Natasha didn't even mind being third dimensional for so much of the time. And Igor felt relieved to see that she was safe and had nice friends, without all that funny business of her childhood. And even if he wished that her partner was Russian, he was impressed that Arjuna was studying astrophysics at Columbia. At the end of their week in New York, Igor headed to the airport happy that Natasha was at last living such a normal life. Masha knew better, but didn't say so to Igor. As soon as Masha and Igor's cab drove away, Ederah and Bereh went directly to the gaming center in the East Village for that evening's big journey to the third dimension on Venus. As Natives of Venus, both Ederah and Bereh were particularly interested to see what had happened when too much heat had gotten trapped on the planet billions of years ago, before their own time on Venus.

The gaming center was crowded when they arrived and took their seats next to Soonam and Attivio. Amutreya and Serapis Bey came on the screen to welcome them and explain that wanderers all over the world would be time traveling together back two billion years, to visit Venus in the third dimension. Hundreds of thousands of gamers from every continent signed in to observe. Amutreya tried to prepare them for what they were about to witness, an arid, desert-like planet with clouds of silicate dust and a surface temperature of over 800 degrees Fahrenheit. "Not only is the surface of the planet broiling hot, but the atmosphere is ninety-six percent carbon dioxide and the clouds are mostly a concentrated solution of sulfuric acid," she explained. "These conditions came about because of the greenhouse effect on third dimensional Venus. The increase in carbon dioxide in the atmosphere trapped in the heat which the planet received from the sun, preventing it from leaving the surface of the planet. As the surface temperature rose, a planet wide catastrophe ensued. Many species were rescued and taken off the planet to safety, but many were lost forever, parts of creation that will never be again. No life that remained on the planet survived. Those of you who have been to Venus in the fourth, fifth, or its current sixth dimensional state will not recognize it as it was in the third dimension."

Lady Venus and Lord Kumara, the Lord Hierarchs of Venus, then informed Serapis Bey that the coordinates and wave length for time travel back to Venus in the third dimension had been set for the group merkaba. Lady Venus explained to all the gamers who were watching that, "It is wavelength that determines which dimension you are in. As you go up into higher dimensions your wavelength gets shorter, and when you go down into lower dimensions your wave length gets longer and has less energy and more density. The wanderers who are traveling back to Venus will change their wavelength and disappear out of this dimension and reappear in the Venus of two billion years ago. When they change their wave length back, after the trip, they will reappear in the third dimension on Earth."

Lady Venus having finished her lesson to the gamers, turned to Amutreya, who gave the wanderers the necessary instructions to change the wave length of their consciousness and reminded them that no one was to leave the merkaba during the journey. She explained that they would not enter the third dimension to view third dimensional Venus, but would observe the searing heat and noxious atmosphere from the fifth dimension. "Expect to return to your human bodies in the third dimension on Earth within twenty minutes. I will tell you precisely when to alter your wavelength to return. Enter the merkaba in your light bodies now. The wanderers and the merkaba instantly disappeared. The gamers watching on their screens around the world would see a projection of how Venus had looked two billion years earlier, when she was a third dimensional planet.

"Your first sight of Venus will be in a few seconds," Amutreya informed both gamers and wanderers.

Venus appeared as a hazy red ball as the merkaba approached. Coming in closer and lowering to an altitude of seventy kilometers above her surface, but still above the cloud deck, the merkaba entered a haze of small particles. Moving ten kilometers closer to the surface, to an altitude of sixty kilometers above Venus, the merkaba passed into yellowish clouds consisting mostly of sulfuric acid. Plunging still lower, it was surrounded by sulfuric acid rain. At about forty-five kilometers above Venus, the atmosphere cleared. The surface of the planet appeared to be a barren landscape, devoid of life. Bereh and Ederah went numb with horror at seeing what their beloved planet had endured. They, and every wanderer in the merkaba, vowed that they would do all in their power to stop this from happening to beautiful, fragile Earth. Gamers, watching the world over, were equally affected when they were informed that this had happened to a once verdant Venus because of the greenhouse effect, which was already heating up Earth's surface temperature into the critical zone. In another ten years, if nothing changed, the coral reefs would be gone and thousands of life forms with them, South Wales would be under water, agriculture in India would be destroyed, all of California and much of the rain forest in Brazil would be on fire, and Africa would suffer a continent-wide drought, killing millions. Seeing what happened to Venus, gamers and wanderers alike re-committed themselves to save Earth.

When the wanderers returned from time traveling, the atmosphere in the gaming center was solemn. Soonam, Attivio, Ederah and Bereh re-entered their human vehicles in silence. The same was true in the London center when Maepleida, Heipleido, Toomeh and Laaroos returned from time traveling and shifted into their third dimensional bodies. No one in the gaming center was speaking. Everyone looked stunned. For a time, no one moved, then Maepleida, her voice choked with pain over Venus and the forever lost plant and animal species, spoke what was in the hearts of all of them. "We can't let that happen to Earth."

Heipleido reached for her hand and turning it over, slowly kissed the inside of her wrist, his tenderness partially restoring her. Toomeh and Laaroos were similarly affected. "We've seen a lot of devastation in many galaxies, caused by war, but seeing Venus like this was a knife in my heart," Toomeh said.

"It's too much to think of the lost species which are gone forever and will never be again," Laaroos said, "and Earth is nearly at the tipping point for the same fate."

"That will not be Earth's fate," Heipleido said. He was, as ever, strong and calm, a powerful presence which reassured them. The four of them left the London gaming center and walked back to the carriage house in silence. Albus and Kenji were at the door meowing hello. Heipleido looked around first at the dragon tree in the living room, then at the tree hydrangea in their bedroom, the plum tree in Toomeh and Laaroos' room, and finally at the red pepper plant in the kitchen. Finding them all at peace he announced, "At least we haven't had visitors in our absence."

Toomeh called up a fire to warm their chilled hearts and Albus and Kenji stretched out on the hearthstone.

"I hope tonight's trip will make a difference in human consciousness about the urgency of global warming, stirring them to get involved," Laaroos said. "Big polluters will resist making the necessary changes to save the planet unless a lot of pressure is put on them."

"Do they somehow believe they will be spared if the worst happens? Or do they not look very far down the road?"

Maepleida asked.

"Humans come in all varieties of consciousness," Heipleido reminded her. "And some definitely don't look very far down the road. We just need enough who do. But I'll admit, the U.S. president is a huge problem." He sat down on the ottoman in front of the sofa where Maepleida was curled up, and took her hands in his. "Now, let's focus on happier things." And reaching behind him, he scooped up Albus from the hearth, kissed his little head and placed him in Maepleida's lap where he coaxed her from the edge of sadness by gazing up into her eyes and purring his sweet song. She lifted him in her cupped hands and brought his nose up to her own. When their two noses met she whispered to him, "Thank you, Albus. May all creatures always feel safe."

Chapter 29

Maepleida Prepares

Galvanized by seeing what had happened on Venus, Maepleida was even more determined to win her election to the House of Commons so she could have an impact not just on poverty, but on global warming. The week after the time traveling, Maepleida, Maggie and Heipleido drove to the family seat, where they planned to stay at the dower house for a week of canvassing. Heipleido loved driving, especially sports cars, but agreed to use Lord Merton's Range Rover when Maggie insisted that they at least have some protection if Heipleido was to be behind the wheel. She needn't have worried as his fifth dimensional aspect affected even his human form, heightening his senses and speeding up his reaction time. With only a few reprimands for his risky driving style, they arrived in one piece and turned into the drive up to the house, passing beneath a long canopy of pink cherry blossoms.

"Late March, cherry blossom time," Maggie announced.

"What a perfect welcome," Maepleida added.

Maggie took the second-floor master suite, and Maepleida and Heipleido settled into a large upstairs bedroom with a fireplace. Their room overlooked an English garden which was maintained beautifully by the caretaker and his wife. Maepleida opened the window and looked down upon hundreds of daffodils, narcissi, and sweet-scented primroses. In a few weeks there would be tulips and lily of the valley. They were even now poking up through the soft earth. A month after the tulips put on their show would come Maepleida's favorites, bluebells, wisteria and lilacs. And finally, in June, the many varieties of her grandmother's roses would bloom to the accompaniment of deep purple irises and honeysuckle. Maepleida imagined all this unfolding as she gazed out of the window. Heipleido came up behind her and followed her thoughts. "Lovely," he said, encircling her waist with his arms. "And what blooms in July?"

"Cosmos, dahlias, and delphiniums," Maepleida answered. "Are you interested in Earth's flowers?"

"My mother had a flower shop in Cairo before we moved to Teheran. Her shop is where my parents met. He saw her arranging flowers through the window and so admired her artistry and concentration that he decided to go in and buy flowers for his mother's birthday."

"Did your mother have a favorite flower?"

"The blue lotus, it was growing on the banks of the Nile outside the hospital room when I was born. Then when we moved to Iran she came to love roses, and grew and sold them to flower shops all over the city. Later she learned how to make rose oil."

Maepleida turned around in his arms to face him and tilted her head up to brush his lips with a kiss. He returned her kiss with a promise of more, which was interrupted by a knock on their door.

"Tea is ready in the drawing room, Miss."

On their first day of canvassing, Maggie was surprised to see how Horus's charm affected the local people. He was particularly handsome when he smiled and spoke in his beautiful deep voice. His height, and charcoal wool trousers and tweed jacket over a fitted blue shirt didn't hurt either, at least with the women. Maggie had to reluctantly admit that Horus was quite an asset. By the end of their last trip, Maggie and Mary had secured five parliamentary electors. This time they hoped to gain five more to have the necessary ten required to stand for the election. The next few days were long and the requests many. Mary listened to them all with care, and promised that if elected she would work tirelessly to address their concerns. And she meant it.

For their last evening Maggie organized a grand dinner and invited all ten of the parliamentary electors who had committed to support her granddaughter in the upcoming election. Since the electors were invited to bring a guest, the party would be a large one. At a quarter to eight Maggie surveyed the dining table set for twenty-three. The silver gleamed, the crystal sparkled, the early spring flowers were fresh and elegantly arranged, and the candles were lit. From the dining room she moved into the drawing room to see that all was in order, the fires warm, the down pillows fluffed, bouquets of narcissi perfectly placed, the room aired and welcoming. The two footmen and the butler Maggie had hired for the evening were impeccably turned out and waiting. Mary had objected to this as unnecessary showiness, but Maggie had insisted that it would remind the electors of her family's history in the district, and encourage them to keep their commitment to her. All was in readiness in the kitchen as well. The caretaker's wife was an excellent cook. She had begun preparing the oxtail soup two days before. It would be followed by smoked trout, then beef Wellington, spring peas and butter potatoes. For desert, she had baked a lemon elderflower cake. And Maggie had selected a different wine for each course, including desert.

Maepleida was considering what to wear in order be seen as mature and serious by her supporters. Nothing too flashy or expensive looking would do. Heipleido sat by the window in his tux watching her as she manifested a black evening suit with wide-leg trousers, then changed it into burgundy silk. No, a suit, even a silk one, was too severe and not her style at all. Next she created a series of dresses. The navy-blue wool dress seemed too functional for a fancy evening dinner party. The red silk with the full skirt felt too flashy and the gold sheath too glamorous.

"Would you like some help?" Heipleido asked.

"No." Then softening, she said, "Well, yes."

A moment later she was standing before her mirror dressed in a long sleeved, full-length emerald A-line silk dress with a boat neck. The dress fell softly over the curves of her body without hugging them. The gold necklace he'd given her for Christmas was around her neck and lay on the emerald silk. She wore no other jewelry.

"You've missed your calling," she said, smiling at him. "Thank you."

The evening was a success. Many local tales of past and present were shared in the relaxed atmosphere, and Maepleida learned a great deal more about the constituency. Heipleido had never doubted it would be a success, though Maepleida had had some anxiety. Even a fifth dimensional being can sometimes think that what they have to offer is not enough. After promising to return in May for the election, the following morning Heipleido drove them back to London, where he got straight to work on his anti-poverty bill.

While Maepleida and Heipleido were away canvassing, Toomeh and Laaroos had been working with Ederah and Bereh to calculate which gamer had won the contest they had set up for *Fifth Dimension.* The winner would be the gamer who had used service to others the most times to defeat the dark side. Gamers around the world had gleaned the message that advancement on the path of light came though service to others, while advancement on the dark path came through taking power over others. The gamers did not know that the wanderers were actually fighting the dark side for real, actually encountering the dark lords. The gamers thought the wanderers were simply advanced players also playing in virtual reality. The question was much debated among the Chohans about when the gamers should learn the truth about the identity of the wanderers. Many of the gamers were likely to be wanderers themselves who had not yet awakened.

Scores were coming in from gaming centers all over the world. The winner would be announced the evening of April first. Laaroos and Ederah were still debating about the prize. Should it be a monetary prize or something like a trip to London or New York for two, to meet the eight wanderers whom the gamers still believed were simply advanced players with special skills. Bereh sat beside the flowering lime tree in their living room with his laptop open, looking at the numbers coming in from Kashmir. The number of players using the dark path and the light path were both very high in Kashmir compared with other similar areas. In fact, there were very few gamers anywhere using the dark path, so these numbers were doubly surprising. He checked them again, ran them by Ederah, then texted Toomeh and Laaroos. They all agreed something was up, possibly more interference with the game by Veldemiron. Bereh and Toomeh apparated to Kashmir to check it out.

Chapter 30

Kashmir

Kashmir had been a bone of contention between India and Pakistan since 1947, when the boundaries for the two countries were established during partition. The fate of Kashmir was left undecided at that time, and both countries claimed it as their own. Pakistan argued that since Kashmir had a Moslem majority it should belong to them. India, desirous of not being seen only as a Hindu country, but as a diverse country, wanted Kashmir as part of herself to help make this point. Things had never been settled.

Veldemiron was well aware of the tension between the two countries, and that this unstable situation between them could easily erupt. So he once again slipped through the quarantine around Earth to incite ill will by fanning the seeds of discontent over Kashmir. He hoped to set the world's teeth on edge by pitting India and Pakistan, two countries with nuclear weapons, against one another. Pulling on the threads of their discontent, he would use gaming to invade the minds of a group of young Pakistani jihadists. Maybe he could even get one of them to be a suicide bomber to kill a busload of Indian soldiers. Then, when India retaliated, the whole world would be frightened of escalation into a nuclear war and he could more easily bring several more world leaders under his control. This wouldn't have been possible under the previous president of the United States, because back then diplomatic channels were operating and many envoys worked around the clock to keep an unstable Pakistan in check. But the current polymorphous orange overlord in the White House hadn't even staffed the American embassy in Pakistan.

Veldemiron decided to take advantage of this situation to act.

First, he would use virtual reality games in order to incite young jihadists to move from gaming to actual violent action in reality. He would play upon the idea that they would be heroes if they did this. His plan was to bring them along carefully at first, only gradually whipping them up. He targeted discontented youths and put it into their minds to go to gaming centers throughout Kashmir. Carefully he directed them to *Fifth Dimension* and pushed them along the negative path of taking power over others. More gamers engaged with them, on the opposite path of service to others, as they played *Fifth Dimension*. The virtual games were lively and grew more and more intense as many more gamers in Kashmir joined on both sides. It was at this point that Bereh, looking at his computer in New York, noticed the numbers and alerted Ederah, Toomeh and Laaroos.

Veldemiron closely observed the gamers to choose his main actor. He needed not only the most violent young jihadist, but the one most easily manipulated. After patiently observing many gamers he made his choice, a nineteen-year old boy originally from Karachi. Filling his mind with the desire to act in reality, to actually kill, Veldemiron fed the boy the idea to plan a suicide bombing to murder Indian soldiers. Once the chosen boy was under his mind control, Veldemiron fed him the information to create the bomb and encouraged him to enlist his friends. Once the bomb was created, Veldemiron directed the group to their target, a busload of Indian soldiers in Kashmir.

Bereh and Toomeh arrived in Kashmir as the massacre was happening. Forty Indian soldiers were dead. India immediately retaliated by flying a bomber over Pakistan. Pakistan shot it down and captured the pilot. Veldemiron gloated. Toomeh and Bereh found a gaming center in Srinagar and logged in to play *Fifth Dimension*. Amerissis, Goddess of Light and Chohan of the Blue Flame of the Will of God, was overseeing the game. Wearing flowing white robes and holding her sword before her she filled the screen, the flame from her third eye rising six inches above her forehead. Both Toomeh and Bereh bowed to her divinity. As they raised their heads, she addressed them. "Let the game begin." Both wanderers left their human bodies at the gaming center in Srinagar and deployed.

Toomeh immediately found himself in Islamabad, inside the very room where the president of Pakistan was being briefed on the downed plane. Coming out of the president's forehead was a red cord about the thickness of a garden hose. None of the ministers or the president himself were aware of the cord. Toomeh followed the cord to its source in the corner of the room, right into the mind of Veldemiron, who hadn't yet noticed Toomeh, who had masked his energy. The cord needed cutting if the president was to see reason and war was to be avoided. Toomeh sent a message to Amerissis. Moments later the Goddess of Light was there, sword in hand. She sliced through the cord right at the point where it entered the Pakistani president's head. The cord immediately snapped back into Veldemiron. Realizing he was no match for Amerissis he apparated to New Delhi to work that end. With the cord gone, the ministers were able to calm the Pakistani president and stop his talk of war. They suggested to him that Pakistan had the upper hand as they had captured the Indian pilot. Toomeh filled the room with invisible violet light rays to transmute the warlike energy, and foster reason and receptivity to a compromise with India.

While Toomeh was calling for Amerissis, Bereh was arriving in a spacious and richly decorated room in New Delhi. He touched his hip pocket to make sure his flask was safe. The Venusian flask, with *Arjuna*, his human name engraved on it, had been a present from Ederah who had told him that the flask would open only at a moment of great need. The President of India was listening to one of his advisors. They had just received the news that their pilot was in the hands of the Pakistani government, and were deciding on the best way to negotiate with the Pakistanis for the return of their pilot when the energy in the room suddenly changed. Veldemiron had arrived. Though invisible to the humans, Bereh was clearly visible to Veldemiron. The next moment he crumpled to the floor and lay in an invisible heap, his life force draining out of him. Veldemiron had penetrated not only the golden sphere around him, but his merkaba as well. Somehow, he had stuck both the upward sun tetrahedron and the lower earth tetrahedron surrounding Bereh. And he was sucking out the vibration of love which had kept both tetrahedrons spinning. Merkabas need love to stay alive, to keep spinning. As Bereh's merkaba slowed, his consciousness faded. The last thing he heard were voices raised in anger, and he realized that Veldemiron had taken over the minds of the Indian president and his ministers and was driving them to retaliate against Pakistan.

The angry voices faded, everything became silent, and Bereh found himself on an ancient battlefield in the open space between two armies readying for battle. Looking down he saw that he was standing in a chariot with his charioteer. Together they surveyed the combatants: ranks of warriors, their adrenaline rising, waiting for combat. For the moment, everything was eerily still. Bereh's charioteer broke the silent stillness and began to speak to him softly, a love song to both the darkness and the light. As Bereh continued to survey the two mighty armies, his charioteer addressed him, calling him by his human name, Arjuna.

I am death, shatterer of worlds,
annihilating all things.
With or without you, these warriors
in their facing armies will die.

Therefore, stand up; win glory;
conquer the enemy; rule.
Already I have struck them down;
you are just my instrument, Arjuna.

{*Bhagavad Gita* — Stephen Mitchell translation}

Bereh lay on the floor, unseen by the Indian president or his ministers, imaging himself on a battlefield, wondering, who is this wise charioteer advising me? Memories floated back of his human father's old, battered, well-loved copy of the *Bhagavad Gita*. "Krishna," he whispered. "It is Krishna, my charioteer is Krishna." As he spoke the name, before his eyes appeared an almost unbearable glorious theophany, the whole universe in God. Standing over Bereh in his limitless, transcendent form, Krishna spoke again.

Those who love and revere me,
who surrender all actions to me,
who meditate upon me,
with undistracted attention,

whose minds have entered my being—
I come to them all, Arjuna,
and quickly rescue them all
from the ocean of death and birth.

{*Bhagavad Gita* — Stephen Mitchell translation}

Bereh felt his strength returning and realized he was no longer on a battlefield but crumpled on the floor in the President of India's office, with his Venusian flask in his hand. He knew he must stand up and be the instrument of God. With determined concentration, he centered himself in his heart and asked the flask to open. Nothing. He thought of Ederah and again focused on his heart as the source of his greatest power. He ran his fingers over the name engraved on its surface. Arjuna. Then he felt it. The flask was opening. Light poured out of it restoring his golden sphere, and reactivating his counter rotating tetrahedrons. Almost as if the flask was speaking to him, he heard the words, "If you do not believe in limitations you can create anything. You are free." Bereh saw himself restored, his merkaba again spinning at the speed of light and he rose to his feet. Veldemiron was facing the Indian president, controlling his mind, when Bereh came up behind him. As he readied himself, Bereh again heard Krishna's words. "Already I have struck him down, you are just my instrument, Arjuna." In one swift movement, he shot Veldemiron with a diamond ray, filling him with light which depolarized his dark energy, weakening him. Veldemiron swung around and struck back but Bereh ducked and the blow hit the marble wall and rebounded on Veldemiron, weakening him further. Furious and too weak to fight on, he fled back to Orion to repolarize. Bereh then entered the negotiations through the minds of the ministers, suggesting a compromise in which Pakistan would return the pilot to India in exchange for no further retaliation by India for the suicide bomber. For the moment, the peace held.

When the compromise had been accepted, Bereh and Toomeh returned to their human bodies at the gaming center in Srinagar and exchanged stories before parting again, each to visit his own family. Caitlin and Aidan, Toomeh's parents, had less than a month left in Mumbai. *The Irish Times* was recalling them to Dublin a little early as there could be trouble on the border between Northern and Southern Ireland due to Brexit. If it went ahead, Northern Ireland would leave the European Union, but Southern Ireland would remain in it. Since there was no physical barrier between the two Irelands there could be a problem. Aidan was needed to cover the upcoming events. Toomeh was as happy to see them as they were to see him, and the trio spent a pleasant day and a half catching up and discussing world politics.

Bereh's mother, Aastha, still lived in their house with its fragrant, flowering, lime trees. And that's where he found her, sitting in the garden with the *Bhagavad Gita* open in her lap. He glanced down at the page which she'd been reading. Leaning over her he read the words.

Those who love and revere me,
who surrender all actions to me,
who meditate upon me,
with undistracted attention,

whose minds have entered my being—
I come to them all, Arjuna,
and quickly rescue them all
from the ocean of death and birth.

There are no coincidences, he thought.

Chapter 31

Contest Winner

Ederah and Laaroos rechecked their numbers. They agreed. The gamer who had won the most virtual games playing on the side of service to others was a seventeen-year-old boy in Mexico. This was the second thing Ederah told Bereh when he returned from Mumbai. First, she threw her arms around him. It had been terrifying to see him lying in a crumpled heap after Veldemiron's attack.

"Your Venusian elixir saved me," he said, taking her in his arms and kissing her. When he kissed her again his urgency to be near her matched hers. For a moment, he held her close and they absorbed one another. "You are my nucleus and I but a lowly electron spinning about you," he whispered, moving his lips close to her ear.

"You would disparage the electron as lowly," she teased. "Both the electrons and the nucleus are necessary for there to be an atom, that most excellent discovery."

"I forgot, it was your friend, that Greek philosopher and wanderer, Democritus, who, for humans at least, first theorized the existence of the atom. In 400 B.C., wasn't it?"

"Yes. And it was brilliant of him. It took humans another twenty-three centuries to invent the microscope and confirm his hypothesis."

"Like all wanderers, he was ahead of his time," Bereh said, smiling at his own joke before tightening his arms around her. When she returned his kiss, he lifted her and carried her to bed. In the six months they had been reunited on Earth, Ederah and Bereh had learned new ways to make love in their human bodies. They could, but they didn't need to, switch to their fifth dimensional light bodies for a powerful sexual connection. Using

231

the central channel running up through the star tetrahedron shaped merkaba encasing each of their bodies they could draw in energy from any dimension by altering the way they breathed. They understood that it is the way one breathes which determines the dimension from which the energy one receives comes from. As they experimented sexually in their human bodies they discovered that holding their breath at the moment they felt their sexual energy rise up their spines to reach their hearts they could prolong orgasm and experience it in every cell of their bodies. In order to do this, when the energy reached their hearts, they would stop breathing, hold their breath, and direct the flow of energy out the back of their hearts and up through the ankh channel around their heads and back down to the front of their hearts. Then, by slowly releasing the breath when it reached the heart again, the sexual energy was preserved rather than lost through orgasm, and it spread to every cell in the body, rejuvenating it as the whole body experienced a prolonged orgasm.

After making love in this way, Ederah lay in Bereh's arms resting in the afterglow, each of their star tetrahedrons spinning at the speed of light. He turned on his side to look into her gray-gold eyes. "You are the beginning, the middle, and the end, without you I am less than half myself," he whispered close to her lips. "It was only the thought of you that allowed the flask to open. Veldemiron's attack sucked all love from my consciousness, stopping the tetrahedrons comprising my merkaba from spinning. I realize now that's how his weapon works. He goes after our merkabas, and stops the tetrahedrons from spinning. If they can't spin, our fifth dimensional bodies are severely weakened and our human bodies die. Our tetrahedrons can't spin without the vibration of love. *The absence of love is the source of all disease.* When I thought of you, love came rushing back to my consciousness and it was as if the motor in my tetrahedrons was being turned on."

"But where did you go when you lay there crumpled? I could feel your absence right through the screen."

"To an ancient battlefield where I was reminded to stand and fight, that there is no death and that I am not the doer, but only the instrument of the doer."

"Krishna?"

He kissed her eyes, "Yes, Krishna."

A reunion was also taking place in London. Laaroos was still trying to decide the best prize for the contest when Toomeh appeared in the carriage house and swept her up in his arms. She leaned back and looked into his eyes, checking him out. Like Ederah, she'd also watched the game in real time, seen Bereh crumple, and heard Amerissis order Ederah not to apparate to New Delhi but to let Bereh manage on his own, that it was important for him. Laaroos had felt Ederah's pain as she struggled between a Scylla and a Charybdis. Should she defy Amerissis and fly to Bereh, or trust her but maybe lose Bereh to the dark side for untold eons? Ederah had watched Bereh lying helpless and maybe lifeless, knowing that *we can never prepare for loss. We can only love completely, simply, intimately, in the only way we know how, for as long as we have.* In the end, she had trusted Amerissis, and then Bereh had risen. Laaroos wondered how she would have handled it had it been Toomeh.

"What would have happened to Bereh if he hadn't risen?" Laaroos said.

"Once he finished fomenting war, Veldemiron would have taken Bereh to Orion and enslaved him."

Laaroos shuddered. "We're playing for real."

"Yes, for real." Toomeh pulled her closer and pressed her to his heart. "But Amerissis was right to stop Ederah from rescuing Bereh. Saving himself allowed him to figure out how Veldemiron's attacks on us work, and how to combat and recover from them."

"If we remember love, we can free ourselves from any thought of limitation, and healing will happen. In fact, only in the presence of love can healing happen," Laaroos said. "They should be teaching us that in medical school. Doctors need to know that it's the absence of love that is the source of all disease. Patients could be spared a lot of tortuous treatments if that was common knowledge."

Toomeh kissed her on the forehead. "Yes, love is the vibration which creates universes."

Later that evening Maepleida and Heipleido returned to the carriage house and sat down in their Egyptian style living room with Toomeh and Laaroos, and the kittens, to discuss the prize winner and the prize.

"So, who is Miquel Angel?" Maepleida asked.

"He's a self-taught computer wizard and gamer who also knows how to make bricks. Here's his statement."

Maepleida took the statement Laaroos had printed and read aloud.

"My name is Miquel Angel Campana. I live in Oaxaca, Mexico, and I am seventeen years old. I attended school until I was fourteen, then I began work as a brick maker, like my father. But this wasn't my joy. My love is for gaming and computers. Now I have a job at a gaming center where I can play for free after work. Since discovering *Fifth Dimension* a few months ago, I can't stop playing the game and watching others play it. I saw the wanderers defeat the dark lord and free the children from their cages at the border between Mexico and the United States. I would love to meet these players. My mother complains that I no longer live in our time. She is a weaver, a maker of baskets, like her mother before her. My two sisters and my aunt help her in the family weaving business. They hand weave indigenous designs into each basket, but lately my mother has been creating pyramids and other geometric shapes as well. She is an artist and puts her heart in each basket. I am happy that I now have work I can put my heart in too. When I learned about computers in school I knew I had found my joy. I taught myself many computer languages at the library. Now I take care of all the computers at the gaming center in Oaxaca. My friend Carlos and I hope to create a game like *Fifth Dimension* one day."

"I want to meet both Miquel and his friend Carlos," Heipleido said.

"In London or New York?" Toomeh asked.

"We could give him the choice," Laaroos said.

"What are they saying in New York?" Heipleido asked. "Shall I send a bubble?"

Moments later they had their answer. "Bereh and I are at Soonam and Attivio's, and we all agree that Miquel and a friend of his choice should decide whether to meet us in New York or London. How does May 15 sound?"

"Maepleida's election is in mid-May, can we say June 1 instead for their visit?" Heipleido bubbled back.

"Perfect." Ederah bubbled. "I'll email him."

Maepleida leaned back into Heipleido's chest and he encircled her with his arms. "What do you suppose Miquel and other gamers think that wanderers are?" Maepleida asked.

"Advanced gamers," Heipleido ventured.

"We aren't free to tell humans we're wanderers unless they're wanderers too," Toomeh said. "It'll be interesting to meet Miquel and see what he is."

"He's only seventeen so he didn't come in our group. Maybe he's been incarnating here for a long time, stuck in the third dimension," Laaroos said.

"Or maybe he's just an ordinary human who loves gaming," Maepleida said.

Across the sea in New York, Ederah and Bereh and Soonam and Attivio were having a similar conversation. It was cool for an April evening. Attivio summoned a fire and they gathered around it on the down sofas. Shiva plopped up and wiggled in between Soonam and Attivio resting his chin in Soonam's lap. Mona took a spot on the back of the sofa, folded her paws under her chest and purred into Attivio's ear.

After talking about Miquel's visit, Soonam changed the conversation and asked Bereh how he had figured out the way Veldemiron's poison ray worked.

"When it first hit me, I felt as if all the light was being sucked from the world. I could feel my merkaba stop spinning. Had I thought of Ederah or love of the Divine right at that moment, maybe I could have counteracted it. After I saw Krishna on the battlefield I remembered Ederah's flask and the thought of loving her opened it. I knew immediately that, as always, love was the answer. Love is always the answer, but knowledge of that goes when Veldemiron's dark ray penetrates your golden sphere and hits your star tetrahedron. Before we go on any mission maybe we could fill the merkabas surrounding our bodies with extra love and light and seal them, as a resource in case we're hit."

Ederah reached for his hand and laced her fingers through his. Attivio shifted as Mona jumped into his lap. "Well done figuring this out," Attivio said. "Love has no limits, but living in the third dimension it's easy to forget that."

"Was it Master Hilarion who taught us that love can manipulate matter, and even create from nothing?" Soonam asked.

"Yes, and the only limitation is what you believe. If you don't tell yourself there are limits to what you can do, then there are no limits," Ederah said.

"With that uplifting thought we'll be off," Bereh said. He took Ederah's two hands and pulled her up. Soonam got to her feet, displacing the lounging Shiva, who licked her hand. Bereh leaned over and scratched him under his puppy chin. Mona gave

Bereh a what-about-me look and he leaned down and bestowed love on her in the form of a kiss on her kitten head.

Soonam, Attivio, Shiva and Mona all accompanied Ederah and Bereh to the front door. Attivio put Shiva's leash on him and the three of them walked over to the Highline stairs with Ederah and Bereh. Mona lay on the carpet in the foyer as the loan guardian of the house, waiting for them to return.

Chapter 32

Telos

Shiva and Mona lay dozing in a patch of sun on the floor beside Soonam, listening to her singing along with Bob Marley as she watered their orange tree. Suddenly all three of them lifted their heads. Attivio came running down the stairs and burst into the kitchen. "There's been another school shooting. I just got an alert on my phone."

"No, after the synagogue shooting yesterday?" Soonam cried. Shiva jumped to his feet and stared at her anxiously. "Sorry, Shiva."

"The man used an assault rifle to target Moslem, Brown and Black children in the classroom. Twenty-seven children are dead."

"Another white supremacist?"

"Yes. The police have him in custody. When they apprehended him, he ranted into the TV cameras, "Death to all Moslems, Jews, Mexicans and Blacks. Long live the president.""

Tears poured out of Soonam's eyes. Attivio's arms were around her the next moment. "I know."

"I have to choose a candidate for president who makes immigration, racism, antisemitism and gun violence a priority," she said into his shirt. "Health care and global warming are essential, but gun violence rips me to pieces."

"Soonam, remember, everyone eventually becomes conscious, even haters with assault weapons. Everyone gets back to Source. There is no death. Those children are on their way home, as are all the people who were praying in the synagogue."

"Yes, but humans don't know that. They just know their child was alive at breakfast and now she's dead."

Attivio kissed her tears. Shiva wiggled in between them.

While Attivio boiled water for tea, hoping to pull her mind from the cliffs of sorrow, he asked her, "Have you any idea yet whose campaign you want to work for?"

"There are four or five out of the twelve still in the race that I really like. The young mayor from Indiana, both young guys from Texas, and the senators from Vermont and Massachusetts. Then there's the former vice president to consider."

"How will you decide?"

"I'll have to go a little farther down the road with each of them, listen to what they say and see who could defeat the current occupant of the White House."

Before she could speak further Ederah and Bereh apparated into the kitchen.

"Have you seen the news?" Bereh asked. "The president's TV network is at it again, like yesterday, denying that the shooter is a white supremacist and saying that children of color weren't the target, even though all of the twenty-seven children killed were Moslem, Black or Latino. They were kindergarteners, five years old."

Immediately following Ederah and Bereh's arrival, a bubble arrived from Saint Germain and Portia.

"All wanderers in the United States are to apparate now to Telos, the inner city of light inside Mount Shasta in the Pacific northwest. Set your coordinates for Mount Shasta, which is at the northern end of the Sierra Nevada Mountain Range in Northern California. Telos is inside Mount Shasta, and is surrounded by a huge etheric purple pyramid which rises more than 14,000 feet above sea level. There is also an inverse pyramid which extends down into the Earth for more than 14,000 feet. Apparate inside the pyramid through the multidimensional portal and make your way to the Temple of Ma-Ra, where Adama, the High Priest of Telos, will speak to you. You will remember him from his visit to Venus. All other wanderers worldwide living outside the United States, please log in to *Fifth Dimension* at your nearest gaming center to hear Adama's broadcast. One hour from now he will address all awakened wanderers incarnate on Earth at this time."

Soonam, Attivio, Ederah and Bereh created a group merkaba and apparated to Telos. They landed in a grove of orange trees in a hydroponic garden. Though inside a mountain, it looked like a perfect, sunny, summer day. A gardener dressed in soft, colorful, knee length robes approached them, and seeing their puzzlement about where the sunlight was coming from deep inside a mountain, pointed out a large glowing orb suspended above them. "That's our light source. We create all our technology with thought."

The wanderers thanked him and asked the way to the Temple of Ma-Ra. He led them through the orange grove and the vegetable gardens to the flower gardens, and then down to the next level, where he pointed them to the Temple of Ma-Ra, a large white pyramid shaped structure. When Soonam admired the structure he told her, "We design everything in Telos using the principles of sacred geometry, including our homes which are circular and made of crystal." He bowed to them and took his leave. When they entered the temple, they saw that there were thousands of other wanderers sitting on crystal chairs. They found four aquamarine crystals and sat down, shaping the crystals for their comfort. The aquamarines welcomed them to Telos and adjusted themselves to make each of them comfortable.

Adama was already in the temple waiting for everyone to arrive. When the group reached ten thousand, he began. "Welcome to Telos, inner city of light. Yesterday, in the United States, forty people were murdered as they prayed in a synagogue. Today, little children, also in the United States, were murdered with an assault weapon. Several of the children recently came to Earth on their own as wanderers, to help with the ascension of the humans. They will return now to the fifth dimension, their job done. I say their job is done because at a soul level each of the twenty-seven children and all forty in the synagogue agreed, before incarnating, to this death as a part of their karmic destiny to bring consciousness. Despite the brutality, and difficult as it is to accept, the men who ended their lives were karmic instruments as well. This was a soul choice by all those who were massacred to move forward to the next evolutionary step. In addition to their growth, and that of their families, their deaths will raise consciousness about prejudice and hatred. Racism and antisemitism appear to be on the rise in the United States and Europe. They are not. Emboldened by the current U.S. president, who wields them like a partisan cudgel, white supremacists are hatching out of the darkness, but they have been there in the shadows all along. Today was another step in bringing consciousness to these realities. Focus on the long arc. You know there is no death. Yes, there is the pain of temporary separation. But that is nothing compared to the pain of not knowing one's own divinity. The end of this ignorance is near for many humans. Consciousness is dawning and yesterday and today brought us closer to that dawn."

Bereh glanced at Ederah. She was smiling at the thought of many humans on the brink of higher consciousness. Bereh turned his attention back to Adama.

"Earth and her surface dwellers are already embarked on the grand adventure of ascension. You and I are here to help. Every day the intensity of light is increasing on Earth. Even now those of us living in the inner cities of light are preparing to come to the surface to live among humans. Already a majority of humans, over sixty percent, can hold enough light in their vehicles to open their hearts and embrace all beings as one. When that number reaches ninety percent we will reveal ourselves and come to the surface to live among humans. That day is coming. It is true that the dark lords are still slipping through the quarantine around Earth to promote selfishness, separation, greed, and desire for power over others. The ripping apart of families, the mistreatment of those fleeing dangerous situations, the taking of land from one group to ensure the safety of another group, the creation of a white elite and a brown underclass, all these are the result of fear. And fear is the opposite of unconditional love for all beings. The dark side manipulates fear to control humans. Our task remains spreading unity consciousness to help humans understand that they are divine beings having a human experience. Every day when you walk down the street your energy is affecting every being within fifty-five feet of you. As your merkabas spin about you in your human form at nine-tenths the speed of light, they give off energy which lifts up all beings near you. Humans also have a star tetrahedron shaped merkaba surrounding them, but many of those merkabas are not spinning optimally. Wanderers around the globe are beginning to give classes to teach humans how to activate their merkabas using breathing techniques. Things are changing very rapidly on Earth now, despite how it appears in the United States under the current corrupt administration. All the poisons in the American culture: racism, greed, self-interest, antisemitism, fear mongering, are hatching out and becoming visible in order to be healed."

Soonam shifted in her aquamarine seat. The idea that all the poisons were "hatching out and becoming visible" was helpful to her in making sense of the dark times they were living through on Earth. She had been more affected by the last two massacres than she felt she should be as a fifth dimensional being who knows there is no death. She told herself she had to do more to keep hope alive in her heart if she was to be a way-shower for other beings on Earth. Attivio glanced over at her. He felt her anguish and self-criticism and telegraphed to her: *My valiant one, you are more powerful than any band of arrogant thugs who think they own this planet.*

Soonam turned her violet eyes to him in gratitude.

"A small group on Earth controls ninety percent of the

wealth," Adama continued, "but this, too, is about to change. These ruthless entities know that their time is coming to an end. In their fear, they are desperately escalating their attempts to stir up hatred and conflict in order to maintain world dominance. Do not be deceived. Their end is near. Hold your resolve that Earth is moving fully into the light. All is well. Peace to all beings." Here Adama stopped and began to bow to them, then, almost as an afterthought, added, "Please stay in Telos as long as you like and explore our city of light. All our citizens will welcome you."

Soonam, Attivio, Ederah and Bereh rose, left the temple and strolled out into a large, open, circular area under a crystal dome. Running off the central circle were a number of streets organized like the spokes of a wheel. They chose one street at random and proceeded down it. Both sides of the street were lined with dome shaped homes made of crystal. Many were quartz or rose quartz, a few were made of amethyst. Soonam marveled at their beauty. When she paused to admire one, the arch shaped door opened to reveal a woman about fourteen feet tall wearing soft white robes which brushed the ground. The woman greeted them and invited them in to have a look. She explained that she and her partner had created their home through visualization, using their heart energy. "First we decided on the diameter and the height, using the principles of sacred geometry. Then we imagined each crystal stone being laid, then we energized the structure by pouring light and love into each stone. When that was done we created the various inside areas to serve different functions. Soonam looked around and saw a crystal table and chairs with a bowl of sweet, fragrant oranges on it. As her eyes moved over the space she noticed a crystal partition. Behind it was a sleeping area with bouquets of multicolored roses on either side of the sleeping palate. Another sector held an altar with several gold and purple meditation cushions before it.

Attivio asked about the fruit and flowers and the woman told him that their gardens, though only covering a space of about ten acres, provided enough flowers, fruits and vegetables for all one million plus residents of Telos. "We eat only for pleasure," she explained, "like you, we are able to live on light."

Ederah wanted to know whether they birthed children in Telos, since the original inhabitants came from Lemuria.

"Yes, but those who wish to become parents undergo a year of training to ensure their commitment and readiness. After the birth, both parents spend full time with the baby for the first two years."

Bereh asked about the animals he'd seen near the orange grove.

"We do not eat animals or use them for labor. Our animals are also vegetarians and do not eat one another. They are our gentle friends, our fellow sentient beings, with whom we communicate telepathically. They teach us about love."

Soonam's heart was full to bursting when she heard this. They all bowed to the woman before taking leave of her.

Out in the street again, they saw floating platforms going up and down to what appeared to be other levels. Stepping onto one of the platforms they directed it upward and arrived at a level with tall trees, running brooks, forests and meadows, and best of all, many kinds of animals they had never seen before. A large animal, looking somewhat like a very large gold-colored dog but with soft cat fur and ears like an elephant approached Soonam and laid one of his large ears against her heart to be cuddled. Melting, Soonam looked into his eyes as he telegraphed his message of welcome. She scratched him under his ear and kissed his forehead as he made soft sounds of pleasure. Communicating telepathically, she asked him about himself.

"I've had over a hundred lives on Earth during the last thirty thousand years, and several thousand lives throughout this galaxy. I came to Telos from Lemuria twelve thousand years ago when Lemuria sank into the ocean. Mostly I have used the quadrupedal form during my Earth lives. My current species, like many species, no longer lives on the surface as we did in the time of Lemuria and Atlantis. Many current day humans use animals in unconscious ways because they don't understand that we are all part of the Divine and when you hurt one part of the Divine you hurt all of it, including yourself."

Soonam put her arms around him and nuzzled her head into his neck, communicating to him her joy at meeting him. That's when he told her his name, Botu. The others wandered around the garden admiring the variety of trees and plants and making their own animal friends. After an hour or so in the garden, Attivio asked, "Are we ready to leave Telos?"

They all agreed. Before leaving the garden Soonam telegraphed to Botu, "I hope we meet again." His answer was swift and sure, "We will."

The four of them joined hands to create a group merkaba. Moments later they were back in New York, in Soonam and Attivio's garden.

Chapter 33

A Troubling Discovery

They'd been at it for hours when Heipleido conceded to his fellow committee members that, "Yes, you're right, our bill for the homeless would be better introduced from the House of Commons than from the Lords. But, our connections are in the Lords. We have no way in though the House, not yet, at least. Let's get through this first reading in the Lords tomorrow and see how we stand."

The bill included provisions for both housing and job training, as well as drug and alcohol rehab programs. It was an ambitious proposal which entailed training the homeless to build the houses themselves in rural areas, using Jimmy Carter's Habitat for Humanity as a model. And for those who were interested, they could receive training in the installation of broadband to reach rural areas. The hard part would be finding the funds. Heipleido had some ideas for this but he needed to do a bit more research that evening, before tomorrow's reading. He'd already given Lord Merton the most recent draft of the bill so he could study it before the reading.

When he returned to the carriage house that evening Maepleida greeted him. She could see that he was preoccupied with the bill. "I wish we could just manifest the money for your bill," she said.

"But that would take the challenge out of it," he answered, pulling her into his arms and commanding her, "Look at me."

Maepleida turned her emerald eyes upward and looked at him.

"You're still upset about the shootings," he said.

"Were we this violent and full of hate and prejudice when we were third dimensional?" she asked.

"No doubt, as it's the task of third dimensional beings to learn about love for all beings as one. Until they understand that, they act unconsciously and we must have, too, when we were third dimensional. Would you like to check the Akashic Records?"

"I don't think I could bear it."

"Consciousness comes to all beings, Maepleida. Don't lose heart. It's only a few humans, fueled by the right wing and the dark side, who pick up assault weapons and mow down their fellow creatures. Their minds are diseased because they have lost the ability to love. Remember, it is the absence of love that is the cause of all disease, mental and physical."

Maepleida rested her cheek on his heart until she felt a soft body rubbing against her ankles and looked down in time to see Albus leap up and cling on to Heipleido's pant leg. He hung there, kitten style, until Heipleido scooped him up with one hand and kissed his little nose, which felt cool and moist against Heipleido's lips. "Come, sit down with me."

The three of them settled on the sofa under the dragon tree and Albus curled up in Maepleida's lap. "It's not a welcoming atmosphere for your bill, is it, with all the right-wing energy up in the world."

"No, but it's when we most need legislation like this to protect the weak and disenfranchised from the efforts of the powerful to dehumanize them. It's not as bad here as it is in The United States, which not only has a crime family in the White House but a corrupt attorney general, guaranteeing the president unlimited power while making him immune even from investigation. With Congress prevented from exercising its function of oversight their republic is in danger of collapsing. They've never had a true democracy because that requires one person, one vote, which they don't have because of the Electoral College."

"Do you think the current president will succeed in becoming a dictator?"

"He's trying, with the help of his lackey attorney general

and the Republicans in Congress. And he certainly befriends dictators while fraying all of America's traditional alliances."

"Don't the American people see it?"

"Some do, but many are fooled by his lies."

"Are we wanderers doing enough to awaken people?"

"There are many fronts to engage on, stopping the dark lords, and the Russian dictator as he attempts to destroy democracies wherever they exist, exposing the power hungry, checking the Chinese, the religious fanatics, and the racists, while at the same time feeding the starving and aiding those in war torn countries. The fight is on, and the enemy has many heads. So, are the wanderers doing enough to turn the tide? I don't know, but we must keep on."

As he said this Heipleido pulled her closer and kissed her forehead before getting up and walking over to the piano. Maepleida leaned back, resting her neck on the sofa to listen. As his fingers touched the piano keys, she exhaled.

Half an hour later and uplifted by Heipleido's rendition of the Goldberg Variations, they heard the front door of the carriage house open. Laaroos and Toomeh walked into the living room as Heipleido's phone rang and he closed the piano. It was Lord Merton. "The first reading of your bill has been postponed. It won't be tomorrow. I'll try to find out who's responsible. I'm sorry, Horus."

"Maybe it's better. That'll give us more time to secure the funding."

"Alright, goodnight."

Heipleido laid his phone on the table and looked at them. "A little delay, that's all. What have you two been up to?"

"We've just been bubbling with Attivio," Laaroos said. "He's got a book deal for his book about wanderers, with a British publisher, John Hunt, and they're arranging a book tour. He's hoping that it'll help awaken some of the wanderers who incarnated with us, and even some from previous missions."

"Well done, him," Heipleido said. "Will Soonam go with him?"

"I don't think so because of Shiva and Mona, unless her father is home to care for them," Laaroos said. "But before Attivio leaves, Soonam wants to go to Washington, D.C. to observe Congress in session. She believes understanding how it operates will help her find her path to the right candidate."

"I'd like to go to Washington myself," Heipleido said. "Today I overheard two Lords talking about a summit the U.S. president is planning to hold in the White House, with the crown prince of Saudi Arabia, the Russian president, and the North Korean dictator. British intelligence picked up word of it."

"Good your hearing hasn't suffered being in a human body," Maepleida said.

"Truth be told, I went fifth dimensional to hear it all, nobody saw, I was in the men's room in a stall. They thought they were alone. Even so, they were whispering."

"What else did they say?" Toomeh asked.

"Only that the summit would be happening soon, under the guise of an agreement about nuclear testing. But no one believes that's the reason for the summit or why would the British, French and Germans be excluded. And there's going to be a state dinner."

"So, what is the real reason those four are having a summit?" Toomeh wondered out loud.

"World domination?" Maepleida ventured.

"A frightening thought," Laaroos said. "We'll have to find out who these four actually are. They could be Greys, Reptilians, Draconians, or even Dark Lords from Orion, like Darpith and Veldemiron."

"They're all capable of posing as human once they slip through the quarantine around Earth. The purpose of these four heads of state seems to be the same, to get absolute power over their citizens," Toomeh said.

"But the dark side doesn't work together, their way is to destroy one another," Maepleida said.

"Maybe they'll do that after they take control of all the humans," Laaroos said.

"We'll have to see them in person and feel their energy to know whether they are human or only posing as human. But it won't be easy to get near any of them," Heipleido said, "we'll need a plan. Did Attivio say when Soonam is going to Washington?"

"In a few days," Toomeh said.

"If she could only touch some of these players, we could know everything," Maepleida said.

"They all have their version of the secret service," Heipleido said, "which makes it difficult to get near them."

"The Chohans must be aware of this summit," Laaroos said.

"My election seems so feeble in the face of these four monsters having a summit to plan world domination," Maepleida said.

"Don't give in to that kind of thinking," Heipleido said, "it will limit you."

Albus stretched in Maepleida's lap and looked up at her as if in agreement with Heipleido's words.

"So, what now?" she asked the others.

"Next week you'll go to your district and win your election to the House of Commons. I'll keep on with my bill in the Lords, Toomeh and Laaroos will prepare for Miquel's visit. He and his friend Carlos can spread word of the game throughout Mexico and South America. And hopefully our friends in New York will go to Washington, D.C. for the summit, and find out who these leaders really are."

"When do Miquel and Carlos arrive?" Maepleida asked.

"The week after your election," Laaroos said. "The plan is for all eight of us to welcome them to London. Miquel chose to meet us in London because his parents did not want him setting foot in the United States. Even though we're providing a visa there is a danger that he could be arrested and detained because of the color of his skin. The brutal immigration policies of the current U.S. president are well known in Mexico."

"Do you think the U.S. president is just a weak, egomaniacal human under the control of either the Draconians or some dark lord from Orion, or is he actually a Reptilian himself?" Maepleida asked.

"He appears such a fool, that either he is very good at playing one, and is actually a Reptilian, or he really is a weak-minded grifter out for his own gain, and perhaps under the control of the dark side as well," Toomeh said.

Chapter 34

State Dinner

Soonam and Attivio walked up the Highline to Ederah and Bereh's apartment as the sun was setting over the Hudson River. Pink light reminiscent of Venus filled the sky, wrapping them both in a soft, peaceful feeling. They paused a moment and gazed out over the water, watching the light ignite the surface of the river. *To love is to give light*, Soonam thought.

Attivio answered with his own thought. *The sun is kissing the river goodnight.*

Soonam reached for his hand and spoke, "Standing here, we don't feel the movement in their relationship. But the Earth travels two and a half million kilometers every day around the sun, like a young girl, infatuated, dancing about her love, telling him a story as they move along."

They stood watching the sun sink below the horizon. When it was gone they walked on to Ederah and Bereh's.

"Lady Portia and Master Saint Germain will be here any minute," Ederah told them. "They have an assignment for us."

This was no sooner said then two violet ovals of light appeared and turned into the Chohans of the Violet Ray of Transmutation. Lady Portia, Goddess of Justice, wore the Maltese Cross over her shimmering violet robes. The cross, which brings the masculine and feminine aspects within all beings into balance, hung about her neck on a chain of amethysts. Her waist length red hair was worn loose this evening, held in place only by the ring of gold circling her crown. Saint Germain stood beside her in a rich violet cloak with a high neck, his violet eyes shining.

"We want the four of you to travel to Washington, D.C., to work for the caterer in charge of the state dinner which the president will have for his three dictator friends from Russia,

North Korea and Saudi Arabia," Lady Portia began. "The catering company, which is called Extraordinary Events, is managed by a wanderer who came to Earth on a previous mission, and chose to remain to help. Her name is Olympia and she is expecting you. The event will be held in a large tent on the White House lawn. You will be the servers assigned to the head table where these leaders will be seated. Each of you will use your powers to discover who each of them really is. We have our suspicions but we would like them verified. The U. S. president is a germaphobe, so it may be impossible for you to touch him, Soonam, but you will be able to touch the fork that has been in his mouth. You may be able to brush against the three visiting leaders while you are serving them. While Soonam will use her skill at psychometry, you, Ederah, will make yourself invisible and listen to their conversation. Attivio, you will watch all four heads of state carefully for signs that they sense the four of you and realize you are not human. If that happens, you will turn time back to before they sensed anything, and Bereh will wipe their memories. Then, if necessary, create confusion by duplicating whatever seems most beneficial at the moment, so you can all make your escape."

When Lady Portia finished speaking, Saint Germain asked if they had any questions.

"Will we be the only four wanderers there, other than Olympia?" Bereh asked.

"Yes. If these four leaders are higher dimensional beings on the dark path, they could easily pick up the energy of a large group of wanderers. You will have to remain third dimensional around them except when you are using your fifth dimensional powers. Soonam was chosen for this mission because she can practice psychometry even as a third dimensional human."

"I'd like to visit the Senate and have a look at that group as well," Soonam said. "Will that be possible?"

"Olympia will arrange it," Portia said smiling at Soonam in

understanding. She too suspected that some of the players in the Senate were from the dark side or at the very least had been corrupted by it.

"When do we leave?" Ederah asked.

"Tomorrow on the 10:00 a.m. train from Penn Station. You will be met at the station in Washington. Olympia will teach you how to serve at a state dinner. Any other questions?" Saint Germain paused and looked at each of them before reminding them, "All is well. Be at peace." He and Portia bowed in acknowledgement of the Divine resting within the four wanderers, turned into violet light and disappeared.

When they were gone Bereh joked, "No one ever told us we were going to be waiters when we volunteered for this mission."

"It might be fun," Ederah said, "as long as we don't spill anything on one of those dictators and get our heads chopped off for it."

"A little spill might allow me to touch them as I wipe up," Soonam said.

"I hope you won't, Soonam," Attivio said picking up her hand and pulling her off the sofa. "Come on, let's go home and take Shiva for a long walk. We're going to be away for a few days and your father is more into letting him go in the garden than actually walking him."

"See you in the morning," Soonam called over her shoulder as they left.

The next day Olympia herself was at the station to welcome them. Tall and light of foot, with large eyes, wearing a casual dress and cardigan and flat shoes, she easily passed as human. But her orange-gold eyes and the music in her graceful movements told the wanderers that she was from Arcturus. Soonam wondered if she knew Toomeh or Laaroos or even Laaroos's mother. Whenever they passed through Washington Square Park, Soonam and Attivio never failed to scour it for Laaroos's mother but they'd never caught even a glimpse of her. In fact, Olympia was the first awakened wanderer, outside of their own group, and those at the meeting in Telos, that they'd encountered since incarnating, and they were full of questions for her.

"Let me get you settled and I'll answer everything," Olympia promised.

Once they were inside her peaceful Georgetown home, away from the rushing world and safely out of earshot of anyone, she served them finger sandwiches and tea and explained that she'd been living on Earth as a wanderer for two hundred years in the same body. She'd had various professions during that time, all in the service of the Chohans. The catering company was her latest venture and had been in operation since the year 1998. She catered all the major political events in Washington which allowed her to gather information about what the government was up to and who the players were. Over the years she'd employed a mix of ordinary humans and wanderers but at the moment was shorthanded and had no one capable of psychometry while in human form, which was why they'd been asked to help.

"But why have you stayed on Earth so long? Soonam asked.

"My job isn't done, and this is an exciting moment on Earth. The whole universe is watching to see how many humans can make the leap to the Fourth Dimension along with Earth."

"How many humans and how many wanderers do you employ at the moment? We're especially excited to meet other wanderers," Bereh said.

"Only one wanderer, at the moment. She incarnated with my original group and reconnected with me twenty-one Earth years ago, when she awoke to her true identity and came to Washington from New York City. Other wanderers have moved through and onto other assignments, but she's been with me the longest."

Ederah felt her skin prickle at the mention of a wanderer who had come from New York after awakening twenty-one years ago. Could it be Laaroos' Arcturian mother? A moment later she had her answer when a woman came into the room. Her orange-gold eyes and copper hair were set in the very face they'd seen under the arch in Washington Square Park twenty-one years earlier, when they'd come to Earth for a day during El Morya's exercise.

"You're Laaroos' mother!" Ederah said.

"I am. Please tell me, she's on Earth, and awakened?"

"Yes, she's in London," Ederah said, "and reunited with Toomeh."

They could all see the joy in her eyes at hearing this. "I have been waiting for this news ever since that day under the arch."

"The Chohans didn't tell you?" Bereh asked.

"No. They said I would know at the right time."

"What shall we call you?" Soonam asked.

"Best use my human name, Sally, for now, as we'll be working around humans." After much talk of Laaroos, Sally invited them to go with her to the kitchens so they could begin training for the state dinner. "The president wanted a grand theme, something befitting his importance. His daughter, who was there when we met with him, suggested Greek Gods and their slaves, with the servers playing the slaves," Sally told them.

Olympia popped her head in and told Soonam, "If you start training now, you can have the morning off and I'll take you to Capitol Hill."

The next morning, true to her word, Olympia took Soonam to Capitol Hill, not into the Senate itself, as there was no vote being held and the chamber was empty, but to the building where the senate majority leader and the head of the Senate Judiciary Committee had their offices. She knew both men well as she had arranged many events for them. She and Soonam would stop by on the pretext of checking some detail for the state dinner. Both senators were always jockeying for the best seat at any presidential dinner and curried favor with her as she had the power to alter most arrangements. However, it wasn't necessary to go to their offices. When the elevator doors opened, they were inside whispering to each other. They stepped out and greeted Olympia, who took the opportunity to introduce Soonam. Thrusting out her hand to shake with first one and then the other, Soonam smiled up into their eyes. Suddenly anxious at seeing something spark in the majority leader's eyes, Olympia pulled Soonam away, telling the two senators that they were late for a meeting.

"I've known those two for twenty years," she told Soonam, "and always thought they were only dark, selfish, calculating humans. They never seemed to pick up that I was anything more than a human, but just now, with you, I felt my heart run cold and was afraid if we lingered they'd see who we truly are."

"They're serpents from Etamin in the constellation Draco," Soonam told her once they were outside. "Their names are Lynseehiz and Mitchhiz. They've been on Earth for five centuries, taking over one human body after another as each body aged and died. Their goal is to enslave humans for Draco. Victory has slipped out of their grasp several times over the centuries, but now they feel their time is once again near as they've found a useful tool in the current president. They plan to use him and his dictator friends to do their work for them. Once all humans live under dictators, they will destroy the dictators and take control. They don't seem to have considered that one or more of the dictators could also be dark beings from a higher dimension, with their own plans for the humans. Also, Lynseehiz and Mitchhiz don't trust one another, and each intends to betray the other once the humans are enslaved. First, they will go after women and minorities by incrementally restricting their rights, using the help of bigoted white men and the Supreme Court. Then they will attack the white men themselves until the whole planet serves Draco. Unlike those from Orion, who don't incarnate as human, but slip through the quarantine to attack as Fifth Dimensional beings, these two have been playing a slightly longer game on Earth."

"Your psychometry skills are astounding," Olympia said.

"What is your superpower?" Soonam asked.

"Hiding in plain sight." The two wanderers smiled at one another knowingly. "I will be interested to see what you pick up at the state dinner."

When they returned to Olympia's house, Soonam found Attivio bare chested, wearing slave sandals and a cloth wrapped around his waist covering barely more than his genitals and buttocks.

"The president's daughter requested that the servers be dressed as slaves," Sally explained to Soonam, "while the guests will be wearing costumes fit for Olympian gods."

Soonam couldn't take her eyes off Attivio. For someone who wasn't usually taken aback, she was speechless. Attivio returned her gaze with a look of commingled chivalry and lust, which promised a passionate night.

"Come here, you're next," Sally said handing Soonam a serpent bracelet for her upper arm, a metallic bra and a long, sheer skirt hung from a metal band which would encircle her hips and expose her belly. Ederah was already dressed in a similar costume, as were a dozen other of Olympia's employees.

"Do you know how each of the four heads of state will be dressed?" Attivio asked Olympia.

"Unfortunately, yes. Their people sent me their choices and I arranged for the costumes when I ordered the pieces for the décor. The president will come as Zeus, naturally, the Saudi prince as Ares, God of War, the Korean dictator will be Apollo, the Sun God, and the Russian leader will be Hades, God of the Underworld."

"Power mongers in love with themselves," Ederah said.

By the time the fittings were completed and a final run through of how the event would proceed was done, it was early evening and Ederah and Bereh strolled out to Olympia's rose garden to enjoy the soft evening light. They sat side by side on her swinging garden bench in the dark watching the moon rise. Bereh stared at the moonlight streaming across Ederah's face amplifying the beauty of it.

"The Earth and the moon are a couple with a timeless bond," Ederah mused. "As Earth's partner the moon stands sentinel and witnesses all the follies and triumphs of her people, their heartbreaks and great loves, kindnesses, envies, genius, and yes, acts of destruction."

"And she makes no comment, ever," Bereh added, "as she sits in the night sky silently witnessing all men's doings."

The screen door opened and clanged shut.

"Here you are," said Soonam, "resting in the quiet before tomorrow evening's spectacle."

"The only spectacle for me will be you in your scanty slave costume," Attivio said, squeezing Soonam's waist.

"Attivio, all these centuries together, and I didn't know you were into romantic bondage," Soonam teased.

"I'm into every tessellated facet of your being," he answered.

Ederah and Bereh smiled at their exchange. After twenty-one years apart both couples were still meeting their twin flames in new ways. Making discoveries about them in their human forms sometimes surprised them as they raced towards the joy in one another. Wind rustled the tree branches overhead disturbing the green silence of the trees and carrying the sweet scent of summer roses to their nostrils. All four wanderers cocked their ears to see if there was a message in the rustling of the branches. Hearing none, Bereh stood up. "Come my untamable love, let's to bed."

"Are you coming?" Ederah called over her shoulder to Soonam and Attivio as Bereh pulled her forward.

"We'll sit a while longer," Attivio said, as Soonam nestled into his chest and gazed up at the branches overhead.

Olympia was relieved when the next day dawned sunny and dry but not too hot. The flowers would survive and the food wouldn't spoil. And no one would faint from the heat while working in the huge tent on the White House lawn. By seven forty-five that evening all was in readiness. The medieval wine goblets gleamed, the low tables were laden with exotic fruit, all the silk cushions were in place and exotic flowers spilled out of hundreds of urns. The vans containing the dinner were behind the tent. The servers, including the four wanderers, were at their stations. Olympia looked around checking every detail, and wondered if the three dictators would enjoy dining while lying on cushions in the style of Roman emperors.

When the guests began to arrive in their Olympian costumes, Soonam observed the two serpents from Draco, Lynseyhiz, dressed as Cronos, the god of time, and Mitchhiz, adorned as Poseidon, slither in and sink into their silk cushions. Relieved not to be serving them, she turned in time to see the three dictators enter the tent alongside the president. They made themselves comfortable on piles of cushions on raised platforms. From there they could look down on all the other guests sprawled on the floor at their feet.

Soonam attended the four leaders. The Russian was the first to hold up his goblet for more vodka after the toasts. Soonam touched his hand as she steadied his goblet to fill it. Human, her touch registered. He was ruthless, egotistical, and dark, but human. His mind was awash with plans for sabotaging every democracy on Earth in order to bring the world under Russian control. He already had his heel on the throat of the U.S. president, who at that moment signaled her to refill his goblet with Coca-Cola. When she approached him with his drink, believing no one could see, he put his hand on her buttocks. He, too, was a human, who despite his bombast was terrified of being discovered as a fraud and a criminal. Next, Soonam attended the North Korean dictator who beckoned her roughly with his arm. He indicated that his napkin had fallen on the floor. She brought him another and touched his fingers as she handed it to him. She had never touched anyone so mistrustful of all other beings. Hungry for power and adulation he was nearly insane with the desire to be seen as a god. But he, too, was human. It only remained for her to make physical contact with the Saudi Prince. But she would have to wait while Bereh and Attivio served dinner to the head table. As Soonam stepped back out of their way she accidentally stepped on Ederah's feet. The waves of love that she felt at this momentary contact with Ederah were sweet relief after touching the three fascist monsters. Invisible, Ederah hovered near to overhear the conversation between the four heads of state while Soonam kept her eyes on the Saudi prince and waited. As if he felt her eyes on him, he nodded and she approached. He grabbed her wrist and twisted it. "You were staring at me? Who are you?" Soonam apologized and he laughed his cruel laugh, as if his remarks had been a joke to frighten and intimidate her. Human! He, too, was human, vicious, power hungry, deceitful, maniacal, and a murderer, like the Russian and the North Korean. Attivio and Bereh cleared the main course. The four leaders now appeared to be jovially conversing with the help of translator buds in their ears. The guests, sprawled on their cushions below the head table, were less jovial and more aware of their lower status. Soonam glanced at Lynseyhiz and Mitchhiz, who were busy pretending cordiality toward those around them. *Snakes*, she thought. As desert was served, Olympia approached Soonam and asked her to step outside the tent. "Are you alright, is any of them onto you?"

"All four of them are human," Soonam informed her.

"I suppose that's good," Olympia said. "But we'll need to know the pecking order among them. Between your and Ederah's work we should be able to put that together."

"Attivio and Bereh may have picked up something as well," Soonam said.

"As soon as the president gets up to leave, walk out and get in my car. Tell Attivio, Bereh and Ederah to do the same. I don't want that grotesque pair, Lynseyhiz or Mitchhiz, to have a chance to make contact with any of you."

When they arrived back at Olympia's after the state dinner, Portia and Saint Germain were already there talking with Sally. Everyone wanted to hear what the wanderers from New York had learned.

Ederah, who had listened to the conversation of the four heads of state with no interruptions spoke first. "Their conversation made it clear that the U.S. president is at the bottom of the pecking order in this group. Several times one or another of them interrupted him or stopped listening and turned away. None of them see him as a threat. There were a couple things of note. The Saudi and the president discussed the president's son-in-law's part in the murder and dismemberment of the Washington Post journalist. Apparently, the murdered journalist discovered that the president's son-in-law was giving classified top secret information to the Saudis."

Attivio and Bereh had picked up bits of this conversation too. "The president was clearly worried that it could come out that he and his son-in-law were in on murder plans," Attivio said.

"The other conversation I heard," Ederah said, "was between the Russian and the Saudi. They were trying to understand why the U.S. president continued to allow North Korea's nuclear testing with no reprisal. They concluded that he was either a stupid muddler or he had some kind of deal with the North Korean dictator? While the Russian and the Saudi were engaged on one side of the president, on his other side, the North Korean dictator commented to him about the democrats running for president, calling them low I.Q. and stupid Americans, and the president laughed and agreed."

Saint Germain then turned to Soonam.

"All four of them are human, grotesque, but human," Soonam reiterated. "Had I not experienced it, I could not have pictured the mental life of such creatures. Each of them is capable of monstrous perfidy. Each has a solely self-interested agenda. The Russian seeks world domination. The North Korean is after status as a major player on the world stage. The Saudi wants to be feared by all and believes his ruthlessness will insure this. The Russian plays a long game. He employs sabotage and subterfuge as well as outright aggression against his neighbors, enemies and allies. The American is terrified of being found out as a crook and a fraud and is desperate to be re-elected as he believes it will protect him from criminal charges being brought against him for requesting dirt from a foreign power on a political opponent. What all four of them have in common with the dark lords from Orion and Draco is that they are all after power over others and are indifferent to human needs and human life, other than their own. To all of them, humans are disposable."

"You also learned something about the senate majority leader and the head of the senate judiciary committee," Saint Germain said.

"Their real names are Mitchhiz and Lynseyhiz. They're serpents from Draco. Like Veldemiron and his minions, they want to enslave humans for their own use. But while Veldemiron slips in and out of the quarantine around Earth, coming and going from Orion, Mitchhiz and Lynseyhiz have been on Earth continuously for five centuries and have not in that time returned to Draco. When I touched them, I felt their detestation for humans. Both are utterly without a conscience. For the last few centuries they have operated mostly in banking, or, as they do now, in government, to create misery and deprivation for the masses, dehumanizing them and grinding them down to helplessness so they will be easier to control. The current president is their newest tool for creating separation, pain and fear in millions of humans, while duping the rest," Soonam explained. "They manipulate both the president and Congress with their attitudinizing."

"Could you sense whether Mitchhiz and Lynseyhiz are aware

of Veldermiron and his minions? Lady Portia asked. "Since they are fighting for the same spoils, they may inadvertently help us by eliminating one another."

"They don't seem to be," Soonam answered.

"Mitchhiz and Lynseyhiz may serve some higher up in Draco," Saint Germain said, "someone who is aware of the competition from the dark lords from Orion."

"In either case, our best hope in this battle is to awaken as many humans as possible to the knowledge of their own divinity. Once they ascend to the Fourth Dimension it will be more difficult to enslave them or to keep them in the dark about their true identity," Portia said.

Saint Germain and Portia thanked them for their work, showered them with violet light and departed.

Chapter 35

Election Day

A June sunset in the English countryside doesn't rush itself. It moves slowly along caressing the honeysuckle, climbing the garden wall, kissing the foxgloves awake before lighting up the purple irises, before falling upon the English roses, igniting them in a blaze of color. Maepleida stood in the center of her grandmother's garden, communing with the flowers and contemplating the light. Each flower was to her a being in its own right. The words of Rilke, a poet she had loved since her school days moved through her consciousness. "There are moments in which a rose is more important than a piece of bread." The ability to be completely engrossed in a rose, despite facing an election the next day, was one of the gifts of being fifth dimensional. If she won the next day that would be good, and if she lost that would be good too. What is, is right. She had long since aligned herself with the will of the Divine as it worked through her. There would be no sorrow or regret or disappointment for her to bite on, no matter the outcome of the election. For this moment she stood surrounded by the magical beauty of the flowers, feeling the earth beneath her feet, breathing in the warm summer evening, and she fell a little more in love with the blue planet.

Caressed by the flowers and confident in her ability to accept whatever outcome the election resulted in, Maepleida made her way back to the large comfortable house and sat down to the country dinner her grandmother's cook had prepared for her. She ate her soup and bread alone, as neither Heipleido or Maggie had been able to leave London. Heipleido's bill was once again scheduled for its first reading the next morning, and Maggie had come down with a mysterious bug. Dinner finished, Maepleida climbed the stairs to bed and opened her window wide to take a last look at the garden below her. It was all in shadow now, resting from the day's exertion of growing. She undressed, brushed her long hair and lay down in her bed enjoying the peace that comes from ordered gardens and settled routines. Before she closed her eyes, she sent a bubble to Heipleido wishing him goodnight and got one back reminding her of his feelings. "I love you because I don't know any other way to live, save loving you. When you breathe in, my chest rises, when you fall asleep, my eyelids grow heavy. Goodnight, my sweetest love."

Feeling safe in her grandmother's home, Maepleida then shut down her upper chakras and allowed herself to become completely third dimensional in preparation for the next day, which she would spend entirely with humans.

Had anyone been outside near the garden they would have witnessed a strange thing. In one moment, every single flower suddenly turned its back and leaned away as two entities passed by moving toward the house. Koultar and Limbat, Veldemiron's proxies, grew more confident and arrogant with each step closer to Maepleida. There was little of courtly polish about these two. Koultar's elongated face bordered on the grotesque with its skin sucked too close to the bone, and Limbat's body looked so much like sausages strung together that it would have been funny in a less evil being. They found Maepleida easily in the empty house, and had her in chains before she was barely awake. Unfortunately, she had been sleeping in her third dimensional human body to rest and restore it.

"No use struggling, my pretty," Limbat hissed. "These aren't ordinary chains. You'll find you're powerless to enter your fifth dimensional body or to apparate or even to send a bubble to that handsome twin flame of yours. Come along. No time to waste. Veldemiron is waiting for you." Limbat and Koultar pulled her along by her chains to the nearby country estate of a recently deceased member of the House of Lords.

"Tell your barbarians to take their hands off me," Maepleida said to Veldemiron on being dragged into his presence. Veldemiron nodded and the two rogues released her.

"Welcome, Maepleida. Did you really think I'd let you win that election?" Veldemiron said, his detestation of democracy evident in his tone. "You do understand that it will be forfeit, since you will not be appearing. Too bad, you came so close."

"What do you want, Veldemiron?" Maepleida asked.

"Oh, many things, but I'll start with bringing you over to serve me on the dark side."

"That will never happen. I will never drink from your poison chalice."

"Shut up," Limbat said, thrusting his blunt muzzle into the conversation. Veldemiron shot him a warning look and he lowered his head and pretended to examine the floor, studying it for some hidden message like an old woman who stares at the bottom of her cup to read the message in her tea leaves.

"You'll find I can be very persuasive, Maepleida, given a little time."

Here was the lacuna in his thinking, Maepleida realized. He wouldn't have much time before it was discovered that she was missing. But he read her mind. "Time enough," he said, smiling, "you don't think I'd let a prize like you, a fifth dimensional being with knowledge of the Chohans' plans for Earth, slip-away do you? Come, you're smarter than that." Veldemiron, intending to keep her guessing, then outlined rather than detailed what he had in store for her. He watched for her to sag in the knees, but saw instead her spine straighten and her chin lift. Momentarily he admired her for it, but then wishing to send her a message he struck her hard across the face. Pointing to a long table he instructed Koultar to chain her down. Veldemiron leaned over her and whispered, his hideous, black, foggy lips close to hers, "You swear fealty to me or I will reach through the golden sphere surrounding your body and its merkaba. You know what will happen when I stop your merkaba from spinning."

Maepleida knew this was a dangerous thing to do to any being. Humans could live with their merkabas not spinning for a time, but for most humans to remain healthy their star tetrahedrons needed to be alive and their merkaba needed to keep spinning at nine tenths the speed of light. The star tetrahedron around a fifth dimensional being, even one temporarily in human form, spins not at nine tenths the speed of light, but at the speed of light itself. If it's stopped, the human body which the higher dimensional being is inhabiting will suffer a quick but excruciating death. Maepleida was in her third dimensional body and knew she could not shift to the fifth dimension with the binding chains on.

Veldemiron's foggy black form bent lower over her, and with his voice close to her ear this time he hissed, "I told you this wouldn't take much time. We could do such great things together. Would you like to reconsider joining me or shall I proceed?"

"I will never go over to the dark side."

"A pity, my dear. But at least there'll be one less wanderer to contend with. And one less member in the House of Commons doing the people's work." He laughed his vicious laugh.

Maepleida thought of Heipleido, *my heart's window,* she thought.

"Touching," Veldemiron said, reading her mind.

She shut him out and prepared to face what he was about to do to her. Choosing death at the hands of a monster felt life affirming. She would never give in. Joining him would be living a life that was a continual death. Better to be gone. She knew there was no final death, of this body, yes, but not of her eternal divine being. Her borrowed atoms which comprised her human body would return to the universe to be recycled. True, she would be separated from Heipleido and her fellow wanderers while they completed their mission on Earth, but not forever.

Angry at her composure in the face of his threats, Veldemiron yanked on the chains securing her to the table, tightening them painfully across her body. His own unmitigated self-interest and disregard for all life other than his own made it difficult for him to understand her choice. But he read her well and knew she was not one such as Darpith. No amount of torture would induce her to come to the dark side. She must die.

"Do you have any final words?" he asked her.

"You can kill my body, but that will only free me. Death will carry me into the presence of All That Is."

Enraged by her calm, Veldemiron hissed, "Won't you miss your twin flame, that gorgeous hunk? Perhaps he'll find another here on Earth and forget you."

Maepleida tried to turn her head away from him, but he twisted it back and looked into her emerald eyes as daylight struck them though the large windows. Momentarily captured by their beauty and fearlessness, he fell silent and stood gazing at her, *darkness considering light*. But lest he become enraptured he pulled back, censuring his momentary weakness. Day was dawning now and he must get on with it. Stepping further back from the table, he made sure he was completely outside the field of her merkaba which was comprised of her star tetrahedron and a flat disk, fifty-five feet in diameter, which passed through the star tetrahedron at the base of her spine. Together the star tetrahedron and the disk looked like a flying saucer. Moving back all the way to the wall in the large room, he focused on this flying saucer, straightened his arm, shook out his right hand and from his fingers released a beam of dark energy. Koultar and Limbat backed up and watched, engrossed to the point of mesmerization as he raised his arm and directed the beams toward the base of Maepleida's spine, the center of her merkaba. The ruthlessness of his act shocked even Koultar and Limbat, who shuddered in horror. The effect was like suddenly inserting a long metal bar into the blades of an enormous fan with two sets of counter-rotating blades spinning at the speed of light. The violence shook the whole mansion. Maepleida left her human body.

At that moment Heipleido awoke with a howl of excruciating pain at the base of his spine. Toomeh and Laaroos were by his side in seconds. "It's Maepleida, something has happened to her." He sent her a bubble and the lack of a response confirmed his worse fear. The three of them apparated to the country, into the bedroom where Maepleida should have just been awakening. The bed was cold. And there was a terrible scent in the room.

"I know that scent," Toomeh said. "I smelled it at the London riots when Veldemiron was torturing Darpith and two of Veldemiron's goons arrived to help him. This is the stench of Koultar and Limbat. They have Maepleida, or Veldemiron does."

"Is the scent strong enough to follow?" Heipleido asked with single minded focus. As they followed the scent his mind curved over Maepleida protectively, like the sky curves over the Earth.

The three of them had little difficulty tracking the abductors to a nearby mansion. Koultar and Limbat were a sloppy and arrogant pair. Heipleido recognized it as the home of a recently deceased member of the House of Lords.

"I think it's empty. I don't sense any life energy," Toomeh said.

"I want to check it out," Heipleido answered.

They approached carefully and entered the mansion silently. The odor of Koultar, Limbat and Veldemiron was strong, but they picked up no life force. Moving from room to room they read the energy. When they reached the dining room they found Maepleida's body still chained to the table, lifeless, but warm. Heipleido freed her and gathered her in his arms. "My heart," he whispered.

Laaroos perceived at once that Veldemiron had stopped her star tetrahedron from spinning, killing her.

"Can you reverse this?" Heipleido looked at Laaroos.

"I don't know. I've never done it. But let's get her out of here in case they return."

With Maepleida in his arms, the four of them apparated to the carriage house which had many protections around it so Laaroos could work in safety.

"I'll notify the Chohans," Toomeh said.

"Ask Master Hilarion to come," Laaroos said.

Heipleido laid Maepleida out on their bed and sat beside her lifeless body.

Laaroos ran her hands over Maepleida's body, her fingers acting like little cameras searching for clues to how Veldemiron had done it. "The point of entry was the base of her spine," Laaroos said. "Veldemiron attacked the center of her merkaba and jerked it to a halt with some kind of dark energy."

"Can you bring her back?" Heipleido asked with more pressure then he intended.

They both turned when an oval of emerald light appeared and manifested into Hilarion, who confirmed Laaroos assessment of what had happened. "We can try to flush out the dark energy and restart her merkaba," he told Heipleido. "Since she can't use her breath to balance the polarities in her electrical circuits to cleanse them, you will use your breath to do it, Heipleido. Lie down on your back and we'll place her body over yours. Toomeh, Laaroos and Hilarion lifted Maepleida's body and laid her on her back on top of Heipleido, her head resting on the side of his neck.

"We'll use the seventeen-breath method of starting a human merkaba. The eighteenth breath, the higher dimensional breath, will be up to her if she returns to human form," Hilarion said.

He then directed the three wanderers to visualize everything he was saying and breathe in unison. "With the first six breaths, we'll cleanse her electrical circuits of the dark energy. Focus on all beings as one. Love all beings as one. Visualize Maepleida's Sun tetrahedron facing upward around her body and her Earth tetrahedron facing downward. Fill both tetrahedrons with the energy of lightning. Use rhythmic breaths and place your hands in the appropriate mudra for each circuit, then breathe in and exhale, six times. With each exhalation, the Sun tetrahedron will drop down into the Earth tetrahedron and a stream of muddy light will shoot out the bottom apex of her lower tetrahedron toward the center of the earth."

Hilarion observed them move through the rhythmic breaths, each time the Sun tetrahedron moved down to the apex of the Earth tetrahedron, he saw a dark muddy stream shoot out of Maepleida toward the earth. They had succeeded at least in moving and cleansing her electrical circuits. But could they reestablish the flow of energy through her chakras?

"For the seventh, eighth and ninth breaths," Hilarion continued, "visualize the central tube running from apex to apex in her body. Fill it with lightning energy from above and below. Allow the energy to meet at her naval, forming a small sphere of blue-white light. On the tenth breath, use the inhalation and exhalation to change the light in the sphere from white to golden, then expand it to the size of Leonardo's sphere, enclosing her body in an orb of golden light. For three yogic breaths stabilize this orb. On the fourteenth breath raise the center of the sphere up to her heart. For the last three breaths hold the consciousness of unconditional love for all beings and again visualize Maepleida's star tetrahedron. If this works, next we'll attempt to recreate the counter rotating fields of a living merkaba around her body. For the fifteenth breath, use the code words *equal speed*. Hopefully this will start her tetrahedrons spinning in opposite directions at one third the speed of light. For the sixteenth breath use the Fibonacci ratio 34/21. And for the seventeenth breath use the ratio 9/10, which will instruct her merkaba to spin at 9/10 the speed of light, which is the speed of merkabas of living humans. Let's begin."

Hilarion watched as the three wanderers followed his instructions. Maepleida still looked lifeless. "Remain in meditation, doing yogic breathing," he directed them. Fifteen minutes passed, then an hour. Maepleida remained lifeless.

"Align your will with the will of the Divine in this and all matters," Hilarion told them before reaching to remove Maepleida's body from Heipleido's. Heipleido's arms wrapped around her. "She's not in there," Hilarion said softly to Heipleido, who released the body and allowed Hilarion to shift it off him and lay it out on the bed.

Albus, who had been watching from a nearby chair, jumped onto the bed, curled up on the pillow next to Maepleida's head and began to lick her cheek with his rough kitten tongue. Heipleido looked away.

"Her parents must be frantic by now, realizing she never showed up to stand for the election," Toomeh said. "Shall I call them?"

"No. I'll do it," Heipleido answered. "They'll want her body for a funeral. And we'll have to let them do what humans do. But please ask Soonam, Attivio, Ederah and Bereh to come. Her parents will expect Attivio, Bereh, you and I to be pallbearers."

The third dimensional human in Heipleido burned to hunt down and destroy Veldemiron. The fifth dimensional being knew that even Veldemiron was part of the Divine and served in his own way, and checked his impulse for revenge.

Soonam, Attivio, Ederah and Bereh were there within moments of receiving Toomeh's bubble. They spent the next week helping with funeral arrangements and comforting Maepleida's parents and grandmothers, who were told that she had died of a cerebral aneurism. When the funeral was over they promised Heipleido they would make short work of this mission to save the humans from the dark side, so they could all be reunited with Maepleida in the Fifth Dimension.

Chapter 36

Miquel and Carlos

A week after Maepleida's funeral Miquel and Carlos arrived in London, as planned, and were welcomed by the seven wanderers. When they asked where Maepleida was, Heipleido told them the truth, that her human body had been killed by the dark side because she refused to submit to them, remaining loyal to the light unto her death.

"I will avenge her death!" Miquel said with exhilarating force, and his words were the more intense because they arose from an honorable source. He had watched Maepleida play *Fifth Dimension* countless times. She was his heroine, and he felt he knew her personally. How could such a one be gone from Earth? Now that garden would be forever shut to him.

But Carlos, rather than seeking to avenge her, was confused. "Did she die while playing *Fifth Dimension*? Can that happen? Both Miquel and Carlos were such avid players that they had come to blur the lines in their minds between the game and reality. When the wanderers were playing, the game was reality, and at a preconscious level both Miquel and Carlos understood that.

"She was murdered by a dark lord from Orion while playing a bigger game," Heipleido told them in a voice shorn of all sentimentality. "You'll come to know about this big game at the right moment, as will all humans."

"What do we do now to avenge her?" Miquel asked, lowering his head like a bull.

"We do what we've been doing. We spread the word of *Fifth Dimension* so that all beings awaken to the knowledge of their own divinity and learn how to defend themselves against the dark side," Heipleido answered.

"But where is she now?" Miquel asked.

"She's on Venus, living in the Fifth Dimension, recovering from the damage done to her merkaba," Heipleido told him. "Lord Sananda and Lady Nada have been using the Resurrection Flame to heal her."

"But how do you know that?" Carlos asked.

"Because she visits me in my dreams. She could not sustain life in the third dimension after the attack because the dark energy not only penetrated her human body, but also affected her fifth dimensional merkaba." Heipleido spoke softly out of intense feeling.

"My grandma visited my mom in her dreams after she died," Miquel said.

"Yes, when people leave the third dimension, dreams are one of the easiest ways for them to contact those they love," Ederah explained, jumping in to spare Heipleido.

"But how did Maepleida get to Venus if her merkaba was damaged?" Carlos asked.

"You know about merkabas? You've learned much from playing Fifth Dimension," Ederah said. "Lord Kumara, who you've met overseeing *Fifth Dimension*, came for her and carried her light body in his merkaba."

Heipleido tried to brush the sadness from his lips as he listened to Ederah talk about Maepleida.

Laaroos came to his rescue, "We can talk more over dinner, but let's get you two settled in your rooms first."

She had added two more rooms to the carriage house, one for her mother, Sally, who had recently arrived from Washington, D.C., and one for the boys, in addition to the two they always had on hand for the wanderers from New York. Nothing was visible from the outside as the inside grew more spacious. While Laaroos showed Miquel and Carlos their quarters, Sally got busy in the kitchen whipping up dinner using a combination of her catering skills and various spells and incantations acquired many moons ago on Arcturus.

Miquel and Carlos unpacked their few belongings in a state of ecstasy. Despite the sad news of Maepleida, being in proximity to these light beings had brought them to near rapture. Though they appeared human, it was clear to both young men that there was something other-worldly about these beings who called themselves wanderers. Toomeh knocked to tell them dinner was ready. In honor of the boys, Sally had created a Mexican feast. The meal began with pozole. While they ate their soup, discussion about Maepleida continued.

"If Lord Sananda and Lady Nada resurrect her merkaba, couldn't she come back to the third dimension?" Miquel asked.

"That would be against the laws that govern Earth. The quarantine forbids it. Maepleida was born here as a human baby for this lifetime, therefore she was permitted to live here. To incarnate again she would have to come again as a newborn. Beings from other dimensions are not allowed to interfere with humans unless they incarnate as human."

"But Darpith and Veldemiron and their slaves weren't born here," Miquel insisted, "they're from Orion.

"You're right, they weren't born here, but they slip through the quarantine. They come and go only as opportunity presents itself," Soonam explained.

"Can't Maepleida slip through the quarantine?" Carlos asked.

"Perhaps at some point, briefly, but not until she's healed," Soonam told him.

At the thought of this Miquel's face crinkled into a smile. "I bet she'll find a way. Maybe the Council will give her a pass."

The soup finished, Sally brought out cemita with milanesa, chilaquiles, cochinita pibil, and flautas with guacamole. Miquel and Carlos, grateful for the sumptuous banquet, ate with relish and gratitude. And when Sally produced churros with chocolate sauce for desert their eyes lit up. With their bellies full and their shirts powdered with crumbs, Miquel and Carlos were the picture of contentment. The wanderers delighted in them, in their simplicity and innocence, their joy and gratitude.

After dinner, Heipleido stood up and hung over the back of his chair to say goodnight. Drooping there, he resembled nothing so much as a weeping willow. He wanted to be alone to think about Maepleida, and withdrew to his room. Nothing about her was extinguished or forgotten in him. She was a soul made for his soul, a deep spring in him, an invincible love. When he had gone, the others discussed plans for the visit. Would they like to attend a soccer match? Visit Buckingham Palace or London Bridge? Go to a show? See Winsor Castle?

"What we'd really like, is to go to your gaming center and play *Fifth Dimension* with you," Miquel said.

"We might be able to arrange that," Toomeh said smiling at the two of them. "But tonight, tell us how you've been spreading word of *Fifth Dimension*. Ederah and Laaroos say it's being played everywhere at gaming centers in Mexico, Central America and South America."

"Yes, even small towns now have gaming centers," Miquel said. "We asked the owner of our gaming center to put a monitor in the window, so kids who couldn't afford to play could at least watch. He did, and the idea caught on and other gaming centers started doing it. Many centers videotape the games whenever any of you are playing and show them in their window monitors over and over. The eight of you are superheroes in Mexico. The game you played at the Mexican/U.S. border, where you fought the reptile and freed the soul of the little girl and straightened out the records, and reunited children with their families, is the most replayed game. The other video that gamers watch over and over is the one where you went back to Venus as it was two billion years ago. No one walks by the window monitors now without at least pausing to check out what's on. New centers are opening every day and some owners are offering times when kids with no money can play for free. The owners have enough business and want to give back. All the kids want to fight on the side of the light."

After Miquel and Carlos had gone to bed, the others discussed how to arrange a game where Miquel and Carlos could play with them. The wanderers usually played alone, with the humans only permitted to watch. Because the wanderers left their bodies at the gaming center and actually traveled to the location, and the humans stayed in their bodies and played a simulated version of fighting for the light, it would be tricky to play together.

"We'll have to ask the Chohans if it's possible," Attivio said. "From the intel we got today from Lord Lanto and Shoshimi it sounds like things are heating up. There is more malfeasance on the part of the U.S. president. Without Iranian provocation, he's beating the drums of war to stir up hatred against Iran. Meanwhile North Korea is shooting off ballistic missiles in violation of international law and he looks the other way as Japan and South Korea, in particular, grow more anxious."

Bereh leaned forward, "Do the Chohans believe that the North Korean leader is acting on his own, with no influence so far from the dark lords?"

"Yes, Attivio answered, "but they feel it's only a matter of time before one of the dark lords, from either Orion or Draco, takes control of him, and of the other three fascists as well: the Russian, the Saudi and the U.S. president."

"Since Darpith's exile the U.S. president has been carrying on his monstrous perfidy himself, getting inhumane ideas from the hosts of his favorite, bigoted, racist news channel," Laaroos added.

"And where is Veldemiron in all of this?" Ederah wondered aloud.

"Lord Lanto conjectured that Veldemiron hasn't felt it necessary to take control of the president as he perpetrates enough damage to the light on his own," Bereh told her. "He also said that Veldemiron has recently become aware of that slimy pair from Draco who run the senate, Lynseyhiz and Mitchhiz, and he's planning to use them as long as he can to further his own plans before eliminating them."

"I missed some of what Lord Lanto said after he told us that Darpith had escaped from captivity in the Andromeda galaxy. My mind kept going back to that, wondering what Darpith will do," Ederah said.

"He'll probably be gunning for Veldemiron," Bereh told her.

"None of us has engaged with *Fifth Dimension* since Maepleida's death," Toomeh said, "it's time we did, but the question is, can we play with Miquel and Carlos as they've requested?"

"The Chohans will send us where we're needed," Laaroos said, "and Miquel and Carlos can participate from the gaming center."

"Will they notice that under our gear it's just the shell of our bodies sitting in the chairs at the gaming center?" Ederah asked.

"We'll give them strict instructions not to move from their seats or speak to or to touch us during the game because it would be dangerous," Laaroos said.

"I'd like to get a crack at Veldemiron," Attivio said, "and his lackeys, Koultar and Limbat."

"We need to bide our time," Bereh cautioned. "He's expecting us to come after him now and he'll be laying traps. Better to wait and strike when the iron is cold."

Soonam had been unusually quiet, thinking about what Lord Lanto had told them about Maepleida, that she was the first awakened wanderer of their group of several thousand, who had been born on Earth twenty-one years ago, to return to the Fifth Dimension. Soonam felt her loss like a crater in her heart. It had been fun to be on Earth in the Third Dimension with her, even for such a short time. Maepleida was volcanic in her passions and full of life in both dimensions, not to mention a fierce and creative warrior. Well, she had shown Veldemiron one thing. Awakened light beings cannot be harvested for the dark side. Almost all of the wanderers in their large group were now awake and working all over the globe. Lord Lanto said it was the most successful group of wanderers ever to incarnate on Earth. He reported that the vibration on Earth was rising, despite the dictators, the proliferation of right wing hate groups and the terrorist attacks by radical religious sects. All the Chohans believed that consciousness was rising on Earth. The poisons were hatching out to be cleared, and each new generation of humans was more centered in the heart, more conscious of taking care of their planet, saving their oceans and atmosphere and forests. And they were more conscious, too, of a brotherhood among men. Soonam turned over all this in her mind while the others spoke. At last she joined the discussion. "Maybe Darpith will take care of Veldemiron for us."

"He won't have any slaves to help him and Veldemiron has already managed to slip several of his minions through the quarantine, so he'll have the advantage," Attivio told her.

"But Darpith is fueled by rage," Soonam said, "and Lynseyhiz and Mitchhiz haven't yet chosen a dark lord to back. Maybe Darpith will manage to commandeer them. He already knows them from when he had control of the president before Veldemiron defeated and exiled him."

"You have a point," Attivio conceded.

"I'm for bed," Toomeh said standing up, stretching and reaching for Laaroos' hand.

"Me too, Ederah said, "I know that there's no death, and we will see her again, but I can't shake my sadness that Maepleida won't be with us for the great battle and the mass awakening of the humans."

Bereh leaned over and kissed her forehead. "Come my darling, I'll tuck you in."

Attivio and Soonam were the only two still up when a violet oval appeared in the room and materialized into Saint Germain and Portia, wearing their high collared, sweeping, violet robes.

"Greetings beloveds," Portia began. "We come with a request that you all report to the gaming center tomorrow at 10:00 a.m. Please let the others know. There is a plan to bomb the great Mosque of Paris, located in the 5th arrondissement. Several wanderers stationed in Paris have penetrated the right-wing group responsible and they are attempting to thwart the plan by disrupting the completion of the bombs, but should they fail or be discovered, we will need you to go to the mosque to thwart this attempt."

Unable to sleep, Heipleido walked into the living room carrying Albus next to his heart, and caught the end of the communication. He bowed to both Chohans. Portia smiled at him lovingly. As she addressed him her hand went to the Maltese cross hanging over her heart, "Greetings, Heipleido."

Saint Germain then spoke. "The bombing is planned to go off during prayer time to injure the most people. We understand that Miquel and Carlos want to play with you. They must remain in London at the gaming center if the seven of you are needed in Paris. El Morya and Amerissis will direct the operation tomorrow and will assign Miquel and Carlos to be lookouts."

"Is this bombing the work of Veldemiron?" Heipleido asked.

"We believe it is," Lady Portia told Heipleido. "But we don't expect him to be there. His part was putting the idea in their heads to blow themselves up along with the mosque."

The next morning when Amerissis and El Morya, Chohans of the Blue Flame of the Will of the Divine, came on the screen, they were all in their gear and Miquel and Carlos had been given their instructions. Miquel smiled when he saw that El Morya and Amerissis would be leading the game. Although he knew the Chohans of all seven rays by sight and had played under the direction of each of them many times, he felt the most connection with the Chohans of the Blue Ray. Amerissis filled the screen, the flame rising up from her third eye blazed as she informed them that Veldemiron had discovered the wanderers who had infiltrated the bombers' group and had taken them prisoner, directing Hannitor to torture them into joining the dark side.

"It's up to you now to stop the bombing," she told the London group. She then reminded Miquel and Carlos to keep their eyes on the screen and their hands on their controls and at no time to speak to or touch any of the wanderers during the game, as it could distract or harm them. They would function as on-screen sentries posted at the entrance of the mosque and were to send an infrared flare into the mosque to warn the wanderers if any of the dark lords or their minions approached. Amerissis gave them the code to ignite the flare and explained that it would be visible only to higher dimensional beings. When the mosque came on the screen she positioned them. As she did this the seven wanderers, dressed as devote Moslems, apparated to Paris, and knelt in prayer at strategic positions around the mosque. Ederah alone did not kneel but made herself invisible and searched the mosque for the bombers. She felt for the misguided youths, who thought they were about to die. She might be able to recognize them by looking for anxious young white men disguised as Moslems. She spotted a jumpy guy and followed his eyes across the room to another boy, who also looked anxious. By watching their eyes, she found all four of them and telegraphed their positions to the wanderers. They were probably waiting for the Mosque to fill up before detonating their bombs, she thought.

Heipleido had an idea. "Ederah, can you remain invisible and tell each of the bombers that you are a divine messenger and that there's been a change in plans. Maybe they'll go for it, since they all look scared to die."

"What kind of messenger?" Ederah telegraphed.

"One from their own Christian god, an angel sent to save them. Go up to each of them and speak while remaining invisible, tell them Jesus does not want them to die today. Then instruct them to leave the mosque immediately, and they will be given the new plan. If any of them looks doubtful, Toomeh will shape shift you into an angel long enough for them to catch a glimpse and be convinced."

"What if they panic?" Bereh telegraphed.

"It is a chance," Toomeh agreed.

"Ederah, apparate immediately if any of them looks like he's about to ignite his bomb," Bereh telegraphed.

"Yes, we will all have to apparate if it comes to that," Attivio agreed.

Miquel and Carlos, at their posts, listened in awe. Amerissis had enabled the controls so that they could hear the wanderers' telegraphed communications.

"There's no time to lose," Heipleido cautioned, "the mosque is filling up."

Ederah approached the bomber who she judged to be the leader. He looked shocked and frightened when he heard her disembodied voice. She felt Toomeh shapeshift her into an angel and she allowed herself to be momentarily visible to the boy, shocking him further. He motioned to the other three with his eyes and she telegraphed her message into their heads, hoping they would pick it up. Two of them nodded to their leader and began to rise, the third hesitated and Ederah approached him, making herself visible as Toomeh again shapeshifted her into an angel. When he saw her, he, too, rose, and the four of them began to make their way to the exit.

When they were nearly at the door, an infrared flare appeared. Heipleido flew past the four bombers and out the door. A humanoid-shaped black cloud was approaching the mosque. Veldemiron. Heipleido summoned the diamond ray and felt it pulsing though his fifth dimensional body, down his arms to his fingertips. Of all the rays, the dark lords hated and feared the diamond ray most. The light of it was unbearable to them as it burned through their negative polarization, weakening them. Heipleido flew at Veldemiron, shooting the diamond ray forty feet across the space between them right into the center of Veldemiron's blackness. He writhed in pain and surprise, spinning and shooting back his poison, but Heipleido was faster. Ducking and dancing in space, he struck Veldemiron again and again. Meanwhile Ederah and Toomeh continued to control the bombers with instructions and angel visions. When they had them outside, Ederah told them to remove the bombs, lay them on the ground and disable them. As a final flourish to convince them never to try this again, Toomeh shape shifted himself into a huge devil with red eyes, claws, horns and a tail, and told them if they ever even threatened to harm another living thing, be it as small as an ant, he would come for them. While Bereh guarded the disabled bombs, Soonam, Attivio, and Laaroos stood ready to aid Heipleido. But Heipleido was getting the better of Veldemiron, who screamed in fury and pain each time the light of the diamond ray pierced him weakening him and depolarizing his negativity until he was so fearful of depolarizing completely that he apparated. Heipleido turned to the others. "Now, when Darpith finds him it will be a fairer fight."

El Morya directed them to return to the gaming center and informed them that a team of wanderers from Madrid had captured Hannitor and freed the wanderers he'd been torturing. El Morya, Amerissis, and especially Heipleido, thanked Miquel and Carlos for their good work.

"Without your warning, I wouldn't have been able to get the jump on Veldemiron and depolarize him so much," Heipleido told them.

"And if Heipleido hadn't engaged Veldemiron in battle, he definitely would have prevented us from getting the bombs," Ederah said. "Well done both of you."

For their part Miquel and Carlos were over the moon. They'd watched in awe as Ederah tricked the bombers and as Toomeh shapeshifted first her, then himself. They'd barely breathed as they witnessed Heipleido wield the diamond ray against Veldemiron. And when they observed Soonam, Attivio and Laaroos's restraint in allowing Heipleido to face Veldemiron without interfering, even when Veldemiron several times came close to hitting him with a poison ray, they marveled at the self-discipline.

"Was it Veldemiron who killed Maepleida?" Miquel asked as he removed his gear.

"He was the one who hurt her, but he didn't kill her," Heipleido said. "She can never be killed. Nor will she ever tremble in the face of evil. She is an enlightened being. You also can never be killed, only your third dimensional body will die, Miquel. You are an eternal light being, as is every human. Most of them just don't know it yet. That's why we need *Fifth Dimension*, to help awaken people to who they truly are."

"Even so, I want to avenge her," Miquel insisted.

That afternoon *Le Monde* ran the story that four disabled bombs had been mysteriously discovered outside the Great Mosque.

Chapter 37

Politics and a Book Tour

"The tempo of things has gotten crazy," Soonam said. "Every other minute there's a new scandal with this president. And just as troubling is the kaleidoscope of confusion he creates by playing on people's grievances without addressing them."

"Do you still think getting involved in politics is the best way to help?" Attivio asked her.

"Yes, if I support a candidate who will serve all the people, someone who will clean up the rubble, prejudice and malice created by the current occupant of the White House."

"Have you decided who?"

Soonam looked up from the carpet of soil where she was kneeling planting basil, mint, rosemary and chives. She brushed her hair back off her forehead leaving a smudge on her face. "I like the young, gay mayor from South Bend, Indiana. Every time I hear him speak I feel his inherent goodness toward all beings. But I'm not sure he has a chance."

Attivio squatted down next to Shiva, who was busy digging a hole, while Mona eyed him from her patch of sun on the back steps as if to say, "What are you doing that senseless activity for?"

"Nature is the best tonic on Earth." Soonam sighed as she pushed a small basil plant into the soil, pressed it down into the earth and watered it."

"Here," Attivio said, "hand me your watering can and I'll refill it. And does it really matter whether or not your mayor has a chance? If you believe in him, fight for him. Help him get his message out. Let people see his goodness. Even if he can't win, his ideas can change consciousness."

"You're right, of course. I see that now that you say it."

Attivio watched her making little holes and pushing the plantings in and patting them down. There was music in her movements. Her shoulders, her hands, even her back, sang as she worked. She was a woman and a poem. With every movement, she inscribed her beauty on the air. As his eyes traveled up her back to her hair, which itself looked like a golden plant, he wondered how Heipleido could bear the separation from Maepleida, from that one Soul, in all universes, who he had admitted to the innermost chambers of his being, who alone inhabited a private world with him, where joy and ease flowed between them. Before they left London, he'd asked Heipleido how he stood it.

"It's being honest about my pain that makes me invincible," he'd answered. "I'm a restless flame without her, but I'll use that flame in battle with the dark side."

Attivio pulled his thoughts back to the present moment. They'd been back in New York for a week already. It was time to think about the tour to promote his book on wanderers. But first, lunch. "It's nearly three. Are you in the mood for avocado toast?"

Soonam smiled up at him. "Just what I was thinking of."

"I'll make it while you finish up."

Take Mona and Shiva inside with you. I want to feed the birds."

When they were gone, Soonam stood up and reached into her pocket. She let a few crumbs drop at her feet to call the starlings and sparrows over. Then she placed a crumb between her thumb and pointer and a small starling flew up from the ground and took it from her. She didn't stop until each of the small birds had eaten a fat crumb from her fingers. For a moment, a memory passed down a sweet corridor of her mind and she saw herself and Attivio on Venus, high up in a tree, face to face with a tiny colorful bird, the day they visited Ederah's parents. A soft chirp restored her to the present and she took another crumb between her fingers. The delight of the starlings and sparrows flying up to her could have engaged her all day had not Attivio called from the porch that lunch was ready. He watched as she danced toward him, over the tender blue of the back porch, the full skirt of her dress flowing around her legs in a rhythm counter to her feet.

Between bites of avocado toast and sips of lemonade, he told her what was being planned for his book tour. "It's not the usual spots, since this isn't a mainstream book. To begin, they want me to go to Mount Shasta, because of Telos, and then to come back East and go on to Washington, D.C."

"I get Telos, but why Washington?" Soonam asked.

"Plans for the city of Washington, D.C. were based on the great cities of light which existed in the Amazon basin during the golden age of South America. Saint Germain worked with the wanderer known as George Washington. Together they lowered the matrix for the city into form. Washington was supposed to be a city of light, a city for the brotherhood of all men."

"That's interesting, given that it's now referred to as a swamp. Is that the whole tour, two cities?"

"No. We're also discussing Palenque in Mexico, the site of the ancient Mayan royal residence, even though it only has a population of 120,000. And Glastonbury, England for an outdoor sunset reading on the Tor, the site of ancient Avalon."

"These would be mystical events then, not just readings."

"That's the idea."

"It sounds perfect. When do you start?"

"Soon, I think. I should hear something today or tomorrow, once they've settled arrangements. Soonam, since Maepleida left the third dimension we've all been careful to always be with at least one other wanderer. I can't leave you alone. I want you to come with me on this tour and when it's finished, in a month or so, I'll go with you to support whichever candidate you choose."

Soonam leaned forward and breathed in the fragrance of

the peonies in the vase before her. She turned to face the open window they had been lunching by and inhaled the perfume of the peony bush itself, mixed with the scent of mint and basil. "Should we consult the Chohans about this?"

"Soonam, you know they'll leave it up to us."

She stood and picked up the vase of deep pink peonies and carried it to the sink to add more water. When she'd filled the vase she said, "You're right. And I haven't even got a plan yet anyway for how to help with the election. We'll just need to have someone for Mona and Shiva if my father isn't back from Europe yet."

Attivio came up behind her and caught her around the waist, kissing her hair, her ears and neck with so much enthusiasm that the cold water from the vase sloshed onto her dress. He took the vase from her hands and set it on the counter. "You're all wet," he said, unbuttoning her dress and exposing her full, round breasts to his lips. She let out a sigh as his teeth gently closed around one nipple then the other, tugging her closer to him. He undid his pants, lifted her dress above her waist, and entered her, blessing her again for her habit of never wearing underwear when they were at home.

A few blocks north of them, Ederah watched Tiger and Lily leap about trying to catch a bee who had mysteriously got into their apartment and was romancing a blossom on their flowering lime tree. Bereh sat nearby working on his laptop, trying to solve a mathematical problem in his hypothesis about why dark matter is invisible in the third dimension. Ederah called his attention to the drama at the lime tree. "My money is on the kittens," he said, closing his laptop.

"No, I'm not having it," Ederah returned. She stood, opened the window, ushered the bee outside into the late afternoon sun, and watched as he flew toward the Hudson River, alive.

"Come and sit beside me," he said. "What's the news from Laaroos? Have Miquel and Carlos sent any new reports?"

"They think we're nearly at the point where *Fifth Dimension* will go viral with millennials and teens in Mexico, Central and South American. But Laaroos is concerned about something else. Heipleido. He's stopped work on his bill for The House of Lords and hasn't even been back there since Maepleida left Earth. She and Bereh are bringing him to New York this evening so we can all be together for a bit."

"He seemed so strong at first, so invincible," Bereh said. "He needs to get involved again with something. He was magnificent at the mosque. When is the next time we're all playing?"

"Nothing is scheduled at the moment. Attivio will be heading off for his book tour. Soonam's going back and forth about which candidate to work for, the new medical students have just arrived at Laaroos' hospital, Toomeh is working on a painting of higher dimensional beings for school, a diptych, I believe. I have a couple of modeling assignments which I can't duck out of, and your head is deep in theories about dark matter. At the moment, we're all focused on our third dimensional lives."

Bereh nodded. "Come on, let's stroll over to Soonam and Attivio's. The light on the river is beautiful this time of day."

"Good idea. Toomeh, Laaroos and Heipleido should be arriving soon," Ederah said.

They walked south on the Highline, enjoying the flowers in the early dusk. It was the time of day when the flowers glowed.

The London wanderers were already there, sitting in the soft green evening light under the trees at the back of the garden when Ederah and Bereh came through the screen door. Ederah embraced Heipleido, wishing to offer him, from her inexhaustible store of love, some small gift to heal the temporary wreckage of his heart.

He acknowledged her intention with a nod of his proud, elegant head. He couldn't tell her that even to think of Maepleida for a fleeting second was to be cast into a memory so real it might be as if he was still dusted with pollen from her lips. Instead he spoke softly of how warm the evening was and how sweet the air. The quiet conversation allowed them all to feel their sadness drawing them closer together. In the background, the crickets took up their song, telling their own story.

Soonam turned to Heipleido. "You have worn out your heart and head with love."

The words had barely left her lips when a bubble arrived from Saint Germain and Portia.

Earlier that day all the Chohans had met on Titan and had chosen two issues for the wanderers to focus on immediately. These priorities were sent to the wanderers in a world-wide bubble.

"Greetings Wanderers. The Chohans of the Seven Rays have a new directive. We wish you to focus on two issues in particular as you continue to work to awaken the humans to their divinity. The first is global warming and the second is preventing the hacking of elections. The time traveling back to Venus in the third dimension helped bring awareness to global warming but we need other efforts as well. One way to prevent further damage to Earth, her atmosphere, oceans and forests, is to elect leaders who will pass legislation to protect her. For this, elections must be secure against hacking by dark players, both human and nonhuman. It will not be just the Russians who hack the next time. The Saudis and the Chinese are getting in the game, too, as is the UAE, and there will be others as well. The Russians interfered not only in U.S. elections, but also in both U.K. and Israeli elections. In the United Kingdom they pushed for Brexit, hoping to foster hatred of immigrants, and to weaken both Britain and the European Union. In Israel, they worked to keep an accused criminal in power, because they believe his right wing policies and harsh treatment of the Palestinians will aid their plan for world domination. All wanderers on Earth will now focus on global warming and safe and fair elections, particularly in countries where autocrats are attempting to seize power. The United States president has already sold high tech bomb parts to Saudi Arabia so they can target innocent civilians and perpetuate famine in Yemen. The Russian dictator continues to fight in Ukraine and to arrest, beat up and jail journalists who expose his corruption. Nobody wants to live with a boot on his neck, but many are afraid to speak up, especially in North Korea, Saudi Arabia and China. Despite the risk, there are courageous protestors. For example, the people of Hong Kong, in huge numbers, are protesting against the Chinese for seizing bookstores, and extraditing and imprisoning their owners. The Sudanese have ousted Omar al-Bashir after thirty years of his atrocities. However, things are far from settled in the Sudan, and we have directed wanderers working in other parts of Africa to go to Sudan to help stem the tide of civilian murders and to restore internet to the Sudanese people. In Russia, too, there are protests, most recently over the arrest of a journalist who dared to expose corruption. However, in other places, like Saudi Arabia, even when a ten-year-old child is accused of speaking against the government and condemned to death, no one has the courage to speak out. Their ruthless crown prince is backed by the current United States president, who colluded with him to murder and dismember a Washington Post journalist. These events can make one feel like there is no progress toward an enlightened planet. Take heart, this is but all the evils hatching out to be seen and healed. Your fellow wanderers and many humans are at work all over the planet to turn the tide against the darkness. There has even been some success in slowing down global warming by wanderers and humans exposing corporations responsible for the large-scale deforestation in Brazil, Peru, Bolivia and Indonesia. As consciousness grows about the cost to the environment of the production of agricultural commodities like beef, soya, palm oil, rubber, and cocoa, many humans will change their life styles. Progress has also been made, thanks to the work of a wanderer making electric cars. The tide is turning against the use of fossil fuels. But, we don't have forever, time is limited for humans to save their planet and to learn to love all beings as one, so they can make the jump to the Fourth Dimension. Continue your work with renewed emphasis on these two issues of global warming and secure elections. Peace be in your hearts. All is well."

When the message ended a silence fell over the garden. Soonam sat still holding a little reed fan she had been using to fan herself and thought over which candidate would best serve these two priorities. Attivio wondered if his book about the wanderers' work on Earth focused enough on global warming and safe elections. Both Laaroos and Ederah silently considered how to get more people involved with *Fifth Dimension* to help with these two priorities. Though there were wanderers already in place there, Toomeh and Bereh couldn't help thinking of the horrific human suffering in places like Yemen, Sudan, Syria and North Korea, and wanting to do something more immediate to stop it. Heipleido wanted to dive into the action against the dark players wherever he could. Right now, the suffering in Sudan was on his mind. Toomeh picked up his thought. "We're not assigned to Africa, Heipleido. Our territory is Europe and North America."

Heipleido nodded.

Soonam stood up and set her little reed fan on her garden chair. "Who's for something long and cool? Attivio made some strawberry lemonade."

Bereh offered to help her and the two of them headed for the back steps. Shiva, always ready for a trip to the kitchen, followed them inside. Soonam switched on the lamp over the kitchen counter and a pool of warm yellow light spilled out the screen door and down the porch steps onto the peony bush. Bereh re-emerged a few minutes later with seven tall glasses and a sweating pitcher on a tray. Soonam stopped to pick fresh mint leaves to add to each drink. As they sipped their lemonade, conversation began to gently flow. Heipleido experienced the music of their mixed voices like a warm stream melting the frozen sea inside him. Soonam's was the voice of a dove, Ederah's that of a mermaid. When Laaroos chimed in, her voice affected him like a cool hand on a fevered brow. Underneath these magical feminine sounds ran the strength and restraint of Toomeh's words, the confidence and amiability in Attivio's voice and the dignity in the cadence of Bereh's speech. What Heipleido felt for Maepleida was a titanic love but here in the garden, listening to the concert of his fellow wanderers' voices, was another kind of love. And Heipleido cherished it.

Chapter 38

Avalon

Attivio's book events in both Telos and Palenque, the site of the ancient Mayan royal residence, both had a touch of other worldly magic about them, but the event in Washington, D.C. lacked any numinous quality. At least it had drawn enough people to fill the venue. So far on the tour there had there been no interference from Veldemiron or his minions. The next stop was Glastonbury, or as the goddesses called it, Avalon. Attivio would give a sunset reading on the Glastonbury Tor. People attending could stop at the Mirror Pools and then the Chalice Well for a drink of water before circling the terraced hill to the top of the Tor.

On the day of the reading Soonam and Attivio arrived early and climbed the Tor. When they reached the top, they looked down over the summer sea surrounded by tall reeds and shrouded in mist. For a moment Soonam imagined she could see a line of young priestesses, robed in plain hooded cloaks, walking along the water's edge, the waving reeds brushing their legs. She saw these daughters of the Holy Isle carrying boughs of juniper and hazel, and a little salt and oil, on their way to make an offering or perform some ritual in honor of the Great Mother. In a past life, when Amerissis was incarnated as Guinevere, she had once wandered too far into the mist and lost her way between the two worlds. Soonam recounted this to Attivio explaining that it was a young priestess of Avalon, and sister to King Arthur, who had found her and led her back through the mist.

"Will Amerissis or any of the other Chohans come this evening?" Soonam asked Attivio.

"Were you thinking of anyone in particular?"

"Amerissis, but really the feminine aspects of each of the seven rays. This is an enchanted isle, home to the priestesses of the old religion."

Attivio smiled at her. "That would be divine," he said pulling her down on the grass beside him. They lay back, side by side on the warm earth, feeling the late afternoon sun on their faces, the grass tickling the backs of their necks, and gazed up at the blue sky. There are moments when the world dissolves and just breathing is enough, as all the tessellated facets of our lives lose their hold on us. For what seemed a long time they lay in the grass, drifting.

The sound of voices called them back to the present and they sat up. It was Attivio's publicist scoping things out and telling his assistant where to set up the little platform on which Attivio would sit for the reading. Seeing them in the grass, he walked over. "Strange place isn't it, feels like chivalry and superstition are still comingled here."

"It's perfect," Attivio said.

"As you don't want to use a microphone we're putting you over there, where the most people will be able to get close. We'll begin in about twenty minutes, while we still have light."

Soonam left Attivio to get set up and walked over to watch the people climbing up the winding path encircling the Tor. Heipleido, Laaroos and Toomeh spotted her. Heipleido waved his long arm in the air to catch her attention. She danced, more than walked, over to embrace them, her gauzy summer dress fluttering about her legs. They all flopped down in the soft grass to catch up while they waited for Attivio to begin reading. Before long they were surrounded by a large group. When he climbed onto the platform and sat cross legged, a silence fell over the crowd and the sweet song of the crickets could be heard. Soonam smiled up at him when he sought her eyes in the audience. He began:

The sky was pink, streaked with gold, as Ederah and Bereh, two natives of Venus, walked along in the throng heading toward the archway into the temple. Green skinned and gold toned beings, some

no more than four feet tall, walked beside black, brown, red and white
ones, some standing more than fourteen feet high. Those with eyes like
melting gold embraced those whose eyes resembled drenched violets.
Many were bipedal, but scattered through the crowd were tri-pedal
and quadrupedal beings as well. Some had tentacles and sensory spots
rather than eyes and ears with which to perceive their worlds. But all
of them had come to Venus for the same purpose. A call had gone out
across the universe from The Council of Nine asking for volunteers for
a mission to Earth.

As she listened to Attivio's voice, Soonam observed a line of
figures in hooded robes moving, as if in ancient time, toward the
platform where he sat. They formed a semicircle behind him and
then, one by one, their hoods and gray robes vanished to reveal
their magnificence.

First, Amerissis unveiled herself and stood shimmering in
white, a six-inch flame rising from her third eye, her sword held
upright before her in her two hands. To gaze on her was to have
one's emotional balance restored, to feel one's will come into
alignment with the Will of the Divine. This gift of emotional
balance she freely bestowed on all those present for the reading.
Soonam looked around to see if the audience could see the
goddesses. Toomeh, Laaroos and Heipleido nodded to her, but
no one else seemed able to see them with their eyes, though
something was washing over all of them creating a feeling of
magic.

Next to Amerissis stood Lady Ruth, twin flame of Paul the
Venetian and Chohan of the Pink Ray of Cosmic Love. From her
emanated the scent of roses which opened every heart and swept
from it the fear of loving. Though unable to see her, the listeners
visibly relaxed as Lady Ruth, resplendent in pink robes with
aquamarines around her collar and hem, stood wielding the ray
of cosmic love to heal all heartache they carried in the tissue of
their physical vehicles.

Beside Lady Ruth stood Lady Nada, who had once walked

the Earth as Mary Magdalene, twin flame of Lord Sananda, then known as Jesus. Nada's long red hair fell to her waist, partly covering her violet and gold robes. Her skin looked as if it had been soaked in flowers. Gazing at Nada, Soonam felt the masculine and feminine within herself harmonize at a higher frequency. Nada directed the gold flame of resurrection to all present bringing into balance their masculine and feminine aspects, creating a new ease in their beings.

Next in line stood the Goddess Amutreya, Chohan of the Ascension Flame. A polished snow quartz rested over her third eye purifying all who gazed on her. For this evening, she permitted it to purify not only all who could see her, but all those on the Tor. Amutreya worked with her twin flame, Lord Serapis Bey, helping to ready as many humans as possible to hold sufficient light in their vehicles so they could ascend to the fourth dimension along with planet Earth.

The fifth in the line of goddesses was Portia, Chohan of the Violet Flame of Transmutation and twin flame of Saint Germain. Around her neck hung a Maltese cross on a chain of amethysts and between her palms she held a golden star tetrahedron. Soonam moved her eyes a few times between Portia's violet eyes and the tetrahedron in her hands, finally resting her gaze on Portia's eyes which seemed to say to her, *together we will usher in the seventh golden age on Earth*. Soonam bowed her head in acknowledgement. Portia offered the gift of subconsciously reminding all the listeners present that they were each surrounded by a star tetrahedron which could be activated to help them travel anywhere in the universe.

Last in the line was Shoshimi, standing still and strong, like a mountain, a gold circlet around her head held her long black hair in place. Representing the Ray of Illumination and Wisdom, her presence felt like cool mountain air penetrating and enhancing one's being. Shoshimi offered the gifts of strength and patience. Soonam pulled her gaze back from Shoshimi and looked on all six of the goddesses at once, and felt the power and beauty of the numinous feminine sweep through her. A moment later they were gone into the mist.

Attivio finished reading and greeted his audience. Once the last few stragglers had made their way down the Tor, the five wanderers stretched out on the grass in the evening light and watched as fireflies began to dance in the air around them.

"Were you aware of the Goddesses behind you while you were reading?" Laaroos asked Attivio.

"I was, and I felt their support and their effect on the audience even though they were invisible to them."

A silence then fell over them as they sat on the Tor amid the fireflies in the growing dark. After a while Heipleido spoke.

"I'd like to visit the mirror pool before we leave Avalon."

They rose and made their way down the path encircling the Tor until they reached the mirror pool. Heipleido took a small pouch from his pocket and opened it. He placed a pinch of salt and a few drops of oil on the surface of the water, and lay small twigs of juniper and hazel beside it as an offering. In his heart, he held the wish to see Maepleida. The others stepped back when Heipleido bent forward to gaze into the pool. The water rippled then stilled and an image began to appear. It was the face of Maepleida, smiling at him. He looked into her emerald eyes with an invincible love, wishing to offer her from the treasury of his being his steadfast strength. He could see that she was recovering under the care of Kumara and Venus. She beat inside him like a second heart and as her image began to fade he trembled at the memory of her lips.

When he stepped away from the mirror pool, Soonam came forward and received from his hands the little pouch of salt and the small bottle of oil. She made her offering and leaned down to observe. The surface stilled, then the scene of a rally in South Carolina appeared. The U.S. president was on stage with life-size posters of four young democratic congresswomen with targets on their backs. As he egged the crowd on they chanted, *"Send her back, send her back."* No one could pretend he didn't have his reckless side, watching him thrust the blunt muzzle of his racism into the crowd. Soonam pulled away from the scene in horror, resolved to fight his re-election with everything she had.

Attivio took the salt and oil from her hands and made an offering. The mirror showed him a movie set where his book about the wanderers was being shot. He was speaking to the director, looking directly at his face when he saw it begin to twitch and the eyes roll back. It was then that he saw Darpith trying to enter the director's head. Attivio must have let out a sound for Soonam was instantly at his side, but the scene had vanished. The surface of the mirror pool was still.

Toomeh took the salt and oil from his hands and gave them to Laaroos. When she gazed at the surface she saw herself on the children's cancer ward at the bedside of a little girl. The child sat dangling her short legs over the side of the bed, telepathically communicating to her. *All the children on this ward are wanderers. We all came to help awaken the families we were born into. Our deaths will be the tool that carries them to fourth dimensional consciousness, even as it is the friend who accompanies us into the presence of All That Is.* Then reaching out to touch Laaroos's hand she added, *We have all been especially happy since you came to work here. We recognized you at once as a wanderer and we feel closer to our home dimension when we see you.*

How did I not realize this, Laaroos thought, as she backed away from the pool and handed the oil and salt to Toomeh who offered a prayer of gratitude as he dropped a few grains of salt onto the surface of the water. He looked down and saw himself at The Royal College of Art's annual show. On one wall were several paintings of scenes from their training on Venus, including images of the Chohans. He recognized them as his style of work, but he hadn't painted them, at least, not yet.

When they finished at the mirror pool it was fully dark, save for the stars, as it was the time of the new moon. They took their leave of Avalon, joined hands to create a group merkaba and headed for the carriage house in Notting Hill Gate. Immediately on entering they knew something was wrong. Albus and Kenji were puffed up and the dragon tree in the living room was shriveled up tight. They checked the other rooms. The plum tree in Laaroos and Toomeh's room and the hydrangea tree in Heipleido's room, even the red pepper plant in the kitchen, were all in distress. Someone from the dark side had penetrated the protection around the carriage house. "It reeks of Darpith," Heipleido said, "he's returned."

Chapter 39

El Paso

After they returned from London and the book tour, Soonam allowed herself a day before tackling the question of which democratic candidate to support for president. She studied all their websites until she understood their positions on every issue, but especially on the issues that mattered the most to her: climate change, a humane immigration policy, and equal justice under law. By lunchtime she had narrowed it down to four candidates: She examined their slogans as well as their positions. "Save our Democracy" was the rallying cry of a female senator running, and the first thing you saw on her website. It struck the chord of an America in crisis, an America losing its grip and destroying its democracy, which Soonam believed it was. The senator from New Hampshire had a short and unifying slogan: "Not me. Us." As a fifth dimensional being who understood that we are all one, this resonated with Soonam. A young mayor also appealed to Soonam. She especially liked him for his calm decency, but she felt he needed to work on his slogan. "A Fresh Start for America," was too vague and too flat for her liking. The former vice president got the tone right, but his slogan was a little long: "We're in a battle for the Soul of America." His other one was shorter, "America is an idea," but it was missing something.

All four candidates supported a Green New Deal and promised to reform immigration and end racial disparity in the justice system. But the female senator had the most detailed plans. And she never diluted her opinions. Soonam admired that. She also never resorted to lazy generalizations, racist solipsism, or shady alibis like the current president and his band of theocratic fascist supporters. The former vice president had the most baggage from being in the Senate for so long. But lots of older people liked him. He was very human, in a good way. The senator from New Hampshire was an articulate fighter who looked like he could easily stand up to the president's arrogance and schoolyard bullying. But had he been around too long? Was he yesterday's news? The young mayor from the Midwest was a fresh face, but short on experience. How would he manage an America menaced by fascism? What would he say on the debate stage to a president who pretended that those he exploited, caged and imprisoned were not human beings? All of the candidates understood that we were living through unpropitious times and that America was no longer seen by the world as a good and hopeful place, a way of living to strive for. Four more years of this polyamorous, greedy, capitalist monster was a definite possibility, and each of the candidates wanted to prevent that. In the end Soonam would work for whoever won the nomination, but for now she needed to choose someone and begin.

To help her decide she studied videos of each of them and watched each of their interviews on Pod Save America. The female senator redefined the word intense. Some would fault her for that or even label her unappealing, too masculine, but Soonam loved her courage and her inclusivity. But it worried her that paying for Medicare for all would be too high a bar. Was she moving too fast for the country?

The former vice president was decent, laid back and folksy, which would appeal to a lot of middle of the road Americans. But he was being smeared big time by the current president who used the power of his office to help himself politically by withholding aid to Ukraine unless they found dirt on his political rivals for him, thus prolonging the war Russia had started by unlawfully invading Ukraine. Many more lives would be lost as a result of this act by the U.S. president, who ran foreign policy for one purpose – his own ends, financial and political. His latest impulsive act to please the Russian and Turkish presidents had caused a genocide.

Then there was the senator from New Hampshire to consider, a man of the people, for real. But he skated too close to anger at times, which turned off the faint of heart. Still, for fifty years he'd been on the right side of every issue, always working for the forgotten and the downtrodden.

The mayor was brilliant, sincere, authentic, personable — but young. He managed to be both measured on policy issues, and a leader capable of inspiring people. Were there enough Americans ready for a gay president, Soonam wondered?

She closed her laptop, and her eyes, and leaned back in her chair at the kitchen table. It was already late afternoon and she'd been at it all day, stopping only to give Mona and Shiva lunch and drink a glass of lemon water herself. She opened her eyes when she heard the front door open. Attivio's hands were on her shoulders a moment later, massaging her. "Come on, you need a walk." He leashed up Shiva and they headed over to the Hudson River. As usual Shiva scoured the streets for a pizza crust or a cupcake paper. The sun was low over the water, covering the surface with sparkling diamonds. They walked out on the pier at Christopher Street and lifted their faces to meet the breeze off the river. "Have you made up your mind about which candidate you're going to work for?"

"I'm almost there, but I thought I'd ask for the gift of a dream to see what my unconscious has to say." Her voice was nearly drowned out by Shiva who started barking to be let off the leash and run free on the grassy part of the pier. Attivio released him and he ran in large circles over the whole of the lawn before jogging back to them, panting and happy. "How about Taco Mahal for dinner? We can sit outside with Shiva," Attivio said.

"Shall we see if Ederah and Bereh want to join us?"

The four of them, with Shiva at their feet, sat at Taco Mahal's outside tables on Seventh Avenue and ate their Indian tacos, the turmeric dressing dripping through their fingers. It was a meal that required several napkins.

"What have you two been up to today?" Soonam asked.

"Bereh has been out among the stars all day working on his paper and taking breaks to explain a little bit of astrophysics to me. These bodies we're wearing now are made of atoms from the inside of giant red stars of long ago. And the gold and uranium in the Earth are there because of a supernova explosion that happened just before Earth formed," Ederah said.

"Yes, and the teeth we're using to chew our Indian tacos are made of calcium from the interior of a collapsing star, so is the iron in Shiva's blood and the nitrogen in all our DNA," Bereh added.

Soonam lifted her mango lassi and offered thanks to all the stars which had gone through their life cycles and bestowed the gift of their atoms to create new life. Attivio, Ederah and Bereh echoed her, "To the stars."

"When are we scheduled to play *Fifth Dimension* next?" Bereh asked as they were saying goodbye.

"Tomorrow morning at nine, NYC time," Attivio reminded him.

The couples said goodnight and parted, Soonam, Attivio and Shiva walking south and Ederah and Bereh west toward the Highline.

When they got home Soonam fed Shiva and Mona and put the kettle on. Even though it was a warm evening they enjoyed a glass of mint tea with little sugared donuts before bed. Attivio was watering the garden when Soonam stepped out onto the back porch and set down the tray holding two glasses of tea and a plate of little powdered donuts. He turned off the hose and opened his arms to her.

"Come here my one, momentarily inhabiting a body created of elements made in the crucible of a red star and baked in the oven of a supernova." Soonam floated into the circle of his arms and laid her head on his heart.

"We're all made of each other, the stars, the flowers, the earth in this garden, the trees and all beings everywhere. It's so intimate."

Attivio held her in a way he'd never held anyone else and whispered the secrets of his heart into her hair. Shiva rubbed up against them wanting to be included.

"Come on, let's have tea and take a shower together," Attivio said.

They sat for a moment on the porch steps sipping their tea and eating the little donuts until their lips and t-shirts were powdered with crumbs. Attivio tossed the last donut to Shiva who caught it in his mouth and seemed to swallow it without even tasting it. Mona looked at him as if to say, "Do you ever even taste anything?"

The water felt soft and luxurious when Soonam stepped into the shower beside Attivio. He soaped up his hands and ran them over her whole back and down around the curves of her bottom.

"Turn around, so I can do your front," he said.

When she turned he rinsed his hands and built up a new lather and applied it to her throat and shoulders before moving his hands over her breasts and massaging them with the rose scented lather. He rinsed and lathered his hands again drawing them over her abdomen and down to the soft inside of her thighs. Gently he separated the lips of her vagina and put his soap covered fingers inside her.

"Stars become silken flesh," he said, when she let out a soft moan. He lifted her up, held her under her bottom and pressed her against the shower wall as he entered her. After her whole body convulsed in orgasm, he set her down. He washed away the semen dripping down her thighs and she tenderly took his penis in her hands and covered it with warm soapy water. It grew erect again at her touch and she suggested they take it to their bedroom. This time they shifted into their fifth dimensional light bodies to unite, and using their breath, hooked their sexual energy into the universe to reach the realm of the Divine. The sexual union of fifth dimensional beings creates a pathway to lift up the vibration of all beings. The energy of the Divine is a continual rapturous orgasm of love for all beings as one. Soonam and Attivio traveled in this ecstasy for several hours before returning to their commitment to be human, on Earth, for this mission. Back in their human bodies they fell asleep in one another's arms, with Shiva and Mona curled around them.

The next morning Soonam and Attivio headed over to the gaming center in the East Village with Ederah and Bereh, donned their gaming gear and sat down in front of their screens. Heipleido, Laaroos and Toomeh did the same at their London gaming center. Master El Morya came on to address them.

"Last night the U.S. president held a rally in which he again stoked fear of immigrants, calling Mexicans in particular rapists and criminals. Since he's been in office the number of hate crimes by those espousing the virulent ideology of white nationalism had tripled, and seventeen million voters of color have been purged from the voter rolls. Because of the president's hate speech at his rally last night, there could again be trouble in El Paso today where a large voter registration drive is getting under way. Eighty percent of El Paso's citizens are Hispanic."

El Morya paused to let this sink in before continuing.

"Your mission is to prevent another massacre like the one in El Paso a year ago. Today's event will be a big one as it's sponsored by a nationwide get out the vote group. You will have access to all your fifth dimensional powers but you will wear your human bodies. Attune to any threat of violence. If people of color are slaughtered while attempting to register to vote it will not only be a devastating heartbreak, but it will deter others from trying to vote. This is what the dark side wants. They prefer dictators who share their values because they're easier to manipulate. America was supposed to be an idea to inspire all people. The dark side wishes to destroy that idea. Remain in El

Paso as long as the registration drive goes on. It is scheduled as an all-day event. All gamers can watch. Only wanderers will play today, with the exception of Miquel and Carlos, who have been given a special assignment. From their gaming center in Mexico they will monitor the grounds outside the tents and warn you of anything suspicious." El Morya appeared to be finished speaking, but then he added, "And one last thing, both Darpith and Veldemiron have again slipped through the quarantine around Earth. Be on the lookout. Veldemiron does not yet know that Darpith has escaped. Activate your merkabas and deploy now."

When the wanderers arrived in El Paso they saw a small medical tent and three large event tents already set up. One tent was set up as a play center for children. It held a large red, yellow and blue bouncy house, a ball pit and a water slide and tank. In a second tent, several local restaurants were preparing tacos, rice and beans, and burritos. Many cold drinks, yogurts and health bar samples were also on offer. The third tent held fifty registration tables. Volunteers bustled about in all three tents. The wanderers spread out. Soonam and Laaroos chose to cover the children's tent. Ederah and Bereh took the food tent, and Toomeh, Attivio and Heipleido stationed themselves in the registration tent.

When Soonam and Laaroos walked into the children's tent, local folk musicians were setting up and doing a sound check. Beautiful bright eyed, brown skinned young children were already playing in the bouncy house and ball pit and lining up for the water slide. Parents stood around holding babies and toddlers and talking while keeping an eye on their kids playing on the equipment. Soonam felt the joy of both the parents and the children. Since the election of this president, care free moments had been rare for this mostly Mexican American group, who, although they were American citizens, some going back several generations, now lived with targets on their backs, and worse, with targets on the backs of their children. El Paso, approximately eighty percent Hispanic, had long been a peaceful community, until the previous year when a white supremacist, echoing the president's hate speech came to El Paso and massacred twenty-six men, women, children and babies. Fear, already high because of the president's repeated hate speech against people of color, swept the city. Today's event was meant to heal some of those wounds as well as to encourage people to register to vote.

Ederah and Bereh wandered around the food tent enjoying the aroma of the fragrant Mexican food. People were lined up in an orderly way at each of the booths waiting their turn for a taco or burrito or a plate of beans and rice. Little kids were drinking various libations from cups and bottles and mothers were feeding little bits of food to their toddlers at the tables arranged in the center of the tent. Ederah looked around at the many happy faces enjoying the simple pleasure of eating delicious food. "Shall we get in line?" Bereh said. I fancy a taco myself." Ederah nodded.

Toomeh, Attivio and Heipleido stood in a clump in the registration tent observing the registration process. Although they sensed no danger in the tent, there was a palpable feeling of discomfort among those in line to register. It was as if they feared that at any moment ICE would appear and haul them away for daring to exercise their rights as citizens. Heipleido checked in with Miquel and Carlos to see if they'd noticed anything or anyone unusual on the grounds. They sent back an all clear. Then a minute later Miquel sent a different message to all the wanderers. He had spotted a suspicious looking white guy with a guitar case approaching the children's tent.

Soonam was standing by the bouncy house listening to the music when she saw the guy come in and kneel down behind the musicians and open what looked like a guitar case. Laaroos was across the tent at the water slide. Soonam watched as the guy pulled something out of his guitar case. It wasn't a guitar.

She rushed toward him into the line of fire as he raised his gun to spray bullets at the children playing on the bouncy house. Darting between him and the children she hit him with a paralyzing ray as the bullets struck her in the chest.

At the same instant Attivio and Toomeh burst into the tent. Attivio cast a shield between Soonam and the gunman, but some of the bullets had already found their mark in her body. Blood was seeping through her summer dress in several places as Attivio lifted her in his arms. Toomeh removed the stunned gunman while Laaroos wiped the memory of every man, woman and child in the tent. Ederah arrived next and made Soonam and Attivio invisible while he carried her to the medical tent.

Thankfully the tent was empty when they entered and Attivio laid Soonam down on the single cot. Laaroos bent over Soonam to assess her wounds and was about to call for master Hilarion when he appeared.

"El Morya alerted me about what happened. Laaroos, ask Ederah to make the medical tent invisible. I don't want to be interrupted while we try to save Soonam's human vehicle."

Meanwhile, Toomeh quietly handed the gunman over to the mayor of El Paso, who was attending the event. The mayor decided to keep the shooting on the down low, so as not to alarm those on the scene or scare off people who might still want to register to vote. Thankfully no one had been hit but Soonam. After handing over the gunman, Toomeh returned to keep watch in the children's tent with Ederah. Heipleido was still in the registration tent and Bereh went to check on things in the food tent. As he entered the tent, Bereh and the other wanderers got a bubble from Heipleido. "Miquel and Carlos have picked up some dark energy roaming the grounds around the tents. They're describing it as a black shadow. I'm guessing Veldemiron has arrived. And Darpith may not be far behind."

The wanderers knew Darpith would be tracking Veldemiron, though Veldemiron himself still believed Darpith was his captive in a far-off corner of the Andromeda Galaxy. Fearful of Veldemiron's wrath if they told him of Darpith's escape, his minions had not informed him of it, and had instead fled themselves to the Triangulum Galaxy.

Laaroos and Hilarion examined Soonam's wounds. Attivio, covered in Soonam's blood, sat on a wooden box next to her cot.

"Will she live?" he asked Hilarion.

"This body isn't Soonam," Hilarion reminded him. "It's only a temporary vehicle which allows her to serve on Earth in the third dimension. We'll try to save it, but it's already lost a lot of blood from seven bullet wounds. The heart itself may have been hit. I'm checking now."

Attivio took her limp hand in his strong one. Just hours before, he'd been inside her human body riding waves of ecstasy. She was his one and he loved her human body as well as her soul, the wonder of it, its warmth, its curves, its softness. He wiped the tears spilling from his eyes and reminded himself that they were wanderers on a mission.

As they scanned the area around the large tents, Miquel and Carlos picked up a second entity with dark energy and alerted the wanderers. Their description sounded like Darpith. Though the entity they observed appeared human, Miquel said that it reminded him of a reptile. Both Darpith and Veldemiron, unaware of Miquel and Carlos's surveillance through the game *Fifth Dimension*, thought they had arrived at the El Paso event unnoticed. Still smarting from losing the battle at the Paris mosque to Heipleido, Veldemiron had come to find Heipleido and settle that score. He'd either destroy Heipleido's human vehicle, as he had done with Maepleida, or capture him for the dark side. Before entering the registration tent Veldemiron altered his appearance so that he looked like a Hispanic man in his thirties. He joined one of the registration lines and looked around in search of Heipleido. But he was impatient, and whereas he should have been able to see through Heipleido's disguise, his own restlessness destroyed his concentration. Forewarned by Miquel and Carlos of Veldemiron's arrival and disguise, Heipleido had changed himself so he appeared to be a young Hispanic woman. His fingers burned to release their searing light and scorch Veldemiron, depolarizing his negative power. But as much as he wanted to capture Veldemiron to avenge Maepleida, he didn't want this event ruined or more trauma to befall the people of El Paso. So, when a young, handsome Latino guy flirted with him, he allowed the attention to further fool Veldemiron, while never losing track of exactly what the dark lord was doing.

Darpith meanwhile was himself searching in vain for Veldemiron. He was sure this was the place he had tracked him to, but where was he? Entering one tent after another he scanned them with his beady eyes. He noted the presence of the wanderers in the various tents, but didn't allow himself to be distracted from his main target. The registration lines were shorter now as the afternoon turned to early evening and the event wound down. The restaurants were packing up and parents were taking their tired children home. The event had been a success. Several thousand new voters had registered in what they believed was safety. El Paso had had a good day. Ederah joined Bereh and Heipleido in the registration tent to keep an eye on Veldemiron. Veldemiron was about to leave in a rage at having been unable to find Heipleido when Darpith entered the registration tent, and sensed that Veldemiron was somewhere nearby. He began scanning every being present to see which one might be him. As registration volunteers packed up materials and the tent company men prepared to dismantle the tent, Veldemiron sensed Darpith's unmistakable energy. He was jolted by the shock that Darpith had escaped. Neither of them had minions with them. Both were in disguise, but it would be only a matter of moments until they honed-in on one another with the meditative power of darkness considering darkness. Then both of them would strike. The wanderers couldn't let that happen here. Ederah acted quickly to make both dark lords invisible to one another. Full of rage that the wanderers had interfered Darpith rounded on Ederah but Bereh was quicker and hit him with a paralyzing ray. Veldemiron, unable to see Darpith or to find Heipleido, and realizing he had lost the element of surprise and was outnumbered, fled. Darpith lay invisible on one side of the tent as a result of Bereh's paralyzing ray. With a single command Heipleido moved his limp body outside and away from the tents and remaining people. The paralyzing ray would wear off in a few hours, once everyone had left.

The wanderers breathed a sigh of relief that there had been no further incidents as they activated their merkabas and returned to the gaming center in New York. Hilarion, Laaroos and Attivio had taken Soonam's body and gone before them. El Morya came on the screen to debrief them, informing them that more than two million gamers worldwide had watched as hope was restored to not only El Paso, but to the larger Hispanic community as well.

The wanderers removed their gear and walked through the village to Soonam and Attivio's. The house was still when Laaroos opened the front door for them. Mona and Shiva did not come to the door to greet them but lay upstairs by Soonam's bed, unmoving. Hilarion and Laaroos had used both the emerald healing ray and the gold resurrection flame to repair the arteries, veins, heart and flesh of Soonam's human vehicle. Then they had worked on her meridians and nervous system, her pineal gland, and finally on all her chakras, intrinsic and extrinsic, but she remained unconscious. Both of them understood that the healer does not heal, they merely offer an opportunity for realignment by channeling intelligent energy as focused light. Regaining consciousness would be the choice of Soonam's etheric body. They all knew that it is the will of the entity which allows her indigo body to heal her physical body, and that this could happen in an instant if the seeker was sincere in her desire to heal. So they waited. And Shiva and Mona waited with them. Shiva climbed onto the bed and laid his head on Soonam's belly. Mona curled up on the pillow beside Soonam's golden hair. Attivio sat on the bed beside her body, his body folded over his guitar, singing her a song of love, asking her to return to them.

Chapter 40

Venus

When the bullets tore into her human body the power of the blast split Soonam's fifth dimensional-self off from her third dimensional-self. She watched from above as Attivio lifted her body and carried it from the children's tent. Then it was as if she was sucked through a vortex. She found herself back on Venus in the palace garden, standing before Lord Kumara, Lady Venus and Maepleida. Resplendent in her light body, she bowed to each of them and they returned her greetings. Lady Venus spoke first.

"Soonam, we welcome you to the palace, but want you to know that you have a choice to make. Your merkaba was not destroyed in the attack on you. You are free to return and re-enter your third dimensional vehicle which Hilarion and Laaroos have made viable again. Or you may choose to stay on Venus and continue working for the humans from here. You have earned that right."

Maepleida looked at Soonam, happily absorbing every detail of her friend and forming a thousand questions in her mind. Kumara sensed that the two friends would enjoy some time alone together and suggested they go for a stroll.

"We'll talk again this evening, Soonam," he said sending them off.

As they walked along, Maepleida told Soonam she missed being on Earth with all of them. She watched every game of *Fifth Dimension* and visited Heipleido during his sleep time whenever she could slip through the quarantine. Her merkaba was strong enough for that now, but not yet strong enough to sustain her for a prolonged time on Earth. Soonam asked how it was going, rebuilding the energy in her merkaba and how much longer it would take.

"I'm not sure, maybe another six months as time is measured on Earth. Daily merkaba meditation is helping."

Maepleida asked many questions about everyone and relished all the little details Soonam provided, especially about Albus and Heipleido's new closeness since Maepleida's departure.

They were passing near to the great temple where they had trained. Soonam looked up to see the diffracted light erupting into many soft colors which shimmered in the air. When she looked down to the ground again she saw Botu, her animal friend from Telos, standing before her. Joy rushed through her at the sight of him and she leaned forward to hug him. Botu was a large animal from Lemuria who had survived by escaping to Telos when Lemuria sank beneath the sea, twelve thousand Earth years ago. He looked like a big gold-colored dog but with soft cat fur and ears like an elephant.

"What are you doing here on Venus?" Soonam asked him telepathically.

"I was logged on to *Fifth Dimension* and saw what happened to you in El Paso. I knew this is where the Cohans would bring you while they tried to repair your human body," Botu responded telepathically. "I wanted to see how you were, so I came."

Soonam caressed his large celestial elephant ears to thank him for his concern.

"Here's our favorite tree," Maepleida said, "shall we sit?" The three of them sat beneath the welcoming tree and for a few moments just drank in one another. It was Soonam who spoke first. "It feels so peaceful to be back on Venus, away from the rushing world of Earth where every morning it feels as if chaos is sitting right across the breakfast table, sipping its coffee, looking for an opportunity to break out somewhere else."

"Events in El Paso saddened all of us in Telos and in all the inner cities of light," Botu telegraphed. "It's a dark consciousness that aims an assault rifle at little children."

"Has the behavior of the current president of the United States slowed the time table for when those of you in the inner cities will come to the surface of the planet and live among the humans?" Maepleida asked Botu.

"We will come in time for the great battle with the dark side. Though it is fast approaching, that time is not yet at hand. This president has allowed all the poisons in the surface dwellers to hatch out, but those poisons were already there in those with a less evolved consciousness, and he has only revealed them. When Earth makes the big jump to the Fourth Dimension, only those who can hold enough violet energy will go with her. He and his supporters will not be moving to the fourth dimension on the path of light. They will either proceed along the dark path of separation, exclusion, self-interest and elitism, to fourth dimensional negative, or they will incarnate on some other third dimensional planet for another 75,000 years, until they learn to love all as one." After communicating this, and satisfied that Soonam was in one piece, Botu rose to take his leave. "Now that I see you're well, Soonam, I'll return to Telos." Soonam encircled his soft furry neck and caressed his elephant ears one more time before she let him go. Maepleida leaned against the tree enjoying the sight of them hugging.

When Botu was gone, Soonam turned to Maepleida, "Are you missing your Earth life or mostly just Heipleido?"

"I miss all of it. I often think of all of you, and of Albus and Kenji, and the pleasures of human life, like tea and toast with orange marmalade in the morning, saying hello to the neighbors in the mews, down comforters, sitting by the fire, snow, the smell of Christmas trees, roses in an English garden, popcorn, olives, cuddling with Albus, horses, dogs, all the animals on Earth really, elephants, hot baths, music, forests, moonlight, the feel of warm sand under my feet, the salty smell of the ocean, making love with Heipleido as humans, which we'll never do again, the weight and warmth of my human body, my human hands, the blue sky. Reluctant as I was at first to incarnate on Earth, I see now what a jewel she is, and I treasure the time I spent on her surface in a human body, among humans. I miss the wonder of the human body itself, but mine died and can't be resurrected. I will most likely never be a human again, but you can be if you choose to, Soonam. Your body was saved and is waiting for you. I'll eventually be able to slip through the quarantine for longer periods or even be granted permission to, because of my service to Earth, but I will have to be only Fifth Dimensional when I'm there."

After this discourse, the two light beings sitting under the tree fell silent. Time slowed as Soonam absorbed Maepleida's words and watched the play of soft pink and gold light on the temple wall. Even a tiny piece of sorrow can stop time.

That evening Soonam and Maepleida joined Lady Venus and Kumara, the Lord Hierarchs of Venus, at the palace. They had a visitor from Saturn. She was an emissary from the Council of Nine, but more interesting to Soonam and Maepleida was the fact that she had once been incarnated on Earth as human and had been a first lady of the United States. She was known then as Eleanor Roosevelt. The five of them sat near a gurgling fountain in the palace garden communicating telepathically about Earth's progress toward the Fourth Dimension. While human, Eleanor, who had gone to Earth as a lone wanderer, had not only been instrumental in setting up the earliest version of the United Nations after her husband's death, but had been the guiding light behind his presidency. Together, with her consciousness guiding his, they created Social Security, the Securities and Exchange Commission, the National Labor Relations Act, and the Federal Deposit Insurance Corporation. Soonam and Maepleida could have sat with her for hours so interested were they in hearing about conditions on Earth in her day and in how she had achieved so much.

After much informative and pleasant discussion with Eleanor,

Venus took a moment to remind Soonam she had a decision to make. Would she return to her third dimensional life and remain there for the great battle for Earth or would she stay on Venus and work from there? Despite the glorious feeling of lightness being on sixth dimensional Venus, in her heart Soonam already knew she would return to Earth and work alongside Attivio and the other awakened wanderers to help Earth join the planets of the light in the coming battle. And Maepleida, Eleanor, Venus and Kumara knew it too. They were all just putting off the moment of parting. Finally, Soonam rose and telegraphed that it was time. The five beings bowed to the Divine in one another and Soonam adjusted her vibration to match that of planet Earth, and disappeared from the palace garden.

When she arrived in New York, in her own bedroom, she saw her body on the bed and Attivio curled around it, asleep, with Mona next to her head and Shiva at her feet. Afraid of startling Attivio, she sent him a dream picturing herself in their room and asking him to wake up. Then she entered her human body through the crown chakra and waited for him to awaken. She watched his eyelids moving and saw him smile in his sleep. A moment later he opened his violet eyes and looked into her own. He held her with his eyes, afraid to let her go lest it only be a dream. She told him with her eyes that she was really back. His mouth found hers and the warm reception he felt as her lips met his made his heart bang against his ribs in a joyous rhythm. A moment later Shiva was barking and wagging, Mona was purring, and the door burst open and Heipleido, Laaroos, Toomeh, Ederah and Bereh poured into the room. Soonam had been gone for thirty-six hours and now she was back. Even Thea, her tree friend in Washington Square Park, had picked up her return and sent a message on the breeze through their open bedroom window to welcome her back.

The next day Soonam found Heipleido alone in the garden, sitting with a rose bush, contemplating a red rose. She sat down next to him and gave him every detail she could of Maepleida's recovery and her life on Venus and her plans to join the coming battle for Earth by slipping through the quarantine and fighting beside him as a fifth dimensional being. Attivio, who couldn't let Soonam out of his sight for long just yet, joined them.

"Did Kumara or Venus send any instructions?" Heipleido asked her.

"Keep on with our work of awakening humans to their divinity by increasing the vibration of love on the planet," Soonam said. "Wouldn't your bill for the poor and homeless be a step in that direction? Maepleida wanted me to remind you that her father loves when you play Shubert for him on the piano and she offered to send him some dreams to further insure his co-operation for your bill."

"That sounds like her. She always had him wrapped around her little finger." Heipleido laughed. "And have you chosen which candidate you're going to support in the primaries?"

"The young mayor," Soonam answered without hesitation, "at least for now."

"He's speaking in Washington Square park tonight," Attivio told her, "if you want to go."

Toomeh and Laaroos came out to the garden to say they were heading back to London to get on with their work. Toomeh had plans for a whole new set of paintings to help awaken humans, and Laaroos wanted to visit the little wanderers on the children's cancer unit before making plans to introduce *Fifth Dimension* to gaming centers in new parts of the Middle East. Heipleido said he was ready to apparate, too, he had some practicing on the piano to do. Ederah and Bereh came outside just in time to say goodbye.

"We're off, too, then," Bereh said. "We'll let you two get reacquainted." He smiled a mischievous smile. To which Soonam responded, "I was only gone thirty-six hours!"

"Yes, but during those hours we didn't know if you would be

coming back," Attivio said with such poignancy that she reached for his hand and brought it to her lips.

"See you soon," Ederah called over her shoulder as they left.

FANTASY, SCI-FI, HORROR & PARANORMAL

Recent bestsellers from Cosmic Egg Books are:

The Zombie Rule Book
A Zombie Apocalypse Survival Guide
Tony Newton
The book the living-dead don't want you to have!
Paperback: 978-1-78279-334-2 ebook: 978-1-78279-333-5

Cryptogram
Because the Past is Never Past
Michael Tobert
Welcome to the dystopian world of 2050, where three lovers are
haunted by echoes from eight-hundred years ago.
Paperback: 978-1-78279-681-7 ebook: 978-1-78279-680-0

Purefinder
Ben Gwalchmai
London, 1858. A child is dead; a man is blamed and dragged
through hell in this Dantean tale of loss, mystery and fraternity.
Paperback: 978-1-78279-098-3 ebook: 978-1-78279-097-6

600ppm
A Novel of Climate Change
Clarke W. Owens
Nature is collapsing. The government doesn't want you to know
why. Welcome to 2051 and 600ppm.
Paperback: 978-1-78279-992-4 ebook: 978-1-78279-993-1

Creations
William Mitchell
Earth 2040 is on the brink of disaster. Can Max Lowrie stop the
self-replicating machines before it's too late?
Paperback: 978-1-78279-186-7 ebook: 978-1-78279-161-4

The Gawain Legacy
Jon Mackley
If you try to control every secret, secrets may end up controlling
you.
Paperback: 978-1-78279-485-1 ebook: 978-1-78279-484-4

Readers of ebooks can buy or view any of these bestsellers by
clicking on the live link in the title. Most titles are published
in paperback and as an ebook. Paperbacks are available in
traditional bookshops. Both print and ebook formats are
available online.
Find more titles and sign up to our readers' newsletter at
http://www.johnhuntpublishing.com/fiction
Follow us on Facebook at https://www.facebook.com/JHPfiction
and Twitter at https://twitter.com/JHPFiction